# Dread Child

## The Dreadmark Arises

## Dreadmark Covenants I

by

J. L. Doty

# Dread Child

## The Dreadmark Arises

## Dreadmark Covenants I

# The Dreadlands

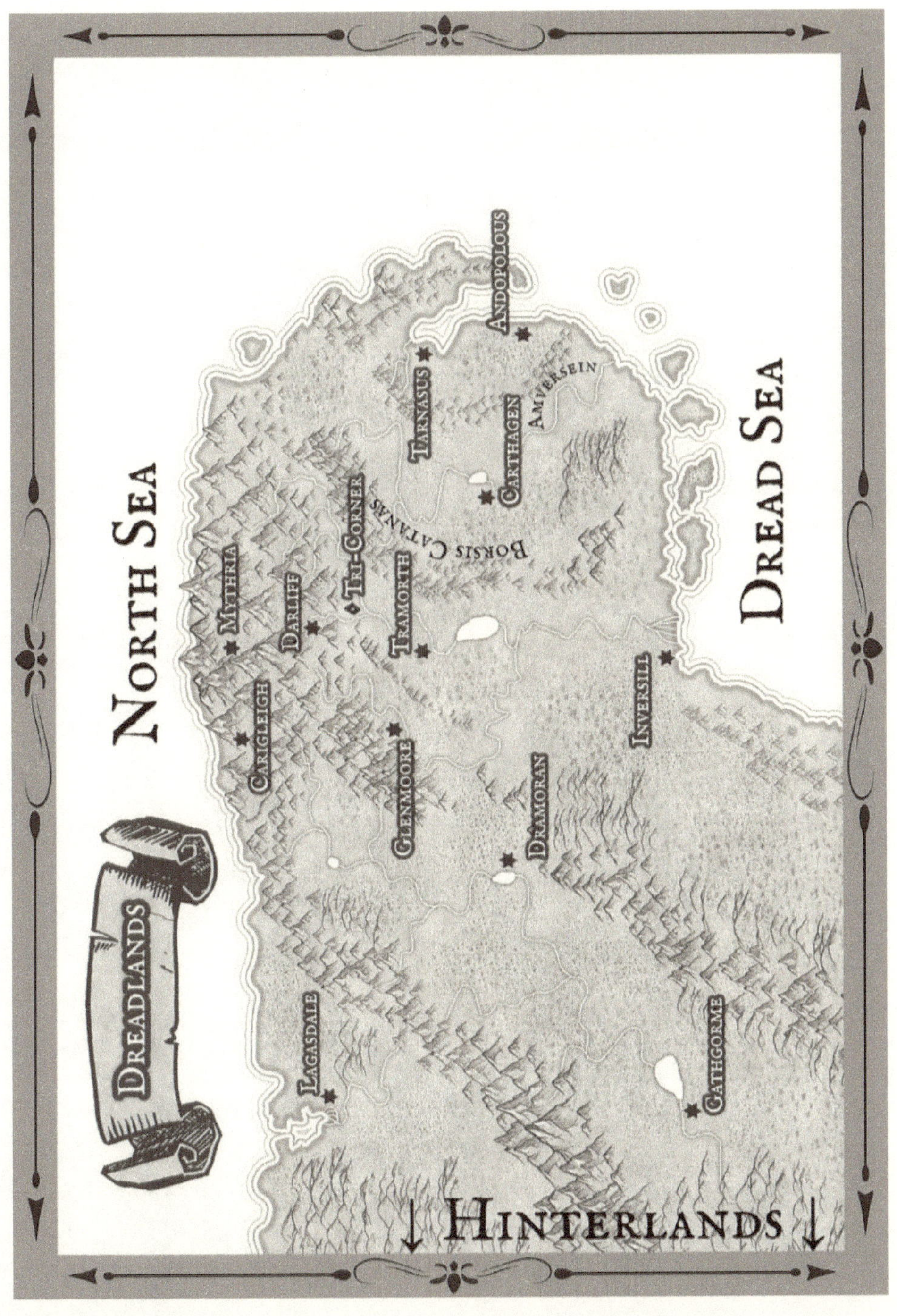

# Excerpt from an Old Scroll:
# Time Lost

*There is no time when time is not lost,*
*and the mark of the dread must find its soul.*

*It deceives and manipulates,*
*bends and shapes all to its purpose,*
*and in time lost its spirit will emerge.*

*Plantonin ahm Carthagen*
*penned in the time of the Withering Wars*

# Prologue:

# The Time of Carnage Past

THE SLAUGHTER WAS done, and triumph now knelt in submission at his feet. Standing on a high bluff, he looked down on the fields of carnage below. The broken bodies of twenty thousand men lay still and silent, in some places piled higher than the stature of a tall man. The stench of death clung to his clothing, his skin, and the air about him, a cloying mix of burned flesh, dismembered bowels, and lost hope.

He looked up into the clear sky. "What brought me to this? What turned me into nothing but a butcher?"

As the rising sun slowly burned away the morning mist, he looked down on the rolling hills and fields. He had climbed to the top of that hill because from there he saw it all: the butchery, bloodshed, and utter waste. Where green meadows and lush countryside had once sprouted rows of ripening grain, they now yielded only a bounty of death.

"My Lord Domaxus, you should not stand so close to the edge. It is dangerous."

Domaxus ignored the man standing behind him and looked down at the ground beneath his feet. Only a hand's breadth of rocky soil separated the toes of his boots from a sheer drop that would mean certain death, a finality he no longer feared.

He raised his right arm and looked at the flesh on the inner forearm. Others saw nothing but a smear of discolored flesh, a common enough birthmark, but he saw a kaleidoscope of ever-changing images. He wondered if they were merely hallucinations, the mad visions of a disturbed soul with a distorted and corrupt mind. Or were they prophesies and portents, a harbinger of the sins he had yet to commit? Sadly, he could never know the answer to that.

He turned about but did not step away from the precipice. His chancellor and closest friend, Claudius ahm Modain, stood waiting for him, an uncertain look on his face. Behind Claudius, a small fire crackled in a circle of stones, a column of smoke rising with lazy indifference into the sky.

Domaxus gave him a sardonic look. "So formal, my friend Claudius. When we were children you called me Dom, or sometimes Little Piss-Ant."

The previous evening, when several smaller victories had removed any question of the battle's final outcome, the two of them had climbed the back side of the bluff, kindled the small fire, and eaten a silent dinner. From there they had watched his army mop up the vestiges of the enemy troops, dispatching the wounded, taking no prisoners. He and his generals had long ago learned the expediency of teaching their enemies the harshest of lessons: resist, and the price you pay will be even greater.

Claudius gave him a pained look. "We are far removed from our childhoods, my lord. Three of the Duchies are all but extinct, and the other four badly weakened. At this moment your generals are reforming your armies to the north. They believe that before the month is out, we can exterminate another two of the Duchies, and the remaining two will fall shortly thereafter. Then we move on to the Mountain Kingdom, and all will be yours."

Claudius's words troubled him greatly. "When did we stop conquering and start exterminating? At this point we sow only carnage and suffering, and leave nothing we might rule."

Claudius lowered his eyes and nodded his head. "A poor choice of words, my lord. What should I tell your generals?"

Domaxus shrugged and tried to conceal his melancholy. "Tell them I'll come down shortly, and we can continue the carnage."

Claudius tried to smile, but the look on his face appeared more like a grimace. "As you wish, my lord. By your leave?"

Domaxus nodded his consent. Claudius turned and walked away.

Domaxus raised his arm and again looked at the strange images flashing on his inner forearm. He wanted them to stop, but they did not relent. He wanted it all to stop. He wanted to go back to the small village where he and Claudius had grown up. He wanted to go back to a time before he had so many august titles. He wanted to go back in time and do it all differently, and looking at the strange marks on his arm, he resolved that he would stop the carnage and destruction. He would stop it now.

He crossed the short distance to the fire, squatted down, retrieved a firebrand, and stood. Several inches of the brand's tip glowed a bright orange-red, with flames crackling upward from it. And even held at arm's length, its heat washed over his face. He transferred the brand to his left hand, looked at its glowing tip, then at the mark on his right forearm. The images did not abate.

He looked again at the brand, then at his arm, then back and forth between the brand and his arm. Then he sighed and pressed the blazing tip of the firebrand against the birthmark. A wave of searing pain washed through his heart and soul, and he dropped to his knees. But he reveled in the agony and did not waver or falter, for it was impartial and just retribution for his sins. As he scraped the brand up and down his forearm, the stink of burning flesh reminded him of the battlefield below. He tried to eradicate any last trace of the cursed mark on his arm, to remove it forever from his sight, to burn the images from his mind.

The blistering torment consumed him for a time, but his thoughts eventually returned from the pain of his memories to the agony of his right arm. He opened his eyes and found himself kneeling near the fire, the brand lying in the dirt in front of him, the inner flesh of his right forearm a blackened ruin. A field of cracks in the charred skin oozed blood and yellow fluids.

Joy filled his heart, for no birthmark remained to flood his soul with disturbing images. It was done. He would go down to his generals and order them to end the carnage. He would disband them, return to Modain, and once again find happiness as a simple peasant from a small village. But as he looked at the charred flesh, an image flashed through his mind, then another, then another.

He threw his head back and screamed, "Nooooo!"

He stood, turned, and charged toward the precipice. The muscles of his legs fought to gain speed, struggling as if the ground beneath him had turned to a sea of thick mud, resisting every step he took. And then he reached the edge and leapt into the abyss of blessed oblivion . . .

# 1

# Dreadmark

THE KITCHENS IN Glenmoore Castle bustled with activity in preparation for that evening's festivities. Kainborne paused one step inside the cook's domain, and took a moment to straighten his long black robes while he scanned the room carefully.

A pretty kitchen-maid stood by a blazing hearth turning a spit of roasting meat. Her pale white skin, amber colored eyes, vertically slit pupils, and the slant to her lids, all marked her as a Scairn bondservant, though her hair covered her ears and hid their points. One of the Mountain Folk, she had probably been taken during a raid of an outlying village. There were several Scairn among the castle's staff, which did not surprise Kainborne in the least. So close to the northern reaches and the barbarians of the Mountain Kingdom, it was not surprising that Lord Kadmarkh of Glenmoore would own quite a few of them.

To one side a hearty fellow dismembered a deer carcass, swinging a heavy cleaver over his head, beads of sweat dripping down his face. Two teenage boys, their backs bent under the weight of a heavy cauldron supported between them, grunted as they crossed the kitchen in short, choppy steps. Three women, one of them Scairn, stood over a heavy table kneading dough and sweating almost as much as the butcher. A maiden carrying a basket of vegetables moved quickly as she slipped behind the women, then danced lightly around the boys with the cauldron. Amid all the noise and chaos, the cook stood among the bedlam issuing orders in sharply voiced commands.

On first impression Kainborne judged the facilities as adequate, but it bothered him that the staff should be thrown into such disarray by the arrival of his master, the newly invested Duke Jarrod of House Dramoran. In the Four Duchies of Kyldaine, Dramoran was second in prominence only to House Inversill, and appearances must be maintained. Kainborne had sent riders out weeks ago to ensure that a minor house like Glenmoore would be forewarned of Jarrod's impending arrival.

Kainborne noticed a small boy seated on the floor in a far corner of the room, his legs crossed in front of him. Clearly older than a toddler, he bent his head in concentration as he held a headless pheasant in his lap and diligently plucked its feathers. On the flagstones next to him lay two featherless chickens, and another pheasant soon to be plucked. The boy raised his head and glanced across the room at someone. He had unusually pale blue eyes, not so light in color that they particularly marked him, but a little beyond the norm.

A flurry of movement at the center of the room caught Kainborne's attention. The cook stood looming over one of her subordinates, anger clouding her features. She pointed a wooden spoon at the fellow like a weapon. "Be careful with that, you clumsy lout."

She held a large bowl nestled in the crook of her left arm, and with the spoon gripped in her right hand she jabbed it into the bowl. She stirred something within it while barking orders at her subordinates. Smudges of flour discolored her dark brown dress, and what appeared to be drippings of fat stained the white apron that covered her ample belly, upon which rested mountainous breasts.

Her plump features glistened with a sheen of greasy sweat as she glanced Kainborne's way. She froze, her eyes widened, then she hurriedly plopped the bowl down onto a nearby table and dropped the spoon into it. She lifted the folds of her apron, and while frantically wiping her hands, she scurried toward him, nodding an awkward series of bows in time with each step. Her breasts jiggled as she bobbed up and down, then she stopped in front of him and performed a poorly executed curtsy.

"Yer Lordship," she said, and all activity in the room ceased, as if an artist had painted a picture frozen in time, with every face turned Kainborne's way.

He could not claim the right to any title of nobility. He was merely the principal advisor and councilor to one of the most powerful noblemen in the land. But he had learned long ago not to waste his breath trying to correct those such as her.

The cook noticed the sudden onset of silence, glanced over her shoulder and shrieked, "On with yuh now. Don't you be gawking at his worship."

The cooking staff returned to their duties, and while the noise and air of frantic desperation resumed, the cacophony remained muted.

The cook turned back to Kainborne. "Me and me staff are at yer service, Yer Lordship."

He had known Glenmoore would be quite provincial, but only now realized to what extent. "I'm here to inspect the kitchen and your preparations for this evening."

He wasn't there to look for anything like poison because he just didn't have to worry about something like that at Glenmoore. But young Jarrod would be displeased if served some foul-tasting mash prepared by an untalented bumpkin.

The woman bowed again. "Whatever you wish, Yer Lordship."

Kainborne focused on the kitchen-maid turning the spit of meat. The top of her dress exposed the swell of small breasts, and her brown hair hung past her shoulders in disarray. Any man with a hunger for Scairn flesh would think her attractive, and some men found a liaison with a Scairn woman an exotic and exciting diversion. But Kainborne had never felt the normal male desire for pleasures of the flesh, not with either woman or man, and especially not with a Scairn trollop. Kainborne thought that taking pleasure with such a woman amounted to nothing better than rutting with live-stock. The Mountain Folk were, after all, no better than the lowest of farm animals.

Kainborne pointed at the young woman. "Let's start with that meat she's roasting."

The cook bobbed another awkward curtsy. "If it please Yer Lordship, follow me."

She turned, marched across the room and he followed, though she repeatedly glanced over her shoulder as if uncertain he would do so. The young girl's eyes widened when she noticed them walking her way. She tried to curtsy without interrupting her duty of turning the spit, and failed at both.

The cook snapped angrily at the young woman, "Give his lordship a taste of the meat, and cut it from the tenderest part near the back of the haunch."

The girl stopped turning the spit, spun about, and from a nearby table retrieved a knife and a pair of tongs. She moved with great care as she cut a slice from the haunch. Using the tongs, she carried it back to the table, placed it on a small plate, then lifted the plate and handed it to the cook. The woman examined it carefully, sniffed the meat, nodded, then extended the plate to Kainborne. He took the plate, tested the slice of meat with his fingers, blew on it several times to cool it, then popped it into his mouth. It proved to be tender and quite tasteful, with a hint of savory spices that didn't overwhelm the flavor of the meat.

"Good enough," he said, not wanting to give the cook too much encouragement.

She then led him from one preparation station to the next, and at each he tasted a sample of Glenmoore's fare. Jarrod would be pleased with that evening's feast.

With his inspection complete, Kainborne turned to leave, but he paused, turned, and scanned the room one last time. The Scairn kitchen maid had relinquished her duty at the spit to another servant. He spotted her as she crossed the room to the young boy busy plucking feathers. The lad had finished the one pheasant and started on the next.

The young woman knelt in front of him and smoothed his ruffled brown hair with her hand. She looked at him the way a mother might look upon her child: an expression of happiness, joy, and love.

Kainborne started, for it had never occurred to him that the boy might be Scairn-draka, a half-breed. His skin appeared a little paler than the norm, but not so that one might think him Scairn. The boy's eyes showed none of the amber of a Scairn, and from that distance Kainborne detected no hint of vertically slit pupils. The lad's eyes did slant downward slightly, not as much as a full Scairn, but now that Kainborne knew his parentage, the difference was there to be seen. His mother had cut the boy's hair just long enough to cover the tops of his ears, which, if they were pointed, would hide that fact from common view. And that was most likely by design.

As the boy pulled a handful of feathers from the pheasant's carcass, he looked up at his mother and smiled. Kainborne noticed a blemish in the flesh on the inside of the lad's forearm. It drew his attention in an unnatural way, and his heart skipped a beat. *No,* he thought, *it cannot be.*

He didn't realize he was moving until he had crossed half the distance between them. He continued without hesitation, his black robes rustling behind him. The cook rushed to keep up while fearfully spluttering questions. When he reached the young woman and boy, he gripped the lad's arm hard enough to make the boy grunt and wince, and looked carefully at the blemish. From across the room he thought he had seen a birthmark in the shape of a tree. But it took considerable imagination to see such an image in the blurred, discolored smudge of flesh, and Kainborne's pulse calmed. He sighed with relief, and chided himself for allowing his imagination to spawn such dangerous thoughts.

As he looked away, thinking a touch of brandy might calm his shaken nerves, the birthmark again demanded his attention. Its edges shifted and flowed, melted and swirled. Some bits of color darkened, and others lightened, forming an intricate network of recognizable hues and shapes. Branches formed, leaves sprouted from them, and the smear of discoloration slowly took on the unmistakable image of an aged oak tree, as if it were a tattoo carefully inked on the boy's arm by a master craftsman. But it wasn't just any oak tree; the birthmark matched the crest of House Dramoran, exactly as tattooed on Jarrod's arm.

"It's just a birthmark, me lord."

The girl's voice drew Kainborne's gaze away from the smudge of flesh. Her eyes had widened with fright, and she spoke with a heavy Scairn accent. He did not try to allay her fears. "The boy is yours?"

"Yes . . ." She spluttered and hiccoughed. "Yes, me lord. We calls him Ket."

Kainborne couldn't hide his confusion. "Ket? That's a name?"

The girl cringed and stepped back a pace. "Aye, me lord. He's a good boy, he is."

The cook pleaded, "Is something amiss, Yer Lordship?"

The plump woman stood next to him just as frightened as the girl. She turned on the younger woman. "Did you do something to anger his lordship?"

She raised her open hand to slap the girl, but Kainborne stopped her. "Stay your hand, woman."

The cook flinched, lowered her hand, and cowered away from him.

Kainborne looked at the young girl and suppressed the shout that boiled up into his throat. He pulled his eyes back to the boy's arm, and once again the smear of flesh appeared to be just a smudge of discolored skin. He looked carefully at the cook and the young Scairn girl, and understood then that only he had seen the true nature of the mark on the boy's arm.

What had allowed him to see what others could not? And had he truly seen it, or just imagined it? He couldn't rule out that possibility, but he'd be foolish to ignore the portent in what had just happened.

"No," he said, realizing he had drawn far too much attention to himself, and the boy, and the lad's birthmark. "She did nothing wrong."

He did not want the kitchen staff spreading rumors through the castle about his strange behavior, and possibly drawing the wrong kind of attention to the boy and his birthmark. He needed to come up with some excuse for his actions, one they would understand. And he had a few questions for the young girl, the kind he did not want to ask in front of witnesses.

"No," he said to the cook. "Nothing is amiss. And the food is quite excellent. His Grace will be most pleased tonight."

The cook beamed a broad smile at him and chortled.

Now, for the excuse they would understand, a subterfuge to cover up his unwarranted attention focused on the girl. He looked at her. "I find this young woman most attractive. Send her to my room tonight after the feast."

The girl frowned.

The cook nodded, grinned, and said, "Yes, Yer Lordship."

• • • •

Caerie's older brother sneered at her. "You're just a girl, and a child at that."

Nick's eleven years of age gave him a one-year advantage on Caerie, and he thought that imparted a level of maturity far beyond that minor difference. She sneered back at him with a knowing smile and tried to ignore him. In exactly two months, as per ancient Scairn custom, she would come of age on her tenth birthday, though that wouldn't make any difference to her brother.

She turned her back on him and crossed the nursery to the only window in the room. Constructed on the third floor of the Myth Palace, it gave an unimpeded view of the flower gardens below.

Behind her, Nicki huffed. "You're ignoring me because you think that'll make me furious. Well I'm not, and I'm going to ignore you back, Caermorgan Mythchild."

Using her formal name as an heir to the Throne of Myth and Legend did not bother her in the least, but she thought it might irritate him if she returned the favor. "But I'm ignoring you more than you are me, Nicklairan Mythchild. Am I not turned away from you, while you stand behind me conversing with my back?"

There came a long moment of silence, then she heard his heavy footsteps as he stormed out of the room. If that had been any kind of victory, she certainly didn't feel victorious. She liked her brother, at least when they weren't arguing. And with the impending birth of a third mythchild and potential heir to the throne, they were all under stress, with none of them on their best behavior.

She looked again at the flower garden below. When winter came the air of the Mountain Kingdom grew icy, and snow blanketed the hillsides to such depths it became difficult to walk. The flowers in the garden below would go dormant, wilt, and became little more than dried, brown sticks. But at that moment she looked upon a glorious kaleidoscope of colors. She loved strolling among the blossoms and taking in their fragrance, but she wasn't allowed to walk the grounds unescorted. And with her mother in labor, and all the women attending her, including Caerie's nursemaid, her guardians had restricted her and Nicki to the general confines of the nursery.

Oddly enough, the gardener had recently planted a small tree in the middle of the garden. The old fellow had once told her he didn't plant trees in that garden because the blossoms in question thrived on direct sunlight and withered without it; so why the change of mind? On second thought, the tree wasn't that small, or perhaps it had grown significantly in just a few heartbeats, which seemed strange. As she looked on, its edges shifted and flowed, melted and swirled, and her heartrate quickened. Branches formed in an instant, grew and lengthened, leaves sprouted, blossoms unfurled, and pollen swirled through the air. An aged oak now stood in the center of the flower garden, tall and majestic with a canopy that extended over a good portion of the garden. But it had an air of unreality to it, like an unsophisticated painting drawn by a childish artist.

A young peasant boy about her own age stood in the shade beneath the oak's branches. He seemed more defined, more real than the tree. He wore crude, homespun clothing, his breeches held in place by a length of rope that served as a belt. Oblivious to her standing in the window above him, he remained statue-still, his right arm extended slightly out, palm up. He stood there staring intently at the inside of his forearm, and from the color of his skin she realized he was not Scairn. If so, he would not be the only servant in the palace born of Lowlands or Duchies stock.

The branches of the tree's canopy cast mottled shadows across his face. A faint breeze ruffled the leaves above him, turning the shadows into an ever-changing swirl of colors and hues that obscured his features. He lifted his chin and looked upward, and she hoped she might see something in his eyes. But the churning shadows made it impossible to discern anything beyond splotches of light and dark. If she were to encounter him somewhere on the palace grounds, she doubted she would recognize him.

The breeze suddenly calmed, and with it the shadows ceased dancing about him. He grew indistinct, and as she looked on, the lines of his clothing blurred. She now saw through him to the trunk of the tree behind him, and slowly he faded, then vanished like a puff of steam from a simmering pot. The tree remained, but then it too lost its hold on the here and now, and in a matter of seconds it followed the boy and disappeared as if it had never been.

# 2

# Worst Fears

THE EVENING'S FESTIVITIES clearly pleased young Duke Jarrod. And while Lord and Lady Kadmarkh were obviously provincial, they spiced the fare with lively and witty conversation. By any account, the event proved to be an unquestioned success. But Kainborne enjoyed none of it.

"Why the long face, Councilor?"

Jarrod's words brought Kainborne's thoughts back to the moment. With the young duke seated in the middle of the head table, and Kainborne at its far end, the duke had raised his voice to reach him, and all there now focused on his reply.

Kainborne struggled to come up with a plausible answer. "We've been away from Dramoran for quite some time, Your Grace. In one week we'll return, and there are a great number of issues that have arisen in your absence."

As the newly seated Duke of Dramoran, Jarrod's inaugural tour of his vassals' estates had taken almost three months. Jarrod smiled at Lord and Lady Kadmarkh. "The man is invaluable. He has a constant stream of riders bringing reports from Dramoran and sending my decrees back to them. He worries about all the things that need worrying about, freeing me to enjoy the pleasure of your company."

The lord and lady beamed at the compliment, and the conversation moved on to matters that did not involve Kainborne.

He struggled through the evening, his thoughts obsessed with the birthmark he had seen on the boy's arm. Had he actually seen such an image, or had his imagination run away from him? He was almost certain what he had seen on the boy's arm was called a Dreadmark, and tried to recall everything he had read about such an omen. He'd come across only a few obscure references to it, and since it had apparently not manifested for many generations, he really hadn't taken them seriously. Kainborne had viewed such reports with considerable skepticism: a rune that heralded doom of some sort; a rune the writer himself and all his contemporaries had never seen. Accounts of that nature were almost always legend and myth, and he now regretted he hadn't paid more attention to them. He chaffed to return to Dramoran, to immerse himself in his scrolls. He would find any and every reference to birthmarks and dissect them meticulously, especially if they also included mention of the Dreadmark.

A high-pitched laugh from Lady Kadmarkh drew Kainborne out of his reverie. He leaned forward to look toward the center of the table. Jarrod clearly enjoyed the company of Glenmoore and his wife, and any hope that the evening might end early disappeared.

• • • •

Ket caught a thermal, spread his wings, and used the air currents to stay aloft without effort. He felt free and alive, with an infinite world of open skies about him. He could go anywhere, do anything, or be anyone, but he was content to just coast on the warm air and scan the ground beneath him. He looked left, then right, and the corner of his eye caught a momentary glimpse of the patch of discolored white feathers beneath his right wing. The white didn't match the mottled reddish-brown that covered the rest of his body, but he paid it no heed.

He caught a hint of movement to his left, so he dipped that wing to circle slowly about, coasting silently above his prey, his eyes riveted to the ground. Might it have been a mouse, or a squirrel, or better yet, bigger game like a rabbit or pheasant? Keeping the position of the sun in mind, he circled wide. He took care to ensure his shadow didn't cross the cluster of thick grasses where he thought his next meal might be hiding.

A tiny spot of dark shadow shifted, moving in a way inconsistent with the gentle sway of grasses in the soft breeze. He dipped his left wing again and circled in closer, still aware of his shadow skating across the ground. It could be a rabbit, and if it was, and he succeeded, he'd have his hunger satisfied for a couple of days.

Another hint of movement. Yes, a brown rabbit, and he had it now. Without taking his eyes off his meal, he dipped the wing deeply, abruptly changing direction and bringing him around into a direct line toward his target. He tucked his wings in and rocketed toward the ground, the grass and the small animal appearing to rush toward him closer and closer and closer. At the last instant, a slight tweak of his wings allowed him to bring his razor-sharp talons forward just as he smashed into the animal. The rabbit let out one squeal of pain, but Ket had it gripped tightly as they tumbled and bounced then came to a stop. The animal lay silent and still in his grip, impaled on his talons.

A woman's voice slithered through the back of his thoughts like the hiss of a snake. "Where is he?" It was not the first time she had come to his dreams. As always, she spoke in the tongue of the Mountain Folk, and sounded like one of the gentle people.

A man's voice answered her, equally chilling in its malice. "I know not, my love." He spoke in the tongue of the Duchies, but with an accent Ket didn't recognize.

Ket started and opened his eyes, confused by the night and darkness that surrounded him. It took him a moment to realize the dream of flying on the wings of a hawk had been only that, a dream and nothing more. His dream had ended with that woman and that man searching for someone, which seemed to happen more frequently now.

Disappointment washed over him as he realized he lay on his small sleeping mat, and the night air of the castle remained still and silent. The small wooden beds where his mother and the other Scairn women slept remained empty. The noble folk must still be enjoying themselves at the feast.

• • • •

By the time the festivities finally ended, Jarrod had consumed more than his share of drink and retired to his suite of rooms, leaving Kainborne to his own devices. As he rushed back to his room, he encountered a Scairn servant in the hallway and cornered the woman. "Tell the cook the feast is done, and I'll be waiting in my room for the girl."

The servant eyed him fearfully. "Yes, Your Lordship." She scurried away.

Kainborne did not need a large room, but had requested one with a lock, using the excuse that it would contain important communications from Dramoran that should not be accessible to just anyone. He hurried up a broad flight of stairs to the second floor, and at the door to his room, retrieved the key from his robes. He unlocked the door, opened it, and stepped through it. To make sure no one disturbed him, he then closed and securely locked it.

Lord Kadmarkh had given him a room clearly meant for guests, though not those of the highest station. It contained a large bed without canopy, a nightstand, and a desk and chair. They had arrived in late evening the day before, and that morning he had sat at that desk reading reports from Dramoran while a maid cleaned the room. He had kept a surreptitious eye on her and took great care not to appear fearful or suspicious, but he allowed no one in that room without him present. When he left the room he always carefully locked the door.

He crossed to a window and looked out at the castle's courtyard below. Flaming sconces lit the grounds in a dim, red glow of flickering fire. It was late on a warm, comfortable evening with stars twinkling in a clear sky. No one moved about below, but there were guards on the ramparts and Kainborne never took chances. He shuttered the window, then turned and walked to a side table that contained three goblets, a pitcher of water, and a small flagon of wine. He poured a careful measure of wine into one goblet, just a few swallows, and carried it to the desk. From a lower drawer in the desk he withdrew a small strongbox. He retrieved another key from his robes and opened the chest. In it were over two dozen small vials that contained his tinctures. He sorted through them carefully, considering the effects they produced. Then he selected one that contained an oily brown fluid, removed its stopper, and placed two drops of the liquid into the goblet. As he swirled the wine in the goblet to mix it, a soft knock on the door interrupted him.

He returned the tincture to the strongbox, locked it, and hid it in the desk's drawer. Leaving the goblet on the desk, as he crossed the room he caught a brief glimpse of himself in a burnished brass mirror. He paused for a moment to examine his reflection. He kept his dark black hair swept back over his ears, with his beard neatly trimmed into a thin mustache and sharply defined goatee. The stress of the Dreadmark's appearance had disturbed him, and without conscious thought he stood there grimacing. That would frighten the young woman, and he needed her complacent and ready to answer his questions. It took an effort to soften the look and relax his features, but he managed.

He turned away from the mirror, walked to the door, unlocked it, and opened it. The young Scairn kitchen maid stood in the hallway with her eyes cast downward.

"Come in," he said as he stepped aside. "Come in."

She walked forward tentatively, walked past him like a small animal not sure of the intent of a dangerous creature nearby. She stopped in the middle of the room and turned to face him, though she stood motionless staring at the floor.

He closed the door and approached her. "You said the boy is yours?"

Her voice trembled as she spoke. "Yes, me lord."

"How old is he?"

"He just turned ten, me lord."

"Who is his father?"

She hesitated for a long moment. "I don't know, me lord."

She didn't seem at all the type, but perhaps she supplemented her meager fare from the kitchen by whoring out to the castle's guardsmen. Or perhaps Kadmarkh loaned her to them to keep them happy. He needed that clarified. "You take many men to your bed, do you? So many you don't know the boy's parentage?"

She shook her head and finally met his eyes. "No, me lord, just the one."

That didn't add up. "And you have no idea who he was?"

She grimaced. "A guest here in the castle, me lord, an older man."

Kainborne considered her words carefully: an older man, a guest in the castle. That almost certainly implied he had been a nobleman of some sort, and it had been ten years ago plus nine months. Thinking of the boy's pale blue eyes, Kainborne's heart quickened.

"Describe this older man."

She shrugged. "He was old, me lord, an aged old man."

To a young woman like her, especially almost eleven years ago, anyone more than ten years her senior would be an *aged old man*. "How tall was he?"

"Tall, me lord. The top of me head barely reached his shoulder."

The girl standing in front of Kainborne was tall for a woman, which meant the father of the boy stood taller than most. "Was he fat or trim, muscled or weak?"

"He seemed quite hearty, me lord. Broad shoulders he had, and for an older man, his waist was not large, and his stomach only stuck out a little. He was kind, he was, and gentle."

Little by little her description of the man, along with the boy's pale blue eyes, appeared to point in only one direction. Kainborne couldn't hide the stress in his voice as he demanded, "Tell me of his hair, woman. Was he bald, or if he had hair was it gray, or black, or brown, or what?"

She cringed and took a half step back. "It was full, me lord, and it was dark brown, not a speck of gray in it."

To hide his reaction, Kainborne turned away from her and closed his eyes. Jarrod's father, the old duke, until the day he died, had been a tall man with broad shoulders and a trim waist. But his most striking features had been unusually pale blue eyes, and a full head of hair that remained dark brown long after it should have gone gray. Jarrod had inherited his mother's brown eyes, not his father's blue. And Kainborne recalled that when Jarrod had come of age, his father had presented him with a valuable bow crafted by the Mountain Folk. That had been on his fifteenth birthday a little less than eleven years ago. To celebrate, the duke had taken his son on his first extended hunting expedition, a journey for which Kainborne's presence was not required. They slept mostly in blankets around a campfire, but had spent a few nights at the castle of a nearby vassal. Kainborne had never asked who that had been, but a casual question or two the next morning should clear that up.

It took Kainborne several seconds to calm his racing heart, and once it slowed he turned back to the girl. "And you said the boy's name is Kit . . . or Kat . . . or something like that?"

The girl lowered her eyes. "Ketcaerm, me lord. His name is Ketcaerm, but we just calls him Ket."

Kainborne had heard or come across that word, but he couldn't recall exactly where or when. "Ketcaerm, a Scairn word, is it?"

The girl continued to stare at the floor. "Aye, me lord."

"What does it mean?"

She shook her head. "I don't know, me lord."

"How long have you lived here in Glenmoore?"

Her voice trembled as she spoke. "Most of me life, me lord."

Given her present age, they had probably taken her as a pre-pubescent child, and she knew little of the customs of the Mountain Folk. He had done a poor job of hiding his anger. "Why did you choose that name?"

The girl's eyes blinked rapidly and she gulped. "It . . . me lord . . . the midwife, one of me kinswomen recommended it, said she heard it somewheres. And I liked it because I wanted him to have a Scairn name."

Kainborne had gotten the information he needed, but he could not dismiss the girl without fulfilling the excuse he had used to get her there. If she told the rest of the kitchen staff all he did was question her about the boy's father, tongues might wag, and he didn't want anyone's attention focused on the boy.

He really wasn't sure how to begin, and he spoke haltingly. "I asked you to come here because . . . well . . . you are . . ."

She frowned, reached up and untied a strap on her dress.

"No," he said. "That's not necessary."

He turned away from her, crossed the room to the desk, retrieved the goblet, returned to her and extended it toward her. "Drink this. It's wine. It'll calm you."

She reached out and took the goblet from his hands, lifted it to her mouth, and took a tentative sip.

He had to make sure she got the full and proper dose of the tincture. "Drink it all. I insist."

She downed the few swallows of wine he had poured into the goblet, then handed it back to him. He turned away from her and placed the goblet on the nightstand next to the bed. When he turned back, he saw that in just those few seconds the tincture had already produced a slight effect. He gripped her shoulders, and as he backed her the short distance to the bed, her eyes rolled about and she grew increasingly unsteady on her feet.

He took her by the waist and lifted her up to sit on the edge of the bed. She groaned and fell back, laid there staring at the ceiling, her head lolling from side to side. She mumbled something incoherent as he lifted her skirts, unfastened her undergarments, and pulled them down to her ankles. He wasn't actually going to do anything, but he must leave her with the impression he had.

With one hand he rubbed at the soft flesh between her legs, and with the other reached up and fondled her breasts like a crude peasant overcome with lust. Inexperienced at such activities, he probably did a clumsy job of it, but that might fix the memories of his actions in her mind all the more. Since the tincture didn't render her completely unconscious, she'd have vague memories of it all. And that he didn't leave his seed in her wouldn't make any difference. It was not uncommon for a man of noble station to finish the job by spilling his seed in his own hand, eliminating the possibility of a bastard heir wandering about, though any half-breed Scairn who came forth as a claimant would quickly find himself hanging from the end of a rope. In any case, the tincture would muddle her thinking, cloud her memories of that evening. If she told the kitchen staff of his interest in the boy's father, it would sound disjointed and unclear.

After several minutes of pretending to take pleasure from her, he walked to the desk and sat down in the chair to wait. She fell asleep for a brief period, and while he sat there waiting he drifted off into a drowsy state of half-sleep. He dreamt of a half-cat, half-bird demon, and jerked awake, his heart beating rapidly.

In one of his scrolls he had come across the Scairn word *ketcaerm*, or something like it. It had been some time ago, but as he recalled, *ket* was their word for a fledgling raptor, like a hawk or eagle, and *caerm* their word for a mountain lioness cub. To the Scairn midwife who had recommended the name to the girl, it had probably meant little more than a pleasant-sounding name she had heard somewhere. It was unlikely either woman knew they had named the child after a mythical demon of the mountain realm.

That was probably all there was to it. He closed his eyes and tried to slow his breathing, but the recollection bothered him, and he swore that once they returned to Dramoran, he would search his scrolls for any references to that word.

After some minutes the girl's eyes fluttered open and she sat up, though she still swayed unsteadily. Had he given her more than a few drops of the tincture, she might have slept the night through.

He stood and crossed the room. "I think you had too much wine."

"But," she said, blinking her eyes rapidly and shaking her head. "I only had a few . . . swallows . . . me lord."

He feigned surprise. "You don't remember? After those first few sips you asked for more, and drank an entire goblet."

She had trouble focusing her eyes. "Yes, I must have."

He helped her pull her clothing back together then saw her to the door. But he paused there, the question of the midwife who had named the boy rising to the surface of his thoughts. "This midwife you spoke of, the one who named the boy. Who is she?"

The young girl shook her head as she tried to focus. "Oh . . . uh . . . she got the cough four years ago . . . She died."

Kainborne opened the door, and the young girl did not look back as she walked down the hall, swaying unsteadily from side to side.

He closed the door, locked it, crossed the room to the desk, once again retrieved the strongbox, and unlocked it. From the many tinctures he selected two. One contained a pale amber liquid; a few drops of that in a person's wine, and the next morning they would exhibit the symptoms of one who had eaten bad meat, though in a few days that would pass without any lasting effects. The second vial contained a bright green powder. Three pinches of that would kill within an hour, while just one pinch might take a day or two.

He considered the two vials carefully, recalling that he, Jarrod, and the young duke's retinue would not leave Glenmoore until three days hence. It wouldn't do to blemish Jarrod's visit with the death of the young woman. Kainborne decided to take no action for the moment, but in the morning, if he confirmed his suspicions, then shortly before their departure he would see to it she received two drops of the amber, and one pinch of the green. The morning after their departure the young girl would fall ill, then a day or two later she would die. And no one would guess that her demise had been caused by anything but bad meat. Kainborne had other preparations to make, but now he knew what must be done, and how to do it properly.

# 3

# The Fledgling and the Cub

THE LITTLE KITTY crouched and stared fiercely at Ket's hand as he walked his fingers across the ground in front of it. With its belly almost touching the dirt, it edged forward to within arm's reach of his hand and froze. It remained inhumanly still for several seconds, then for a moment its butt and tail waggled rapidly, and it pounced.

The kitty was faster than Ket and caught his hand before he yanked it away. As he laughed, it growled and snarled, wrapping its body around his hand and killing its newfound prey. But it must know they were only playing, for while it clamped its jaws on his fingers, its teeth never penetrated the skin. He got a few scratches from its big clumsy paws, but the game they played was far too much fun to worry about that.

The kitty released his hand, backed away, turned, looked Ket in the eyes, and emitted a throaty growl. But while Ket's ears heard the growl of a kitten, his head heard the voice of a young girl saying, "Again."

Ket extended his hand, walked his fingers across the ground, and again the kitty pounced. It growled and hissed while Ket laughed until tears filled his eyes. He leaned back to catch his breath, and looking up he saw a pretty young girl standing in a window above him. And even from that distance he recognized the amber eyes and vertically slit pupils of a Scairn girl.

A hand gently shook Ket's shoulder. "Ket, me boy, time to wake up."

Ket opened his eyes and realized the kitty had been just a dream. His mum stood over him smiling kindly. "Time to fire the ovens, me boy."

• • • •

With her belly almost touching the ground, she crouched low on all fours and eased forward through the tall grass, one step at a time. She hesitated, pushed up slowly with her front paws, and lifted her muzzle just above the top of the grasses. Approaching the small herd of deer from downwind, she easily caught their scent on a light breeze. She lowered her front quarters back to the ground and continued forward.

Caerie marveled at the power and strength in her limbs. Her mouth watered at the thought of tasting the deer's blood, and crunching its bones in her powerful jaws. And even though the air carried a chill, the sun high above warmed the fur on her back. She continued forward another ten paces then paused, and again raised her muzzle to confirm the deer had not moved.

The time had come where discipline and caution were most needed. So close to the kill, the temptation to prematurely rush forward hammered at her, but she resisted the urge.

She reached the edge of the tall grasses, lowered her body to the ground, and rested her jaw on her front paws. About twenty paces from her, six deer foraged beneath the canopy of a small stand of olive trees, picking at ripe fruit dropped to the ground. Occasionally a buck or doe raised a head to glance about, but the yellow color of Caerie's fur blended perfectly with that of the grass, so she did not fear discovery.

A yearling doe meandered a little closer to her hiding place. But if she attacked now, and it saw her the moment she moved, the distance would still be a challenge. Then the doe turned aside, probably following a trail of ripe fruit. Caerie scanned the other deer and noted that they were all angled away from her, and would have to crane their necks and look over their shoulders to see her. And then the yearling turned away from her as well.

She lifted her belly off the ground and tensed, judging the moment, and decided her chance had come. She shot forward, charging with all the power and strength her muscles could deliver. Luck was with her and she covered half the distance to her target before any of them understood the danger descending upon them. And then in an instant they all moved like lightning.

The yearling darted to one side, and Caerie dug her paws into the ground to change direction. It wasn't enough, but as she passed the doe she threw one paw out with her claws extended, and caught the yearling's hindquarters, striking it with enough force to knock it to the ground in a sprawl. Caerie spun about and reversed direction just as her prey recovered. But she spotted blood on the doe's hip, and smelled it in the air. Her claws had done their job and the doe moved with less speed and agility.

At the next pass Caerie caught the yearling with another swipe of her claws, then was upon her, clamping her teeth on the doe's throat, pulling her to the ground.

Caerie crushed the deer's throat, and lay there to wait for the inevitable, her heart pounding in her chest. She would feast well that night.

Caerie snapped awake and lay still for a moment, trying to get her bearings. The lioness's hunt and kill had been exhilarating beyond belief, and her breathing came in rapid bursts as she slowly calmed down. Dawn had come to the nursery and a shaft of sunlight spilled through the window.

She sat up in bed and rubbed sleep from her eyes. She wanted to lie back and return to the power and glory of the lioness's body, but that was simply a dream, though not like any she had ever had before. It had been so real, so thrilling, almost intoxicating.

She swung her legs off the bed, slid her rear off the edge of the mattress, and lowered her bare feet to the cold stone floor. She didn't want to wake her nursemaid, so she took care to make as little noise as possible. The woman had assisted in the delivery of Caerie's new younger brother. And with the dangers of a difficult birth now behind them, she, along with most of the castle, needed more rest than a single night could offer. Caerie also had an ulterior motive.

She picked her slippers up off the floor, tiptoed across the room to a plush chair, sat down and pulled them on. She threw on a robe, then walked as silently as possible to the window that overlooked the flower garden. Thankfully, unlatching the shutters produced no noise. But as she slowly opened them, their hinges creaked and she hesitated. Caerie paused with the shutters half open and waited, but her brother Nicki didn't storm into the room demanding an explanation for why she had arisen early. When no one else reacted, she carefully opened the shutters fully.

She looked down at the morning mist that enveloped the flowers in the garden and saw no tree, no peasant boy. The image of the tree had intrigued her because she had seen it's like before, but at the time couldn't recall exactly where. She thought it had something to do with one of the noble houses of the Four Duchies. And after seeing the vision of the boy and tree the first time, she had gone to her mother's library and hunted down a leather-bound book on the houses of Kyldaine. She had only recently started to read, and most of the words she saw in that tome were indecipherable to her. But on one page a charcoal sketch beautifully displayed an image like the tree she had seen in the flower garden. She now suspected the image she had seen was not just any tree, but the Mark of House Dramoran. After that she returned to that window several times, hoping the tree and the boy would reappear, hoping she might finally see his face. But looking now, she saw only a garden of flowers. She realized her vision the previous day had been nothing more than a transient hallucination, a flight of her own fancy. Nicki had told her many times she had an overactive imagination, and after he said that, they would then argue.

Thinking of Nicki, she glanced over her shoulder just to be certain he hadn't snuck up behind her, which would be so like him. Satisfied that she remained alone she looked again at the garden, and there she saw the peasant boy seated beneath the canopy of the ancient oak. The tree again appeared as if it were a clumsy painting by a childish artist. The boy wore the same clothing, the same homespun shirt and breeches, the same short length of rope that served as a belt. He looked her way and smiled, though since the mottled shadows beneath the leaves of the tree obscured his features, she couldn't say how she knew he smiled.

Something on the ground in front of him jumped, drawing her attention. A small cat paced back and forth in front of him. He played with it, walking his fingers across the ground in front of it and allowing the animal to pounce upon an imagined mouse. The cat was barely a kitten, with yellow fur, and paws much too large to be those of an ordinary cat. The paws were the clue she needed, and she realized then he was not playing mouse to a simple cat, but to a mountain lion cub, a female, a small caerm.

A woman's voice hissed through the back of Caerie's thoughts. "Where is he?" The voice held such malice and hate it frightened Caerie.

A man's voice answered her. "I know not, my love."

It surprised Caerie that the man spoke the common non-Mythrian tongue with a refined Lowlands accent, while the woman had spoken High Mythrian of the court. But regardless of language or accent, both bore the same malevolence.

The vision vanished, Caerie gasped, and she staggered back from the window.

Thankfully, no one heard her. Nicki would have rushed in to accuse her of being childish, or her nursemaid would have fawned over her, fearful some miasma had taken her. She vowed then she would reveal her visions to no one.

• • • •

Each morning Kainborne met with Jarrod to review important dispatches from the duchy. On the morning of the second day of their stay at Glenmoore, as the young duke signed an order for the execution of a recently captured highwayman, Kainborne casually said, "Your Grace, this is your first visit to Glenmoore, is it not?"

Jarrod finished scribbling his signature, then looked at Kainborne and shook his head. "No, councilor, not quite. Father and I spent a few nights here once. Remember when I came of age and Father took me on that hunting expedition? We grew tired of eating game burned over an open fire. Our guardsmen were good at keeping me and Father alive, but they weren't good at cooking. Oh, and I stayed here for a single night a few years back, though Father wasn't with me at the time. By the way, I still cherish that bow Father gifted me, though it hasn't seen much use of late."

Kain waited patiently, and the day before they departed from Glenmoore, with his suspicions now confirmed, he visited the kitchen one last time. Using the same excuse, he instructed the cook to send the young kitchen maid to his room that night. Prior to her arrival he again prepared the goblet of wine and added a few drops of the oily brown tincture. To that he added a pinch of the green and two drops of the amber.

She came to his room as instructed, and again he made her drink the wine. The brown tincture produced the same drowsy effect in her, and he repeated his feigned performance at lust. Again, she fell asleep briefly, again she awoke, and again he sent her on her way. Then he cleaned the goblet carefully. It could complicate matters if someone used it for a quick drink of water and received a hint of the tinctures he had given the girl.

With that part of his plan in place, he made his way down to the barracks where the guards in Jarrod's retinue bunked. As he approached the building, he heard the din of soldiers arguing, laughing, and probably telling stories that none of them believed. But when he stepped into the room, silence descended and all motion stopped.

Two rows of cots lined the walls on his right and left, with an aisle down the middle. At the far end of the room a group of soldiers sat at a table, all focused on a game of dice. Several others sat on their bunks, sharpening weapons or repairing tack. Kainborne didn't spot the man he sought until the fellow stood, stepped out into the aisle between bunks, and calmly walked his way. The fellow wore his pale brown hair down to his shoulders, had a scar on his right cheek, and several on his forearms. He stopped in front of Kainborne and smiled, though the puckered scar on his cheek wrinkled into something more like a grimace. "Master Kainborne."

Kainborne acknowledged him with a nod. "A word with you, Zarkoffa."

Zarkoffa's smile broadened.

Kainborne turned and walked out of the barracks, and heard the fellow's footsteps as he followed. He employed the man for special assignments, frequently involving activities the duke might frown upon. The man was a talented assassin, though Jarrod knew nothing of such nefarious skills.

Kainborne stopped in the middle of the castle's courtyard well away from any structure, satisfied no one could hide nearby and eavesdrop on their conversation. He turned to face the fellow and lowered his voice. "You identified the boy?"

The man's face could have been cut from stone for all the expression it held. "As you instructed, I passed through the kitchens and spotted him easily; the blue eyes are quite telling. I checked further and learned he sleeps on a mat on the floor in a room with the girl and several other female servants, all of them Scairn. I'll have no trouble getting him when the time comes. What do you want me to do with him?"

One talent Kainborne valued in the man was his ability to think, which meant Kainborne didn't have to spell everything out for him. "Tomorrow, when we depart, you'll remain behind. I've told Lord Kadmarkh you're carrying dispatches in a different direction from that we'll be traveling. By tomorrow morning the girl will be quite ill, and by tomorrow evening close to death. Under the cover of darkness, and the confusion caused by her impending demise, spirit the boy away and take him to the monastery in the Vale of Tramorth. And above all, make sure you're not seen and do not harm the boy."

Kainborne had thought long and hard about what he would do with the lad. A quick death would be a simple and easy solution, but until he knew more, that course of action was much too irreversible. "Tell the abbot I want him to treat the boy well and care for him. I have to gather more information before I decide exactly what to do with him, and in a month or two I'll give the abbot more detailed instructions."

The man nodded. "As you wish."

Kainborne lowered his voice further. "For now I want the boy alive and well, and out of the way and under my control. But I may eventually require you to make him disappear completely. Regardless, you'll be paid well."

The man grinned. "I always am."

# 4

# To Tramorth

KET SAT ON his sleeping mat on the floor, his back to the stone wall, knees pulled tightly up against his chest, eyes closed. He had tried desperately to sleep, but worry and fear had prevented him from finding any rest. His mum suffered from some horrible illness; had eaten bad meat, they said. That morning he had watched her empty the contents of her stomach all over the floor, then grow steadily worse as the day progressed. By late afternoon she didn't even recognize him. His mum didn't even know him, and then they took her away.

"You poor lad."

Those words had been spoken in the tongue of the Mountain Folk, which they used among themselves when only Scairn were about. To speak it in the presence of others might earn one a flogging.

A hand ruffled his hair. He opened his eyes and looked up to see one of the older Scairn women standing over him. Her amber eyes seemed to glow faintly in the late afternoon light as tears streamed down her cheeks. A teardrop spilled off her chin and spattered on the back of his hand. He desperately needed to know. "How's me mum?"

She sniffled and ruffled his hair again. "We'll take care of you, lad. We'll take care of you just fine."

Her chest heaved with sobs as she turned and walked out of the room. "You poor lad. You poor lad."

Ket closed his eyes and lowered his head to his knees. He eventually drifted off into a kind of half-sleep, but a heavy hand shook his shoulder.

"Up with you, boy," a gruff voice said. "You're to come with me."

Ket opened his eyes. Night had come and darkness filled the room. Dim light splashed through the doorway from a sconce in the hallway. It illuminated a silhouette standing over him. "Come on, boy, we got no time to waste."

A man with shoulder-length hair stood over him, though Ket saw nothing of his features because the darkness and shadows hid his face.

"Where are we going?"

The dark man leaned closer and whispered. "To see your ma."

Ket climbed quickly to his feet. "Is she okay?"

The man gripped his arm just above the elbow, clamping his fingers around it painfully. "Only the physikers can answer that question, boy."

The fellow hustled Ket out of the sleeping room. Ket stepped quickly to keep up with the man's long strides as he marched down the dimly lit hallway. It was clearly late because the halls were empty and they encountered no one. When they came to an intersecting hallway, the dark man stopped and peered around the corner before moving on. The man led him out into the castle yard, and they didn't march straight across it, but moved through the shadows of the sheds and buildings lining its periphery.

The dark man stopped at the castle gate and spoke briefly to a guard. He handed the fellow something and said, "Remember, you never saw me or the boy."

The guard grunted some sort of reply.

The dark man kept his painful grip on Ket's arm. Once outside the castle wall he quickened his pace, and Ket ran to keep up. He pleaded, "Where's me mum?"

"Be silent," the man snarled.

The man didn't slow his pace until they entered a small copse of trees. Then he stopped, turned to face Ket without releasing his arm, and looked down at him. "Be quiet and don't make a sound. If you make any noise I'll be very angry, and you won't like it if I get angry."

"But where's me mum?"

The dark man shook his head. "She's gone. You ain't never gonna see her again. If she ain't dead yet, she will be soon."

His mum was dead, and Ket couldn't hold back his tears. He sobbed, but at the sound the dark man reached out with his free hand and gripped Ket's throat even tighter than he gripped his arm. As Ket struggled to breathe the fellow leaned down and Ket smelled garlic on his breath. "You can cry, boy, but do it quietly. Remember, you don't want me angry, so don't make no noise."

A faint glow from torches on the castle's parapets cast the only light among the trees. But it was enough for Ket to see the man's eyes for the first time, and he saw only cold, uncaring indifference. He choked back his sobs, but couldn't stop his tears.

In the copse of trees, the dark man led him to a saddled horse tied to the limb of a tree. The fellow lifted Ket easily and plopped him into the saddle. From that height

it seemed a great distance to the ground, and he feared the horse might buck and un-
seat him.

The dark man untied the horse's reins, then led the horse out of the trees while
Ket clutched desperately at the saddle. When they reached the road, the stranger again
lifted Ket, but now placed him straddling the horse's shoulders just in front of the
saddle. Then he climbed into the saddle behind Ket, took the reins, and spurred the
animal into a terrifying trot. And even though the man's arms enclosed him, Ket
gripped the horse's mane and held on for dear life.

The man smelled of leather and sweat, and the night smelled of fear and sorrow.

• • • •

"Come on, boy, wake up."

Ket started awake and gasped, bright rays of light blinding him as the sun rose
over distant peaks. He still sat on the horse's shoulders in front of the saddle, the dark
man's arms enclosing him. They had come to a stop and Ket wondered why.

The saddle creaked and joggled as the man shifted his weight then stepped down
and stood on the ground beside the horse. He gripped Ket under his armpits and lifted him as if he weighed nothing, then placed him on the ground to stand facing him.

Ket looked up at the dark man, seeing him for the first time in the clear light of
day. Thick, pale brown hair hung down to his shoulders in oily strands. A puckered
scar on his right cheek extended from the edge of his mouth to his ear. A much
smaller scar bisected his left eyebrow.

"We're gonna rest for a bit," he said. "We made good time, got far enough away,
nobody's gonna follow us. If you got to shit or piss, take care of it in the brush. But
don't go far. There's wolves in this forest, and the occasional big cat. You won't be
much of a meal for 'em, but that won't stop 'em from eating you."

Ket glanced about. They had stopped in a clearing near a small creek that crackled
with flowing water. He saw no sign of a road, but a game trail passed through the
clearing. Ket did need to pee, so he turned away from the man and stepped out of the
clearing, though he didn't go more than a few paces. He untied the short length of
rope that kept his pants up and relieved himself, then laced his breeches and retied
the rope.

When he returned to the clearing the dark man knelt over a small pile of sticks.
He held a heavy knife in one hand, and struck the back edge of the blade against a
flint. It showered a stream of sparks over a small puff of what looked like fuzzy,
frayed cloth. Ket had heard of flint and steel, but in the kitchens at Glenmoore, at
night they simply banked the fires in the ovens, then brought the coals back to life in

the morning. That had been Ket's job, to help his mum fire the ovens each morning. Thinking of her, tears welled up in his eyes, and recalling the man's words from the night before, he choked back his sobs, but not his tears.

As the dark man coaxed a fire to life in a small pile of sticks, Ket sat on the ground opposite him. The fellow wore a waist-length leather jerkin over a cloth blouse of some sort. The leather sleeves of the jerkin ended at his elbows, and he'd rolled the cuffs of the blouse up, exposing his forearms, where Ket noticed several scars. "How did you get those scars?"

The man paused, held up his right arm and looked at it for a moment. "Knife work," he said. "Close-in knife work." He pointed the blade of the heavy knife at Ket to make his point. "If you ever gotta kill a man, best do it from a distance with a crossbow, or a bow and arrow. If you gotta do it close, sneak up on him from behind quiet-like and cut his throat so he can't shout, then finish him with the blade in his heart."

Ket wasn't sure what the man was trying to say.

"Here," the man said.

Ket looked up just in time to see a leather pouch arcing through the air toward him over the fire. He had only an instant, but he reacted quickly and caught it.

"Eat your fill," the man said. "We won't get to the Vale of Tramorth until late to-day, and you won't get nothing else 'till then."

Ket opened the pouch and found strips of dried meat. His stomach growled, and while the meat didn't look terribly appetizing, he had no trouble selecting a piece and shoving it into his mouth. It was hard and salty, and choking it down required water from the creek and a lot of chewing. The man sat on the other side of the fire also chewing jerky as they ate in silence.

When the man finished eating, he stood, turned about and stepped to the edge of the clearing. He unlaced his breeches and peed on a bush. Then he turned back, and while lacing his breeches he said, "I'm going to get an hour's sleep or so. Sit quiet and don't wake me. And don't go wandering through the forest. If you get lost, I probably won't find you, but them wolves will."

He retrieved a blanket from the horse and laid down on his back by the fire. He rested his head on a rock, closed his eyes, and became completely still. Ket couldn't tell if he'd immediately gone to sleep or not.

If it was an hour that the man slept it seemed like an eternity. Little noises filled the forest, and Ket imagined that every creak, crack, chirp, or flutter was the sound of one of those wolves stalking him. When the tall stranger did finally awake, he seemed to transform from sound sleep to stand fully upright in an instant. "Up with you, boy. Time to move on."

The man lifted Ket back up to his place on the horse's shoulders, climbed into the saddle behind him, and aimed the horse down the game trail. To Ket's surprise, they reached the road in about a hundred paces.

Ket had never heard of the Vale of Tramorth, had no idea what or where it might be. He spent the day sitting on the horse in front of the man. Sometimes he cried quiet tears for his mum, sometimes he dozed in shallow and fitful sleep, sometimes he watched the countryside pass by, bored by the monotony of never-ending fields, forest, and hills. They occasionally passed someone going by in the other direction. The first time that happened, the dark man said, "Don't say anything. Don't even move."

Interestingly enough, everyone who passed them looked away and didn't make eye contact with the dark man. Ket thought he understood why.

In late afternoon they crested a low rise in the road, and below them Ket saw a green valley with the mists of early evening settling over it. Smoke rose from a dozen chimneys interspersed over the valley floor. All appeared to be small farmhouses or steadings, with thatched roofs and mud-brick walls. But in the far distance, a large, stone structure stood out by its size. Enclosed within a wall of stone blocks, to Ket it looked much like the castle where he had grown up. The road wound across the valley and passed close by the walled structure.

"The Vale of Tramorth," the dark man said.

• • • •

It took two days to travel from Glenmoore to Dramoran. Thankfully, after months journeying from one liege lord's holding to the next, Jarrod was eager to return to home, hearth, and fire, and did not delay them with any foolish side excursions. That eminently suited Kainborne's own desires.

They arrived late in the afternoon on the second day of travel. Since they had sent out riders ahead of them, the cook had a hearty meal ready and waiting. Jarrod was not in the mood for a feast and ordered dinner brought up to his rooms, where he closeted himself with the meal, a flagon of wine, and a couple of his favorite whores. That suited Kainborne's wishes. He ordered dinner brought to his workshop, and intended to closet himself there with his oaf of an assistant, and his most important scrolls.

Shelves of scrolls, jars of ointments, vials of tinctures, and the preserved skeletons of various strange animals made his workshop a crowded space. When Kainborne stepped into the room, his assistant sat slumped in a chair snoring loudly, his mouth open and drooling a stain of spittle on his shirt.

"Up with you," Kainborne shouted.

The idiot started, jumped up from the chair, and banged his head on an over-hanging shelf, opening a gash in his scalp. With blood trickling down his face, he bowed deeply. "Master Kainborne, I'm at yer service."

"Of course, you're at my service," Kainborne shouted as the fellow cringed. "We're going to be working all night. I want every scroll that mentions a tattoo or a birthmark, and I want them now. And don't get any blood on the bloody scrolls or I'll have you flogged."

The fellow bowed, dripping blood on the floor. "Yes, master. Right away, master."

The fool was a moron, but he could read in a rudimentary fashion, which lent him some value. Kainborne tried to recall the fellow's actual name but couldn't, which didn't really matter since he always thought of him as simply *the oaf.* He sat down at his workbench, his heart calmed, and he realized that shouting at the idiot had been therapeutic.

A kitchen maid showed up with a tray of food. As the oaf rushed about mumbling and gathering scrolls, Kainborne sat down to eat. He had gone to a lot of trouble over the years to index and categorize his scrolls, which facilitated the oaf's ability to assist him. Kainborne selected a chicken drumstick from the tray, took a bite, and considered his next actions. He desperately wanted to find something that would allow him to take the simple expedient of having Zarkoffa strangle the little brat and bury his body in a shallow grave in some forest somewhere. Then he'd be done with strange and unsettling portents.

He hadn't asked for scrolls mentioning the Dreadmark, and would not do so. That might be a strange enough request for the oaf to remember it, and he did not want that word bandied about the castle. But in his vague recollection, every reference he had come across had been associated with a tattoo or birthmark, so that should be sufficient for the time being. Later, on his own, he'd conduct a more thorough search in case there were any references that weren't associated with a tattoo or birthmark.

The first scroll the oaf brought him discussed birthmarks, with no mention of the Dreadmark. A wealthy woman had authored it, and in it she discussed how the shape of a birthmark foretold a newborn child's future. It was pure drivel and a complete waste of time.

The next scroll was a lengthy volume penned about three hundred years earlier by a wealthy recluse who fancied himself a physiker, a practitioner of thaumaturgy, and an alchemist. But it read more like the ravings of a madman. The fellow believed that the bearer of the Dreadmark will . . . *defile the land and bring it to heel in the yoke of his degradation.* And because the Dreadmark had manifested, *oceans and seas will burn in the inferno of the netherworld until they are consumed and become deserts of blowing sand.* Kainborne rolled his eyes as he read. Apparently, mountains would also crumble and cities fall into rubble.

He leaned back and considered what he had just read. If there was any truth to that scroll, he'd definitely have Zarkoffa dispose of the boy. But before acting, he needed evidence more substantial than the hallucinations of some psychopath. Or he at least needed to establish that the lunatic wasn't a complete lunatic.

He read through that entire scroll just to be certain he had missed no references to birthmarks, tattoos, or the Dreadmark. It took more than an hour to do so, and by that time the oaf had piled ten more scrolls on his workbench. Since Kainborne had indexed them all, like the first, he'd find and read the appropriate references fairly quickly. But at the time he'd indexed them, references to the Dreadmark had sounded more like fanciful imaginings, and he hadn't taken them seriously. And like the first, after the initial scan, he'd have to read each scroll in its entirety to ensure that he hadn't overlooked any mention of the Dreadmark, no matter how trivial.

He looked at the pile of scrolls on his workbench and sighed wearily. He had anticipated a long night, but now knew it would take several nights and days.

# 5

# Unsettled Rule

THE OLD MAN lying in bed wheezed in a failed struggle to draw in breath. He was not as old as he looked, but two years of the wasting sickness had slowly sapped the strength, vitality, and vigor of the ruler of Carthagen, leaving but a shell of the once-vibrant man Aurelius remembered as his father. Where a year ago Marius's hair had been dark and full, there now remained only wispy strands of thin gray. And during his illness the skin of his face had faded from the olive hue characteristic of their family, to a sickly sheen of pale flesh stretched tightly over skeletal bones. It gave him a spectral appearance like something from a child's nightmare.

Seated at the old man's bedside, Aurelius's mother wore black mourning garb and seemed indifferent to the fate of her husband. Divonia's diamond-sharp beauty had not diminished with the years, and a few streaks of gray only added dimension to her dark black hair. When her mouth tightened with anger, as it so often did, only a smattering of faint creases surrounded her lips. Wealthy and influential men still sought her companionship, and her bed. Divonia sat near her dying husband trying to pretend she cared, and succeeded only a little.

A faint sob nearby drew Aurelius's attention. He looked to his right, found that his sister Porcia had entered the room and stopped beside him. A true beauty that any healthy man would covet, it was unlike her to leave her boudoir in a disheveled state. She would normally take care to have her hair arranged atop her head in a fashionable coif, but now it hung past her shoulders in a disarray of uncombed ringlets. And no makeup, no lip paint, nothing around her eyes, or on her cheeks. She was still a beauty without it, but he could not reconcile the frazzled woman standing next to him with the image that came to mind when he thought of his sister.

He reached out, put an arm around her shoulders, and pulled her against his side. She buried her face in the lapels of his coat, and more sobs ensued. Aurelius wanted to shed tears too, but he had already shed more than a year's worth. And in his heart he felt at peace with the old man's impending demise, for death would relieve Marius of the agony in which he now lived.

Porcia's sobs drew Divonia's attention. She looked their way, and her eyes focused on her daughter like daggers of sharp crystal. She stood and marched across the room, the folds of her black skirt fluttering behind her.

She stopped and faced Aurelius squarely. "What is going on here?"

Anger welled up in Aurelius's heart. "Our father is dying, Mother, and some of us feel sorrow."

"Yes, of course," she said, spitting her words as if expelling iron carpenter's nails from her mouth. "Don't state the obvious. The end is quite near, and that means you'll be playing a much more important role in the Senatus and all of Carthagen. If you state the obvious, those vultures will tear you apart. You're going to have to be on guard every moment of the day and night, and watch every word you speak."

She turned her anger on Porcia. "And you, you look atrocious. Do something about your appearance. How are you going to get an influential husband looking like a beggar on the street? And what will people think of us? Pull yourself together . . . daughter." The last word erupted from her mouth like a curse.

Divonia's head suddenly swiveled side to side in sharp jerks, like a hawk searching for its prey. "Where is Maximillian?"

Aurelius knew anything he said would only invite her wrath, but poor Max was in no shape to deal with her at that moment. "He's taking this much harder than the rest of us. He was closest to Father."

Interestingly enough, Aurelius did not begrudge his older brother his close relationship with their father, for Marius had been kind, loving, and fair to them all.

Divonia dismissed his words with a slash of her hand. "I know. I know. But we don't have time for sentimentality. It's going to be a nasty fight, but we will prevail and Max will inherit the Supremus. I will tolerate nothing less. He will be the Senatus Supreme, and I don't care who I have to kill to make it happen."

Her eyes focused past Aurelius at something behind him. "Come with me now." She stepped around him.

Aurelius turned to watch her leave as she marched toward the room's entrance like a general on a military campaign. She shouted, "Guards! Guards!"

Behind Aurelius, Porcia said, "I know it's rare for Mother to speak the truth, but she meant it when she said she'd kill anyone. How many do you think are going to die tonight?"

Aurelius turned back to face her. "None, if I have anything to say about it. Trust me, Father made plans that specifically account for her bloodthirsty nature. I'll tell you about it when we have more time. Right now I'll handle Mother. Why don't you stay with Father?"

She smiled and grimaced at the same time. "Thank you." She stretched upward on her tiptoes and kissed his cheek, smearing his face with tears.

Aurelius turned and followed in his mother's wake, which was easy to do; simply follow the shouting. Just outside the entrance to his father's bedchamber, he encountered Captain Brunasus of the Palace Guard, and his father's chief councilor, a man named Janus.

To Brunasus, Aurelius said, "The end is quite near. Seal the palace, and for the next few hours no one is to speak with anyone outside its walls. I'll rescind those orders as soon as I've been able to calm Mother and make a few arrangements."

The soldier bowed his head. "As you wish, Dominus Aurelius." He spun on his heel and marched away.

Marius had been an astute ruler, and during the last year, when it became clear he would die, he had carefully orchestrated his own demise. He had regularly assembled Aurelius, Maximillian, Janus, and a few of his most trusted councilors. It had been especially astute of him to exclude Divonia so thoroughly she hadn't even been aware of their planning.

Janus lowered his voice. "As we discussed, we'll notify the city guard so they can prepare for any unrest. I have messengers ready to deliver the news of your father's passing to each of the members of the Senatus, and as planned we'll give them as little notice as possible. They'll hear about your father's demise only moments before the rest of the city. That should minimize any opportunity they have to provoke unrest."

At least someone in the palace was thinking clearly. "Thank you," Aurelius said. "And I believe Mother has personally enlisted the aid of a few key senators, which should help some."

Janus had demonstrated time and again his capacity for discretion. He didn't even raise an eyebrow; if Divonia had *personally enlisted the aid* of a few senators, she had probably done so by inviting them to her bed.

Aurelius continued. "Now I need to . . . try to control my mother. But I'll be available at any time of the day or night."

He started to turn away, but Janus said, "One more thing, Your Grace."

"Yes," Aurelius said. "What is it?"

Janus lowered his voice even further. "Your father told me and a few others that . . ."

It was unlike the man to hesitate. He continued. "Your father told me your brother might take his passing rather hard, and for a time we might need to look to someone else for guidance. He told us to look to you until your brother recovered from his initial grief."

Again he hesitated, then blurted out, "But we can't ignore your mother."

Aurelius took a deep breath and let it out slowly. His father had thought of everything. "Let me handle my mother. I'm going to stay by her side throughout the night. But after that, if she . . . tries to do something untoward, warn me first. As I said, day or night."

Janus displayed a faint smile. "I thought you'd say that, and when I tell the others, they'll be as relieved as I that we can count on you. Now, I've taken up enough of your time."

Aurelius found Maximillian sitting on the floor in a corner of his apartments, their mother standing over him, berating him. Thankfully she hadn't yet raised the volume too high. Maximillian simply sat there rocking back and forth, his eyes staring at something a thousand leagues in the distance. He said nothing, cried no tears, though the salty remnants of earlier tears still stained his cheeks.

Seething with anger, Divonia looked at Aurelius. "Is your brother even capable of the Supremus?"

Aurelius grimaced. "It's not his choice, is it?"

Both corners of her mouth curled upward, though what Aurelius saw on her face didn't really qualify as a smile. "No, it's not."

Aurelius braced himself for a long, tedious night.

• • • •

The Mountain Folk held the Priestesses of Mythrian Legend in great esteem, and attributed all sorts of mystical powers to them. After all, when the ruler who sat upon the Throne of Myth and Legend abdicated or died, the priestesses selected the new ruler from among the offspring of the old, the mythchildren, attributing their decision to divine insight. Damuel Barasha viewed their rituals with some skepticism, if for no other reason than that their rites and ceremonies employed a fair amount of unnecessary dramatic flair. He appreciated the need for pomp and circumstance, but now and then one of them had a vision and started wailing and caterwauling. When that happened, more than once Damuel had watched a few of the more restrained members of their sisterhood roll their eyes at such spectacle.

As Damuel stepped into his sister's birthing chamber, he noted that the gathering had considerably thinned from those present during the birth, though the room remained crowded nonetheless. His sister, Selene Barasha, Crown Mother of the Mountain Realm, lay comfortably in bed with the newborn child suckling at her breast, while two midwives examined her. Four priestesses stood nearby, watching closely, all exhibiting the intricate tattoos that circled their amber eyes, then ran down their cheeks and necks to their upper chests. And while all had clothed themselves from neck to ankles, the diaphanous materials that covered their bodies hid almost nothing. Damuel was a healthy man with normal appetites, and with women near his own age, some younger and some older, the images visible through the sheer fabric of their gowns did not leave him unaffected. But on one as ancient as the High Priestess Melceinnia, such revealing clothing did not appeal to him.

One of the younger priestesses noticed him looking their way. All Scairn had amber eyes, but hers were particularly striking, though he couldn't say why. She gave him a coy smile, an inviting smile. Upon occasion he had availed himself of the sacred rite of carnal worship, though when he did he never found it within himself to utter any prayers during the act. And it had been quite some time since he had taken advantage of that pleasure. The priestesses offered themselves freely for such deeds of veneration. He had always suspected the sisterhood gave them extensive training in the ways of pleasing a man, especially a high-ranking nobleman such as him. Afterwards he went through the motions of saying the requisite prayers with the woman, then offering the optional—but actually required—alms of penitence. He thought it possible that might be the primary source of income for the Priestesses of Mythria.

Scanning the room again, Damuel saw no sign of the noble consort Sander deVries. He was probably out celebrating, perhaps worshiping with a priestess or two. Nick and Caerie stood to one side of Selene's bed; Nick nervous and wringing his hands, Caerie as always calm and unperturbed. She carried herself with the demeanor and maturity of a woman older than her true age, and that saddened Damuel.

Caerie glanced Damuel's way, their eyes met, she smiled and spoke softly. "Uncle Damuel."

At her words, Selene looked his way and she extended a hand toward him. "Brother."

He crossed the room and took her hand in his, clutching it to his breast.

The older of the two midwives straightened and announced, "She is healthy and hale, and so is the child."

Selene had borne the child five days ago, so the entire event was unnecessary theatre. If anything had been wrong with Selene or the boy, they would have all known about it long ago. But the laws of Mythria required an official examination exactly at the hour of birth five days later, accompanied by the declaration that all was well and good in the kingdom. It was now Damuel's responsibility to pen a formal declaration to be posted at strategic intersections across the city and read aloud by palace criers. He also needed to send the same message by fast rider to Carigleigh and Darliff. Then each of the three principal cities of Mythria could spread the word to outlying villages. He had already prepared a draft that included several flowery phrases implying omens of good fortune for the entire kingdom. All he need do now was review it carefully before issuing the proclamation.

He and Selene chatted briefly. He hugged her, Caerie, and Nick, then excused himself with, "The kingdom awaits the official word, and if I dally the rumor mongers will undoubtedly come up with all sorts of fearful inaccuracies."

His sister excused him with a smile and a nod.

Damuel returned to his study, sat down at his desk, and retrieved the draft announcement he had prepared. He took a moment to read it one last time in case any changes occurred to him. As he did so, a knock on the door interrupted him. He stood, stepped around his desk, and opened the door.

The young priestess who had given him the inviting smile stood in the hallway. She looked at him with those striking amber eyes and gave him that smile again. She had dark hair, and like all of them the tattoos around her eyes immediately drew his attention. Patterns of color continued down her cheeks and throat, then along her upper chest and across the cleavage exposed above the top of her gown. The ink ended there, but as she gained more rank in the sisterhood, they would extend the tattoos down her chest, across her breasts, and down her belly.

The translucent fabric of her gown was so thin he could easily discern the outline of her areolas, which would have been obscured, had the tattoos extended that far. He tried not to notice the points of her nipples protruding prominently through the garment, and wasn't sure if he succeeded.

She smiled. "Councilor Barasha, I am Zalestria, only recently elevated from my novitiate's robes. May I have a word with you?"

He stepped back and to one side. "If Mistress Melceinnia desires my service in some fashion, I will of course do whatever is within my power to aid her."

Her smile broadened as she stepped past him into his study. "I'm not here at her behest."

She paused in the middle of the room, which placed her between him and his desk. She turned toward him but stopped with her body in profile, rotating her head slowly to look him in the eyes. Three candles in the candelabra on the desk behind her vividly illuminated the curves of her breasts through the near-transparent fabric of her gown, and he wondered if she had chosen that position intentionally. As if she read his thoughts she smiled coyly. "I have a question of my own I want to ask you."

He tried to keep his voice neutral. "By all means, ask away."

The smile on her face shifted from coy to calculating. "Damueltarn Mythchild, do you hate us for choosing your sister above you? Do you hate us for leaving you the Unchosen?"

Taken aback by such a brazen question, he struggled to compose his thoughts. "I am no longer mythchild. That ended when you women chose my sister."

The smile disappeared from her lips and she completed the turn, now facing him directly. She stepped forward, standing barely half a pace from him. "You said, 'you women,' but I was barely a child then. Had I been vowed and consecrated, I would have chosen you. And you haven't answered my question."

He shook his head. "A question not worthy of an answer."

She shrugged and spoke softly. "Perhaps your prevarication is answer enough."

She moved forward, halving the distance between them, her breasts barely a finger's breadth from his chest. "You have the potential to wield great power, and if your sister were not Crown Mother, I could help you in that. It's a shame, don't you think, that—"

He snarled, "Enough."

She gave him that inviting smile again, reached up and traced a finger along the line of his jaw. "Very well. But if you ever wish to talk further, in private, you need only ask. I would be happy to help you . . . worship any time you feel the . . . desire."

He did not turn to follow her as she stepped around him, but heard her open the door behind him, then close it softly.

Selene had told him the priestesses had a crude insult they used only among themselves: *Her husband must be a very wealthy man.* Since priestesses didn't wed, when applied to another priestess, it implied she took many men, and spent so much time worshiping on her back, she must be bringing home a sizeable income accumulated through alms of penitence. He wondered if that adage applied to Zalestria, though if not now, he suspected it would soon.

# 6

# The Monastery

AS THE SUN settled toward dusk, the dark man led the horse along the road that crossed the valley floor. Near the walled stone structure, he turned onto a cart path that ended at a large wooden gate in the wall. Were it not for the carefully tilled fields around it, the place could be deserted. The dark man followed the path, and as they approached the monastery, Ket realized its walls stood easily as high as those of Castle Glenmoore, though there were no crenellations atop them. The dark man stopped about ten paces from the heavy gate.

He startled Ket when he bellowed, "Hail, you have a visitor here."

He waited for several seconds, then shouted, "Come forth. I'm not going to stand out here all night."

Again he waited, but when nothing happened he growled, "Bloody hell!"

He shifted his weight, the saddle creaked, and he dismounted, leaving Ket seated precariously in front of the saddle, clutching desperately at the horse's mane. The dark man walked toward the gate, drawing the heavy knife from a sheath on his belt. Gripping the knife in his fist, he pounded the butt of its hilt against the gate. "I'm here on the affairs of House Dramoran, blast you. Don't leave me out here in the cold or your benefactor will be mightily displeased."

He stopped pounding on the gate and stood there waiting, though when nothing happened, he once again raised the knife. But an instant before he struck the gate, a small shutter in the middle of it slid aside. It revealed an opening just large enough to display the grimy face of a young man with a smooth chin. He spoke in a frightened whine. "What do you want?"

To Ket, the dark man seemed to speak only in a growl. "I'm here on the affairs of House Dramoran. I need to see the abbot. Now open the bloody gate and let me in."

The fellow behind the gate demanded, "But how do I know you're who you say you are?"

The dark man slammed the hilt of the dagger against the gate. "Because if you don't open this bloody gate right now, I'm going to climb over your bloody wall, beat you to a bloody pulp, and open the bloody gate myself."

The young man's voice now trembled. "But I don't—"

"Here, here," an older voice said, interrupting him. "Stand aside. Let me see."

Another face appeared in the small opening, an older man with a scruffy black beard. His chin stood out prominently beneath gaunt, hollow cheeks, and his face appeared almost skeletal. "Yes, I know this man. Now open the gate as he requested, you idiot."

Ket heard a grunt, as if the older man had struck the younger fellow. There followed the mechanical sound of a latch disengaged, then the gate swung back on creaking hinges. The man with the skeletal face and scruffy beard stood beneath the arch of the gate, his hands clasped in front of him. He was slight of build and his head barely reached the dark man's shoulders. He wore drab, ankle-length robes with a hooded cowl thrown back. Behind him the younger fellow pushed the gate fully open.

The older man nodded. "I'm Brother Markus. You're Zarkoffa, are you not?"

Zarkoffa gave a silent nod.

Brother Markus seemed eager to please the dark man. "Good. I've seen you here before in the company of Master Kainborne. You say you want to see the abbot?"

Zarkoffa stood statue still. "Aye."

Markus turned to the boy. "Take his horse to the stables. And tell Brother Atticus to see to the animal himself." He cuffed the lad in the side of the head, knocking him to his knees.

The young man scrambled to his feet and rushed forward. The dark man sheathed his knife, stepped around to the side of the horse, and lifted Ket off its shoulders. Glad to once again stand on solid ground, Ket waited for Zarkoffa to tell him what to do while the other boy took the horse's reins and led it away.

Markus nodded his head to one side. "Please follow me."

He turned and marched away. The dark man followed, leaving Ket standing there. Not sure what to do, Ket rushed after him, running to keep up with the older man's long strides. The monk led them across the central courtyard, where several other monks toiled silently at various tasks. Many threw surreptitious glances at Zarkoffa, and Ket was glad their attention did not focus on him.

Markus stepped into the gap between two smaller buildings, and hurried up a narrow walkway there, his robes fluttering behind him. The narrow walkway ended when they stepped out into an open area at the center of the walled compound. In it, neatly tended gardens surrounded a two-story stone structure. Tall double-doors easily twice the height of the dark man marked the front of the building. Markus led them to a smaller door off to one side, opened it, and stepped into the dim interior of the place. Zarkoffa followed, and Ket followed him into a massive hall. Rays of the fading sun spilled through windows high above, dimly lighting the place in shadows.

The dark man and Ket found Markus speaking in hushed tones with another monk, a big fellow who stood head and shoulders above Markus. Ket caught only a few of their words, "Abbot Benedictus . . . Kainborne's man . . . study." The monk Markus had cornered wore a patch over one eye, and was clean-shaven, with several days of stubble sprouting from his face. He nodded to Markus, turned, and walked away.

To Zarkoffa, Markus said, "Brother Obregon will fetch Abbot Benedictus and we'll meet in his study. I'll show you there now."

The dark man did not respond, but his head slowly turned to watch Brother Obregon's retreating figure. He rested his hand on the hilt of the large knife in his belt. Ket thought he saw distrust in the man's face, thought he probably distrusted everyone.

Markus led them to the back of the great hall, then down a narrow passageway dimly lit by a lone sconce. He opened a door, and they entered a room lit only by the wan light of the setting sun slanting through a large window. A heavy desk commanded the back of the room, with racks of scrolls on one wall, and leather-bound books lining another.

Markus turned to face the dark man. "Please make yourself comfortable. Reverend Brother Benedictus will be with us shortly."

Zarkoffa slowly swiveled his head from side to side, crossed the room to a large chair, and dropped into it. He leaned back and stretched his legs out in front of him. Ket stepped back into the shadows at the edge of the room, hoping they'd all pay no attention to him. He wanted his mum, but when he thought of her he recalled the dark man's words, "If she ain't dead yet, she will be soon." Tears welled up in his eyes, and anger flooded his heart.

Ket was not aware the room had a second entrance, and started when the other door shot open. It revealed a fellow standing in the doorway, panting as he caught his breath. He wore robes cut much like those of the other monks, but they reminded Ket more of the fine garments the noble people wore, not the homespun of those like Markus. The top of his bald head glistened as if burnished with boot polish. From the sides and back of his head, greasy, curly black hair hung down to his shoulders.

Brother Obregon stepped into the room behind him, and it was the first time Ket got a close look at the man. Neatly trimmed gray hair on the back and sides of his head surrounded a shiny bald top. A jagged scar ran from his forehead to his cheek, disappearing for a short distance beneath the patch on his left eye. A large man, he stood far taller than Markus, and a head taller than the fellow in fine garments. He'd rolled up his sleeves, and Ket saw several scars on his right arm not unlike those Zarkoffa bore, though his left arm contained only a few such marks.

"Master Zarkoffa," the fellow in fine robes announced grandly, speaking in a high-pitched voice like that of a woman. "What brings your noble presence to this humble abbey?"

The dark man's leathers creaked as he stood. "I am not noble and this abbey is not humble, Benedictus."

"Yes, of course," the abbot said. "But we are ever humbly grateful for the endowments His Grace bestows upon us, and always happy to care for one of his subordinates."

The dark man shrugged. "I'm sure His Grace is aware of the endowments, but it's Master Kainborne who ensures that they are sufficient for your needs. And as long as you continue to collect rents for His Grace in a proper and timely fashion, my master will continue to see that the endowments flow your way."

The abbot smiled, though the smile extended only to his lips and not his eyes. "We will do our utter best to fulfill His Grace's needs and your master's requirements. And what, pray tell, may we do for him now?"

Zarkoffa's head swiveled slowly to look directly at Ket, and the look in the man's eyes cut into his soul like an icy knife. "Step forward, boy, so the abbot can see you."

Ket dearly wanted to stay in the shadows, but dare not disobey the man. Keeping his eyes downcast he took two steps forward.

The abbot's eyes widened. "A young lad?"

Zarkoffa returned his attention to the abbot. "Master Kainborne wishes you to care for the boy for a time. Treat him well, and in a month or two my master will send further instructions for you regarding him."

The abbot looked at Ket and his eyes narrowed. "Come here, boy, so I can see you properly."

Ket carefully crossed the room to stand in front of the abbot. He kept his eyes focused on the floor.

"Don't look at the floor, boy, look up at me."

Ket lifted his face to look at the abbot. The man looked into Ket's eyes for several seconds, then he turned to address the dark man. "He seems like a nice young lad. Blue eyes are not terribly common in these parts, and he is not unattractive. Why is he here?"

To Ket it appeared the dark man didn't care too much for the abbot. "He's here because Master Kainborne wants him here. That's all you need to worry about."

Benedictus cleared his throat. "I take it Master Kainborne . . . fancies the boy in some way?"

The dark man stiffened, then he moved quickly and took two steps forward, his boots thudding on the floor. The sudden movement startled Ket, and startled the abbot as well, forcing him to step back. Standing nose to nose with the abbot, the dark man spoke with hard steel in his voice. "Not in the way you might think. You may discipline him if you need to, but don't overdo it. And take great care how you treat the boy. If you or one of your colleagues touches him in the wrong way, Master Kainborne will send me here to cut off your balls right after I cut off theirs. And then I'll make you eat them."

"Yes," the abbot said, gulping and breathing rapidly. "We'll take good care of the lad . . . uh . . . good . . . and proper care."

The dark man slowly looked the abbot up and down, then nodded. "I think you get the message."

Brother Markus stepped forward and demanded, "Is the boy's birth of any significance?"

The dark man looked at Markus, the lines of his face hardened, and Ket saw distrust in his eyes. "Why do you ask?"

Markus lowered his eyes and spoke softly. "Are we to . . . educate the boy . . . or not?"

The dark man stared at Markus for several seconds, then his head turned and he focused on the abbot. Benedictus quickly lowered his eyes. The dark man turned his gaze upon Obregon. The eyebrow above the old man's good eye lifted slightly, he did not look away, and Ket thought he saw humor in the look the fellow returned.

The dark man shook his head. "The boy's birth is not your concern. Just treat him well unless you hear otherwise from me or Master Kainborne."

He spun suddenly and marched to the door, speaking as he did so. "I'm hungry. Get me something to eat. And get something for the boy as well. I'll be leaving in the morning, so I'll need a place to sleep for the night, and not a cot in the bunkroom with those fool guardsmen Duke Jarrod lent you. And I'll need provisions for my ride tomorrow." He stepped out of the room and closed the door behind him.

Brother Obregon broke the silence, speaking with a thick, common accent much like Ket's. "Well now, he made himself rather clear, didn't he? And I do fancy keeping me balls intact, so I think it best we make sure Brother Antiphinees never finds an opportunity to be alone with the boy."

"Aye," Brother Markus said. "And that applies to Brother Willowby as well."

The abbot nodded rapidly. "I'll speak with them myself, warn them to keep their attentions . . . focused elsewhere." He looked pointedly at Markus, then Obregon. "And you two keep an eye on the boy."

The look on Markus's face soured.

Obregon merely shrugged and said, "Aye, Willowby will be a good boy, but we'll have to keep a close eye on Antiphinees. He's a sneaky little shit."

Benedictus looked at Ket. "Zarkoffa didn't say one way or the other, but do we educate the boy or not?"

Both Markus and Obregon shrugged their shoulders.

Still looking at Ket, the abbot's eyes narrowed. "If we don't educate him and we should have, Master Kainborne might be displeased. On the other hand, if we do, and it turns out to be unnecessary, no harm done. So for the time being let's assume we must. You two will be in charge of that."

"Me!" Markus said. He looked at Ket. "The boy's obviously a peasant." He hooked a thumb at Obregon. "And he's a peasant too."

Obregon planted his fists on his hips. "Well you ain't no nobility yerself, are yuh? Taking on airs all the time."

"Be silent," the abbot shouted. He focused on Markus. "Yes, you, with Brother Obregon. And I don't care if the boy was fathered by a pig. We're going to do whatever it takes to keep Master Kainborne happy."

From the look on his face, Markus was none too pleased with that. He approached Ket, looked him over carefully, and Ket realized the monk stood only a hand's breadth taller than him. He leaned close to Ket's ear and hissed, "You'll learn boy. You'll learn good and fast, or my switch will taste the skin on your backside."

Obregon impolitely elbowed the man aside. "Come with me, boy. His Most Grand Imperial Lordship Brother Markus here'll probably just let you wander about until you get lost. I'll get you settled."

Obregon took Ket by the hand and led him out of the room. As soon as he closed the door and the two of them stood alone in the hallway, Ket heard Brother Markus's shouts muffled by the door.

Obregon gripped Ket's shoulders and faced him squarely. "Let me see yer ears, boy."

The man didn't wait for permission, but reached out and pushed Ket's hair back over his left ear. The older man nodded. "Pointed, as I thought, but not as pointed as most Scairn."

"Aye," Ket said, trying to hide his shame. "Scairndraka."

Obregon grimaced. "Don't ever use that word, boy. I know the Mountain Folk use it for a half-breed, but it's a mean, nasty word with a very unkind intent."

He leaned close to Ket and lowered his voice. "The Scairn, they really ain't no different from us. They got villains and scoundrels and thieves and murderers among them, and they got their prejudices and they don't like half-breeds. But they got plenty of noble and good folk too. Learn to be one of the good ones, boy, and don't let no one around here see them ears."

# 7

# A War of Dreams

*I am an old man now, but I still remember that day with vivid and stark recollection. I waited with his generals for the longest time, and when he didn't come down from that high bluff, we found his body at the base of the cliff, twisted, shattered, and lifeless. I remember how earlier I watched him stand at the very edge of that precipice, tempting fate with his bravado, or possibly with his melancholy. Perhaps chance intervened that day and he slipped, but a darkness had enveloped his soul in those last months. And recalling his mood that morning, I fear the only chance involved was his desperate need for peace, for release.*

*The scorched and burned flesh of his right forearm surprised and confounded his generals, but they did not know my old friend, as did I. That birthmark haunted him. Why, I cannot say, for when he tried to explain the fear and trepidation that came to him when he looked upon it, I heard only the disjointed ramblings of a mind near the breaking point.*

*After that day our armies faltered, and eventually returned to the lowland fells where they dispersed, which, I think, is what he wanted.*

*Claudius ahm Carthagen neh Modain
penned some years after the Withering Wars*

Aurelius leaned back in his chair and pondered the words Claudius had penned so long ago. He had read that passage many times and it always disturbed him. Had Domaxus taken his own life, as the words in the scroll seemed to imply? And what was it about the birthmark on his arm that haunted him so? Aurelius had asked himself those questions time and time again, and well knew he would find no answer.

He had come across that scroll many years ago buried deep within the vaults of the Deoclation Palace, and even as a much younger man knew that it must never see the light of day. Their histories heralded Domaxus as a vaunted hero, conqueror, and the founder of modern Carthagenian society and its ruling structures. In Carthagen they taught that after taming the Seven Duchies by exterminating three of them, he had withdrawn to the Lowland Kingdoms to rule over a peaceful and prosperous land. But the Four Duchies sought revenge, and one of their assassins murdered him shortly before his triumphant homecoming.

Aurelius leaned back in his chair and worried at the meaning in Claudius's writings. He had kept the contents of that scroll solely to himself, and only he knew of its existence. For if the words in that scroll ever became common knowledge, it would shatter the basis of their most formidable myth, Domaxus the Conqueror, hero and legend. Aurelius didn't know what that might do to Carthagen.

He stood and scanned the small study his father had granted him. Lit by a lantern on his desk, and augmented by dim rays of sun that leaked through one small window, tapestries on the walls and a small hearth warmed the place. But it remained an austere cell, and that he preferred.

He carefully rolled up the scroll and bound it with simple twine, then crossed the room to a large oaken closet where he stored all his scrolls. He opened one of its doors and placed that special scroll at the bottom of a pile of similar documents, though none of them contained writings of such import. Two more scrolls penned by Claudius lay in that chest, with a few more penned by others who had accompanied Domaxus on his campaigns. Aurelius had considered placing those parchments in a separate compartment behind a locked door, but that would only draw attention to them. Divonia in particular would have wondered at such precautions. So he had decided to simply bury them in small piles of other scrolls of no significance. But he knew each of the important scrolls intimately and could easily find them.

As Aurelius turned to leave his study, he wondered if he should simply burn them all and be done with them.

•  •  •  •

The vision had come twice, and now several days had passed with nothing. The mountain lion cub in her previous vision must have had some meaning, but she feared to speak of it to anyone. And the boy! He and the aged oak tree were the only common thread in the two visions. Caerie stood at the window looking down at the flower garden and wondering what to do, fearing she must do something, but knowing not what.

The sharp cry of a bird of prey startled her, and she looked up to the skies. It was probably just a hawk, but one never knew. She searched for several seconds and finally spotted a dark spot high in the sky. She watched it circle slowly, descending with each turn. With no frame of reference in which to judge its size, it could be nothing more than a small falcon or kestrel, but feathered only in black, that limited the possibilities.

As it continued to descend, she thought it might be larger than her first impression, with a wingspan perhaps the height of a grown man like her Uncle Damuel. Then just as it came to the top of a tower above her, it flared its wings and settled upon a crenellation there. Covered in coal black feathers with a black beak, the bird looked at her with blood-red eyes that glowed like burning embers, a raken, a raptor out of pure legend. The priestesses claimed raken were mythical birds of danger and portent. No, Caerie would speak of this to no one, especially them.

The raken opened its beak and cried out a sharp screech that pierced at her heart and hurt her ears. Then it looked down, and she followed its gaze. The young boy and the ancient oak had reappeared in the middle of the garden where they did not exist. He sat beneath the tree's canopy, again playing cat and mouse with the lioness cub. The young cat's oversized paws made it clumsy, and the boy emitted a laughing squeak, a pleasant sound to Caerie's ears that contrasted sharply with the harsh screech of the raken. And then the raken cried out again, drawing Caerie's attention upward.

Once again the raptor's burning eyes met hers and it nodded, as if acknowledging her and demanding her attention. Then it slowly turned its head, shifting its gaze to the other side of the garden. On the parapets high above, two outsized ravens perched atop crenellations, and both birds stood easily as tall as the raken.

One raven squawked, but Caerie heard the hiss of a woman's voice. "We've found him." It was the same voice she had heard before, and the malice and hate had not lessened in the slightest.

The other raven flared its wings and hopped to the next crenellation, looking at Caerie with coal-black eyes. "But only in her vision, my love. We have no power over her vision." Again he spoke with a refined Lowlands accent.

The female raven screeched, "Then we must kill."

Across from them, the raken cried out in anger and challenge. It spread its wings, displaying a wingspan easily the height of a tall man.

The two ravens hopped off the crenellations, swooping toward the helpless boy.

In response, the raptor pulled its wings in and tucked them tightly about its body, then toppled off the tower into a head-first dive. It rocketed down toward the boy and lion cub, and screamed out a warning. The boy and cub ceased their play and looked up. At the sight of the raken and ravens diving toward them the boy froze, but the lion cub's shape blurred as it shifted and changed. Its shoulders broadened, its tail lengthened, and in an instant a full-grown lioness stood beside the terrified boy.

Caerie assumed the raken and the ravens had targeted the boy. She tried to cry out to warn him, but her throat seized up and she managed only a faint squeak. The three monstrous birds shot toward him, and Caerie thought they would tear him limb from limb. But at the last instant the lioness pounced, leaping into the air and catching one raven in her jaws. At the same moment the raken extended its claws forward, exposing talons the length of Caerie's hands. Then it flared its wings and swooped past the boy's head, slamming into the other raven. Both of them collided with the lioness, forcing her to spill the first raven from her jaws. All four tumbled to the ground, but recovered quickly.

The lioness and raptor faced the two ravens, the boy standing to one side, his face filled with fear. The smaller of the two ravens squawked, and Caerie heard the hiss of the woman's voice. "He is ours."

The raken screeched out its defiance with an ear-splitting cry. The lioness growled and roared like thunder in a dark storm, but Caerie heard a young girl's voice. "He is us."

In that instant all four of them lunged and crashed together, the raken and ravens fighting with beak and talons, the lioness with teeth and claws. The ravens tore chunks of fur from the lioness's hide while she and the raptor ripped feathers and chunks of bloody meat from the ravens.

The boy pleaded, "No. Don't. Please don't."

They ignored him, the massive bird and lioness locked in a battle to the death with the ravens. And little by little, as they fought they all dwindled, became less, until nothing remained but a scattering of black feathers and tufts of lion fur. The young boy dropped to his knees, buried his face in his hands, and his shoulders shook with uncontrolled sobs.

Caerie staggered back from the window and gasped.

"Caermorgan Mythchild," a deep, male voice said, addressing her by her formal name.

• • • •

Caerie stood statue still at the window as Damuel Barasha stepped into the nursery. Hoping to avoid startling her, he called out to her, using her formal name. "Caermorgan Mythchild."

She didn't answer, didn't turn and greet him, didn't appear to have even heard him. She simply stood at the open window with her back to him, her head tilted slightly downward, probably lost in thought. He didn't want to surprise her, so he crossed the room quietly and stopped beside her. He spoke softly. "Caermorgan Mythchild."

Still, she didn't move. He leaned slightly to one side to get a better look at her face. Her eyes appeared to be focused on something in the flower garden below. He glanced that way and saw nothing out of the ordinary, then looked again at her face. Even at ten years of age she had strong features. Like all his kin she had dark hair and fair skin, though she tended toward the lighter shades while Damuel appeared more weathered by his years. In time she would become a beautiful woman and a valuable asset to the Throne of Myth and Legend, whether she sat on that throne, or lived her life Unchosen.

He had now stood beside her for several seconds and she had yet to blink. Had she taken some malady, or had the madness of those damn priestesses touched her? He dearly hoped she didn't start having visions and spouting drivel like some of those unhinged women.

Without warning she gasped and stepped back from the window, but did not otherwise react. Then she again froze into stillness.

He spoke again, spoke more harshly. "Caermorgan Mythchild."

A few seconds passed, then her chest expanded as she took in a breath and released it. She blinked, and her head turned slowly toward him like a machine on old cogs. She looked him over carefully, as if she didn't recognize him.

He tried again. "Is something wrong, Caerie? You seem distressed."

Once more he thought she might not answer him, might again drift off into whatever had transfixed her. But then she shook her head as if to clear her thoughts. "No, Uncle Damuel." She hesitated, as if struggling to find words. "I was just enjoying the view of the garden, but I was a bit distracted as well."

He heard truth in her words, but the tremble in her voice told him of the lie there as well. He didn't call her on it.

"She's always distracted."

Damuel glanced over his shoulder to see Nick marching toward them. "How do our mother and new brother fare?"

Damuel nodded. "As you know, both are well, and the throne now has another potential heir, another mythchild."

The young boy grinned. "That'll make those old women's decision harder."

Damuel didn't want to get into that discussion. "When your mother dies or abdicates, the priestesses will choose. I don't know if their decision will be difficult or easy, but one of you will rule, and the others will serve, as do I." He didn't add that there wasn't much choice in the matter once one became Unchosen.

Caerie tugged on his sleeve, and when he glanced down at her, she gave him a pained look. "Was it hard for you?" she asked. "Was it hard when they didn't choose you?"

The fear and pain on her face were stark and real. Damuel glanced at Nick and saw the same concern etched on the young boy's face, and he thought it a travesty that two children should suffer such anxiety. Raised from birth to rule, of the three of them—Nick, Caerie, and their younger brother—two would never realize that destiny. He resolved never to answer such a question with the truth.

For whatever reason, Selene had always believed that Damuel would be chosen above her, believed it with absolute and undisputed certainty. And she had instilled in him her own unquestioned confidence that he would eventually sit upon the Throne of Myth and Legend. He'd grown up believing that, had carefully prepared to rule, and had lived with the certainty of that every day of his life. Then the day had come, he had expected to become Crown Father of Myth and Legend, and the walls of un-realized expectations had crashed down around him. That foregone conclusion had made it even more difficult to accept. And for that, he could only blame his sister. But in answer to Caerie's question, he shrugged. "No. I think it's harder for her. She has all the worries and headaches, not me."

Caerie frowned, and for a moment he wondered if she'd heard the lie in his words.

• • • •

In the Primus Council Chamber of the Senatus, each of the senators stepped forward one by one to kiss the casket of Dominus Marius Supremus, then leave a single tea leaf on top of it. He had lain in state now for three days, and when the ceremony in the Chamber ended, they would parade his casket through the city on an open car-riage. They'd finish at the tomb of Kings, where they would lay him to rest.

Standing beside Aurelius, Porcia said, "It's a rather boring show, don't you think? Not terribly entertaining. I would think they'd want to liven it up a bit. Perhaps bring in some of those Mythrian priestesses with all their tattoos. They could perform that carnal worship I've heard so much about, do it with half a dozen senators in front of us all. I, for one, would find that a lot more entertaining than this dreary parade of old men."

Aurelius didn't need to look Divonia's way to see the diamond hard look she gave her daughter. "Don't be crude, girl."

Standing next to Divonia, Maximillian choked back a laugh. "She's right, you know. It is a tedious procession of old men."

Aurelius leaned close to his sister's ear and whispered, "Give it a rest, please."

She wrinkled her nose and whispered back, "Oh, I'm sorry, I'm making it harder for you, aren't I?"

He answered that question with a pointed look.

She grinned and lowered her voice even further. "That sour look on your face; did you learn that from Mother?"

Divonia hissed. "I heard that. At least he's taking this seriously."

Aurelius noticed Janus standing at the Chamber's entrance. Their eyes met, and Janus cocked his head slightly toward the exit. Aurelius turned to Divonia. "Something has come up. I won't be gone long."

She perked up. "I'll come with you."

He shook his head. "No, Mother. It would be unseemly for you or Maximillian to leave the ceremony. I don't count because I'm just excess baggage." That was a bit of a reach, but the last thing he needed was her meddling in a carefully orchestrated transition.

Aurelius stepped back, and with as little commotion as possible, slipped between onlookers to the back of the crowd, then edged his way along the periphery of the Chamber to Janus. The two of them stepped out into the hallway beyond where Captain Brunasus of the Palace Guard awaited them.

Janus said to Brunasus, "Tell Dominus Aurelius what you told me."

The captain kept his voice low as he spoke. "This morning I visited the commanders of each constabulary precinct. Your father's preparations worked well: no organized unrest. A few drunks, a few lone anarchists spouting drivel; they quietly manacled them, tossed them each into a cell, and are keeping them in solitary confinement. They'll hold them there for a couple of days and nothing will come of it. And when they release them, they'll keep an eye on them for a few days as well, just to be certain."

Aurelius nodded. "Thank you, Captain."

The man bowed, turned, and walked away, leaving Aurelius with Janus.

Divonia had sent a few hired assassins after certain senators. Aurelius asked, "What of my mother's henchmen?"

Janus nodded. "We intercepted them all, and lent each senator a small contingent of trusted constables for their protection. As a byproduct, a few of those senators are quite grateful to you."

Marius had had a strong faction of supporters in the Senatus, and many of them helped Aurelius monitor the rest, but it wouldn't hurt to add new eyes and ears to those already enlisted. "I'd like their names, and I want to meet with each of them individually, in private, as soon as possible."

Janus knew exactly what Aurelius was thinking. "As soon as this morning's ceremony is done, I'll come to you with a list. And before the day is out, I should have those meetings arranged."

As Aurelius returned to the Primus Council Chamber, the look on Divonia's face precluded any possibility of a peaceful family afternoon. Earlier, Porcia had stood between him and his mother, but as he approached them his sister stepped to one side, forcing him to stand next to Divonia. Either Porcia had done that on her own so he could shield her from her mother, or Divonia had insisted she make room for him at her side.

She didn't allow him a moment's respite, but immediately asked, "And what, pray tell, was so important?"

He stared straight ahead, watching the next senator step up to Marius's casket. "Just a little unrest, but nothing organized; mostly misfits and drunks. Nothing came of it."

Without looking her way, in the corner of his eye he saw her turn her head to look his way, no doubt with a rather pointed and unpleasant expression on her face. "I could have helped, but you thwarted my assistance."

Maximillian chuckled. "Assistance, Mother, you mean those assassins?"

She spun her head to look at Max. "How do you know about that?"

Aurelius did finally look her way. "You were not subtle or discreet, Mother."

Her head snapped back to look at Aurelius, and he continued. "Had you succeeded, everyone would have known they died at your hand. We could have had civil war, and it would have been a bloodbath."

She shook her head. "Those I targeted were not that important or powerful."

He held back a weary sigh and tried to keep his voice flat and level. "No, but those who are important and powerful would have wondered if they were next, and taken action against us. As it is, Max will ascend to the Supremus, and there will be no problems."

She said nothing in response, but lifted her chin proudly and returned her attention to the ceremony at the center of the Chamber.

Aurelius did the same, and he thought it ironic how Divonia's murderous instincts, in failing, might actually bring a few new allies his way, and help him cement Maximillian's ascension.

# 8

# Speak Properly

BESIDES TATTOOS AND birthmarks, Kainborne also tasked his assistant with finding any references to mountain lion cubs or fledgling birds of prey. He never mentioned the word *ketcaerm*.

In three days of scouring through his scrolls he had learned a lot about tattoos and birthmarks, but only a little about the Dreadmark. Its last known manifestation had occurred about three centuries before his time, shortly before the madman had penned the scroll filled with psychopathic ravings.

In another scroll from the same period, a monk named Plantonin detailed how he had discovered the Dreadmark on a young girl. To save civilization he had poisoned the child, and after her death had seen to the cremation of her remains. Thirty years later Domaxus the Conqueror led the armies of the Lowland Kingdoms in The Withering Wars, devastating three of the then Seven Duchies. Everyone knew something of the dark times surrounding Domaxus's bloodletting. Bards told stories of the slaughter and devastation, though in their quest to entertain, they filled such tales with exaggeration. Interestingly enough, at the height of his power, and in a position to continue northward, most historic references agreed that Domaxus would probably have been victorious, might have even marched past the Duchies and conquered the Mountain Folk. But after his greatest victory, something had abruptly stopped his armies' advance. They had continued the fight, but they won fewer battles, and the Duchies eventually expelled them.

According to certain scrolls in Plantonin's possession, Domaxus had borne the Dreadmark. But those documents had not survived the passage of time, so Kainborne couldn't confirm Plantonin's account. Domaxus's age at the time of the wars placed his birth shortly after the death of the girl, and Plantonin surmised that killing the girl had been fruitless. The death of its bearer could not prevent the Dreadmark from fulfilling its destiny—it would simply find another poor soul to carry the burden.

Plantonin concluded that if one discovered the Dreadmark early, one could not stop it altogether, but might influence its destiny with small but subtle changes in the circumstances surrounding it and its bearer.

Kainborne found himself grinning like his fool of an assistant. If he controlled a dominant portent like the Dreadmark, he might become a very powerful man, perhaps even more so than Archduke Macallan of House Inversill, Regent Monarch of the Four Duchies. In any case, killing the boy was no longer an option—the Dreadmark would simply find a new bearer, and like Plantonin, Kainborne might not discover his or her identity until too late, if at all.

The oaf shuffled up to his workbench carrying a scroll. "Master Kainborne, I thinks I found me something real interesting."

Kainborne focused on the moment. "And what would that be?"

The idiot's nose drizzled snot on his upper lip, and Kainborne prayed he didn't drip any on his workbench or the scrolls. The oaf nodded his head with excitement. "Found me a reference to both a lion cub and a raptor all in the same scroll. It's got some sort'a weirding name in the mountain talk, but I can't makes it out. It's some kind of demon what's half cat and half bird."

Kainborne's heart raced, but he dare not show any excitement in front of the fool. He casually waved a hand at the edge of his workbench. "Put it down there. It's probably nothing, but I'll get to it eventually."

The idiot had several scrolls tucked under one arm. He took a second to wipe the snot from his nose with his free hand, then the blasted fool used the same hand to sort through the scrolls tucked under his arm, contaminating them all with his vile fluids. He placed one scroll on the workbench, though it stuck to his hand for a moment and he had to shake it free. Kainborne winced, but said nothing.

Kainborne didn't want to display his true level of curiosity, not in front of the oaf. So as the fool walked away Kainborne pretended deep interest in the scroll in front of him, when in fact all his thoughts had focused on the new scroll contaminated by the oaf's snot. After a few minutes he casually rolled up the scroll he'd been reading, and reached for the new one.

To his great surprise it had been penned by a noblewoman of the Mythrian Court, a former mythchild whose sibling had been chosen to sit upon the Throne of Myth and Legend, leaving her Unchosen. She had decided to devote herself to scholarly pursuits, and her writings were clear and distinct, without any of the fanaticism or ideology common among those of unstable character. The oaf had been unable to decipher much of it because, while many sections of the document were written in the common tongue of the Four Duchies and the Lowland Kingdoms, others had been written in the Mythrian script and language, for which the fool had no proficiency. Even Kainborne struggled with some of those passages.

It surprised him to learn that the demon could not be whole until the lioness and the raptor became one. But to do that the lion cub, the caerm, must first mature into a lioness, and the fledgling raptor, the ket, must mature into a fearful raptor out of legend called a raken. And they must do *something* with *the flame and the crucible*. The author did not elaborate on what the flame and the crucible might be, and had penned those words as if anyone who read them would automatically know what they meant. As to the *something* they must accomplish, Kainborne had wrestled with a single Scairn word that could be translated as either *battle* or *free*. So that begged the question: would the lioness and raken battle the flame and the crucible, or would they free them?

Kainborne shook his head sadly and muttered, "Another blasted legend."

Seated in a chair, half asleep and drooling on his shirt again, the oaf perked up. "Eh, does Yer Lordship need something?"

"No," Kainborne shouted. "Shut up and go back to sleep."

The Mythrian scroll proved nothing, but did fill in some gaps in Kainborne's knowledge. In any case, the demon ketcaerm was nothing more than a myth, so unless he found some compelling evidence to the contrary, he'd focus all his work on the Dreadmark.

• • • •

Brother Markus's face burned red with fury as he shouted, "For that, five strokes of the switch. Bare your backside, boy."

Ket cringed and trembled as he untied his rope belt and dropped his pants, then reached over his shoulders and lifted his shirt to expose his back.

Markus gripped the back of his neck, digging his fingers in painfully, then raised the willow branch high. Ket closed his eyes as the monk brought the switch down, lacing a line of fire across his rear. He flinched, but gritted his teeth to keep from crying out.

"One," Markus said, counting the stroke. "If you don't learn to speak properly, you'll taste this switch every day of your life."

As he spoke he brought the switch down again, and again, and again. With each stroke Ket gritted his teeth and his anger grew. The man considered crying a sign of weakness, so Ket held back his tears.

"Two," Markus snarled.

Ket had learned that the man didn't know how to count, or grew so furious that he simply lost track of the strokes. If he said Ket would get five, it usually meant ten or fifteen. And the unfairness of that angered Ket even more, but he dare not let that show.

"Good," Markus said. "Two strokes, and none of that sniveling or whining. You're learning."

Ket had also learned that anything he might say frequently earned him another stroke of the switch, so he kept his mouth shut. After a week in the abbey his backside burned where a mass of red welts covered his butt and back, all placed there by the application of Brother Markus's switch.

Markus continued the punishment, applying the switch with considerable anger and fervor, counting only about one in three strokes. It took every bit of willpower Ket had to not cry out, but he managed, and when the ordeal ended Markus released his neck.

"Turn and face me, boy."

To delay for even the tiniest of instants might earn Ket another stroke, so he quickly spun, pulling up his pants as he did so. He focused on bits of food stuck in the monk's scraggly beard as the old man spoke. "You need to learn how to speak properly, boy."

Markus raised the willow branch and looked at it as if to admire it. "Until you learn to speak properly, you and this switch are going to be the best of friends."

Markus also sometimes switched the young smooth-chinned boy who had first greeted the dark man at the gate. His name was Thadamous, and even Ket understood he wasn't smart enough to avoid a thrashing or a cuff in the side of his head.

The monk pointed at the door of his cell with the switch. "I believe you've got a lesson with that peasant Obregon. So off with you now, boy."

Ket had also learned that the less he said to Markus, the fewer strokes he earned. "Yes, Brother Markus."

The monk jerked forward and shouted, "Go! Now."

Ket spun and raced out through the door of the cell. He charged down the hall a short distance, then slowed his pace to a brisk walk, let the tears flow, and tried to control his anger. The building contained a maze of hallways that connected the cells of the more senior monks, and as he turned a corner he almost ran into an old Scairn bondservant. The fellow stopped short and frowned at Ket. "What yuh crying for, Scairndraka?"

The other Scairn servants in the monastery were all men. Ket had accidently revealed himself to one of them by speaking to the man in the Mythrian tongue, and word of his half-breed heritage had quickly spread among them. Other than Obregon, the monks remained oblivious to that fact.

The old bondservant had spoken in the tongue of the Duchies. Ket responded in the tongue of the Mountain Folk. "I got a switching."

Anger clouded the old servant's features. "Don't speak that foreign gibberish to me, boy."

The man elbowed Ket aside, slamming him against a wall. Ket cringed, fearing a beating, but the old servant turned and walked away. Something like that had happened several times now, and Ket didn't understand why the other Scairn disliked him so.

He noticed a little peasant girl standing at the end of the hall holding a cloth bundle of something, a frown on her face. He wiped away tears as she cautiously walked his way, looking right and left as if fearful the man might return and harm her.

She stopped a pace short of Ket. "Why'd he hit you?"

Ket shook his head. "I don't know."

"And why you crying?"

He didn't know how to explain Markus.

She leaned to one side and frowned. "The back of yer neck's bleeding."

She edged to one side. "And there's more blood coming through yer shirt. Who did that to yuh?"

All he could think to say was, "I got a switching."

"Ah," she said. "You poor boy."

He feared being late with Obregon. "I gotta go, or I'll be late."

He turned away from her and continued on his way to Obregon's cell. He tried to put the memory of the Scairn bondservant out of his mind, thinking instead of the pretty little peasant girl with brown hair and eyes. His highest priority should be to figure out what Brother Markus wanted of him. Or maybe he could leave, escape the monastery and never suffer Markus's switch again. But he feared he had no hope of doing that anytime soon, and his poor backside would suffer the consequences for some time to come.

They had given Ket a pallet on the floor in a corner of the kitchens. He slept there, and rose each morning with the sun to fire the ovens, much as he'd done at Glenmoore, though without his mum. For breakfast they gave him scraps from the previous evening's meal. Then he reported to Markus for lessons, and following that, Obregon.

The door to Brother Obregon's cell stood open so Ket stopped several paces short of it and used his sleeve to wipe the tears off his cheeks. He also struggled to calm his anger so Obregon would see no hint of it.

Ket walked forward, stopped short of the doorway, and peered into the opening. Obregon sat at a small writing table reading something, his back to Ket. Somehow he knew Ket stood there. "Don't stand out there gawking. Come on in, boy."

Ket stepped cautiously into the monk's cell. So far Obregon had not punished him, no switch, nothing, but that didn't mean he couldn't start. And given the size of the man, a beating could be quite painful.

The old man turned to face Ket. "Got another switching, did you, boy?"

Ket nodded. "Aye."

Obregon's eyes narrowed. "Ain't no fun, is it?"

"Aye," Ket said, "me backside hurts."

The monk grimaced. "Let me see."

Ket turned around and lifted the back of his shirt.

"Damn!" Obregon said. "Couple of those gonna leave a scar. I have something that might help. Strip down."

Ket dare not disobey and quickly removed his clothing, while the monk rifled through a trunk at the end of his bed. He retrieved a small clay pot and nodded. "Come here, boy, and turn around."

Carrying his clothing in a bundle, Ket crossed the short distance to the monk and turned.

"This'll help a little, lad. It's really meant for burns, but it'll cool the pain a bit."

Obregon applied some sort of salve to Ket's back, and it did help. As he worked, the older man said, "Do you know why he switches you?"

Ket shook his head. "I don't know what he wants, and he don't tell me, just says I need to speak proper like."

"He said that, did he?"

Ket nodded. "Aye."

The man finished. "There! Now put your clothes back on."

Ket moved quickly to do so, then turned to face the monk.

Obregon's eyes twinkled as if he found some humor in Ket's dilemma. "Told you to 'speak proper like,' is that what he said?" Before Ket answered, the old man continued, "But he didn't say that, did he? I'll bet he really said, 'speak properly,' didn't he?"

Ket didn't hide his confusion. "Ain't that the same?"

Obregon's cell had a single window through which a shaft of sunlight glistened off the top of his bald head. "That old coot puts on airs, he does. And he wants you to talk like him, not like me. But I can talk like him if I wants to, and now you're gonna learn to talk like him too."

The old monk laughed, then cleared his throat, and when he next spoke he sounded like a different person, more like one of the noble folk at Glenmoore. "Yes. Along with all the other stuff, I guess I'll be teaching you how to speak properly. At least you don't speak with a retched Scairn accent. Let's start with no more *ain'ts* and no more *ayes*. From now on you'll say *isn't* and *yes*. And do you speak any Mythrian?"

"Mythrian," Ket asked. "What's that?"

Obregon grinned. "The tongue of the Mountain Folk. Since no one else here speaks it, I need someone to practice with."

Ket switched to Mythrian. "Uh-course I speaks the tongue. In the castle that's all we talked when there was just us Scairn about. Didn't talk it in front of Scairnessa."

Obregon frowned and spoke in Mythrian. "Scairnessa, what's that mean?"

"Not Scairn," Ket said.

The old monk winced. "Even in Mythrian you sound like a peasant. We'll have to fix that too. So you learned from the older Scairn bondservants, did you?"

Ket nodded. "Aye."

Obregon eyes hardened. "I said no more *ayes*."

Ket flinched. "Yes, I learned from them."

Obregon leaned back and rubbed his chin. "Were they taken from Mythria, or born into bondage?"

Ket didn't understand the old man's interest in his native tongue. "Mostly taken, I think."

Obregon grinned and nodded. "Good. That means you probably don't speak it with an accent." He frowned and hesitated. "Well, you do speak it like a peasant, but you won't have a foreign accent like we from the Duchies might. And that'll help me clean up my accent. We'll learn from each other, boy."

Ket had noticed the scars on the monk's forearms, not unlike the scars on the dark man's arms. But Zarkoffa had an equal number of scars on both arms, while most of Obregon's scars marked only his right forearm. "How did you get them scars? You got scars on your arms like the dark man."

Obregon frowned. "The dark man, you mean Zarkoffa?"

"Aye," Ket said. "Uh . . . I mean . . . yes. He says he got 'em doing knife work. Is that how you got yours?"

Obregon lifted his hands, looked at his arms and grinned. "Knife work? No, I got these on the shield wall."

He lowered his hands and looked carefully at Ket. "Maybe someday I'll tell you about that. And it's *those* scars, not *them* scars."

He leaned close to Ket and lowered his voice. "Why are you here?"

Ket didn't understand the question. "The dark man brought me."

The older man squinted with his one good eye. "But why did he bring you?"

Ket shrugged. "Me mum died. They said she ate bad meat."

Obregon shook his head. "Why not just leave you at Glenmoore? Lot less trouble if they let the Scairn bondservants take care of you. Why bring you here? And Zarkoffa doesn't even sneeze without orders from Kainborne. Why did Kainborne have him bring you here?"

That was a name Ket hadn't heard before. "Who's Kainborne?"

Obregon wrinkled his nose. "A sneaky little shit. When he's involved, no good comes of it."

The old man lowered his voice even further. "And you'd be wise to not mention Mythrian to that old reprobate, Markus. Don't tell anyone we're going to be practicing the Scairn tongue."

Ket's heart beat rapidly. "Will I get a switching?"

Obregon winked. "Not if you don't mention Mythrian to anyone."

# 9

# Unstable Transition

*The whore awaits her freedom, and only the bearer can fulfill her desire. She con-
nives and cajoles, a temptress beyond life, a seductress of the soul, a sorceress of
malign enchantment. She offers the fulfillment of all desires and hopes, a siren of
carnal need and material delight, and yet she gives naught but destruction and
damnation. The bearer will succumb, and all mankind will perish.*

*Decritos ahm Tellargan*
*penned after the fall of Tellargan*

The city of Tellargan had perished about six hundred years ago, and some years
back Kainborne had visited the ruins. Scavengers had long ago taken any stonework
that wasn't broken or poorly sized, and only a landscape of tumbled brickwork and
shattered masonry remained.

The scroll penned by Decritos disturbed Kainborne. The man had filled the entire scroll with a vitriolic rant against women, his words marked by unmistakable fanaticism. He also referred to one woman in particular whom he called *the whore*, apparently some sort of witch. He sometimes called her *the flame*, and Kainborne recalled
that the ketcaerm must *battle the flame and the crucible.* Could it be that the flame was this
witch? And did that mean that the crucible was a person as well? But who?

If one discounted village shamans and healers who practiced a combination of
herbal medicines and simple slight-of-hand, real witches did not exist. Kainborne had
found many spells and enchantments in old tomes and scrolls, and had diligently tested each of them. A few had worked, some only when augmented by his tinctures, but
none yielded powerful magics like those described in legend and myth. Kainborne had
concluded that truly powerful magics existed only in the tales told by bards and story-
tellers.

A muffled shout in the distance pulled Kainborne's attention away from the scroll in front of him. He scanned his workshop, wondering where the oaf had gotten to, but didn't give that much thought and returned his attention to the scroll.

The door to his workshop burst open and the oaf charged into the room, panting and sucking air into his lungs. "Master Kainborne, the Duke wants to see you . . . a messenger from Inversill . . . said you was to come right away."

From Inversill and for Jarrod! That would be a message from Archduke Macallan. Kainborne stood, leaving the scroll on his workbench. "Where is the duke?"

The oaf gulped. "In his study, Master Kainborne."

Kainborne found Jarrod pacing back and forth, holding a partially crumpled piece of paper in one hand. At Kainborne's appearance, Jarrod stopped pacing and half shouted, "Marius is dead, and there's chaos in the Lowland Kingdoms. Macallan thinks they'll be weak for months to come, so he's going to probe their borders."

They had all known that Marius suffered from the wasting sickness and would not last much longer. Kainborne had his own sources in Carthagen, had in fact grown up there, the son of a middling merchant who proved to be a poor businessman and died destitute. At least the man had provided him with an education, which Kainborne leveraged into a position as a young scribe. He'd barely survived.

Kainborne extended a hand. "May I see that, Your Grace?"

Jarrod handed him the piece of paper, and returned to pacing while loudly making plans to conquer the Lowland Kingdoms.

Macallan had received a message from one of his sources that Marius had died, and he'd passed exactly eight days ago. In the message Macallan speculated Carthagen would be weak for some time to come. Infighting among the factions in the city might even delay Maximillian's ascension to the Supremus for months, and the Duchies might take advantage of the fragile political state there. Macallan wrote of raiding their cattle and sheep herds, perhaps even annexing some valuable grazing land and water rights east of Inversill.

Kainborne paused for a moment and did the math. "Your Grace, might I suggest a note of caution?"

Jarrod stopped expounding on the largess to be had from a weakened Carthagen. Kainborne's failure to join him in his excitement clearly disappointed him. "What is it, man? Speak up."

Kainborne chose his words carefully. "This message places Marius's passing exactly eight days ago. A fast rider pushing his horse hard could reach Inversill in three to four days, and it would take another three to four days for a fast rider to carry that news from there to here. That means that the information Archduke

Macallan received left Carthagen no later than a day or two after Marius's death. So we really have no idea how the situation has developed in the aftermath of his passing."

Kainborne remained silent for several seconds while he watched Jarrod do the math. In an instant the young man's excitement disappeared and was replaced by deep disappointment. He shook his head sadly. "Yes, it's all speculation. None of it is true. How foolish of me!"

Kainborne loved moments like that. "Yes. But I have my own sources in Carthagen. In the next week or two, I'll be receiving updates from those sources, as will Archduke Macallan from his. There are always weaknesses after a change in power, and when we know what they are, we'll take advantage of them."

Jarrod's face brightened. "I knew I could count on you, councilor."

"And," Kainborne said, holding a dramatic pause after the word, "I noticed that Archduke Macallan invited you to guest at Inversill come the spring. By then we should know enough to judge whether you should bring armed troops with you. You'll want them there if you and he are going to be raiding the lowland fells."

Jarrod's face brightened even further.

• • • •

Seated atop his horse, Aurelius glanced about at the wealthy houses and estates on either side of the street, and listened to the fighting one street away as it echoed through the night. Muffled by the distance, he heard sword ring against sword, and the cries of men and horses.

With three palace guardsmen blocking his way, his impatience rose to the boiling point. His father had told him to never trust an officer who didn't lead his men in battle, but he had also told him that at some point, a general must stand back and let his troops do the fighting. His father had also taught him to never countermand the orders of one of his officers, saying, "Your choices are: dismiss him, hang him, or keep your mouth shut." Brunasus had ordered the three soldiers in front of Aurelius to protect him, with an implicit order to keep him out of the fighting, and he had too much respect for the man to dismiss him, or hang him.

As the minutes ticked by, the noise of struggle and strife slowly dwindled, then ceased altogether. By that time Aurelius's patience had reached its limit. Some minutes passed, then a horse and rider emerged far down the street, charging toward them. The three guardsmen drew their swords and turned their mounts to face the man, but as he approached, they recognized him as one of their own and relaxed. The fellow pulled his horse to a halt in front of them, both he and the animal breathing heavily.

"Dominus Aurelius," the man gasped, struggling for breath. "We've taken Garrien alive, and Captain Brunasus says it's safe to proceed."

Aurelius spurred his horse into a canter, almost knocking one guardsman off his mount. He and the animal covered the distance to the end of the street in seconds, then Aurelius turned the horse down a broad avenue littered with about a dozen corpses. A hundred paces down the lane, a crowd of palace guardsmen and city constables had clustered in front of the entrance to a moderate estate. They parted as Aurelius approached.

He guided his horse through the gates of the estate, and more corpses lay sprawled on its grounds. One of Brunasus's officers stood at the main entrance to the house. As Aurelius dismounted, the man saluted him and said, "This way, Your Grace."

Aurelius followed him into an elaborately decorated foyer, its floor littered with the broken remnants of a statue. The man led him toward the back of the house past more corpses, broken pottery, and shattered statues, then into a guest parlor as damaged as the rest of the house. In the center of the room Captain Brunasus and the Captain of Constables of the fifth precinct stood over a man seated in a chair and tied there securely. A bloody bandage strapped around Brunasus's left upper arm testified to the intensity of the fighting. Tied in the chair, Garrien's hair hung in a sweaty and tangled mess, while a trickle of blood from a cut on his forehead had drizzled down to his chin. Behind him, his wife and three daughters stood in a corner, all wearing bed clothing and clutching fearfully at one another.

As Aurelius approached, Garrien looked up at him with hate-filled eyes. "How dare you? You have no right. I will protest this before the entire Senatus—"

Brunasus raised a hand to strike him, and Aurelius shouted. "No. Hold."

Brunasus froze, his hand still raised.

Aurelius knew another shout would not be as effective as a pointedly worded command. "Do not strike him. That is an order, Captain."

Brunasus lowered his hand, which was all the signal Garrien needed to continue his righteous tirade. "The Senatus will not tolerate the unwarranted abuse of one of its members. You'll be . . ."

Aurelius ignored his rant and walked forward calmly, reaching beneath the lapel of his coat into a pocket there. He stopped one pace in front of Garrien and withdrew a carefully folded piece of stationery. A hand-inscribed border decorated the edges of the paper, a flourish that must have cost a small fortune. Aurelius made sure Garrien saw it clearly, and the man's voice trailed off.

Aurelius looked him in the eyes. "Let me read you something."

He was not one for dramatic flair—that was his mother's way—but at that moment he tried to imitate her. He carefully unfolded the paper, held it up, then began reading. "To his most serene Highness, Regent Monarch Archduke Macallan, of House Inversill. As we have discussed in our previous missives, the winds of fortune might present us both with opportunities for mutual benefit. Most recently, here in Carthagen, the passing of Dominus Marius Supremus may seem to be no more than a simple transition in power, but might I recommend you look at it from a different perspective—"

Aurelius stopped reading, locked eyes with Garrien, and stared at him while he refolded the paper and returned it to the lapel pocket. By the time he finished, Garrien trembled like a deer in the jaws of a lion. "How did you get that?"

Aurelius shrugged. "You were not as discreet as you thought." He recalled saying something similar to his mother.

Aurelius leaned down and stopped with his nose only inches from Garrien's face. He kept his voice calm and even. "Senator Garrien, there are many factions here in Carthagen, all seeking power in one way or another, some in the most nefarious ways. And they are tolerated because this is Carthagen; that is what we do. But there is one thing that none of us will abide: betray us to the Duchies or the Mythrians, and we'll all unite against you."

He straightened. "We have more than enough samples of your handwriting in the archives of the Senatus, and have easily confirmed you penned this yourself. Much too sensitive to trust to a scribe, eh? In any case, the Primus Council has already met on this matter. Three days from now you'll be hung in the square in front of the Senatus, and you'll hang there until the crows have picked your bones clean."

Garrien's wife stepped forward, though the two guards crossed swords in front of her, blocking her way. "Dominus Aurelius, my daughters and I knew nothing of this."

Aurelius hesitated. Garrien's youngest daughter appeared to have barely reached her teens, and the thought of her hanging from a gibbet next to her father sickened Aurelius. If it actually came to that, he'd find some way to spare the younger girls' lives. "You'll have an opportunity to present your case before the Primus Council two days hence, and you have my word you will be judged fairly. If you are innocent, you will not be harmed." There was no need to state what would happen to them if they shared her husband's guilt.

Divonia would want the woman and her daughters hung as a matter of course. But Aurelius's father had always taught him that the Senatus must take responsibility for the innocent. If they were truly without guilt, he'd do everything in his power to see to it they didn't hang with Garrien.

He didn't return to the palace until sunup, and even though exhausted by a sleepless night, he joined Janus and three scribes in his office. The Primus Council had prepared a statement to go out to all members of the Senatus regarding Garrien. It included excerpts from the man's letter to Macallan, with details on his proposed betrayal. Aurelius had held back sending them out until he knew Garrien's fate, but now he gave orders to have them sent immediately.

In less than an hour several responses came back with questions that needed an immediate reply. At mid-morning Janus reminded him he must prepare for Maximillian's ascension to the Supremus at noon. He left the rest of it to the councilor.

He washed away the smell of sweat and horse, then shaved, and combed his hair into some semblance of order. He finally sat down in a chair to catch his breath for a moment or two. When Porcia and Maximillian woke him, he had trouble orienting himself for several seconds.

He stood, and Porcia looked him over carefully. "We heard you've had a rather exciting night."

Maximillian grinned. "Garrien, eh?"

"Yes," Aurelius said. "The evidence was overwhelming."

Maximillian abruptly spun about and crossed the room to a side table. From a pitcher he poured a goblet of wine, returned to Aurelius and extended it to him. "You look like you need this."

Aurelius waved him off. "If I drink that, after your ascension, everyone who attended it will talk about how I slept through the entire thing."

Maximillian grimaced. "Yah, that would look bad."

He looked at the wine in the goblet for the longest moment, then raised it to his lips and downed the entire thing.

Porcia said, "A little early for that, isn't it?"

Maximillian shook his head. "I'm making an exception today. I need this to calm my nerves."

• • • •

Three days after Macallan's message to Jarrod, a rider from one of Kainborne's sources delivered a detailed account of the transition in power in Carthagen. It had been penned one week after Marius's passing. After reading the dispatch, Kainborne immediately sought out Jarrod and found him in the stables.

As Kainborne stepped into the darkened interior of the stables, he spotted Jarrod standing outside the stall of his favorite horse. He stood with his fists on his hips while saying something to someone in the stall. Jarrod glanced his way and Kainborne raised the piece of paper above his head. "Your Grace, I've just received an update on the events in Carthagen."

Jarrod's eyes brightened; he broke into a trot and jogged the short distance to Kainborne. Extending the dispatch toward the young duke, Kainborne asked, "Do you wish to read it?"

Jarrod dismissed the question with a wave of his hand. "No, no. Just give me the salient details."

Behind Jarrod, at the stall he'd been standing in front of, a groom peeked out and looked their way cautiously. Kainborne nodded toward the groom. "Perhaps we should step out into the sunlight."

Jarrod glanced over his shoulder, then turned back to Kainborne. "Yes, excellent idea, councilor."

Together they walked out of the stables into the castle yard, then Kainborne turned to face the duke and lowered his voice. "It's not all good news. My informant believes Marius planned carefully for an orderly transition after his passing. The members of the Senatus learned of Marius's death only shortly before the family supremus announced it to the populous. The constabulary precincts were all placed on alert before that, and were backed by contingents from the Supremus Guard, not by officers of the standing army."

Jarrod's eyebrows rose and he nodded, clearly understanding the significance of that.

"Unrest was limited to a few individuals of no real significance, and their efforts were quelled quickly. My source believes that Maximillian's ascension to the Supremus is all but assured. It will happen about a week after this missive was penned, which would be about now."

Jarrod's shoulders slumped. "I confess I am greatly disappointed."

Kainborne cherished moments like that. "It's not all bad news, Your Grace."

Jarrod perked up and his eyes brightened. "What am I missing?"

Kainborne smiled and gave him a knowing look. "Reading between the lines, the palace does not completely trust the officers of their standing army. We should be able to make some use of that. And it is common knowledge that Maximillian will be a weak ruler. In fact, the only strength behind the Supremus is his younger brother, Aurelius, who has no official capacity other than his own seat in the Senatus. Maximillian's greatest strength is that those in power believe Aurelius will keep him from making one mistake after another."

"Yes," Jarrod said. "A weak ruler, we can use that."

It was time to see how far Jarrod wanted to go. "And I have an idea . . ."

Jarrod's eyes brightened. "Yes, man. Spit it out."

Kainborne gave Jarrod a devious smile. "I can contact . . . some of the more disreputable elements in Carthagen. We shouldn't act without consulting Archduke

Macallan, but with your authorization and his, I might be able to arrange for Aurelius's demise sooner rather than later. If we can remove the strength behind a weak ruler, I must believe any number of options will open up."

Jarrod's lips curled into a smile to match Kainborne's. "Excellent, councilor, excellent! I'll prepare a message proposing just that and send it to Macallan right away."

Fearing Jarrod's enthusiasm had gotten the better of him, Kainborne spoke quickly. "But we must be cautious, Your Grace. Such a message could be of great value to many people. If a messenger took a bribe, or were simply waylaid, and your message fell into the wrong hands . . ."

Jarrod's enthusiasm morphed into a deep frown. "Of course, of course, it would forewarn the Lowlands of our intentions."

"Yes," Kainborne said, nodding slowly, "but worse than that it could precipitate open war, and we can gain far more by slowly picking at the corpse of the city-states. If I can suggest, merely hint to Macallan that we might have a means of adjusting the situation in Carthagen to our advantage, but don't be explicit. Even use my name, if you wish. Tell him you'll discuss it in more detail when you meet face-to-face in the spring."

Jarrod smiled and nodded slowly.

Kainborne was most pleased with the conversation, especially if it brought him to the attention of Macallan. If he became councilor to the Archduke of Inversill, the horizon of his ambitions would expand far beyond Dramoran.

"Yes," Kainborne said. "I think it likely that if we plan wisely, you and Archduke Macallan might still enjoy good sport next summer."

As to Carthagen, Kainborne didn't harbor any great loyalty to the city of his birth, would in fact enjoy contributing to its demise. As a young scribe in Carthagen, he almost starved. But he eventually found employment with a wealthy dowager. Her failing eyesight forced her to hire one such as him to facilitate correspondence with her contemporaries. And perhaps because of his youth she came to trust him more than she should have. He embezzled a little here and there from her accounts, though he didn't take much, but it made the difference, until he had to run for his life. The city constables had hunted him mercilessly, and would have stretched his neck at the end of a rope had they caught him. No, he would shed no tears for Carthagen.

# 10

# No Simple Solution

AS KAINBORNE'S HORSE followed his escort down the road into the Vale of Tramorth, a gust of icy wind battered him and he shivered at the thought of the coming winter. It had taken him over two months of long days and late nights to scour all his scrolls for any references to the Dreadmark. Some of the writing descended into lunacy and referred to the most fanciful imaginings. But from several authors Kainborne had learned a number of important details.

The appearance of the Dreadmark sometimes altered civilization through great and momentous events, and sometimes through insignificant incidents. The bearer of the Dreadmark might slaughter untold thousands of people, as had Domaxus the Conqueror, or prove to be a great leader, or a great villain. The bearer might also be a simple person of no account, which meant the Dreadmark could have appeared regularly without discovery by anyone.

Kainborne had found one reference connecting it to the mythical ketcaerm of the Mountain Folk. Penned about six hundred years ago, the author implied it had something to do with an ancient curse. He further speculated that the combination of Dreadmark and ketcaerm portended something even more ominous.

Kainborne wondered if he should reconsider his decision to allow the Scairn brat to live, and leaned heavily toward that course of action. He also decided to make certain discreet inquiries of traveling merchants in the hope of acquiring some of those lost manuscripts.

A guardsman in his escort broke away from the group and rode ahead at a gallop. To ensure that Abbot Benedictus was prepared for his arrival, they had sent riders out each day of the five-day journey to Tramorth. And as they approached the walls of the monastery, its gates stood open, with Benedictus waiting for Kainborne in the middle of the gateway. Had he not been there, Kainborne would have been sorely displeased.

Riding beside him, Zarkoffa leaned close and lowered his voice. "The smarmy lump is foolish enough to fear only a lessening of the endowments you send his way." Zarkoffa understood the abbot had much more to lose than that.

Kainborne had concluded his wisest move would be to eliminate the boy. He looked Zarkoffa in the eyes. "I'm going to speak with the boy. I'm not sure what I will ultimately decide, but after that I'll probably ask you to eliminate him. Can you do so quietly, perhaps spirit him away and dispose of him with no witnesses connecting you or me to his disappearance?"

Zarkoffa grinned. "If that's your decision, Master Kainborne, then after we leave I'll hide nearby in the forests for a few days, and I'll be careful no one sees me. Then one morning the boy will simply be gone, and no one will have seen him leave. And no one will ever see him again."

Kainborne smiled. "I knew I could count on you."

Zarkoffa's grin broadened. "Of course you can, as long as I can count on being paid."

The guardsmen brought their horses to a stop just in front of the monastery gate. Benedictus squealed in his high-pitched voice, "Master Kainborne, such a great pleasure to have you visit us."

He trudged the short distance to stand beside Kainborne's horse. Zarkoffa and the guardsmen dismounted first, and Kainborne noticed Benedictus eyeing the assassin with a fearful sidelong glance. Zarkoffa had told him of Benedictus's presumption that Kainborne's interest in the boy was tainted by unwholesome desire. Kainborne would do nothing about that now, though if the man ever again implied something of that nature, he'd have Zarkoffa garrote the fellow.

Kainborne dismounted and faced the abbot, who gave him a smarmy smile. "Master Kainborne, if you'd like to wash the dust of the trail out of your throat, I have chilled refreshments waiting in my study."

Kainborne nodded. "That would be most welcome. By all means, lead the way."

Benedictus turned about. "This way, if you please."

In his study the abbot pointed Kainborne to a comfortable chair upholstered in brocade fabric. As Kainborne sat down, the abbot served him refreshingly chilled white wine, which piqued his curiosity. "Do you have ice brought down from the mountains?"

The abbot shook his head. "No need, good sir. This close to the Mountain Kingdom, most raiding parties stop here for a night or two before proceeding up into the higher elevations. They return with shackled Scairn bondservants—their primary merchandise—but frequently they also bring cartloads of ice back to trade for other goods."

Kainborne enjoyed the wine, but impatience pushed him to inquire about the main reason for his journey. "And how is the boy doing?"

Benedictus shrugged. "He grieved for his mother for a time, still sheds a tear or two now and then, but we're seeing less of that each day. Brother Markus found it necessary to switch him a few times, but that too has become less necessary with time. And Brother Obregon says he is reasonably intelligent. By the way, what did happen to his mother?"

Kainborne shrugged. "I'm told she ate some bad meat."

Benedictus cringed. "Oh, that can be an unpleasant way to go."

Kainborne finished the wine quickly. "I need to see the boy alone. I'll use this room for that. Please have him brought here."

Benedictus smiled. "I did anticipate that. The boy is waiting just outside. If it pleases you, I'll have him sent right in."

Kainborne nodded, and the abbot turned and walked out of the room. After several seconds the door opened again. Benedictus stepped halfway through it, stopped, and looked toward the outer room. "Come on, boy. Stand up straight and give Master Kainborne a good look at you. And be sure to address him properly."

The young boy stepped into the room still dressed in his peasant garb, his hands clutched in front of him, his eyes downcast. Benedictus stepped out through the door and closed it. The boy stood silent and unmoving.

Kainborne tried to sound kindly. "Come forward, lad."

The boy didn't look up from the floor, but crossed the room and stopped an arm's length away. Kainborne leaned forward, reached out and gripped the lad's right wrist. He pulled the boy toward him, forcing him to take a step, and twisted his arm so he held it palm up. The birthmark on his inner forearm remained simply that, just a smudge of discolored skin, and not an ominous portent. Kainborne wasn't sure what he would have done if it had flared and again shown the mark of House Dramoran; probably give Zarkoffa orders to murder the boy then and there, and damn the consequences.

As he looked at the smudge of discolored skin, he recalled that he'd been exhausted that day in the kitchens at Glenmoore. They had arrived only the night before after several days on horseback, during which they had slept on the ground wrapped in blankets. He'd only seen the Dreadmark on the boy's arm that one time two months ago. And sitting in Benedictus's office, looking at nothing more than a blotch of purple skin, he concluded weariness and sore muscles had caused him to imagine something that had not been.

While he looked again at the smudge of skin, its edges shifted and flowed, melted and swirled. The simple purple smudge darkened in places, lightened in others, and changed color elsewhere, forming an intricate pattern of recognizable hues and shapes. Yellow fur formed, with large clawed paws raised high, and a lithe body supported on powerful haunches. Again, the smear of discoloration slowly took on the appearance of a tattoo carefully inked there by a master craftsman. But this time it wasn't an oak tree. Now Kainborne saw a lioness rearing up almost erect on her hind paws, her fore paws clawing at the air in front of her, the right paw above the left. In the birthmark he saw a lioness rampant, exactly matching the crest of House Inversill as tattooed on Archduke Macallan's inner forearm.

Something in Kainborne's chest turned over. He shouted, lashed out blindly, and stood, breathing rapidly. He took several breaths and managed to orient himself. The boy lay on the floor in front of him, his eyes wide and fearful, a trickle of blood running down his cheek.

The door to the office opened and Benedictus stepped in, stopping just within the doorway, his eyes blinking rapidly. "I heard a shout. Is something wrong, Master Kainborne?"

"No," Kainborne shouted. "Leave us. I'm not done here."

The abbot made a hasty exit.

Kainborne once again sat down in the chair. The boy remained on the floor, motionless like a frightened animal.

Kainborne shook his head to clear it. "Stand up, boy. I won't hit you again. And come here."

The boy hesitated for a long moment, then slowly rose and approached Kainborne, remaining just beyond arm's reach.

Kainborne snarled, "Closer."

The lad again hesitated, then took a cautious step forward.

As he'd done before, Kainborne reached out and gripped the boy's wrist, turning it palm up and exposing the birthmark on his forearm. Now it appeared to be nothing more than a smudge of discolored skin.

Kainborne couldn't keep an angry snarl out of his voice. "What do you see there, boy?"

The lad still did not meet Kainborne's eyes, and his voice trembled as he spoke in the crude accent of Glenmoore's kitchen staff. "Nothing, me lord."

"You see absolutely nothing, no birthmark, no tree, no lioness?"

The boy shook his head. "No, me lord, just purplish and smudgy skin."

*Purplish and smudgy skin*, Kainborne liked that. He released the boy's arm and the lad stepped back. The damn Dreadmark haunted Kainborne as nothing else could, and he now feared any action he might take regarding the boy. He thought it best to simply take no action at all and just let the boy live, at least for the time being. He could always change his mind later.

"Look me in the eyes, boy."

· · · ·

When the strange man said, "Look me in the eyes, boy," Ket raised his chin, looked into the man's face, and a chill swept through his heart. Where the dark man radiated physical danger, Ket couldn't name the sense of dread he got from this man. "Kainborne," Benedictus had called him. He wore black robes, had black hair pulled back over his ears, with a mustache and beard trimmed to a sharp point beneath his chin. But something in Kainborne's black eyes told Ket his life depended upon every word he spoke in the man's presence. Obregon had referred to him as a ". . . sneaky little shit," and clearly didn't like or trust the man.

The man's eyes narrowed with distrust. "Tell me again what you see when you look at that birthmark."

Some instinct warned Ket it would not be wise to *speak properly* in front of this man. "Just a smudgy birthmark, me lord, like everyone sees."

Kainborne nodded slowly. "Like everyone sees." He leaned forward, his eyes boring into Ket's face as if searching for something. "Nothing more than that? You see nothing but smudges of discolored skin?"

"Aye, me lord. Nothing."

The man leaned back in his chair, steepled his fingers in front of him, and stared at Ket for a long moment. Again, his eyes seemed to search for something. "Have any of the monks touched you . . . inappropriately?"

Ket didn't know the meaning of the word *inappropriately*, and wasn't about to ask. "Brother Markus switches me sometimes."

Kainborne raised an eyebrow, and his lips curled upward into a faint smile. "Brother Markus switches you, does he? Well you probably earned it, and that won't really hurt a young lad like you."

Ket disagreed with him on that, but kept his thoughts to himself. Just the thought of Markus and his switch sent him into a spiral of anger, and to maintain his sanity he struggled to control it. *Someday*, he thought. *Someday*.

Kainborne waved a hand at him dismissively. "You may go. And tell Abbot Benedictus I wish to speak with him."

"Aye, me lord," Ket said. He turned and struggled not to race for the door. He opened it and stepped out into the hallway beyond.

The abbot stood just outside the door, clutching his hands nervously in front of him. "You didn't anger Master Kainborne, did you? If you did, I'll switch you myself, and I'll switch you like you've never been switched before."

"No," Ket said. "He wants to see you again."

Benedictus's eyes widened. "Brother Obregon's expecting you and you're late. Off with you."

He brushed Ket aside, almost knocking him to the floor, swept past him and through the door. Once again alone in the outer room, Ket raised his arm and looked at the birthmark there. It was just an oval of purplish and smudgy skin.

As he walked to Brother Obregon's cell he encountered a Scairn boy headed in the other direction. The young man appeared to be in his mid-teens, far younger than the old grouch, though several years older than Ket. As they passed in the hallway, hoping to make a friend, Ket greeted him kindly in Mythrian, using one of the *speak-properly* phrases Obregon had taught him. "A pleasant morning to you, good sir."

The young Scairn halted abruptly in his tracks and turned to Ket, his eyes blinking rapidly. He spoke in the common tongue. "What did you . . ."

The boy's eyes narrowed angrily, and he lunged. Ket saw the blow coming, saw the fellow's arm swing out, but fury was the last reaction Ket expected. The open palm of the boy's hand connected with the side of Ket's face, knocking him against the wall of the corridor. He bounced off it and landed on the floor on his shoulder, wrenching it badly. The boy kicked him in the ribs, then drew his foot back to kick him again.

"Stop that."

The shout startled the boy, but Ket recognized the young peasant girl's voice. The boy cringed, turned, and ran, even though he stood taller than her and outweighed her considerably. That her shout had struck such fear in him surprised Ket as much as the boy's attack, and for the first time he understood the status of all Scairn.

The girl walked up to Ket and stood over him. "You poor boy."

She helped him to his feet. "Why did he do that?"

The boy's attack had been a revelation. To the other Scairn, Ket was not Scairn, he was Scairndraka, and they looked down on him the same way the Four Duchies people looked down on Scairn. But the peasant girl would never understand that.

Ket shook his head. "I don't know."

She appeared to be about his age, and he had learned her name was Peta, that her mother had died a few years ago, and her father raised her alone.

He smiled. "I'm Ket, and you're Peta."

She smiled back, one of the few kindnesses anyone in the monastery had shown him. "I know me own name, and I know yers too. No switchings today, eh?"

He grimaced. "Not yet, but I never know."

She nodded. "Well let's hope yer luck holds. And stay away from that Scairn boy."

She gave him another smile, then continued on her way. He headed for Obregon's cell, thinking that if he truly wanted to escape Markus, he'd have to come up with a plan, not just start running.

• • • •

The events of the afternoon had greatly upset Kainborne, and he declined Benedictus's offer to share the evening meal with him, choosing instead to have dinner brought to his room. As he ate he carried on a running argument with himself. On the one hand, he wanted to be done with the whole mess and have the boy eliminated, but on the other he could no longer deny what he had seen. Twice now the Dreadmark had appeared on the boy's forearm, once as the Mark of House Dramoran, and once as the Mark of House Inversill, the two most powerful duchies in Kyldaine. Would it manifest again in the form of the two lesser houses, Lagasdale and Gathgorme? And what did it mean?

Dramoran and Inversill; power beyond belief. If Kainborne controlled the boy, could he control those two Duchies? An intriguing thought, that! But how might he accomplish that? At best, the damn scrolls gave him only obscure and disjointed instruction. He needed to find the lost manuscripts referenced in that one scroll, if they still existed. But it would be exceedingly dangerous to let it be known he sought information on the Dreadmark. Someone might then connect his inquiries to the boy, which would complicate matters no end. He could spread the word that he would pay handsomely for scrolls with information on successful warlords. He had a few names besides Domaxus, men who had organized armies and fought historic battles, some who won, and some who lost, but all bearing the Dreadmark in their time. Gathering such information would align nicely with his responsibilities. He'd simply be studying historical military tactics so he could properly advise young Jarrod, should the need arise.

He thought he just might get a good night's sleep after all, but a soft knock on the door interrupted his thoughts. He crossed the room and opened it. A pretty young peasant girl stood in the hallway, her eyes downcast. She spoke with a heavy accent. "His Holiness wants me to see to your needs."

They had cleaned her up, washed her hair, probably even bathed her, though they couldn't do anything about the chipped and grimy fingernails. Kainborne nodded. "See to my needs, eh, is that what he said?"

"Yes, Yer Lordship, whatever it is you're a-wantin'."

Kainborne stepped aside. "Then enter. By all means, enter."

He would employ the same subterfuge he'd used on the boy's mother: drug her, grope at her breasts and crotch for a few minutes, and leave her with a confused impression he'd done what other men would do. He didn't want Benedictus to realize that Kainborne did not suffer the same desires as other men. The abbot would clearly misinterpret that information, and Kainborne now needed the man to ensure that damned boy lived long enough for him to figure out what to do with him.

# 11

# The Flame and the Crucible

PEERING INTO A polished brass mirror, Caerie examined the elaborate makeup her mother had helped her apply. Its color and pattern mimicked the tattoos of the priestesses. It started with her eyes, then continued down her cheeks, throat, and across her upper chest where her gown exposed a small amount of skin. Caerie thought it obvious the design was meant to draw a man's gaze first to the eyes, then pull them down to the priestess's breasts. Unfortunately, Caerie didn't yet have any breasts that might draw a man's gaze. And thankfully she didn't have to wear a translucent gown that left her all but naked in front of everyone in the room. It was embarrassing enough to have such a flat chest, and would have been absolutely humiliating had she been required to expose herself the way those priestesses did.

Standing behind her, her mother sighed as if reading her thoughts. "Don't worry, dear. In another year or two, you'll be a pretty young girl with all the attributes you could hope for."

Looking in the mirror, Caerie saw her Uncle Damuel standing behind her mother trying to suppress a smile. Neither of them understood.

"She's a pretty young girl now," Damuel said. "I think she's just relieved she doesn't have to walk among us almost naked in one of those sheer gowns. I was terrified when I came of age. It was bad enough having to put on all that makeup, but wearing one of those outfits; no one told me I didn't have to beforehand."

Perhaps he understood, just a little.

It was Caerie's tenth birthday. Early that morning at the hour of her birth she had officially come of age and become eligible to inherit the throne. When the time came to name a new monarch, custom dictated that the priestesses select the heir to the Throne of Myth and Legend only from among those mythchildren who had *come of age*. That almost frightened Caerie more than if she were to become an Unchosen like Damuel.

Still looking at her mother in the mirror, Caerie watched her make that subtle shift from parent to monarch. She couldn't say exactly what the woman did, but Caerie had seen it a hundred times before. And when her mother spoke, the words were not those of a parent to child, but that of queen to subject. "Come. The court awaits us."

Caerie turned about and gave a slight bow to the Crown Mother. Selene turned and led the way, with Caerie following, and Damuel behind her.

Her father and brother waited for them just outside the nursery. Crown Consort Sander beamed a broad smile. "You look stunning, my child."

Caerie tried not to appear pained as she returned his smile. "Thank you, Father."

Her brother leaned close to her and whispered. "It was a nightmare removing all that makeup, so when this is done I'll help you get rid of it."

She loved Nicki, but at that moment she truly liked him as well, a claim she couldn't always make.

Damuel made his own way to the festivities while the royal family took a back passage through the palace, which allowed them to enter the Great Hall of Myth and Legend through its main entrance. The entire court of the Mountain Kingdom had assembled for her coming-of-age, a crowd that filled the enormous hall. A contingent of the royal guard waited for them at the closed double doors that formed the main entrance. As they approached, Caerie heard the din of the crowd's conversations as a faint muffled roar.

They stopped in front of the doors for a moment and Selene asked, "Are you ready?"

Caerie wasn't ready, would probably never be ready, but she simply nodded. "Yes, Mother."

Selene nodded to the captain of the Mythrian Guard. He and a couple of his men put their shoulders to the doors, and they swung them open on creaking hinges. No longer confined by the thick planks of the doors, the roar of the crowd blossomed and assaulted Caerie's ears. Then the crowd became conscious of their monarch standing just beyond the entrance, and the din died slowly. The assembled courtiers parted to form an open aisle up the middle of the hall.

Selene led them at a stately pace, with Caerie following, Nicki behind her, then Sander. At the far end of the hall they ascended the dais to the throne, where Selene sat. Sander sat in a smaller throne on her left, with Nicki standing on his left. Then Caerie took her place to stand at Selene's right hand.

At that moment, Caerie's thoughts shut down. A little over a year ago she had stood at Sander's left while Nicki wore the makeup and stood at Selene's right for his coming-of-age. It was a tedious ceremony that required nothing of her but to stand there, look good, and be the center of attention.

High Priestess Melceinnia presided over the festivities. She wore the formal gown and feathered mask of her order while she carefully chanted the rituals and rights of

Caerie's coming-of-age. At one point, one of the younger priestesses cried out, howled for a moment in a strange tongue at some vision, then fainted. Melceinnia ceased her chant, shook her head sadly and rolled her eyes, a gesture only Caerie saw. She spotted Damuel in a private gallery above the main floor. Their eyes met and he returned a sympathetically sardonic smile.

After more than an hour the ceremony ended and they adjourned. Caerie was free for a short time, though there would be a parade through the city, then a reception that evening for only the most notable of merchants and nobles. Unfortunately, she would have to wear the makeup until she went to bed that night.

As they filed out of the hall, High Priestess Melceinnia approached her. "A word with you, child, if it pleases you."

The old woman's words may have been a request, but from Melceinnia it was an absolute command that even Selene would hesitate to defy. Caerie nodded. "At your pleasure, mistress."

Melceinnia gave her a nondescript smile. "Please follow me."

With royal guards accompanying them, the old woman led Caerie to the temple attached to the palace, and there to her private quarters. The guards waited outside.

Melceinnia casually waved a hand at a comfortable chair. "Sit down, child, and relax. I thought you might need an hour's respite from the tedium."

Caerie let out a sigh of relief and sat down.

The old woman peeled the feathered mask off her face, tossed it to one side with irreverent indifference, and turned to a small side table. She poured something from a pitcher into two goblets, handed one to Caerie, then sat down facing her. Caerie tasted the liquid in her goblet: chilled white wine.

Melceinnia raised her goblet to Caerie in a half-hearted toast. "The wine has been watered with unfermented grape juice, so the alcohol content is low. You needn't worry about getting tipsy."

Melceinnia touched her own goblet to her lips and Caerie relaxed further.

"So," the old woman said, "you are now of age, Caermorgan Mythchild. Did you know you were born under the realm of the lioness?"

Caerie didn't understand the reference, though she had heard of the realms of the stars. "I don't understand."

Melceinnia's face remained expressionless. "I study the stars and aspects of the moon to help me . . . understand things."

Caerie took great care not to roll her eyes, or give any indication of her skepticism. "I have only a little understanding of that. You believe groups of stars have shapes, and those shapes have meaning, am I correct?"

Melceinnia shrugged. "The meaning of the stars changes with the aspects of the moon."

Caerie spoke carefully to ensure her words and tone conveyed not a hint of disrespect. "I thought such magics had fallen out of favor."

A faint smile touched Melceinnia's lips, as if she understood Caerie's cynicism. "It's not unlike our gods. We once believed in a pantheon of them, truly believed the stories were historical documentation of fact. And now we regard them as nothing more than myth. The realms of the stars are much like that in many ways. Their study is not a sorcerous art, or a magic of strange powers. It doesn't reveal great portent, or give me prescient thoughts to glean the future. It simply helps me think, helps me consider possibilities, helps me organize my thoughts. Or at least . . . that's all it does most of the time. But upon occasion, it does surprise me."

That was an open invitation Caerie did not want to take, but she couldn't avoid it. "It surprises you?"

Melceinnia took a sip of her wine and her eyes met Caerie's. "No one else really studies the stars anymore. And that's why I think only I realize you were born under the sign of the lioness."

The old woman was leading her to something, and she had no choice but to follow. "Does that have some special meaning?"

Melceinnia shook her head. "No, not in and of itself. It might portend that you'll be a strong and powerful leader, or merely just a good mother, like a lioness. Or it might portend nothing at all."

The woman had now aroused Caerie's own curiosity. "Is there . . . something else then, something that adds to the meaning?"

Melceinnia lifted an eyebrow. "Caermorgan Mythchild, the stars were the same ten years ago at the hour of your birth, and today at the hour of your coming-of-age. But you were born under a full moon, which meant you were born under the realm of the lioness. And today you came of age under a dark moon, which means you came of age under the realm of the raken."

Caerie saw nothing of significance in that, and she pondered the old woman's words for a moment. "A lioness and a raken, I don't understand."

Melceinnia's lips turned upward in a malicious grin. "A raken and a lioness. A fledgling raptor and a lioness cub. A ket and a caerm."

Caerie gasped and spilled her drink in her lap. She stood and demanded, "What . . . what are you implying? I have no connection to a ketcaerm. I don't believe in that drivel. And in any case, a grown lioness is not a lion cub."

The old woman's lips curled upward in a predatory grin. "No, she's not. But at the time you were born under the realm of the lioness, you were an infant, a cub. And that's why I recommended your mother name you Caermorgan."

Caerie struggled to regain her composure. "That's just meaningless superstition."

Melceinnia placed her goblet on a side table, stood, and took two steps to stand facing Caerie. She leaned down and touched the fabric of Caerie's dress where she had spilled the wine. "You'll have to change your gown before the rest of the festivities today. But child, your reaction tells me a great deal. You are without doubt the lioness, but I wonder who might be the raken. And I think it's time you tell me what you're hiding from us all."

．．．．

*We thought we extinguished the flame and broke the crucible. But I fear the flame will fire the crucible once again, even if from the grave.*

*A hundred priestesses joined in unison to hold Cerciea and Damodian enthralled while they burned. And after the fires cooled, as we collected their ashes to scatter them to the winds, a conspiracy of a thousand ravens blanketed the sky. Squawking and shrieking, they swooped down upon us, attacking the way an army and its generals might. They ripped out the priestesses' eyes with their beaks, and tore out their hearts with their talons. The foul carrion-eaters bathed in the ashes of their master and mistress, covering themselves like gray, ghostly specters. Then they rose into the sky higher and higher until one by one each burst into a brilliant orb of flame.*

*We believed we extinguished the flame and broke the crucible, the witch and the sorcerer, the whore and her lover, but did we?*

*Author unknown*
*penned in an unknown time long ago*

Aurelius had come across the scroll in a small shop, where he found it buried in a pile of other worthless scrolls. He might have missed it completely had it not rained that day, a sudden deluge so intense it forced him to step off the street and take cover in the nearest shop. It was the kind of place that offered cheap imitations and manuscripts of questionable provenance, and he immediately regretted that he hadn't braved the downpour long enough to take refuge in another shop nearby, one that might offer merchandise of more interest. To kill time while the rain thundered down, he browsed about, not really paying attention to what he saw, his mind preoccupied by his brother's transition in power.

He might have missed it completely had not the parchment been reused. Its most recent author had taken an old scroll, and penned a new missive on the back of its parchment. Then he had reversed the scroll as he rolled it up, protecting the newer lettering on the inside, with the older exposed on the outside. And for that reason, on that day, during that storm, with his thoughts focused on the transition in power, Aurelius glanced down for a brief instant and saw a strange glyph. He didn't know it's meaning, but had seen it's like before, and that pulled his thoughts into the moment.

He had a certain scroll that purported to translate an ancient cuneiform script into a more modern tongue. He had only glanced at it briefly, and had never found it of any use. But he thought the strange glyph on that scroll in that shop appeared quite similar to that older script. On a whim he bought the scroll, paying only a pittance for it.

Upon his return to the palace he didn't have time to translate the thing, but thought he'd take a moment to see if the older writing on the new scroll matched that ancient script. Four hours later he sat at the desk in his study stunned beyond belief. The older writing purported to be an eyewitness account of a mythical tale, a scary story told to Scairn children on a stormy night to elicit shrieks of fear and laughter. Aurelius knew of the story only because a few years ago he'd come across it in a parchment written by a Scairn academic. Cerciea and Damodian, Scairn witch and Lowlands sorcerer, the flame and the crucible, the lovers who committed a crime of such unspeakable atrocity, they were burned and their ashes scattered to the winds. As to the scroll he'd found in that shop on that rainy day, the author had either been a prankster or a madman, because to believe him meant the story was far more than just a tale for a stormy night. To believe him meant the lovers had actually existed, had not perished, and intended to return.

Aurelius had translated the older scroll onto paper. He crumbled that piece of paper and tossed it into the blazing hearth in his office. Then he stored the untranslated scroll among the other scrolls of no importance, swearing he would never look at it again.

• • • •

Zalestria had no responsibilities during the coming-of-age ceremony of a mythchild. She spent the time carnally worshiping with an old merchant, and he demonstrated his devotion with a generous tithe of alms of penitence. After he left, she visited a young lieutenant in the royal guard, and worshiped with him. He was much too junior to be as generous with his tithe, but he made up for it in energy and stamina while worshiping. She thought she might encourage him to worship with her regularly.

From there she had to rush to arrive at the coming-of-age ceremony before it ended. She found a place near the back of the Great Hall of Myth and Legend and waited. And when that old priestess finally finished the ceremony, Zalestria held back. Once the hall had emptied of all but a few stragglers, she stepped into a shadow.

Most laypeople were not aware of the small pouch all priestesses carried. Suspended by a pale leather thong tied around her waist, it hung between her legs, though not in such a way that it might impede pleasurable activities. And in the shadows there, it was all but invisible, even beneath the translucent fabric that revealed everything else.

From it she retrieved a small vile of colorless ointment that all the priestesses carried. It produced almost no effect in women, but when applied to the skin of a man, it would quickly arouse him. And the intensity of his excitement would be directly proportional to the amount she applied. But for her purposes that day, she only needed a tiny smear. She applied some of it to her lips on top of her lip paint, then a small dab of it to the tip of her index finger.

• • • •

During the ceremony, Damuel's rank and station allowed him a seat with other dignitaries in a private gallery above the main floor. And when the rather tedious ceremony ended, he held back. He remained seated while everyone else in the gallery stood and joined the assembled masses below. Sitting quietly, he watched them file out of the Great Hall, his thoughts drifting to the other two realms.

With the passing of Marius, the unrest and instability in the Lowland Kingdoms worried him. Macallan would undoubtedly test the strength of the Lowlands borders, and their resolve to defend them. In some ways that would be a blessing: if the archduke focused his efforts on the Lowland Kingdoms, he might put less effort into raiding Mythria's border villages. But that contributed to the overall instability of all three realms, so that would be a mixed blessing.

Damuel glanced around; the other occupants of the gallery had departed. He stood and leaned on the gallery rail. Down on the main floor only a few stragglers remained, speaking quietly in small groups here and there. He quickly scanned their faces, and didn't see anyone who might waylay him on his way out. He pushed off the rail and crossed the short distance to the spiral staircase that led down to the main floor. But a figure hidden in the shadows blocked his way.

A female voice said, "So pensive!"

The young priestess with the striking amber eyes stepped out of the shadows. He had to think for a moment to recall her name: Zalestria.

She gave him a coy smile and took another step forward, stopping at an intimately close distance. She reached up and used the tip of her finger to delicately trace the line of his jaw. "So pensive, one would think you bore the weight of all three realms on your shoulders. You serve the throne so diligently, do you have no needs of your own, no desires?"

Looking at her, something within him stirred, but he ignored it and shrugged. "I have what I need."

She raised an eyebrow. "Most men want a legacy, an heir, something—"

He shook his head. "I have no need of an heir. That would only . . . complicate matters."

With her finger she traced a line down his throat and along the top of his neck. "You know, the women of the court gossip about you, the handsome brother of the Crown Mother. It's common knowledge you don't even have a woman with whom you carry on a casual relationship of convenience."

Conscious of the translucent near-nakedness of her gown, he found it difficult to speak. "Such a relationship would generate even more gossip."

She smiled and continued to trace the finger across his throat. "You don't strike me as the type of man who concerns himself with the trivial gossip of a bunch of women."

He tried to focus on her words and not her body, but found that more difficult with each passing second. "One must always be concerned with appearances."

She leaned forward and brushed her lips across his cheek. "It's also common knowledge you're not a lover of men, and as a priestess, I know for a fact you haven't worshipped carnally for quite some time. All men have needs, and I very much doubt you're the celibate type."

Many women had tried to seduce him purely because of his rank and station. Their advances, and the potential complications that might ensue, rarely swayed him. But this young priestess sent a thrill through him he struggled to resist.

She smiled as if she understood the thoughts roiling through his mind. "And I'm not the celibate type either."

He kissed her, and her tongue probed his mouth as he tasted her lips. The hunger he had suppressed for a long time rose within him. Her fingers gripped his wrist, then pulled his arm up and pressed the palm of his hand against her breast.

He ended the kiss. He was not one to lose control, and didn't understand why he had done so now with her, but he wanted her with an intensity he could not resist. "Should we," he said, trying to control his breathing. "Should we adjourn to the temple, and—"

She pressed a finger against his lips. "Carnal worship?" She shook her head. "No. No worship, but definitely the carnal part. Just pleasure, desire, want, need—here and now."

With one hand she lifted her gown, and with the other she pulled at the laces of his breeches. He lost himself in his need, though at one point he thought he heard her whisper, "And perhaps an heir." But the taste of her skin called to him, and he ignored that.

# 12

# Ambitions

AS MAXIMILLIAN STEPPED into the drawing room, Divonia turned on him and shouted, "We have to expand our army. We can't let Macallan get away with this."

Maximillian stopped in his tracks just inside the door. He gave Aurelius an apologetic look, and said, "Aurelius tells me he's just testing us, now that father's gone. Wants to know if I'm weak."

Divonia gave Aurelius an angry look, but focused her ire on Maximillian. "And you have to show him you're strong. That's why we have to expand the army. And we have to do so immediately."

Aurelius stepped forward and stopped in front of Divonia, standing between her and Maximillian. "That's not necessary, Mother. We have more than enough men to patrol that border and repel any skirmishes he sends our way. We'll kill a few of his men and send the rest of them back to him badly bloodied. He'll quickly tire of losing good men, and we'll return to the status quo without starting all-out war."

Aurelius knew Divonia didn't care what he thought; after all, he had no real power. She stepped around him and marched toward Maximillian. "You could rule so much more than just this city if only you took the initiative. Expand the army and become someone your father would be proud of."

Her words stunned Aurelius. He should have seen it before. Divonia had no interest in a strong and healthy Carthagen. She wanted an empire. She wanted a conqueror who could *rule so much more*. He could probably do nothing to thwart his mother's ambitions, or to prevent the inevitable eruption between her and Maximillian, but he had to try. "Mother, we've discussed some of this before. Perhaps we could put it aside this once."

Porcia stepped up beside him and lowered her voice. "You're wasting your time, Brother."

Divonia turned away from Maximillian and aimed her anger at Aurelius. "Put it aside? Through your father the three of you are direct descendants of Domaxus the Conqueror. And as the eldest, Maximillian could rule it all."

Maximillian rolled his eyes and crossed the sitting room to a side table. He lifted a decanter of wine and poured a healthy draft into a goblet, turned and raised it in salute. "To Domaxus the Conqueror." He swayed as he hesitated, frowned, and shook his head. "No, that's not the right salute. How many men died because of his conquests? Thrice ten thousand? A hundred thousand?"

He raised the goblet again. "To Domaxus the Butcher. Yes, that's much more appropriate."

Porcia whispered, "I predict she'll get him so furious he'll throw the goblet against the wall and storm out of the room."

Maximillian touched the goblet to his lips, gulped heartily, upended it, and downed the entire thing.

Divonia's eyes flashed with anger, and her fair complexion paled even further. "It's barely mid-morning and you're already drunk."

Maximillian shook his head. "No, Mother, I'm not in the least drunk. That was only my second drink of the day. It'll take at least another hour to get completely drunk, so I doubt I'll be drunk before noon, but I fully intend to get there."

Divonia's lips stiffened into a tight slash of a line, though only a few faint creases marred her otherwise stunning beauty. Aurelius watched her tamp down her anger before she spoke. "If you handled this properly, you could quietly expand our army, and that would put you in a position to rule more than merely Carthagen."

Maximillian shook his head. "You would have me rule the cities of Andopolous and Tarnasus as well? I think *they* might have something to say about that. And I can't imagine that the Senatus would sit idly by if I tried to turn Carthagen into a military encampment."

Divonia's eyes widened as she lifted an eyebrow. "Andopolous and Tarnasus are weak. Their armies are small and little better than city police. We have eight hundred city constables to keep the peace here in Carthagen. But your late dear father saw to it we also have a standing army of two thousand men that train continuously to be ready for any conflict. That is why Andopolous and Tarnasus dare not make a move without consulting you, the Senatus Supreme. And while the Senatus is not without influence, they are purely advisory. If you enlisted the aid of a few key senators, the Senatus would not dare oppose you."

Maximillian uttered an exasperated sigh. "Enlist their aid? You mean bribe them, don't you?"

Divonia curled her hands into fists and planted them on her hips. "Yes, I mean bribe them, at least some of them, but there's more to it than that. Most of the men I'm thinking of, and in fact the most important of them, cannot be swayed simply with coin. Offer them opportunity, greater wealth, power. Each is different, and one must—"

Maximillian cut her off. "Of course they require more than merely coin. I'm thinking in particular of Lucius, whom, I believe, you're fucking. And don't deny it."

Divonia's jaws clenched and her eyes hardened. "Don't be crude. Your father is no longer with us, so if I choose to spend some time with a companion, you have no right to—"

Maximillian demanded. "And who else are you fucking? Do you intend to fuck every one of these men you're thinking of? Or maybe you're simply going to fuck the entire Senatus. You could get that done in a week or so, if you took them on three or four at a time and gave each a different hole to fuck."

She lashed out with her hand and slapped him across the face, striking him with such force he staggered back a step and dropped the brass goblet. It clattered on the floor then came to a stop.

He threw his hands up in the air and shouted, "By the ancient gods!" Then he turned, and stormed out of the room.

Porcia whispered, "I may have been wrong about the goblet against the wall, but I was right about the storming-out-of-the-room part."

Aurelius had seen the same drama play out again and again, though it was the first time he'd glimpsed Divonia's true motives. And Maximillian had never pushed her so far that she struck him. Carthagen was preeminent among the lowland city-states, but his mother wanted more.

She turned to Aurelius, still breathing rapidly and struggling for control. "If only you were my eldest son. If only you could inherit the Senatus Supreme. If only—"

Aurelius didn't want to hear any more of that. "Don't say it, Mother. Once Max marries and produces an heir, I cannot inherit and that will not change."

Divonia was a woman of action, and he watched the look on her face shift from stark anger to cold calculation. His words had prompted some sort of idea in her head, and if she allowed her thinking to continue down that line of thought—

"You know," Porcia said, still keeping her voice to a whisper, "the look on Mother's face makes me think she's considering her options regarding our dear brother's continued tenure as Senatus Supreme."

Aurelius had tried to prevent his thoughts from going down that path, but as always Porcia understood their mother better than anyone. Aurelius did not hide his anger as he crossed the room in a few long strides, stood more than a head taller than

Divonia, and purposefully loomed over her. "And if you attempt in any way to change that, I will not support you."

She calmed and grinned, giving him a sly look that said she wouldn't need his support for a fait accompli.

He turned, but did not storm out of the room like his brother. Instead, he walked calmly out of her presence, though it took every bit of control he had.

• • • •

Throughout the winter, Jarrod and Macallan regularly communicated via messenger. Jarrod had not forgotten Kainborne's caution about putting dangerous specifics in a written message, and frequently asked Kainborne to review what he had penned before sending it. Small, enticing hints that they might have the means to influence the political situation in Carthagen had clearly sparked Macallan's interest, and with the onset of spring he and Jarrod were eager to meet face to face and cement their plans.

At the first hint of milder weather, before he and Jarrod even began making plans for their journey to Inversill, Kainborne sent Zarkoffa to Carthagen with instructions to contact certain acquaintances of his. If the man moved quickly, he could reach the city, complete Kainborne's business there, then return to the Duchies and arrive at Inversill about the same time as Kainborne and Jarrod.

A few weeks later the trip to Inversill proved to be a muddy slog through rainy weather, though otherwise uneventful. At Inversill, Macallan greeted them in a large foyer as they shook rain from their clothing and scraped mud off their boots.

"Jarrod, my friend," he said, gripping the young duke in a hearty embrace. "I remember when you stood knee-high to me. I do miss your father, but I see you're quickly filling his boots."

The lord of Inversill was a large man with a full beard. He kept his wavy, shoulder-length brown hair brushed back and tied in a warrior's knot behind his head. Releasing Jarrod, he turned to Kainborne and nodded politely. "Master Kainborne."

Kainborne bowed deeply. "Your Grace."

Macallan looked him over, appraising him carefully. "We've met before, but never really had the chance to get to know one another. And apparently you can help us with the situation in Carthagen."

Kainborne smiled politely. "I spent some time there as a young man, and through the years have maintained relationships with old associates. Some are not the most . . . savory sort of character, but are useful nevertheless, and sometimes more useful because of their . . . questionable backgrounds."

Macallan nodded, but otherwise showed no expression. "I have a few unsavory acquaintances of my own, but none in Carthagen. Before you leave, let's make sure we get better acquainted."

Kainborne lowered his eyes. "That would be my pleasure."

"By the way," Macallan said. "Your man Zarkoffa arrived early this morning, was rather evasive as to why he wasn't travelling with you."

Another implied question, and Kainborne spoke carefully. "I sent him to Carthagen to remind certain colleagues there that I may soon require their services."

Macallan's lips split into a broad grin. "Would you like to speak with him?"

Kainborne nodded. "By your leave, yes."

"Stay here," Macallan said. "I'll have him brought to you."

With that, Macallan spun about. "Jarrod, I have some strong brandy that'll warm your gut." He lowered his voice. "And a right pretty whore to warm your bones."

The two men left the room speaking of brandy and whores. Some minutes later a rain-soaked Zarkoffa stepped through the outer door, cursing and shaking rain from his cloak. "Master Kainborne," he said. "I hate this bloody weather."

The two of them were alone in the room, but Kainborne still approached the man and lowered his voice. "What of Martonian?"

Zarkoffa lowered his voice as well. "I found him, though the shit didn't even pretend to trust me, only trusted me a little after I mentioned that name you gave me, then trusted me a little more when I gave him that coin you provided."

Martonian had been Kainborne's fence when he needed to convert a bauble he stole from the old dowager into coin. Kainborne wasn't foolish enough to give Zarkoffa his own true name, had instead told him to tell Martonian, "I work for a man you know. You and he have a mutual acquaintance named . . ." And there, the name of a long-dead old woman meant a great deal to the fence.

Kainborne shrugged. "I'm not surprised he didn't trust you. They don't like Duchies men in the Lowland Kingdoms."

Zarkoffa frowned. "How'd he know I'm a Duchies man?"

Kainborne merely said, "He would know." He didn't add, *Because of your atrocious Duchies accent.* After Kainborne had left Carthagen, only one step ahead of the hangman, it took him several years of careful practice to eliminate his Lowlands accent and sound like a proper Duchies man. "What of Garrien?" he asked.

Zarkoffa froze, looked at Kainborne pointedly and raised an eyebrow. "Oh, I saw Garrien all right. He's come up in the world, got to be one of them senators, but now he's hanging from a gibbet in the square in front of the Senatus. Been there about six months. They told me they'll take him down when the crows have picked his bones clean, though his bones looked pretty clean to me."

"Interesting," Kainborne said. "The traditional Lowlands punishment for a traitor. Did you learn what he did?"

Zarkoffa shrugged. "Word has it he tried to contact Macallan directly to cut a deal."

Out of curiosity, Kainborne asked, "Did they hang his wife next to him?"

The assassin frowned and shook his head. "No, he was hanging there all by himself."

The Senatus would have thoroughly investigated Garrien's plot. If evidence pointed in any way to the woman's complicity, they would have hung her next to her husband. And depending upon who controlled the Supremus, they might have hung her regardless, along with her children. Kainborne suspected someone had intervened to temper the city's ire.

Zarkoffa didn't have much more to report. He had reached two more of the names Kainborne had given him, which meant they didn't need Garrien.

Kainborne joined Jarrod, Macallan and several others for a hearty dinner, then retired early, leaving the two dukes to their brandy and whores.

The next morning Jarrod and Macallan went out hunting with Macallan's young son Clarahm. Kainborne thought the castle staff would leave him to his own devices and steeled himself for a thoroughly boring day. But shortly after the two dukes left, Macallan's chief steward approached him.

"Master Kainborne," the fellow said. "Duke Jarrod mentioned you study old scrolls, and Archduke Macallan has several here that no one has ever bothered with. He thought you might find them of interest."

Kainborne's heart raced, though he tried to appear casual about his interest. "Yes, I do find historical records of interest. It's a diversion of mine."

Macallan's steward summoned a couple of servants, then led Kainborne to a storage room in the back of the castle. A thick layer of dust on everything made it clear no one had touched anything there in years. At the steward's direction, the two servants dug through piles of old clothing, hides, and other discarded refuse, exposing a large wooden chest about the size of a coffin.

The steward nodded his approval. "Archduke Macallan told me he discovered this as a young man. Apparently, his great grandfather was an avid collector of such lore. But the present archduke has no interest in old scrolls and has never bothered with them."

The servants muscled the chest into the center of the room, but when they tried to open it, the lid refused to budge and they forced it loose with a crowbar. The archduke's ancestor had filled it to the brim with old scrolls, but to Kainborne's disappointment, some of them had rotted away.

"I'll leave you to it," the steward said. He turned, and with the servants following him, he left the room.

Kainborne knelt down in front of the chest and carefully lifted one scroll. It appeared intact, but when he unrolled it, half of it disintegrated into flakes of moldy hide. Each morning for the next week, Jarrod, Macallan, and Clarahm went out hunting, while Kainborne spent the time on his hands and knees in front of that chest. Some scrolls disintegrated on first touch, and he learned to recognize those before opening them. He carefully put them aside, thinking that if he ever had the chance, he'd treat them with the greatest of care and copy their contents to paper. It would be a painstaking task, for he'd have to replicate every character and glyph.

He came across tantalizing and exciting hints. Several references to the Dreadmark tempted him to dig deeper, but he focused on preserving the information for later study. Each afternoon, the two dukes and Clarahm returned from their hunting and Kainborne put aside the chest of scrolls. They spent afternoons and evenings planning various ways to take advantage of the turmoil in Carthagen.

Near the end of the second week Kainborne stood in front of the open chest looking at the wealth of scrolls in contained. He now realized it would take him months, perhaps years, to get to the last of them. He already had a small pile of those he needed to copy, and each would require an effort of three or four days. He sighed and was about to kneel and continue the effort, but he heard shouts muffled by the walls that surrounded him, some sort of commotion in the castle yard.

Kainborne turned and walked hurriedly out of the storage room, then through the castle proper and out into the yard. The sun had only climbed about halfway to noon and the hunting party had returned.

"It's Archduke Macallan," someone shouted. "His horse threw him and he's badly hurt."

They had brought Macallan back on a make-shift stretcher. He was conscious, but crying out in considerable pain. Two physikers descended upon him and issued orders to carry him inside. Kainborne, Jarrod, and Clarahm followed them, the young boy wringing his hands.

Kainborne asked Jarrod, "What happened?"

Jarrod grimaced. "His horse stepped in a badger hole, went down bad and fell on Macallan's leg. Had to put the animal down."

Kainborne stepped forward to look over the shoulder of one physiker as he examined the archduke's leg. His right foot appeared twisted at an odd angle. As Macallan screamed in pain, Kainborne asked, "How bad?"

The physiker continued to probe at the ankle and foot as he spoke. "Skin's not broken, so we don't have to worry about festering. Maybe nothing broken, just a lot of torn muscle and ligaments." Macallan screamed again and thrashed about while four servants tried to hold him.

The physiker growled. "Keep him still."

It was then that Kainborne realized he could help them all, and perhaps considerably improve his standing with the archduke. He leaned close to the archduke's ear and shouted to get the man's attention. "I have a tincture that will help the pain."

Macallan grabbed the front if his robes and pulled him down. "Anything," he screamed. "Anything!"

Kainborne shouted, "No, Your Grace, listen to me."

Macallan went silent, though he trembled and his eyes blinked rapidly, but Kainborne had his attention. "The tincture is dangerous. It will cloud your thinking. You will not be yourself, you will not be sane for a day or two, but you will feel no pain."

Macallan gritted his teeth and shook as he spoke. "Do it."

Kainborne rushed back to the small cell they had given him. He opened the strongbox containing his tinctures and selected the one he had in mind. Macallan was a big man, so he drizzled six drops of it into a goblet, then diluted it with a splash of water. He closed and locked the strongbox, then picked up the goblet and rushed back to Macallan. He had to shout to be heard above the archduke's screams. "Sit him up so he can drink this."

The servants lifted the big man's shoulders and got him into an upright position. Kainborne put the goblet to his lips. "Drink it all."

Macallan obeyed, desperately gulping the mixture. They laid him back down and he continued to scream while the physikers and several others in the room gave Kainborne skeptical looks. But after some minutes Macallan's screams turned to groans and the skeptical looks disappeared. Then the archduke sighed and lay back, murmuring a discordant stream of gibberish. Besides eliminating pain, the tincture Kainborne had given him twisted the mind in strange ways.

Kainborne didn't see Macallan for four days, but then the archduke summoned him. The large man lay in his bed propped up on pillows, with Jarrod and Clarahm standing nearby. As Kainborne stepped into the room and bowed, Macallan demanded, "Do you have more of that stuff you gave me?"

"I do," Kainborne said, "but it is extremely powerful and dangerous. A single use will not harm you, but repeated use can kill."

Macallan frowned. "Can kill, eh?"

Kainborne nodded. "Yes, my lord. Now that the pain has abated, I recommend strong willow bark tea, but not the tincture. It's much too dangerous."

"Well," the archduke said. "I thank you nevertheless. My physikers tell me that once I fell into a stupor, they reset the ankle quicker and better because I was still."

The incident had worked out nicely for Kainborne. "I'm glad I could be of help."

"By the way," Macallan said. "I'm told you found those old scrolls of interest."

Kainborne didn't want to pass up any opportunity to leverage the man's good will. "Yes, my lord. Would it be possible to take a few with me when we leave?"

Macallan gave a casual wave of his hand. "Take the whole bloody chest. I have no use for it. And speaking of leaving, when Jarrod returns to Dramoran, perhaps you can stay here at Inversill for a bit. I have some issues I'd like to discuss with you in more detail, not least of which is Carthagen."

Kainborne kept the look on his face neutral. "With my liege lord's permission—" Jarrod smiled and nodded. "I'd be most happy to."

That night, as Kainborne lay in bed, the talk of Carthagen and his former acquaintances there had stirred old memories. The old dowager had discovered his theft, and when she confronted him, he had no choice but to murder her to keep her silent. It was her fault actually. Had she minded her own business, they could have continued an excellent relationship, and he wouldn't have stolen too much from her.

He escaped the city one step ahead of the hangman, but pilfered her mansion before doing so, and came away with a small purse of jewels and coins. It hadn't been much, but it allowed him to create a new life in the Duchies and eliminate his Lowlands accent. It took several years to meet the right nobles, make a good impression, demonstrate his worth, and slowly work his way up the hierarchy to his present position with Jarrod. He fell asleep thinking that with his new relationship with Macallan, he might go even higher than House Dramoran.

# 13

# Hessian

AS A MATTER of convenience, Aurelius had limited the meeting to a select group including Maximillian, Councilor Janus, Captain Brunasus, the ambassadors from Andopolous and Tarnasus—two ancient diplomats—and finally Senator Lucius, Chairman of the Primus Council of the Senatus. They sat around a large table while Porcia and Divonia, who were not officially participants, stood near the entrance behind Aurelius. Divonia at his back always made Aurelius nervous.

Standing while addressing the rest of them, Councilor Janus continued his report. "We know the Duchies were hoping for the worst, and were disappointed that the transition proved uneventful."

Naerin, Ambassador from Andopolous, appeared to be napping, but Aurelius knew better.

Victicus, Ambassador from Tarnasus, leaned forward. "I wouldn't call the incident with Garrien uneventful."

Janus gave a slight shrug. "Interestingly enough, it was. After Marius's death, everyone expected something to happen. And then we caught Garrien red-handed and hung him. So something did happen. We thwarted it expeditiously, and everyone breathed a sigh of relief. I should mention that a search of Garrien's villa uncovered evidence he has been working with someone in the Duchies for quite some time. We haven't identified his contact there, but it was clearly not one of the four dukes, probably someone of considerably lower station. We suspect Garrien wanted to move farther up the chain of command, hence, his ill-conceived letter addressed directly to Macallan."

Naerin perked up. "And what of Macallan?"

Janus raised an eyebrow. "He sent a few sorties into border villages, but we repelled them easily, and he has since ceased testing us."

Victicus asked, "What about the Mountain Kingdom?"

Janus's brow wrinkled in thought. "Since we don't raid their villages for Scairn bondservants, the Mythrians are probably keeping a close eye on us, but fundamentally staying out of it."

Aurelius had already heard it all in considerable detail. He had assembled them there for the benefit of the Primus Council and the two ambassadors. They needed to reassure the political factions in all three city-states that commerce, trade, peace, and tranquility would proceed without interruption.

Lucius, Victicus, and Naerin had several questions. Aurelius chafed at the extra time they took, fearing he'd be late for an important appointment, and chiding himself that he hadn't allowed more slack. When the meeting did finally break up, he hurriedly excused himself, but as he turned to leave, Maximillian gripped his arm, halting him. Porcia joined the two of them as Maximillian lowered his voice and spoke with a hint of desperation. "You'll be back before I convene the Senatus, won't you?"

Aurelius nodded. "Yes, of course, I have plenty of time."

His brother grimaced. "I hate it when you leave me alone with Mother."

"Don't worry," Porcia said, "I'll be there."

Maximillian closed his eyes. "I know you wouldn't leave if it wasn't important, so go before someone else delays you."

Aurelius turned away from them, and to his great relief, no one else intercepted him. Tribune Denian, a trusted lieutenant, stood outside the room waiting for him, dressed in common street clothing. "This way, Your Grace."

Two palace guardsmen waited for them in the stables, also dressed in common clothing. With them stood a rough-looking fellow whom no one would mistake for anything but a thug. Denian handed Aurelius a bundle of clothing. Aurelius stripped down and changed into a simple pair of breeches, old scuffed boots, a plain linen blouse, and a threadbare coat over that. Like his four companions, he no longer looked the part of a nobleman.

He turned to the ruffian standing with the two guardsmen. "You are?"

The man gave him a grin twisted by an old scar on his lower lip. "Ganda. I report directly to Hessian, but you already know that."

Aurelius returned his grin. "Just wanted to make sure. Short swords allowed, right?"

Ganda shrugged. "That's what Hessian said, though if it was up to me, I'd have you walk in naked."

Aurelius stepped up close to the man and stood a finger's length taller than him. They locked eyes and he said, "But it's not up to you." The man lowered his eyes.

Aurelius turned back to Denian, who handed him a sheathed short sword. He strapped it on, they all mounted horses, and Ganda led them out of the stables.

By prior agreement, for his first meeting with the Slum Boss of Campo Adrina, Aurelius, Denian, and the two guardsmen did not know where Ganda would lead them. They could easily guess which section of the city, but not a specific street or location. Aurelius had already had two similar meetings, and the meeting with Boss Hessian would be his last. If all went well, that afternoon's work would put the last cog in place so the city could continue to prosper as it had under his father's rule.

Ganda led them into Campo Adrina, the largest of the city's three slums. They turned down a narrow street filled with vendors and hawkers of various wares, though most were probably cutthroats or pickpockets as well. Hessian had guaranteed their safety and possessions, as long as they weren't foolish enough to try anything stupid. But their greatest protection was that everyone wanted to maintain the status quo. If Hessian betrayed them, Maximillian would send in two thousand armed, fully trained soldiers, and they'd burn Campo Adrina to the ground. It would be bad business for all concerned.

Ganda pulled his horse to a stop in front of a soothsayer's shop. They dismounted. A fellow wearing filthy clothing and a wooden peg for a left leg stepped out of the crowd and asked, "This them?"

Ganda nodded. "Yah."

To Aurelius, Ganda said. "He'll watch your horses while you come with me."

Denian looked like he might object, but Aurelius caught his eye and shook his head. If it went bad, one man, alone, on that street, would not stand a chance. Better to have him with them.

Ganda led them into the soothsayer's shop, then out a back door into an alley, down the alley, into another shop, then out another back door into another alley. They finished in a haberdashery where they followed him down a flight of stairs into a large room. A crowd of about twenty stood milling about, mostly men looking as thuggish as Ganda. Dim tapers lit the subterranean chamber poorly, and a haze of greasy hemp-leaf smoke hung in the air. They paused at the base of the stairs, and the crowd slowly parted before them.

At the far end of the room a woman sat in an ornate chair that almost mimicked a throne. Long black hair hung in a disarray of ringlets that ended just below her shoulders, with spikes of hair sticking out here and there. She wore a man's blouse open down the front, and pants and knee-high boots like those of a man. Makeup shadowed her eyes, and bright red lip paint darkened her lips. But the dim light, shadows, and smoky haze in the room made her lips appear black from that distance, and he thought she might be painted like a trollop. She sat casually leaning back, one leg thrown out in front of her and resting on its heel. In one hand she held the bowl of a pipe with the end of its long stem tucked in the corner of her mouth. Her eyes appeared black, though that could be because of the dim light and haze. She sucked on the pipe, then blew a short sequence of smoke rings. They drifted away from her and dissipated into the haze of the room.

Aurelius hadn't known what to expect; certainly not a woman. But any woman who rose to the rank of Boss in Campo Adrina had done so by being better than most men. And as the most powerful of the city's three slums, in effect that made her the boss of bosses.

Aurelius walked forward slowly, careful to make no sudden movements, and stopped about three paces in front of her. Standing much closer to her now, to his surprise the lip paint was truly black, her cheeks were not caked with rouge like a trollop, and the makeup around her eyes gave her a dark and foreboding appearance. Beneath all the makeup and costume, he thought she might be quite attractive.

She smiled pleasantly, as if she knew his thoughts. "Dominus Aurelius," she said in a soft contralto, "a pleasure to meet you. And if you and I are to get along, you'll have to stop Bapo-Anto's efforts to encroach on my territory."

Aurelius had met with Bapo-Anto a week earlier, and had gotten an earful regarding the strife between the two slum bosses. He shook his head slowly. "No, you're going to have to stop trying to encroach on his."

She leaned forward, propped one elbow on a knee, and since the man's blouse she wore was open almost down to her navel, she exposed more cleavage; he suspected by design. She pointed the stem of the pipe at him. "My territory ends two blocks north of the Palisades Market, and he's trying to take that from me."

Again, he shook his head. "No, the north end of Campo Adrina ends at the north side of the Palisades Market, and has ended there for more than a hundred years."

She leaned back and her eyes narrowed. She took another puff on the pipe, and repeated the smoke rings. As they dissipated she stared at him for a long moment, and he refused to react or look away. She smiled. "Why is it I get the impression you could draw a map of the boundaries of Campo Adrina exactly as it was six months ago when your father died? And I'll bet you'd not be off by more than the width of my boot."

He returned her smile. "I could do that. I could also draw you a map of its boundaries as they existed a hundred and fifty years ago, which were different back then. I could also draw a map as they were three hundred and eighty years—"

She abruptly stood, silencing him. He had expected her to be tall with round and overly developed curves, like a prostitute on the streets. But he realized now she stood average height, with attractive curves that were muted. And nothing about her stood out in a spectacular way, nothing but her personality.

Standing to one side, Ganda said, "Be careful, Hessian. He maybe walks and talks like a fancy lord, but I wouldn't want to face him in a fight, at least not a fair one."

She stared at Aurelius for another moment, then abruptly marched forward, crossing the distance between them. She stopped with her breasts almost touching his chest, and with her tongue she slowly wetted her lips. "That you would make such an impression on Ganda impresses me no end. Perhaps we can . . . work well together . . ." She gave him a knowing grin. ". . . you and me."

He didn't like women who used their femininity to intimidate others, so he slowly and carefully lowered his eyes to look pointedly at her cleavage, did rather enjoy doing so, but wasn't about to let her know that. While the blouse was open almost to her navel, somehow she kept it from flaring open and exposing her breasts completely. He took care to adopt a visibly lurid look. "I suppose we can . . . if we must." He looked into her eyes. "What kind of work did you have in mind exactly?"

She threw her head back and roared with laughter in a way no stately woman of the court would dare. She looked at Ganda. "I think I see what you mean, friend."

Ganda winked. "I told you so."

Someone laughed, then others laughed as well, and the tension in the room dissipated. Hessian ordered drinks for them all, and they sipped at mediocre brandy while they agreed she would stop trying to acquire additional territory at Bapo-Anto's expense. After all, the status-quo had heretofore been quite profitable for them all.

Aurelius, Denian, and the two guardsmen followed Ganda on a circuitous route back to their horses. But just as they mounted up, a sharp whistle echoed up the street. Then Ganda rose up in his stirrups, lunged at Aurelius, and he thought the ruffian had betrayed them. Ganda hit him, wrapping his arms around him. Aurelius heard a hiss just as something stung his side and he cried out. They hit the ground. Ganda landed on top of him, knocking the wind out of him. An arrow thumped into the dirt inches from his nose.

As he struggled to regain his feet, he heard cries and shouts up and down the street, swords clashing, the hiss of arrows. A horse reared, a crossbow bolt embedded in its hip. Then all went still and quiet.

Aurelius grunted with pain as Ganda and one of his men pulled him to his feet. They stood him up against a horse, using it for cover while Denian examined the wound in his side.

Aurelius looked Ganda in the eyes. "Did you betray us?"

The thug shook his head. "No."

"Then Bapo-Anto?"

The man continued to shake his head. "Them wasn't his men neither. Wasn't slum people at all. Them was hired assassins. You didn't tell me I needed to worry about assassins."

"No puncture," Denian declared. "Crossbow bolt took a nice chunk of flesh out of the side of your rib cage, but no puncture."

Ganda wouldn't let them leave without him. And with a dozen of his men accompanying them, he got them back to the palace. Porcia took over from there and called in his personal physiker. As Maximillian joined them, the surgeon looked at the wound and declared, "No puncture, no squirting blood. There's some shredded tissue that won't heal. I'll have to cut that away, which is going to hurt, but you'll live."

To Porcia he said, "He's lost some blood so make sure he rests."

Maximillian said, "But . . . I have to convene the Senatus."

The surgeon shook his head. "You'll have to do so without him."

In response, Maximillian marched over to a sideboard, poured a goblet of wine, downed it in a gulp, poured another and carried it back to them. To Aurelius he said, "Since you're not going to be there, I need this to calm my nerves." He gulped the wine down, returned the empty goblet to the side table, then turned and walked out of the room.

Porcia leaned close to Aurelius's ear and lowered her voice. "He's been doing that a lot lately. More often than not he uses Mother as his excuse, but today you were handy."

# 14

# Escalation

ZARKOFFA SHOULD HAVE returned from Carthagen more than two weeks ago, and his absence did not bode well for the success of his mission. And when Kainborne heard he had finally returned, he did not wait for the man to come to him, though inside he felt none of the outer calm he displayed as he made his way down to the castle yard. In the stables he found the man yielding the reins of his horse to a stable hand. Zarkoffa did not look happy.

Kainborne waited as the man crossed the distance between them, then turned and they walked side by side out of the stables. "From your late return and the look on your face, I take it something went amiss?"

The man grunted a reply, clearly seething with anger. "Something bloody well went amiss, all right. The bloody slum dwellers bloody well thwarted us."

"Martonian delivered, did he not?"

Zarkoffa abruptly halted, turned to face Kainborne, but glanced about before saying anything further. "Yah, he came through, three experienced assassins. We had our chance with Aurelius in Campo Adrina. He had an escort of only four, and all they carried were short swords. They were down in the street and we had a rooftop advantage. But someone spotted us, and all hell broke loose. Bloody slummers came out of the woodwork, killed two of the assassins, and I barely made it out of there with my own skin."

Kainborne thought he now understood. "The assassins Martonian supplied, Carthagenians?"

Zarkoffa shook his head. "No, Tarnasus."

Kainborne closed his eyes and tried to calm his nerves. "The slummers are a tight-knit group. There must be ten thousand in Campo Adrina, but they can spot anyone who is not one of their own in the blink of an eye. It should have been done outside the slum, or done with Campo Adrina assassins."

Zarkoffa grumbled. "Spent two bloody weeks on the run from the damn city constabulary, almost didn't make it back."

When they parted, Kainborne sought out Jarrod, thinking how he would break the news to the young duke. Then he'd have to compose a carefully worded message to Macallan. He needed someone to blame the failure on, but using Zarkoffa for that would be a waste. He'd have to think on it, but he'd come up with an appropriate scapegoat.

• • • •

With Obregon's help, Ket slowly learned to *speak properly*, and as the months passed Brother Markus administered fewer and fewer switchings, though he never stopped completely. It seemed that Markus needed to give someone a switching now and then, and if too much time elapsed without some poor soul deserving punishment, Ket got a switching. Frequently, poor Thadamous did something stupid and he got the switching instead of Ket. It now seemed obvious the older boy was a bit daft.

Other than his lessons with Markus and Obregon, the monks by and large ignored Ket. Brother Antiphinees frequently looked at him strangely and invited Ket to join him in his cell, but Markus had warned him that if he did so, he'd get a switching far worse than anything he'd ever gotten before. And he'd once overheard Markus shouting at Antiphinees about them all getting their balls cut off. Markus had called the other monk, "You bloody idiot," and "You damn fool." After that Ket rarely even saw Antiphinees, and then only from a distance.

They put Ket to work in the gardens helping Brother Christolus grow vegetables for their meals. And frequently they gave him minor jobs, or had him run errands, though none that ever took him outside the walls of the monastery, a fact that did not escape his notice. But other than that, and his almost daily lessons with Markus and Obregon, they ignored him the way the gentlefolk at Glenmoore had ignored all the servants. Ket's mother had told him that during an argument or intimate conversation between nobles, a servant often learned the most interesting details. "Keep yer mouth shut," his mother had said. "Like a rabbit in the forest, don't move or do anything to remind them you're there, and they'll talk as if you ain't."

In the castle at Glenmoore the Scairn women had protected him and he had not needed to learn such lessons, but he did so now. Interestingly enough, when Obregon and Markus got into one of their heated arguments, Ket got the impression Obregon said things to Markus that seemed more intended for Ket's ears. Sometimes Obregon baited Markus, driving the stick-thin little man into a fury, and Ket frequently learned something that might someday be of use.

As the weather grew warmer in early spring, they put Ket to work in the fields. He rose with the sun and spent each morning at his lessons with the two monks, then worked through the afternoons in the fields next to peasants and Scairn. It was hard work with pick and shovel and hoe, and at first his hands blistered, but they soon callused over. Labor in the fields was much harder than working with Christolus in the gardens, but as long as Markus hadn't given him a switching that day, Ket enjoyed the physical release, and slept well each night when he went to bed. And working in the fields was the first time they had allowed him outside the abbey's walls. That proved to be the biggest change, and he thought more and more of escaping. But if he just took to his heels and ran, how would he eat, where would he sleep?

In the fields he worked shoulder to shoulder with both Scairn and peasants under the supervision of farmers and landholders. One day he overheard two farmers discussing their rents, one fearful that he might not meet his next payment. The next morning he asked Obregon about that, and got a lesson in land ownership and rents. Duke Jarrod owned all the land and everyone paid rent. "We all pay rent," Obregon said. "The abbot pays rent to the duke, the farmers pay rent to the abbot, and peasants and Scairn pay rent to the farmer in sweat and sore muscles."

While working outside the walls of the monastery, Ket frequently saw travelers pass through the valley. Once he saw a man with dark brown skin, something he'd never seen before. The man walked down the road near the field in which Ket toiled, passing not ten paces away. Ket must have been staring, because the fellow stopped, looked Ket over, grinned, and spoke with an unfamiliar accent. "Never seen someone with skin like mine, eh lad?"

Ket shook his head. "No, good sir, never."

The man's eyes brightened. "Good sir, is it? A boy with manners. Well, there's plenty that look like me, but not hereabouts." He turned and continued up the road.

Sometimes, while Ket worked in the fields, gentlefolk passed by in a carriage or on horseback, sometimes a farmer with an ox and cart. He had a vague memory of the differences in dress and manner among the people at Glenmoore, but he hadn't been conscious of the vast difference in station between the gentlest of the gentlefolk, and the lowest of the bondservants.

One day, after one of Markus's switchings, his thoughts returned to the idea of escape. Could he simply start running and never stop? If he left the monastery, Markus could no longer switch him, though he'd miss Obregon. It was an intriguing thought, but as he considered it he looked up at a peasant working beside him. The man stood almost twice his height, literally towered over him. He didn't know where to go, would just end up running and hoping for the best. And where would he find food? And where would he sleep? They'd catch him, and Brother Markus would switch him as he'd never been switched before. Maybe when he was older. Maybe then he'd run away, but not that day.

It was during that time that he came to understand he had a unique place among peasants and Scairn. In the fields outside the walls, working shoulder to shoulder with them, he learned that the gentlefolk looked down on the peasants, the peasants look down on the Scairn, and the Scairn looked down on the Scairndraka. The only exception was that little peasant girl Peta. In the fields, she ran errands for the monks, farmers, and peasants. She frequently trudged through the fields carrying a small leather bucket of water, offering the laborers a drink from a clay cup.

One day she approached Ket, stopped and looked around, an odd look on her face. "Why do they treat you different?"

He paused, stood up straight, and leaned on his hoe. "I'm half Scairn and half peasant."

She wrinkled her nose. "You don't look Scairn."

He reached up and pulled his hair back, uncovering his right ear. Her eyes widened. "Pointed they are, but kind of cute."

Ket lowered his hand, had never thought of his ears as cute.

A nearby Scairn spit out, "Scairndraka!"

Peta leaned close to Ket. "Why doesn't he like you?"

Ket shrugged. "I'm only half Scairn. Same reason peasants don't like me."

Peta frowned. "You seem like a nice-enough boy. I like you, and I'm a peasant." She offered Ket a cup of water.

One of the peasant men stopped her. "Off with you, Peta. Don't you be talking to no half-breed."

Peta's frown deepened, she turned, and trudged away.

Until then, Ket had always gotten his own water, but after that Peta found ways to give him a quick drink with none of the others watching.

• • • •

Lucius's fully gray hair gave him the distinguished look of a handsome older man, which he used to good effect. Aurelius watched him enter the room with Divonia on his arm and wondered at her intent in arranging a meeting in the absence of Maximillian. Porcia followed close on their heels, glancing Aurelius's way and raising an eyebrow. Like him, she probably wondered what scheme Divonia had hatched with Lucius.

"Aurelius, my dear," Divonia said, smiling pleasantly, "I think drinks would be in order. Please do the honors?"

They all agreed that chilled white wine would be delightful. Aurelius turned to a side table and served the two women first, followed by a goblet of wine for Lucius. For himself, he decided on a glass of strong brandy, which he thought might help him get through the evening while he navigated Divonia's scheming.

Lucius raised his glass. "To Carthagen! May our beloved city remain prosperous and grow strong."

Aurelius raised his glass to his lips and took a sip, savoring the fiery liquid as it burned its way down his throat. He decided to ask the obvious. "Where is Maximillian?"

Divonia frowned. "He's unable to join us this evening. He's . . . indisposed."

Standing where neither Lucius nor Divonia could see her, Porcia wrinkled her nose and silently mouthed the word *drunk*. It occurred to Aurelius that she could have spoken the word aloud, for Maximillian's *illness* was not a well-kept secret.

Divonia would normally be livid that her oldest son missed a meeting with an important senator because of drink. But that evening she seemed not in the least upset at Maximillian's folly, almost appeared pleased by his absence. It occurred to Aurelius that she might have purposefully arranged the meeting for late in the evening, choosing a time when she could count on Maximillian's indisposition.

"Come," Divonia said. "It's a comfortably warm evening. Let's adjourn to the back terrace."

Lucius opened a set of large double doors, and he and Divonia stepped out into the gardens beyond. Aurelius followed, but as he passed Porcia she gripped his arm, forcing him to pause for a moment. She lowered her voice as she spoke. "Why does Mother not want Max here?"

Aurelius thought it best not to answer that question. "We should join them, and I suspect we'll quickly learn exactly what she does want."

Porcia took his arm and they walked out onto one of the Deoclation Palace's many garden terraces. Decorative lanterns marked carefully laid out pathways through which one might stroll and enjoy the warm night air. Lucius and Divonia waited for them in a small gazebo, him standing, she seated. Porcia took a seat next to Divonia while Aurelius stood with Lucius.

They chatted about trivialities for a while, and then Divonia mentioned the weather in Tarnasus. In response, Lucius frowned and swirled the wine in his glass, looking at the pale liquid as if he might glean some dark meaning there. "I've heard Tarnasus is expanding its constabulary."

"Oh really," Divonia said, her eyes widening. "Is that a problem for us?"

Lucius shrugged. "Not if it's just a few extra constables, but my sources tell me it's more. And they haven't had an uptick in crime lately, so I don't see the need, unless they have other intentions."

Porcia caught Aurelius's eye. Her brow furrowed, and her lips puckered into a straight, thin line.

Divonia gave Lucius a vacant look. "It's just Tarnasus. Why should that concern us?"

Aurelius had learned long ago that when Divonia played the stupid woman, one should look to one's back for a sharp blade.

Lucius shook his head, pretending to consider her question. "I don't yet know. I'll have to bring it up tomorrow in the Senatus, and some there might consider it a provocation. They might think we should respond in kind."

"Respond in kind?" Porcia asked, her voice tense and hard. "What do you mean?"

Lucius again swirled the wine in his glass. "We may have to match their expansion with our own, man for man, perhaps even exceed it. Purely out of caution, mind you."

As a senator, Aurelius had his own sources in the other city-states. Since he would inherit no actual power, he had nurtured them carefully, hoping to be of some use to his brother during his rule. Tarnasus had embarked on an expansion of its constabulary only in response to Carthagen's supposedly secret expansion of its own.

The conversation moved on to the coming harvest and stockpiling of grain for the winter months. But it was clear Lucius and Divonia considered the real purpose for the meeting well and done.

They finished their drinks and returned to the sitting room. Lucius ended the evening with, "I have a busy day tomorrow. I should take my leave."

After he left the room, Divonia stood and faked a yawn. "This talk of expanding the constabulary has taxed my strength. I think I too shall retire."

She kissed Porcia on the cheek, then did the same with Aurelius, and walked out of the room.

Porcia looked Aurelius's way and rolled her eyes. "Is there any doubt that Lucius will shortly join her in her bed?"

Aurelius grimaced. "Lucius may have a busy day tomorrow, but I think he's going to have a busy night tonight."

Porcia turned serious. "Out in that gazebo, did you get the impression we were watching a well-rehearsed play?"

Aurelius and his sister thought alike in so many ways. "You noticed that as well."

She frowned. "Our dear mother is so predictable. And I fear we've only seen the first of a carefully orchestrated three-act structure. Is Tarnasus really expanding their constabulary?"

Aurelius shrugged. "No, just like us they're actually expanding their military, and pretending it's their constabulary."

# 15

# Failed Empire

*Domaxus did not truly understand what he had, and but for his ignorance, he could have had it all. After the annihilation of the first three Duchies, we could have simply stumbled down the path that lay before us. All we needed to do was complete the destruction of the Duchies, then move north to subdue the Mountain Kingdom. Civilization would have knelt at our feet like a supplicant on the street begging for alms. We could have had it all and he squandered it, threw it away as if it were nothing. He could have ruled all men, all time, all places, all things. He could have been the master of all, of everything. Kings and Queens would have bowed at his feet and bent the knee before him, but he was a fool, an imbecile who wasted the power we fought so hard to attain.*

*At his death our armies grieved along with the populous. For the sake of expediency I feigned sorrow and anguish, but inside I seethed with insurmountable anger. It was not the loss of our great leader that angered me, but the loss of opportunity, the loss of conquest, the loss of empire. He was a fool, and he failed us all.*

*Octovian ahm Carthagen*
*Invictus General*
*upon return from the Withering Wars*

Kainborne had slowly accumulated a list of names, all men who had at one time borne a strange birthmark that might have been the Dreadmark. Under the guise of learning military tactics for Jarrod's benefit, Kainborne had let it be known he would pay well for any scrolls that referenced those names. That had yielded mixed results.

Octovian ahm Carthagen had been a high-ranking general who commanded several of Domaxus's legions. Historical records claimed Domaxus retired to Carthagen after his victories over the Duchies, but only lived a short while before malcontents assassinated him. In his writings, Octovian complained that Domaxus had squandered the power he had accumulated, which did not conform to those records. That troubled Kainborne.

His horse shifted its weight beneath him, bringing him out of his reverie. He and the guards accompanying him had just reached the crest of a low rise in the road, and before him lay the Vale of Tramorth. One year had passed since he'd seen the boy, and it was time to check on him.

. . . .

Caerie returned to that window overlooking the flower garden many times, but a year had passed and she had not again seen that boy. Standing there in her nursery and looking down on the garden, she saw nothing but flowers and wondered if it had been just a whim of her imagination? It saddened her he might never come to her again, and she recalled with fear and sorrow the last time she had seen him beneath that aged oak tree. The ket and the caerm, the raptor and the lioness, had battled with those monstrous ravens, and oblivion devoured all four of them. The boy had wept and pleaded with them to stop, which left Caerie with tears of her own running down her cheeks.

Melceinnia proved to be absolutely relentless. She clearly had told no one else of Caerie's birth connection to the ket and the caerm, but she constantly made cryptic references to it. If they attended some ceremony that placed the two of them standing side by side, the old woman might lean down and whisper something like, "Is it the ket today, or the caerm?" Once, during a discussion on protecting outlying villages from Duchies raiding parties, Caerie proposed they strengthen their standing army and provide regular patrols of the villages in question. One of the older men had looked at her askance, clearly displeased that one so young might express an opinion, or perhaps displeased that a woman might offer an opinion. Melceinnia had nodded and said, "When she is grown, she'll be quite the lioness, won't she?" No one else saw beyond her words, but Caerie looked into Melceinnia's eyes and the older woman returned a smug smile. If the High Priestess thought her taunts would weaken Caerie's resolve, it had the opposite effect, and Caerie vowed no one would ever know of her visions.

Caerie pulled her thoughts back to the moment and looked down at the flower garden. Her heart quickened, for the oak tree had once again appeared and beneath it stood the peasant boy. He seemed taller, and his homespun rags fit him poorly, had clearly not been replaced as he grew during the past year. The lion cub pranced about his feet, but he stood with his right arm extended and stared intently at the inner forearm, ignoring the caerm. Again, the everchanging, mottled shadows beneath the oak obscured his features.

His image shifted. He grew in height and stature, and stood easily as tall as her Uncle Damuel, with broad shoulders and the trim waist of a young man. But now he looked to be a young warrior, with brown hair that hung down past his ears. On his shoulders, chest, and belly he wore segmented layers of shiny, hardened leather armor that extended down to mid-thigh. Boiled leather greaves protected his lower legs, and stiff bracers his forearms. He stood before a small campfire, and as she looked on he stripped the bracer off his right arm, then stared at his inner forearm for long seconds, standing as still as a statue. The lion cub prowling beside him had grown into a lioness.

When the young man finally moved he startled Caerie. He bent, and carefully lifted a firebrand out of the fire, one end of it glowing bright red. Looking carefully at the tip of the brand, then his arm, he pressed the glowing end of it against his forearm. He threw his head back and cried out, and the lioness let out a roar of fear and pain. Caerie's heart lurched and tears streamed down her cheeks as he dropped to his knees, while the lioness paced in a circle about him. Again and again he pressed the red-hot brand against his arm, and again the flesh there crackled and smoked, and again the lioness roared. And while the lioness's roars continued, the young man's cries slowly dwindled to plaintive whimpers.

When he finished he dropped the hot brand and remained motionless, kneeling in front of the fire, the lioness pacing about him. He stared at the damage he had done to his arm, and even from that distance Caerie saw it easily as if she stood next to him looking over his shoulder. No skin remained on his inner forearm, for he had burnt it down to the muscle, leaving a blackened and cracked landscape of flesh oozing blood and unhealthy fluids.

In that moment he disappeared. The tree, the boy, the lioness, the warrior, the ancient oak; they all vanished, and she now looked upon nothing more than a garden of flowers.

Caerie staggered back from the window, wondering what she had just seen, what portent or meaning the vision held. She glanced over her shoulder and was relieved to find no one standing behind her, no older brother to berate her, no ancient priestess who might interrogate her about demon ketcaerm and visions of a strange young man. She wiped the tears from her eyes and cheeks, still recalling the pain and sorrow in the young man's cries, and the lioness's roars.

After so many months, why had the vision suddenly returned? And why had the young boy grown into a warrior and mutilated his arm so horribly? And why hadn't the lioness stopped him, saved him somehow? For in Caerie's heart she knew it was up to the lioness to save the boy.

Caerie tried to think back to the day she had first seen the vision of the boy. It had been exactly two months before her tenth birthday, her coming-of-age, and now it was two months before her eleventh birthday. The vision had returned exactly one year to the day after she'd first seen him under that oak tree. She vowed to return to that window on that day next year, and each year after that, and would continue to do so again and again, even if he didn't come to her, even if she didn't see him again.

. . . .

Ket rarely encountered Abbot Benedictus and wondered if the man had forgotten he even existed. Then one day Obregon said, "Come with me, Ket. The abbot wants to see you."

Obregon escorted him to Benedictus's office, and as Ket stepped into the abbot's hallowed sanctum, the man rose from a chair. He seemed excited and fearful as he said, "Come here and stand before me, boy."

Ket crossed the room quickly and stopped a pace from the older man. Benedictus reached out, grabbed Ket by his shoulders, and spun him about. "Yes, you'll do. A little worse for the wear but you look fine."

Ket still wore the only clothing he had, the homespun his mother had given him and the rope belt that held up his trousers. Benedictus's concern for his appearance made him conscious of the fact that his sleeves, which had been arm-length when he came to the monastery, now ended just below mid-forearm, exposing quite a bit of wrist. And his trousers now ended well above his ankles. He had grown some.

Benedictus nodded his approval. "Now that you've been with us a year, Master Kainborne has come to check on you. Be on your best behavior—" Benedictus leaned down and his eyes hardened. "—and don't anger him or I'll make use of Brother Markus's switch."

A short time later Kainborne stepped into the room, and Benedictus left the two of them alone. Kainborne sat down in the same chair he had sat in a year earlier. He seemed unhappy as he growled, "Come here, boy."

Eager to please the man, Ket crossed the room quickly. Kainborne reached out, gripped his wrist, tugged him forward and twisted his arm palm up, sending a shock of pain through his shoulder. Ket bit his lip and managed not to cry out. The man peered intently at his birthmark for several long seconds, then snarled, "Nothing. Nothing at all."

The last time he'd looked at Ket's birthmark, he'd shouted, struck out, and knocked Ket to the floor, opening a cut in his cheek. Ket cringed, fearing he might do so again, but Kainborne released his wrist with a shove, pushing him back. Ket stumbled, but stayed on his feet, stopped a few paces from the seated man, and lowered his eyes to stare at the floor.

"Don't stare at the damn floor like a dimwit."

Ket looked into Kainborne's face. The man squinted at Ket, his mouth a sharp straight line. "What am I to do with you, boy? With all this portent, why is nothing happening?"

Ket didn't know how to answer that. "I . . . I don't know, good sir."

That appeared to calm the man. "No, of course you don't." He sighed and seemed upset about something. "Patience. I'll just have to be patient. Do you still see nothing when you look at your arm."?

"No," Ket said, shaking his head, "I do see something."

Kainborne's eyes widened and he leaned forward. "What? What do you see?"

Ket desperately hoped to avoid the man's anger. "The birthmark, kind sir. The purplish and smudgy skin."

The man sat unmoving for the longest moment, his eyes blinking rapidly. Then he threw his head back and roared with laughter. "Yes, yes, purplish and smudgy skin, and here I thought—"

The door to the office opened and Benedictus stepped in, stopping just within the doorway. "I heard a shout. Is something wrong, Master Kainborne?"

Kainborne wiped tears from his eyes. "No, nothing at all, not if you don't count purplish and smudgy skin."

Benedictus frowned and gave Kainborne an uncertain look.

Kainborne took a deep breath and sighed. "Close the door on your way out. I'll let you know when I'm done here."

As the abbot hastily exited, Ket recalled they had just repeated almost the exact sequence of events from a year earlier.

Kainborne quizzed Ket further about his birthmark, then dismissed him, mumbling something about, "I guess I'll just have to be patient."

Both Benedictus and Obregon stood waiting for him in the hall outside the abbot's study. Benedictus gripped Ket by the shoulders and shook him angrily. "Is he angry? Did you make him angry?"

"No," Ket pleaded. "He said he has to be patient."

The abbot shook him again. "Why did he say that?"

Ket shook his head. "I don't know."

Benedictus released him and shouted at Obregon, "Get this boy out of my sight."

He spun away from Ket, and disappeared through the door into his study.

Obregon sighed as he knelt down in front of Ket and looked him in the eyes. "What is it Kainborne sees in you? His interest borders on obsession, and that I find strange."

Ket extended his arm. "He always wants to look at my birthmark."

Obregon reached out and gripped Ket's wrist, but for such a big man he did so with a gentleness that belied his size. He stared at the birthmark for several seconds, then shook his head. "Just a smudge of discolored skin. What is it he's looking for?"

They walked back to Obregon's cell and resumed Ket's lessons.

It surprised Ket that an entire year had passed. He had never thought about keeping any sense of time, never thought about counting the days or months to keep track of an entire year. He remembered being ten at the time the dark man had taken him from Glenmoore, taken him from his mum, and he'd never seen her again. At the thought of the dark man and his mum, he recalled that when he had asked about her, the man had said, "If she ain't dead yet, she will be soon." Something about that had always bothered Ket. Only physikers knew if someone would live or die, and the dark man was no physiker, so how would he know something like that? Such thoughts confused Ket, made him long for his mum, and he tried to put them out of his mind.

He'd been ten when the dark man took him from Glenmoore, and now he was eleven. Ket thought more and more of the dark man's connection to his mum and what the fellow had said: "If she ain't dead yet, she will be soon."

One day during his lesson with Marcus, he asked the monk, "May I ask a question?"

Markus waved a hand impatiently. "Yes, yes. This is a lesson. I'm teaching you and you're supposed to ask questions."

Ket carefully composed the question. "How do physikers know if someone is going to live or die?"

The monk wrinkled his nose in thought. "It's a matter of knowledge, boy. They take lessons and they learn, just as you're taking a lesson from me, and you're learning. Eventually they become knowledgeable about such things. That's how it works. You gain knowledge, and you know things. And that's what you're doing right now, gaining knowledge so you'll know things."

Ket did learn something from the man that day. The fellow confirmed what he had already begun to suspect: if the scrawny little monk didn't know something, he was loath to admit it and invented something to cover his ignorance, or simply gave Ket a switching. But when Ket asked the same question of Obregon, the big man said, "Had a little experience with physikers when I was on the shield wall. Some are good and some are bad, and all of them are mostly guessing, and hoping they're right."

So if the physikers couldn't predict with any confidence if someone would live or die, on that dark night long ago how had the dark man been so certain Ket's mother would die? As Ket pondered that question, his heart raced and anger consumed him. Something didn't add up, but he didn't know what, and he didn't know where to direct his anger. Breathing carefully, he slowly calmed his racing heart, thinking he should focus on escaping, and forever leaving the monastery behind. But the same issue remained: How would he survive?

For the past year Ket had been completely unaware of the passing months. He realized he should keep track of the time somehow, and as more time passed he tried to count the months, which he could now do because Obregon had taught him numbers.

After summer ended, autumn arrived uneventfully. But that winter a horse kicked the stable boy in the head and he died. And since Brother Christolus's vegetable garden produced nothing during the colder months, they assigned Ket to Brother Atticus to help in the stables. He learned how to care for horses, repair tack, saddle a horse, and harness a horse to a cart or wagon. He even learned to ride a horse bareback, as long as he kept it at a slow walk, though he remained leery of any animal large enough to trample him.

Ket learned that three of the horses were there for six guardsmen Duke Jarrod had assigned to the monastery. The men were there to help the abbot collect rents and to maintain the peace in the valley. He had occasionally seen them about, but they looked much like the guardsmen at Glenmoore, and they didn't really concern him.

Kainborne showed up again a year later, and again the following year, and each time he looked at the birthmark on Ket's arm. And each year, in his dreams, Ket saw that pretty Scairn girl in the window high above. But from one year to the next, nothing ever changed.

# 16

# Injustice

WITH WINTER ALMOST over, the farmers in the Vale of Tramorth were eager to plant seed. After three years living in the valley, Ket understood that a bad year for the farmers meant a bad year for everyone. And with spring approaching, his duties shifted from the stables to planting. He didn't actually put seeds in the ground, but labored with the other men using pick, hoe, and shovel.

During planting season, he started each morning at his lessons with Markus and Obregon. But the first day he reported to the fields, he saw none of the hectic activity associated with planting. One of the other men told him, "Farmer says dirt's too cold and wet. Gotta wait."

Delays like that were not unusual, so Ket reported back to the stables and spent the day repairing tack. But the same thing happened the next morning, and the next, and after three weeks of delays, the mood in the valley turned somber. Then one morning it all changed.

The head foreman gathered all the workers and announced, "We can't wait any longer. We have to get seed in the ground now. The south end of the vale is warmer, so we're all going down-valley to help them. We'll work our way north as the soil warms."

Ket picked up his shovel and joined the column of workers walking down the road. About a league south of the monastery they joined other workers, and spent the day in a frantic effort to get seed in the ground. At the end of the day, the overseers fed them a meal of boiled potatoes with a little salt, then herded them into a barn to sleep. Ket approached a foreman and said, "But I'm supposed to report for me lessons in the morning. They'll be mad if I don't." He was thinking specifically of Markus.

The man shook his head. "Don't you worry, boy. Planting's all that counts now."

The southern workers joined them as they worked their way north, and over the next two days, they labored at a hectic, almost desperate, pace. Nothing changed when they reached the fields near the monastery. Ket simply shoveled dirt and sweated with the others. It was lonely, mindless drudgery, and he let his thoughts drift to his mum. He'd been happy at Glenmoore, and he missed her.

Something stung his face, burning a fiery line across his mouth from his upper left cheek to his lower right. Then someone shoved him and he fell, landing heavily in the dirt and wrenching his shoulder. He rolled onto his back, looked up, and saw Markus standing over him, switch in hand.

"Where have you been?" the monk shouted, his eyes wide, his face red with anger. He lashed out with the switch, and it scored a line of fire across Ket's arm and chest. "Three days you've skipped your lessons. Where have you been?" He lashed out again. "Hiding from me, I'll bet."

"No," Ket pleaded. "They made me stay to work."

"Lies," Markus shouted. He struck with the switch again, and again, and again. Ket raised his arms to cover his face, and Markus lashed his belly and legs along with the back of his arms.

"You lazy, ungrateful whelp. I give you my valuable time, and you spurn my efforts."

Ket rolled over and tried to crawl away on his hands and knees. And even though he wore a homespun shirt, Markus's switch cut into his back through the cloth. As he crawled, blows landed on his head, neck, arms, and legs, one after another, each a burning a trace of fire as the willow branch scored his flesh. He kept moving, but the blows didn't stop. And only when he struggled to his feet and ran did the blows end. He ran with all the speed he could muster, ran past the other workers who stood silently watching him, ran past the edge of the field and kept running. He didn't think of any direction or destination, he simply ran and didn't stop until his legs gave way beneath him. And then he collapsed and lay in the dirt.

• • • •

The atmosphere in the Privy Council had grown tense. Seated at the room's large table with her mother, uncle, councilors, and generals, Caerie thought it best to keep her mouth shut. Next to her, Nick leaned close and whispered, "I think Mother is upset."

Seated at the head of the table, Selene Barasha's amber eyes hardened as she focused her attention on the Chancellor of the Exchequer. "Do you not recall that we discussed this matter last autumn?"

Chancellor Palmath nodded and spoke cautiously. "I do, Crown Mother, and I had intended to allocate funds in early spring before—"

Selene cut him off. "Winter is coming to an end, and those bloody raids will be upon us sooner rather than later. We need soldiers in place as soon as possible."

Palmath didn't seem terribly frightened by Selene's wrath. "Yes," he said, "but the early spring thaw produces ankle-deep mud on all the roads, so the raids don't begin in earnest until—"

Selene stood and slammed her fist on the table. "But there are always Duchies noblemen eager for sport after a long cold winter. I'll not stand for one more Scairn forced into bondage. I want armed troops stationed south of Darliff and east of Carigleigh, with messengers making regular rounds of nearby villages, and scouts watching all trails coming up from Glenmoore, Tramorth, and Lagasdale. Let's make sure those soldiers can prevent a raid because they know it's going to happen before it does."

She pointed a finger at Palmath. "Release those funds now."

She pointed a finger at Command General Kailill. "Call in the levies now."

He nodded. "It will take time to equip and train them."

Selene placed both palms flat on the table and leaned forward. "I want those outlying villages protected. So how do we get soldiers in place before the spring thaw?"

"Crown Mother," the captain of the city patrol said. "I can lend them some men. Crime is always at its lowest during the winter months, and doesn't really pick up until late spring."

Kailill leaned forward. "By then we can have the new men trained and in place, so you can have your people back. And Carigleigh and Darliff might contribute men from their city patrols as well. After all, they're closer to the border, and their outlying villagers suffer the brunt of Duchies raids."

Selene pushed off the table, straightened, nodded, and sat down. "Good. Do it."

It was Caerie's first time in attendance at the regular meeting of the Privy Council. With her thirteenth birthday well behind her, her mother had decided she should become more involved in the art of statecraft. She wasn't sure if it suited her, but she had long ago outgrown playing with dolls. And for once she was thankful to have Nick close at hand. A year ago when he first attended, he had bragged about it, telling her she was still too much of a child to do so.

She leaned close to him and whispered, "Is Chancellor Palmath in trouble?"

He hissed, "No. Mother tears into one or two of them at every meeting."

The next item of business was a report by General Kailill on Carthagen's expansion of its standing army. He concluded with, "It's only a few hundred men a year, so unless they accelerate that, we should keep an eye on it, but not be overly concerned. I should add that it is straining their relations with Tarnasus and Andopolous."

At that point one minister gave a report on grain inventories, then Palmath provided details on tax revenues. Caerie feigned interest in those and other mundane subjects, while her thoughts drifted to the peasant boy in her visions. She had seen him again each year on the anniversary of the first vision, had watched him grow much as she had grown. The lioness cub always appeared with him, with the raken perched on a crenellation atop that tower above, watching over them both. Sometimes the two ravens appeared, attacked, and the raptor and lioness fought them to oblivion, with never a clear victory for either side. Sometimes the female raven spoke in the snakelike hiss of that woman's voice, sending a chill up Caerie's spine. And when the ravens failed to appear, the raken merely watched over the boy and the caerm, and preened its feathers. Thankfully, she did not again see the young warrior put a firebrand to his forearm.

· · · ·

Ket awoke shivering, his teeth chattering. Darkness surrounded him, with a half-moon in the sky providing faint illumination. He'd never been outside the walls of the monastery alone at night, and feared wild animals would hunt him down and eat him. Though he didn't really know if he should fear such dangers.

He rolled over and struggled to his feet. Still shivering in the cold night air, he hugged himself tightly to stay warm. But that sparked the return of fire in many of the wounds Markus had inflicted with his willow branch, and it felt as if the scrawny monk had lashed every inch of his back and legs.

He'd collapsed in a field of fallow ground gone to weed, but did not know where. Turning full circle, he saw no lights or other signs of life. And with no idea where he'd ended up, he simply started walking. The moon provided enough light to avoid tripping over anything obvious, but he still needed to take care where he stepped.

He had no sense of time or distance, and couldn't say how long or far he walked, but after some time the sky lightened enough to tell him dawn was not far off. When he approached a copse of trees, he turned away to avoid it, fearing wolves or some other danger might lurk within its shadows. But near its edge, he noticed a dark sil-houette obscuring a section of stars on the horizon. He turned, walked that way, and as he approached it, his nose caught the scent of livestock. That clue helped him rec-ognize the shape in front of him: one of the larger barns in the valley. He had stum-bled onto the steading of a prominent farmer, and with dawn close at hand, he had no time to waste.

He crouched and moved forward cautiously. A hog snorted nearby and he looked that way. In the dark it took him a moment to recognize a fenced-in pen built against the side of the barn. He heard another snort, and saw a couple of shapes moving around within the pen.

The barn had a simple door with a wooden latch. He opened it only enough to slip inside, but it still squealed on its hinges. He heard a horse snort, probably a draft horse, and moving by touch in that direction, he located a crude horse blanket draped over the wall of a stall. It wasn't large, but it covered his shoulders and warmed him a little.

Still moving by touch, he worked his way along one wall and located a large wooden bin containing hog feed. He ate a dinner of bits of maize and sweet-potato root, with a small amount of wheat grain and oats. It was tasteless, but it filled his gut. Then he slipped out of the barn, closed the door, and with false dawn slowly lighting the landscape, he took his chances in the copse of trees.

Ket found a spot where a shaft of sunlight warmed him, and he hid through the day. He slept a little, but spent all his waking hours wondering what he would do next. He had decided long ago to formulate a plan to escape Markus, but through fear he'd always put it off. And now he had run away with no idea of what to eat, where to go, how to survive.

At thirteen years of age, he'd grown since coming to the vale. And were it not for Markus, he could bide his time, and wait until he'd grown up before venturing out into the unknown. But Markus had destroyed any chance of that, and he hated the man for it.

As darkness settled over the copse of trees, he huddled in his blanket and slept fitfully. He awoke well before dawn, still with no plan, and his anger at Markus didn't warm him or fill his gut. Hunger led him back to the barn, and the bin of pig feed. As he chewed on some hard maize, he heard a voice and froze.

"Smart of you to come for us this morning. Think it might be him?"

Another voice answered. "Could be. I told you I heard something yesterday just before dawn when I got up for the day. And when I checked the barn, there was a horse blanket missing. I think he's come back for more."

A third voice said, "Thief or the runaway, it don't matter."

The first voice said, "Thief wouldn't be stupid enough to come back. But the boy probably is."

The door to the barn squealed on its hinges as they pulled it open, and a shaft of light from a lantern blinded Ket. He couldn't see anything, so he ran. But someone tripped him up, and he tumbled into a sprawl on the ground. Three men held him down as they bolted his hands into heavy iron manacles in front of him, then lifted him to his feet. In the lantern's glare, he recognized two guards from the monastery. The third man wore a simple shirt, breeches, and boots; probably the farmer.

The sun rose as they tied a rope to the manacles. Then the two guards mounted their horses, and with one holding the end of the rope, they nudged their animals into an easy walk. They moved at a pace that allowed him to walk as they headed down the road back to the monastery, and they didn't mistreat him. An hour later they passed through the main gate of the monastery and into its central courtyard. Several monks busy at their morning chores all paused to stare at him.

The guards led Ket to the stables and removed the rope from his manacles. Then they secured the cuffs to a metal ring in a stone hitching post. They left him there, so Ket sat down to wait for whatever came next.

Exhaustion weighed heavily on him, so he lowered his head and dozed off. But when he heard footsteps approaching, he snapped awake. Ket didn't care anymore and didn't look up, didn't care if Markus had come to beat him with his switch.

"Why did you run away?"

Ket recognized Obregon's voice. He raised his head and looked the man in the eyes. And while he couldn't see it himself, he knew a nasty welt ran in a line across his lips from his upper left cheek to his lower right. He also had welts on his forehead, neck, and shoulders.

Obregon grimaced, then squatted down, reached out and gently gripped Ket's chin. He turned Ket's head to the left, then to the right. "Oh bloody hell!"

Word of Ket's capture must have spread quickly, because behind Obregon, Ket saw Benedictus, Markus, and a farmer walking toward them at a brisk pace. They stopped next to Obregon, and the farmer squatted down beside him. When he looked at Ket, his eyes blinked rapidly, his face turned red, and he shot to his feet. He spun about, lurched toward Markus, and loomed over the little monk, screaming at the top of his lungs. "You said you didn't whip him, that my workers were lying. And you clearly did, so they think you whipped him for planting. I'm going to have trouble with all of them."

Markus sneered at him. "Then give them a taste of the whip too."

The farmer's face reddened even further.

Benedictus waved his hands frantically. "Everyone calm down." He addressed the farmer. "Tell them he was whipped for disobeying, not for planting."

The man shook his head. "But he wasn't. We didn't let him come back because planting comes first."

"It doesn't matter," Benedictus said, beads of sweat running down his cheeks. "Just tell them it was for disobeying, not for planting. That should mollify them."

The farmer closed his eyes, took a deep breath, exhaled loudly, then opened his eyes. He looked at Markus and lowered his voice. "If I ever see you in my fields again, I'm going to tie you to a post, and whip you until there's no skin left on your back."

He turned his back on them and walked away.

Large sweat stains now decorated Benedictus's armpits. "Everyone listen to me. This never happened. We're just going to pretend it didn't, and never speak of it again."

On that day, Ket learned that certain farmers in the valley held considerable sway.

# 17

# An Heir

ZALESTRIA WAS TRULY a beautiful young woman in every sense of the word. But Damuel understood they shared no love between them. When they were apart he didn't long to be with her the way two people in love might, to chat and converse about trivialities and all the things that true lovers did. He did frequently long to be with her, but only to fuck her, and when they met, as soon as she touched him, the passion between them proved undeniable and all-consuming. But no, they did not share love, nor did they even share love-making. They shared pleasure, desire, and rutting, though he did rather enjoy those aspects of their relationship. *Her husband was probably a very wealthy man*, he thought, but he didn't care about that either. And it occurred to him she probably didn't have it in her to love someone.

Lying beside her in bed, both of them naked, he traced a finger along her hip, then up her belly and across her breast.

She perked up. "Again?" She sat up, glanced at his crotch, and scrunched her face into a pout. "No. Apparently not. At least not now."

He shrugged. "Perhaps, in a bit."

She leaned over and kissed him on the cheek. "You know I'm always ready."

If nothing more, his time with her took his mind off the escalating situation with the Duchies. As Mythria augmented more and more border pickets with city patrolmen, they would soon have in place a means of protecting their outlying villages. But in so many ways, that was nothing more than a further escalation of a steadily worsening situation, and he feared it would only lead to more conflict.

"Darling," Zalestria said, pulling him out of his reverie.

He focused on her. "Yes."

She smiled uncomfortably, which was so unlike her. "I'm with child."

He replayed her words in his thoughts several times to understand them. He assumed he wasn't her only lover, if for no other reason than that she must have some sort of responsibility to the sisterhood regarding carnal worship. Then again, that too was an assumption. And even if she didn't have obligations required by Melceinnia and the others, he didn't think her the type to limit herself to just one lover.

He had to ask. "Do you know whose it is?"

She nodded. "Yours."

"How do you know that?"

She lowered her eyes, and appeared every bit the insecure young woman. "When Melceinnia heard you and I were lovers, she suspended my other duties regarding men. You're the only man I've been with for more than a year."

She hesitated. "And it's a boy."

He wasn't buying the insecure young woman act. "You know that, do you?"

She nodded. "Once it's conceived, we have ways of determining the child's sex. You will soon have an heir."

He shook his head, trying to conceal his bewilderment. "I have no need of an heir. I have nothing to give an heir, nothing for him to inherit."

The insecure young woman disappeared. "Then you have to come up with something. Perhaps you don't need to serve the throne so diligently. It takes up all of your time, all of your mind, all of your thinking. Perhaps you need to think of yourself for once. And now you definitely must think of your heir."

Damuel tried to calm his racing thoughts.

"After all," Zalestria said. "You deserve to be on that throne every bit as much as she does."

• • • •

For three years Aurelius had kept the expansion of their army to a minimum. But Divonia had outmaneuvered him in the Senatus and they had recently begun to recruit new soldiers in earnest. Hoping to keep Tarnasus and Andopolous unaware of their expanded efforts, Aurelius had moved the soldiers to two training camps outside the city. But that created a serious problem he had not anticipated.

Standing at a window in his apartments on the third floor of the Deoclation Palace, he watched a hired carriage pull into the courtyard below. A footman opened a door in its side, and assisted a woman as she stepped down onto the cobblestones. She wore a garishly colorful dress and a fashionable bonnet that, because of his vantage above her, hid her face from view. The footman helped three more women out of the carriage. Two of them wore brightly colored dresses and bonnets like the first, but the last wore clothing and a bonnet in more subdued tones. Aurelius had expected three women, not four.

A servant escorted the four women into the palace. A few minutes later Aurelius heard footsteps behind him, and turned to see that Janus had entered the room. The councilor cleared his throat. "Dominus Aurelius, your . . . guests have arrived. As you instructed I escorted them to the Blue Drawing Room, and served them refreshments. They seem to be enjoying themselves."

"I invited three," Aurelius said, "but four arrived."

Janus bowed his head. "Yes, Dominus, a . . . Miss Hessian accompanied the three ladies you invited. She said you would not object. I can have her removed, if you wish."

Aurelius shook his head. "No. I'll meet with all four."

The Blue Drawing Room boasted the most extravagant and sumptuous styling of almost any room in the palace, but Aurelius had chosen it for this meeting because of its reputation: the family supremus entertained only the most important personages there. Hopefully, his guests would take that as a compliment, which might lessen the degree to which he must humble himself before them.

As Aurelius approached the entrance to the room, two guards opened its tall double doors. Through them Aurelius spotted one of the four women standing at a sideboard arrayed with various whiskeys and brandies. She had painted her lips in the darkest red, with heavy purplish shadows around her eyes, and thick rouge on her cheeks. As he stepped into the room, she lifted a glass of amber liquid to her mouth and tossed it back in a single gulp, then glanced his way and spoke in a thick street accent. "Bloody good whiskey you got here."

Janus had briefed him thoroughly on his three guests. "I'm glad you like it, Madam Lascivien."

Aurelius scanned the room. While Madam Lascivien stood at the sideboard downing shots, two of his three invited guests sat demurely on a couch. Madam Pleasuria appeared younger than expected, while Madam Dominatia seemed ancient beyond belief. Like Lascivien, both appeared to have applied their makeup with a paintbrush and trowel. Not for the first time he wondered what true names they'd been given at birth, and marveled at the lewd names they adopted when one ascended to the position of Madam in a brothel. He also wondered if they painted themselves that way as a matter of preference, or because that's what their customers expected of them. Or maybe they had done it for him, because that's what he expected of them.

Their appearance contrasted sharply with that of his uninvited guest. Hessian stood to one side, a knowing smile on her face. Gone were the black lip paint and foreboding shadows around her eyes. Instead, her makeup had been discreetly applied, could have been put there by one of Porcia's handmaidens. She wore a dress of muted colors, with her hair piled atop her head in a stylish coif. At their previous meetings, she had worn a man's blouse open down to her navel. But now she'd removed all the sharp angles and harsh flairs of the slums, and could have passed for a pretty young Domina of considerable standing. Looking at her, and for the first time seeing a beautiful woman, the thoughts that coursed through his mind at that moment made him uneasy.

Her eyebrows rose, as if she understood his discomfort. She walked toward him, moving slowly but deliberately, and stopped in front of him.

Recalling how she had tried to intimidate him almost every time they met, he looked her up and down. "You're not wearing men's pants and boots. I almost didn't recognize you."

She curtsied like the finest of courtiers, straightened, and looked him in the eyes. "Does my appearance meet your approval?"

He cocked his head slightly to one side. "You do appear more refined. But I suspect my approval is of no concern to you."

Her smile broadened, she leaned close to him, and lowered her voice. "I'm a woman of many talents and abilities. After all, one must always look the part. And your approval is of concern to me. I can't seduce you, can I, if I don't show you my more sophisticated side?"

Old Madam Dominatia grumbled, "So you're going to seduce him, are you?"

Young Madam Pleasuria perked up. "Can I seduce him as well? He is rather handsome. In fact, I'll do it for free. Or we could do him together. Think he can handle us both?"

Still displaying the knowing smile, Hessian shook her head. "No. You can't seduce him. And on second thought, nor will I, because—" She leaned away from him and looked him up and down. "I think *he's* going to seduce me. He certainly wants to. I can see it in his eyes."

Aurelius struggled to maintain a bored, indifferent look.

Behind Hessian, Dominatia gave her a sour look and shook her head. "The look on his face doesn't bode well for your success, my dear."

Aurelius decided enough was enough. To Hessian he said. "I invited them. May I ask why you're here?"

Her smile disappeared. "Today I represent all three slums. And they—" She tilted her head toward the three madams. "They own the three most profitable brothels in Carthagen, but today represent more than fifteen of their colleagues, as you well know."

He nodded. "That's why I invited them. You still haven't said why you're here."

She sighed, as if frustrated by the need to instruct a dimwitted child. "Most of the commerce in Carthagen is deeply interdependent. If you do something that adversely affects the revenue in one of the more significant segments, it almost always affects commerce in many others. You moved all of those soldiers out of the city. We want you to move them back."

He shook his head. "I can't."

Young Madam Pleasuria abruptly stood, her face sharp with anger.

Before she spoke he continued. "I can't have that many soldiers wandering about the city. And I can't properly train them here. But I understand your needs, and I think I have a solution that will accommodate us all."

Hessian's eyebrows rose and she turned slightly to look over her shoulder, taking a few seconds to glance individually at each of the three women. Aurelius didn't see them nod, blink, or do anything to communicate with her, but apparently they did in some way. She turned back to him and smiled pleasantly. "We're listening."

The soldiers in those camps had grown restless with nothing to occupy their spare time but dice and cards. Aurelius should have anticipated that, should have anticipated the issue with the brothels' revenue as well, and chided himself for such a lack of forethought. As a group, the madams in the city held considerable sway for many reasons, including that they contributed nicely to the city's tax revenues.

He chose his words carefully. "The camps are not far outside the city, less than half an hour by coach from its outskirts. We need to feed, clothe, and train those men, and where needed, we're building facilities to house their wives and loved ones. Soon those camps will become small cities in and of themselves. We also recognize that we must see to . . . all the needs of our men, as well as the needs of important independent businesses here in the city. To that end, Carthagen will provide accommodations for your employees as well, though, at the moment, they may be a bit spartan, but that will improve quickly. We'll be happy to provide transportation to and from, and as we recruit more soldiers, I think you ladies will find there's more than enough business to keep all of your people gainfully employed, perhaps even expand your operations a little."

Madam Pleasuria planted her fists on her hips. "I'm still in charge of me girls."

Dominatia growled, "That goes for all of us."

Aurelius nodded. "The Senatus recognizes we would be fools to insert ourselves into a business in which we have no experience."

Lascivien let out a hearty laugh. "I can name quite a few senators who have considerable experience with me girls."

Pleasuria added, "Me too."

"Yes," Dominatia said, standing and leaning heavily on a cane. "And I. But it occurs to me that you, Dominus Aurelius, are not among them." She looked a question at Pleasuria, who shook her head in answer, then at Lascivien, who did likewise. To

Hessian, she said, "For the good of us all, make sure he doesn't take too long seducing you."

Aurelius ignored her remark. "It appears we agree. Now, I have a busy day before me, so I'll have Councilor Janus see you ladies to your carriage."

He turned to summon Janus, but Hessian stood between him and the door, one eyebrow arched sharply upward. She acknowledged him with a coy smile and a faint nod of her head, but didn't step aside.

She liked to play her game. City business or Senatus issues forced them to meet two or three times a year. And he took care to never be alone with her because she might actually get serious, and looking at her now he wasn't sure how enthusiastically he'd resist her. He kept the look on his face neutral as he walked around her and found Janus waiting just outside the drawing room.

He gave the councilor instructions to see the ladies to their carriage, then returned to the window in his apartments. The hired carriage had waited there in the courtyard during their meeting, and he watched Janus assist three of the ladies up into its interior. All three wore brightly colored dresses and bonnets. The carriage pulled away from the front entrance, then through the palace gates, and into the city streets.

Aurelius heard soft footsteps behind him and the rustle of petticoats. He didn't turn about, but continued to look out the window as he spoke. "Janus is not one to breach protocol this way. What lie did you tell him?"

He heard Hessian's footsteps as she crossed the room and stopped just behind him. "I told him you and I have some unfinished business to discuss, which is not a lie."

He finished the sentence for her. "And then you told him I asked you to stay?"

"No," she said flatly.

He turned to face her.

She stood barely an arm's length from him, but she stepped forward half a step. "I told him you *wanted* me to stay. And that was the truth I saw in your eyes. If he misinterpreted that as, *You asked me to stay*, well, that was his mistake, not mine. And I'm right, aren't I?"

She leaned forward on her tiptoes, stretched upward, and brushed her lips lightly against his throat.

All his earlier thoughts came back in a rush. "It doesn't feel too much like I'm seducing you."

She leaned back, her lips barely an inch from his. Her nose scrunched and she grinned. "No, it doesn't. But you have all this business-of-state occupying your thoughts. So it's only fair if I accept responsibility for the seduction part. But we won't tell the madams I'm breaking the rules, will we?"

"No," he said. "I've noticed you do that a lot; break the rules."

She brushed her lips across his. "That makes it more fun."

He reached out and took her in his arms.

She lifted an eyebrow. "There, you see, it does appear as if you're seducing me."

He shook his head. "If I cared about appearances, I wouldn't be doing this."

She smiled and kissed him, the first of many kisses that afternoon. The business of state took a holiday for a few hours.

# 18

# The Sport of Spring

WITH HIS HORSE moving at an easy walk, Kainborne had trouble keeping his eyes open. But a loud, barking laugh from Macallan startled him.

About twenty paces ahead of him, Kadmarkh of Glenmoore rode next to Jarrod and Macallan, with Macallan's young son Clarahm riding sandwiched between them. Kainborne listened to the three men regale the young boy with stories of past raids on Scairn villages.

Zarkoffa leaned close to him and lowered his voice. "You think any of their stories are true?"

Kainborne kept his voice equally low. "I suppose some are."

"Aye, lad," Macallan told his son. "Just wait 'till you take one of them sweet, young Scairn wenches. It's a treat, let me tell yuh."

It occurred to Kainborne that the boy was hardly old enough to have such urges. He was about the same age as the half-Scairn boy with the birthmark. That thought reminded him that in a few months he must go see the lad for his annual visit, though since previous visits had yielded nothing, he considered skipping a year.

Macallan had brought his son north from Inversill for some sport in the Mountain Kingdom. He'd spent a couple of weeks at Dramoran, then along with Jarrod and Kainborne, continued north with about twenty soldiers to Glenmoore, where they stayed for another week. Near the end of their stay the lord of Glenmoore had grown increasingly ill at ease. Kainborne suspected that it strained his coffers to simultaneously host both dukes, but the man dare not complain. From Glenmoore they had ridden north toward the Mountain Kingdom.

Kainborne was not a fighting man and would not normally join such an expedition. But after raiding a village, there were always Scairn captives more spirited and resistant than the rest, which limited the number of bondservants they collected. Recalling the way Kainborne's tincture had made him utterly complacent, Macallan wanted Kainborne to do the same to those more spirited captives. They could collect more and accomplish in one expedition what normally required two or three.

In midafternoon the road narrowed to a trail, forcing them to ride in single file, and they gained altitude. A short time later they entered a small clearing and Macallan brought them to a halt. "We're going to split up here," he said. "Three groups, one lord in each group. If you're spotted, looks more like a single nobleman escorted by a half-dozen soldiers. My men all know the rendezvous point. We'll meet up late tomorrow."

Kainborne and Zarkoffa accompanied Jarrod along with a few soldiers. Kainborne asked one man, "You've used this rendezvous before?"

"Aye," the fellow said. "Four, five years now. Good place to meet up, camp, and setup raids on nearby villages."

To Kainborne it seemed cavalier to be so predictable. "What if the mountain folk are watching for us and they call in soldiers?"

"Nah!" he said. "Them villagers are like sheep. They run around and bleat while we kills off their men and gathers up the women." He turned to one of his comrades and said, "Bahahahah."

The fellow responded with, "Bahahahah," and they both got a good laugh out of that.

A third one said, "When I take me a Scairn woman, does that make me a sheep fucker?"

That produced a chorus of loud guffaws, with all of them imitating bleating sheep.

Jarrod glanced over his shoulder and gave them an angry look. "Silence!"

They obeyed with only a little grumbling.

They spent that night at the edge of a pasture in the foothills of the Cairngaede Mountains, then continued the next morning. And while the weather in the lower elevations had warmed in late spring, as they climbed higher the temperature dropped with each clop of a horse's hoof. One by one, throughout the day they all pulled on more layers of clothing.

Near dusk they reached the rendezvous point, a slash in a granite shelf that produced an overhang of rock, and protection on two sides from the harsh mountain winds. The archduke had taken the shortest route to their rendezvous and had arrived several hours before them. The camp appeared well established, with crackling fires and simmering pots of stew.

As they dismounted Macallan greeted them. "I've already scouted out a couple of villages. Grab something to eat. Kadmarkh should be here in an hour or so. We'll give them a chance to fill their guts, then we'll have some fun."

As night descended, Kainborne, Jarrod, Zarkoffa, and their small group of soldiers sat around a fire and ate a meal of mediocre stew. Kainborne picked at the meat in the bowl, and was about halfway through it when a shout broke the relative quiet of the night.

Zarkoffa stood. "That was a perimeter guard."

More shouts followed the first.

Jarrod asked, "Kadmarkh?"

Zarkoffa stared out into the darkness. "Probably, but something's wrong."

Kainborne stood as Kadmarkh limped into the camp walking his horse, a bandage on his left forearm. Five soldiers accompanied him, a few also wearing bandages, but he had started with seven.

"Scairn cavalry," Kadmarkh said. "Ambushed us, like they knew we were coming."

A horse whinnied somewhere, then Kainborne heard the unmistakable sound of steel swords clashing. A rider on horseback charged through the camp, his sword flashing in the light of the campfires. He cut one of the nearby soldiers down as another rider followed him. Shouts of anger and pain erupted everywhere.

Kainborne stepped back from the fire, looking for a place to hide, but a rider on a charging horse bore down on him, his sword raised high. Kainborne froze, had only a moment to see his own death reflected in the man's amber eyes. But from one side a heavy sword slammed into the Scairn's chest, sweeping him from the saddle. He landed in the dirt as the horse raced past. Zarkoffa stepped out of the darkness, stood over the downed Scairn warrior, raised his sword high, and buried it in the man's chest.

Realizing the light of the fire made him a target, Kainborne bent into a crouch and dashed away from it. He found a small bush at the edge of the camp and squatted down behind it. But as quickly as the Scairn riders had appeared, they disappeared into the night.

Kainborne waited and did not move. He didn't want to risk a stray arrow or crossbow bolt, and watched from the darkness as Macallan's soldiers got the camp reorganized. But then Macallan marched to the middle of the camp holding a heavy sword. He stopped and shouted, "Kainborne. I need you. Now."

Kainborne weighed the risk of a stray arrow versus the loss of the archduke's good favor. He stood and hurried toward the man. "What do you need, Your Grace?"

Macallan growled, "My son."

A sword-stroke had cut entirely through the boy's right calf. The bone of his leg had prevented it from severing the leg completely. Kainborne didn't need a physiker to tell him the boy would probably lose the leg, and even then it would likely fester and kill him. The boy kept crying out in pain.

"Your Grace," Kainborne said. "I'm not a physiker. I only know the most rudimentary of their skills."

The big man shook his head and did not hide his anger. "We know how to field-dress a wound. Just give him something for the pain. Give him that stuff you gave me. Then we'll get him to Glenmoore and Kadmarkh's physikers. You just keep the pain at bay while we get him there."

The next three days were an ordeal for them all. Ten of their soldiers had died in the initial attack, with five more badly wounded. The Scairn harried them, but didn't again attack in numbers. When they reached Glenmoore, Kadmarkh's physikers took one look at Clarahm's leg and confirmed Kainborne's earlier diagnosis. "We have to remove the leg. At least it'll be below the knee."

"A cripple," Macallan said. "The bloody Scairn have made my heir a cripple. This means war. I'll not rest until I've buried or enslaved every last one of those barbarians."

Clarahm came close to death, but survived, and would learn to walk with a wooden peg for a lower leg. Kainborne spent the rest of the summer at Inversill, using his tinctures to lessen the boy's pain. He had spoken truly when he'd told Macallan the special tincture that produced a stupor was dangerous if repeatedly used. He gave the lad a different tincture that reduced the pain for several days without inducing the stupor, and that saw him through the ordeal of his initial injury. But unbeknown to Macallan and his son, that tincture was highly addictive in an unusual way. If the boy didn't receive another dose, there'd be no ill effects for some months, but then his joints would ache to the point where he'd become bedridden. It would appear to be an unrelated malady, but then Kainborne would cure it with another dose of that tincture, and Macallan would be most grateful.

It occurred to Kainborne that if Macallan were to fall ill and die of some malady, the new Archduke Clarahm of Inversill would be dependent upon Kainborne for the rest of his life. He'd have to think on that.

• • • •

Another year passed, but Kainborne didn't come to look at Ket's birthmark. Ket worked in the stables, in the fields, and learned how to lead a cart pulled by an ox or horse, then later a large wagon pulled by a team of two horses. It became one of his regular duties to lead a horse-drawn wagon and follow Brother Sylander when he made the rounds of the valley to collect rents. He did that twice a year, accompanied by the six guardsmen, three on horse and three walking with Ket, while Sylander rode in the back of the wagon.

The Scairn still mistreated him, but as he grew they did so less often.

Peta continued to bring him cups of water. He hadn't seen any other children in the valley, and assumed the nearby population must be just old people, monks, him, and Peta.

He liked Peta, and sometimes noticed her watching him from a distance. She usually looked away when he caught her at it, though frequently she looked back and gave him a shy smile. She too had grown, and changed, though he couldn't say exactly what was different about her. He enjoyed looking at her too, liked that a lot.

One day while helping Brother Christolus in his vegetable garden, she walked by carrying a large basket of laundry. She stopped and gave him that shy smile. "Hi, Ket."

Ket stood and brushed dirt off his hands. "Doing laundry today?"

"Aye," she said, "for Brother Benedictus. He likes his fine pretty robes washed careful like. But he wants them in a hurry so I gotta run."

She walked away, but briefly glanced over her shoulder and smiled. He watched her go, noticing how her hips swayed from side to side as she walked. But then something slammed into his back, knocking him face down in the dirt. He rolled over to find Brother Markus standing over him, waving his willow switch at him. "You put your base carnal thoughts of that trollop away. If you succumb to your disgusting, animalistic desires of the flesh . . ." He waved the switch in front of Ket's nose. ". . . I'll use this to teach you the error of such wanton urges."

Ket's anger at the man boiled to the surface and he shot to his feet. He faced the scrawny monk, his fingers curled into fists, and didn't know what to do next.

Markus grinned, raised the switch in front of him and waggled it side to side. "Come on, boy. Give it a try, and I'll beat you to a pulp."

At fourteen, Ket almost matched the little monk in stature. But even if he succeeded, what would he do, beat the fellow to death? Then he'd have to face six guards, and they'd probably hang him from a tree.

Ket unfisted his hands and lowered them to his sides.

Markus's grin widened, and like a bolt of lightning, he lashed out with the switch and scored a line of fire across Ket's chest. Ket cringed, and the monk hit him, knocking him off his feet. He landed in the dirt, and waited for the beating he knew must come. But it didn't.

Standing over him, Markus leaned down. "Learned a valuable lesson today, didn't you? Don't ever forget it, boy."

Markus kicked him in the ribs, then stepped over him and walked away. Ket waited until he was well and gone before climbing to his feet, his mind reeling with confusion. Markus had used a lot of words he didn't know, and like so many things with the man, Ket couldn't fathom what he was supposed to do, or not do, to avoid another switching. He gave Brother Christolus a questioning look, but the monk merely shrugged, rolled his eyes, and returned to tending his vegetables.

Ket had grown in the four years he'd lived at the monastery, and he no longer felt like a tiny mouse among predators. During that time he had frequently thought of escaping, but survival out in the world had seemed so daunting. On the other hand, he had promised himself long ago he would plan his escape carefully. If he did so, and took his time, prepared in advance, didn't rush anything, perhaps it could work.

Ket studied with Markus and Obregon, and when Markus failed to restrain himself while punishing Ket, sometimes Obregon used his salve to cool the burn of the strokes left by the willow branch. Sometimes Peta found him crying, and they talked for a bit. And more and more Peta's company soothed his hurt as much as Obregon's salve.

At the end of the following summer Kainborne again didn't come to look at Ket's birthmark. Two years in a row! If Kainborne never again came to stare at his birthmark, that wouldn't bother Ket in the least, because he really didn't like the man. Then again, the next time Kainborne came, maybe Ket wouldn't be there.

• • • •

Ocean air and southern breezes moderated the winters in Inversill. And while a light drizzle had settled in that morning, the same weather would have produced ankle-deep snow in Dramoran. With summer drawing to an end, as Kainborne and the guardsmen accompanying him approached Macallan's castle, he looked forward to spending the winter there. He now spent more time there than Dramoran.

To Kainborne's surprise, as he rode his horse through the castle gates, Lady Claireen stood just outside the main building's entrance. Ten years younger than Macallan, the Lady of Inversill had yet to show any signs of age, and any man would find her desirable. She huddled out of the rain in a shallow alcove, wringing her hands anxiously. They had sent a rider ahead that morning, so she knew when they would arrive, and must have been waiting for them.

Kainborne dismounted and handed his reins to a guardsman. Paying no heed to the mud in the castle yard, he hurriedly crossed the distance to her. "Your Ladyship, you shouldn't stand out here in this weather."

She grimaced. "Clarahm has taken a turn for the worse. Can you help him?"

"Oh dear!" Kainborne said, giving her a worried frown as if he deeply cared for the lad. "I'll do what I can. Please, lead the way."

Kainborne had managed Clarahm's addiction by proactively giving the boy a dose of the tincture shortly before symptoms manifested, and withholding it at other times. He always dosed the lad before leaving the castle for an extended period of time. In that way the ache in the boy's joints appeared only a couple times a year.

In the vestibule of the main building Kainborne handed his rain-soaked cloak to a servant. But as he took a moment to scrape the mud off his boots, the lady said, "That's of no concern. Clarahm needs you now."

Kainborne followed her into the heart of the castle, leaving a trail of muddy boot-prints behind.

Clarahm lay in bed with his eyes closed, a tall physiker standing by his side, a slight grimace on the boy's face the only sign of his pain. The physiker looked their way as they stepped into the room, but Clarahm didn't respond. Lady Claireen gripped the boy's hand and said, "Master Kainborne is here."

Clarahm opened his eyes and produced a strained smile. "A welcome presence indeed. You'll help me, won't you?"

Kainborne nodded and spoke the lie he'd used before. "I will try. But as I've told you before, my tincture doesn't treat your ailment, just the pain, so I never know if it will actually work."

Kainborne asked the physiker, "What is his ailment, exactly?"

The man shook his head sadly. "He suffers from the ache of old bones due to an excess of humors, a rare malady in one so young, but not unheard of. It is not an ailment for which there is a cure."

Knowing the boy would need treatment, Kainborne had come prepared. He didn't want to open the small strongbox containing his tinctures in front of anyone. The many tinctures in it might spawn unwanted curiosity, and that could lead to the wrong kind of questions. That morning he'd selected the tincture Clarahm needed, and placed the vial in a small pocket of his robes. He retrieved it, dribbled a few drops in a goblet, added some water, and gave it to the boy. The lad gulped at it hungrily.

Those few drops were not enough to completely alleviate the pain, but that meant Kainborne stood vigil over the lad through the night, incurring even more gratitude from the Lord and Lady of Inversill. In the wee hours of the morning, with no one looking over his shoulder, he dosed the boy again. And by noon of the following day, Clarahm had improved sufficiently to stand and walk short distances. Kainborne drew out the boy's suffering for two days, after which Clarahm could function again.

With the boy greatly improved, Kainborne feigned exhaustion, as if he'd gone without sleep that entire time. Lady Claireen thanked him with tears in her eyes.

On the third day after his arrival, Macallan summoned him to his private study where they met alone. Worry clouded the archduke's features. "I'm afraid there's no hope for my son."

Macallan needed some guidance. "Your Grace, the ache of old bones doesn't portend an untimely demise."

"No," Macallan said. "But it makes him weak when he needs to be strong. I need a strong heir."

He lowered his voice. "That's why I now spend a few hours each night in my lady wife's bed. I need a spare."

Kainborne did not want a new heir complicating the situation. He considered giving the Lady of Inversill a tincture to ensure she conceived no child, though he couldn't be sure it actually worked. But if it did, and Macallan persisted, Kainborne would have to spend all his time at Inversill to keep the woman properly dosed. Better to wait, and if the man did produce another heir, Kainborne would have plenty of time to kill the child before it matured.

# 19

# Rebellion

SEATED ON THE throne of the Senatus Supreme, Maximillian took a sip from his tankard of ale, and Aurelius watched Divonia struggle to control herself. With the ambassador from Tarnasus about to arrive any minute, it wouldn't do for the two of them to engage in one of their high-volume blowups. Divonia knew that as well as anyone, as did Maximillian, and she and he appeared to have come to an unspoken agreement. If the day's schedule contained any important business for the Senatus Supreme, he held off and kept his drinking to a minimum, and she didn't berate him. But once they completed the last of his responsibilities, all bets were off. Every day he got falling-down drunk, while the two of them competed to be heard throughout the palace. Their accommodation didn't always work, and upon occasion Aurelius filled in for his brother. And when that wasn't possible, they postponed the event with some phony excuse everyone knew they had contrived.

Maximillian looked longingly into the tankard, but sighed and did not take another sip. He turned his attention on Aurelius. "Tell me again, Brother, why does tiresome old Victicus want to meet with me?"

Divonia's control slipped. "Aurelius told you that yesterday, briefed you fully, as I recall. And you don't remember a thing, do you?"

Aurelius gave her a pointed look and she cringed. The briefing he had given his brother the day before had come after they had completed the day's business, and at the time Maximillian could barely stand.

His brother rolled his eyes. "Yes, Mother, I do recall that. But it wouldn't hurt if he refreshed my memory."

Aurelius tried to calm his thoughts. If he sounded in any way patronizing, that could set Maximillian off as easily as a harsh word from Divonia. "They have their spies here in Carthagen, just as we have ours in Tarnasus. So they know of our expanded military capability, and of late they've grown quite nervous about that."

Maximillian closed his eyes, rubbed his temples, and spoke tiredly. "And how expanded is our military capability?"

Aurelius had done everything to oppose the expansion. But other than his lone seat in the Senatus, he held no official power, Maximillian just didn't care, and Divonia had carefully marshalled her contacts within the Senatus. He hated to admit it, but she was probably fucking most of them. The expansion of their military, not the fucking, was a bone of contention between Aurelius and his mother.

He spoke carefully. "We've been strengthening our numbers since shortly after your ascension, a little over five years, and we now have over eight thousand men."

Maximillian focused his eyes for a moment long enough to give Aurelius a pointed look. "Do we really need that many constables for the city guard?"

Aurelius shook his head. "Initially, we kept recruitment to a minimum, just three or four hundred a year, and we put them in constabulary uniforms, hoping to conceal the expansion. But two years ago the Senatus accelerated our efforts, and the numbers grew beyond any possibility of concealment, though we continued to try. At that time we moved them into two large training camps outside the city. But now there are four such camps."

Maximillian lifted an eyebrow. "Eight thousand soldiers wandering the streets would be rather obvious."

Aurelius grimaced. "Unfortunately, while the camps are somewhat isolated, it's fundamentally impossible to hide the existence of that many soldiers."

Maximillian lifted the tankard of ale to his lips. Divonia tensed, but he merely sipped and didn't guzzle, so she remained silent.

Maximillian nodded, his eyes focused in the distance. "And what is the purpose of Victicus's request for an audience today?"

If Maximillian took an interest, Aurelius might marshal support in the Senatus to avoid conflict with Tarnasus. "About a year after we started our expansion, Tarnasus's Senatus decided to match us man for man. And for the last few years they thought they had succeeded because our efforts to conceal the numbers were somewhat successful. Right now their standing army numbers about half ours. Unfortunately, they recently discovered the true numbers, and now they're quite upset that we have them badly outnumbered."

"And so," Maximillian said, "old Victicus is here to whine and complain."

Divonia bristled at that comment. "Just be polite, treat him with respect, and at least pretend you're listening to him. Aurelius and I will handle him after you're finished."

Maximillian stiffened, but before he responded a servant stepped into the room and bowed deeply, waiting to be acknowledged. Hoping to cut off the argument he saw building, Aurelius spoke before either of them threw the next barb. "Yes, man, what is it?"

The fellow announced, "Ambassador Victicus has arrived. Domina Porcia greeted him and is escorting him here now."

Aurelius had asked Porcia to intercept the old lecher. Beautiful young women were the old man's weakness, and distracting him before the meeting could only help.

Aurelius remained where he stood while Divonia stepped forward to stand at Maximillian's left hand. A few seconds later Porcia and the old fellow stepped into the room walking arm-in-arm, and it was clear she had had the desired effect.

She had donned a very revealing low-cut gown that exposed an indecent amount of flesh, and she did have a fair amount to display. The nipples protruding through the fabric of her garment added to the effect, and made it clear she wore no undergarments beneath the dress. And while Aurelius could never look upon his sister the way other men did, he couldn't blame the old lecher for his inability to take his eyes off her breasts.

Victicus said something to her, speaking too softly for Aurelius to hear, and she emitted a girlish laugh. She leaned close to him, whispered something, and in doing so accidentally pressed the flesh of her breast against the back of his hand. Then she glanced about the room and said, "Oh yes, you're here on some sort of business, and I was so enjoying our conversation."

Giving the old man a sly look and pulling him even closer, she walked him across the room to stand in front of the seated Maximillian. Only then did she release the ambassador. She spoke in formal tones. "Dominus Maximillian Supremus, may I present His Excellency, Dominus Victicus, Ambassador from Tarnasus?"

Maximillian at least responded properly. "I welcome His Excellency with open arms."

As Porcia stepped away from them and walked Aurelius's way, Victicus responded with an equally formal phrase. When Porcia stopped beside Aurelius and turned to watch the proceedings, he decided to let Divonia handle the situation.

Porcia whispered, "Is he sober?"

Aurelius didn't shrug or move. "Sober enough. In fact, more so than usual."

She glanced his way. "I didn't hear any shouting, so I assume Mother held back."

"As much as she could."

She grimaced. "I guess that'll have to do."

He glanced down at the exposed cleavage, let her see him doing so. "Pouring it on a little thick, aren't you?"

She smiled coyly. "As I recall, it was you who asked me to distract him with my girlish charm."

He looked again at her cleavage. "That's quite a bit of girlish charm you're displaying. And don't you think you overdid it when you *accidentally* pressed your breast against the back of his hand?"

She sighed. "I suppose I'll have to let the old lecher seduce me."

Aurelius didn't want that for her. "Don't whore yourself out for anyone. Trust me. I'll make it work without that."

He heard the weariness in her voice. "Oh Aurelius, we're both whoring ourselves out to make up for Max's weaknesses and Mother's unbridled ambitions."

A shout from Victicus brought Aurelius's attention back to the ambassador. "And I protest. You are acting in bad faith, and if this continues it will mean war."

Aurelius moved quickly, marching across the room toward them as Divonia said, "Well if it's war you want—"

At that moment she saw the look on Aurelius's face and clamped her mouth shut. As Aurelius stepped up beside Victicus, Maximillian tried to placate the ambassador. "Ambassador Victicus, please do not mistake my mother's comments as a sign that Carthagen has any desire for armed conflict with Tarnasus."

Victicus did not appear to be at all soothed. "Then why do you now maintain a standing army of almost nine thousand men?"

Aurelius intervened. "Ambassador, our concern is aggression from the Four Duchies. In the last couple of years Macallan has expanded his forces, and as you know we are closer to that border than you. It is for that reason we have always maintained a standing army. After all, when they raid, it's not Tarnasus or Andopolous who suffer their aggression. And the frequency of their raids has increased of late. The Duchies are also now fighting regular skirmishes with the Mythrians, so we are merely anticipating an unstable situation on the border."

That was close enough to the truth, and it appeared to placate the old man, but not completely. The only thing that appeared to smooth his ruffled feathers was the nearness of attractive women. When the meeting ended, Porcia and Divonia each took one of his arms to escort him back to his carriage, and he clearly had trouble deciding which pair of breasts he wanted to look at more.

Maximillian started drinking in earnest, and Aurelius retired to his apartments. It occurred to him that he should mention to his mother the considerable benefit that would incur if Victicus looked favorably upon them because of a personal connection to their family. Divonia might then decide to seduce the old reprobate and save Porcia the unpleasantness. But he needed to carefully consider how to approach his mother on such a delicate subject. And then there would be the issue of fitting the old fellow into her busy seduction schedule.

Aurelius sat down and tried not to think of the dangers they faced in the coming year.

• • • •

Another year passed, and Ket wondered if Kainborne would come that year, wondered if he would ever come again. If he did, it would be somewhere near Ket's sixteenth birthday. He didn't really know the date of his birth—that had died with his mother—but had a vague idea it occurred sometime in late summer.

To facilitate his escape from the monastery, Ket had accumulated a small stash that consisted of a few stolen pennies and some extra clothing. He kept the stash hidden beneath hay in a far corner of the hayloft in the stable. And since he was the only person who ever climbed up there, he needn't fear someone might discover it. He had no experience with money, so he didn't know how far the pennies might take him. But with the onset of spring and warm weather, he planned to steal as much food as he could carry, then sneak off in the middle of the night and run, though at the thought of doing so, his gut tightened with fear. He resolved he would not let that stop him.

He spent the afternoon working in the fields. It was a warm spring day, though it had rained the day before, which made for a muddy day with shovel and hoe. At the end of the day he trudged back to the monastery.

When he returned from the fields covered in mud, if he didn't wash down first thing, Markus gave him a switching. So he had developed a cleanup routine that worked reasonably well. In the stables he retrieved a leather bucket, filled it from a horse trough, and poured it over his head. He scrubbed, poured another bucket of water over his head, and with more scrubbing removed most of the mud and dirt from his clothing. That done, he retrieved a third bucket of water, carried it into the stables, and found a clean stall that had been mucked out that day, its floor covered in fresh hay. In the stall he stripped out of his clothing, and hung it to dry over the chest-high wooden fence that separated that stall from the next. He used some of the water to finish cleaning his shirt and pants, and the rest to clean the last remnants of the field off his body.

"Ket!"

He froze and listened carefully.

"Ket!"

Peta, calling for him.

"Ket, are you back here?"

In the stable not far away.

He spun around, water dripping off his shoulders, and had not an instant to react as Peta stepped into view at the open entrance to the stall, her eyes focused on the ground in front of her as she gingerly stepped around a pile of horse dung. She turned his way, took a step toward him, and only then looked up, saying, "I thought I'd find—"

He stood two paces from her, wearing not a stitch of clothing. Her eyes widened, she put a hand to her mouth and squeezed her eyes tightly shut. He covered his crotch with his hands.

"I—" he said. "I . . . uh . . ."

"I—" she said. "I just—"

She tried to back step with her eyes closed, but stumbled, tried to correct, and fell onto the hay at his feet. He reacted instinctively and reached out to stop her from falling, but didn't move quickly enough. He only caught one of her hands and ended up standing over her wearing nothing but his own skin.

"What filth are you two up to?"

Markus's words froze him where he stood, bent forward, his hands extended toward Peta. The scrawny monk stood in the open stall entrance holding his willow switch, his face a mask of fury. "When she followed you in here I knew you two were up to something."

Like a snake striking, his hand lashed out with lightning speed, and the switch laced a line of fire across Ket's arms and chest. He cried out and staggered back. Markus advanced, hitting him again and again as Ket cowered against the back wall of the stall. The switch struck his back, his arms, his legs, and all he could do was beg, "Please . . . stop. It hurts."

Markus shouted, "You're no better than a rutting pig. You're both just filthy animals, satisfying your base desires like cattle in the stables."

Ket crumbled to the floor under the onslaught of the switch as it struck his head, arms, and shoulders, and then Peta shouted, "Stop it! Stop hurting the poor boy."

"You slut," Markus screamed.

Ket heard a loud smack, then the sound of ripping cloth, and the hiss of the switch, but didn't feel any of its fiery pain. Someone else screamed.

"You filthy cow!"

Again the hiss of the switch, and that scream.

"You wanton trollop."

The hiss of the switch and the scream.

"You shameless whore."

The hiss, the scream, but no pain, and then Ket realized the voice behind the scream was Peta's.

He opened his eyes, saw the switch flash down and mark a thin bloody line across her raised arms. It came down again, scoring a line of bloody welts across her bare chest. Markus had torn away the thin, home-spun shift she wore during warm months, and she tried to cover her small breasts. Another bloody line of welts on her chest, and one across her face, testified to the damage the switch had already done. But the tears streaming down her cheeks pulled at Ket as nothing else could.

Markus stood over her, his eyes wide with burning hatred, jaw clenched, teeth gritted. "You unholy seductress." He struck again, and she cowered and screamed.

A strange, roiling anger climbed up Ket's throat, and something in him changed with each strike of the switch, and each ragged scream from her throat. At that moment the thing that arose within him was not natural, kind, or forgiving. It was simple fury. He roared, "Nooooo!"

He didn't know where he found the strength, but he erupted from the floor and charged. He plowed into the monk, slamming him against the opposite wall of the stall. They both bounced off it and staggered back.

Markus stumbled away from him, raising the switch, holding it between them, his eyes filled with hate. "Now you've done it, boy. You've gone too far. You're going to pay for that with the switching of your life."

He raised the switch high, but before he struck, Ket charged again, wrapped his arms around the scrawny little bastard, and tackled him to the floor. Markus landed on top of a pile of horse dung. Ket landed on top of him and heard a satisfied grunt of pain as he knocked the wind out of the monk. Ket jumped to his feet, saw the switch lying to one side where Markus had dropped it. He picked it up, looked at it for a moment, then swung it high over his head and brought it down across the man's face.

Markus screamed and tried to crawl away from him.

Ket hit him again, and again, and again.

"Stop," Markus pleaded. "Please stop."

Ket heard Peta screaming. He heard Markus screaming, and he didn't care. He hit the horrible little man over and over, kept at it and had no intention of stopping. And then something slammed into him, knocking him to the floor. He fought and struggled, but there were six of them, the guardsmen.

A fist slammed into his face, a boot into his ribs. Then something smashed into the side of his head.

# 20

# Unstable Borders

AT THE MEETING of the Privy Council, during the discussion of grain and live-stock inventories, Caerie struggled to keep her eyes open. Then Palmath recited revenue numbers and statistics, and Caerie stayed awake by recalling the last time she had seen the peasant boy in her vision. Standing beneath the canopy of the oak tree, he had looked down at the lioness curled up and sleeping at his feet. And though the mottled shadows of the tree's leaves hid his features, she imagined him smiling. When he looked up at the raptor perched high above and shielded his eyes from the sun, she imagined him smiling at the bird as well. Then he looked at Caerie, and she imagined him smiling at her.

If she could see his face, she thought she might like his smile. But something changed and he frowned. Then his image blurred, and he stood there bent in a crouch, bloodied, beaten, his wrists and ankles locked in irons, wearing nothing but a loincloth.

She saw him now every year without fail exactly two months before her birthday. He had grown into a young man with broad shoulders, just as she had become a young woman with bumps and curves. In a sense, he and she had grown up together.

"Command General Kailill," Selene said, sitting at the head of the table. "What's the situation on the border?"

As Kailill stood, Caerie perked up.

The old general said, "Macallan is still building his forces and we've had three serious skirmishes just this month. He's definitely probing our defenses."

One of the councilors asked, "Do you think he intends war?"

Kailill hesitated for a moment and took a breath. "I don't know how to answer that. During a couple of the skirmishes we experimented by withdrawing. They definitely don't fight well on mountainous terrain, especially at the higher elevations. As long as he comes at us with probing skirmishes, we're going to fight and repel him at the lower levels so his troops don't learn anything about fighting higher up. And if he finally comes at us in force, we're going to withdraw and take him on where we have the advantage. We should be able to repel him, but that kind of push will make his intentions clear. And I fear it's not a coincidence that it's early spring. That gives him several months to probe and experiment, then eventually attack in force without worry of cold weather higher up."

That produced a considerable amount of discussion and a few arguments, but all seemed satisfied with Kailill's plan and the talk ended there.

Caerie's Uncle Damuel said, "Before we close, I have some concern regarding the Lowland Kingdoms. I'm hearing rumors from merchants, and it appears Tarnasus and Carthagen are close to war. And if they fight in earnest, Andopolous will get involved as well."

Selene nodded. "We've all been watching that situation. What's your point?"

Damuel shrugged. "One Lowlands city against another, they don't have to worry about winter up here in the mountains. So the timing may not hold them back. I think we should keep a close eye on that border as well."

Selene looked a question at Kailill.

He acknowledged her with a nod. "I'll double the patrols along both borders."

With that, Selene asked if there were any further issues. No one spoke up, so the meeting ended. But as Caerie rose from her seat, Selene said, "Daughter, please stay. I'd like to have a word with you."

Caerie didn't sit down, but remained standing by her seat while the rest filed out of the room. As the last of them walked through the door, Melceinnia stepped into the room. Caerie's first instinct was to march past her and get out of there, but the priestess closed the door.

Selene stood and approached Caerie from one side, while Melceinnia approached her from another. Caerie took a deep breath and tried to remain calm.

Selene gave Caerie a sharp look and snapped words at her. "Do not find yourself with child, my dear."

Caerie had not been expecting that. "Uh . . . what . . . what do you mean?"

Her mother put her fists on her hips. "You're sixteen now. I got that itch between my legs when I was your age, and just like you I found a handsome young boy my age to show me how to properly take care of it. Well, actually, he was a miserable failure at it because he was just as inexperienced as me. But I got rid of him and found an older boy with some experience, and he did it right."

Melceinnia said, "Crown Mother, please calm down."

Memories flashed through Caerie's thoughts of slipping away from a reception with a handsome young friend, then groping at each other in the dark. "I . . . I don't know what you're talking about."

Her mother took in a sharp breath, but Melceinnia raised a hand and Selene released the breath with a loud, "Humph!"

Melceinnia said, "The boy from the Skelain clan."

Caerie's gut tightened and she sighed. "You know about that?"

Selene snapped, "Of course we know."

Again Melceinnia raised that hand, and in response Selene spun on her heel and walked across the room. She stopped with her back to them.

Melceinnia spoke in a calm, soft tone. "You've been having a passionate affair with him for over two months."

Caerie tried not to sound as if she were pleading. "What's wrong with that?"

"Nothing," the priestess said. "How do you feel about him?"

Caerie didn't know how to answer that. "He's . . . fun . . . and he . . . pleases me."

"You're not in love with him?"

"No," Caerie said, "of course not. He's just . . . convenient. What do you want me to do, play with dolls?"

Selene turned around and walked back to them. She spoke without the sharp edges of anger coloring her voice. "At least you picked a boy with some experience. That first time for me was horrible."

Melceinnia added, "Enjoy yourself with him, but don't find yourself with child. And by the way, I can help with that."

"Really," Caerie said. "How?"

The old woman grinned. "I'm a priestess, and we do know a few things, especially when it comes to issues regarding women."

Her mother said, "And the Skelain boy, he's just not right for you. Enjoy him for the time being, but don't become attached."

"No," Melceinnia said, grinning. "He's definitely not the ket to your caerm."

Selene frowned. "What do you mean by that?"

Melceinnia stepped around Caerie and took Selene by the arm. "I have a story to tell you about the realms of the stars."

No longer pinned between the two women, Caerie decided not to wait for her mother's reaction to that. She turned, didn't look back as she marched to the door, opened it, and stepped through it before either woman called after her.

She paused in the hallway and thought of the Skelain boy and their passionate groping, and how that had led to so much more. She had enjoyed herself, but whenever they met, and afterwards, the peasant boy beneath the oak tree occupied her thoughts. That, she would never reveal to anyone.

• • • •

Anthon Barasha had inherited the striking amber eyes of his mother, and when he grew up, young Scairn girls would find that most attractive. Zalestria and the three-year-old boy sat on the floor facing each other, a small kitten prancing between them as they played with it. The kitten jumped in the air; the boy emitted a piercing shriek, and Zalestria clapped her hands. Seated in a comfortable chair, Damuel watched the boy's face light up. That was one of the few genuine pleasures he enjoyed, other than rutting with Zalestria.

During Zalestria's pregnancy Damuel had wondered every day if he could truly trust her, constantly wondered if she had told the truth when claiming he had fathered the child. But the boy inherited Damuel's facial structure, and even at birth, and more so as he grew, any question of his parentage had been moot. Damuel never voiced his early doubts to anyone.

With parenthood, Selene had granted Damuel a larger apartment, a fairly luxurious space with several rooms. Once Zalestria gave birth, she resumed her duties as a priestess and now divided her time between the temple and their apartment in the palace. It was Zalestria who pointed out, "Doesn't it bother you that you must depend on your sister for everything? You should have been chosen, not her."

It had never bothered him before, but once she mentioned it, he frequently recalled her words. He owned nothing not granted to him by the good graces of the Throne of Myth and Legend. And the Crown could take it all in an instant if those good graces faltered. He couldn't deny that Zalestria's view had some merit, and the more he thought about it, the more his situation grated on him. He had nothing to give his son beyond the hope that whoever sat on the throne would look upon him with favor.

Damuel stood. "I must be off."

Zalestria stood, leaving Anthon to the cat. She crossed the room and gave Damuel a kiss on the cheek. "Must you go?"

He shrugged. "Selene is expecting me."

Zalestria's eyes darkened, but she didn't say what was clearly on the tip of her tongue. Instead, she took his arm and turned for a moment to look at their son. "He should be mythchild. And he could be, if she weren't on the throne."

Damuel left her there and made his way to Selene's apartments. His sister wanted to discuss the results of the last meeting of the Privy Council, as well as strategize for the next. He met her in a drawing room she used more as a large working space. When he stepped into the room, she looked at him and smiled. "How is Anthon?"

Damuel couldn't help but smile when he thought of his son. "He's well, and quite enjoying the kitten you gave him."

She frowned. "You know, when you and Zalestria petitioned Melceinnia to bear a son, I didn't approve. But Melceinnia felt it would be good for you, and she was right. But it would still bother me if you became attached to that trollop."

That made him pause. "Petitioned Melceinnia . . . a son?"

She spoke while rifling through some papers, her attention focused there. "Yes. The sisterhood would not have suspended Zalestria's duties to other men if you and she hadn't agreed in advance that she would bear you a son."

She glanced his way for a moment. "And then Melceinnia watched her rather closely, because I wouldn't put it past her to take any number of men to her bed. Her husband is probably a very wealth—"

He snarled, "Don't say that."

She winced. "Sorry." She returned to rifling through the papers.

He thought it good that at that moment she wasn't looking his way, because while he wouldn't allow Selene to apply that insult to Zalestria, he had begun to think of her that way himself. "They can dictate the sex of the child?"

She found what she was looking for and selected a piece of paper, looking at it while she spoke. "Oh, yes, of course. They can control it all, the gender, and if and when to conceive."

He took care to control the look on his face.

She finally looked his way. "I still don't approve of Zalestria. As far as I'm concerned, she's just a whore, but I love that little son of yours."

Zalestria had lied to Melceinnia, telling her he had wanted a son with her. She had lied to him as well, led him to believe that the child had been unplanned. He had never really approved of Zalestria, except for the physical pleasure they enjoyed, and she had given him a son he did love. He could live with that, but he'd have to keep an eye on her.

• • • •

With an escort of forty soldiers led by Tribune Denian, and riding with light rations, Aurelius forced them to push the horses to the limit. It still took a day and a half to reach the border between Carthagen and Tarnasus, a boundary no one could define with any accuracy, and one that shifted constantly. One day the border might be a waist-high stone wall at the edge of a farmer's property, and the next a babbling creek a league or two north of that. No one had ever really cared that much, because for several centuries they had enjoyed the benefit of peaceful relations—at least until recently.

Carthagen's military numerical superiority had frightened Victicus and his colleagues in Tarnasus, and they had called in all available levies. That had increased tension on the frontier, and a couple of overzealous centurions decided to settle the matter with open war. The Carthagenian prefect commanding that section of the border had immediately withdrawn all troops, then sent a messenger to Carthagen. Aurelius wanted to kiss the man for his restraint.

Late on the second day of riding, after a break to allow the horses to rest, they returned to the trail and kept the pace at a slow walk. They followed a dirt-track road headed northeast, and near dusk they spotted one of their outriders in the road ahead, riding hard toward them. Denian halted their advance, and the outrider pulled his horse to a stop next to them.

"Tribune," he said to Denian. "Their camp is up ahead, and they're expecting you."

Several minutes later they rode into an encampment with tents neatly lined up in rows. Smoke rose from the fires in field ovens in a semi-permanent kitchen near its center. Prefect Parthan stood outside his tent waiting for them.

As Aurelius and Denian dismounted, he saluted them. "Tribune Denian. Dominus Aurelius."

Aurelius demanded, "How many dead and wounded?"

Parthan grimaced. "On our side, two dead, four wounded, but one of the wounded took a gut wound. I doubt he'll make it. On their side, probably much the same."

"And the centurion responsible?"

Parthan shook his head. "A twenty-year man, Your Grace. He's the one with the gut wound."

Parthan got Aurelius and Denian seated near a blazing fire with a bowl of warm stew and a mug of ale for dinner. As they ate, he brought forward each man involved in the skirmish one at a time, and Aurelius questioned them thoroughly. The incident simply boiled down to two centurions, both hot-heads, exchanging words at the border. The words escalated into shouts, and in short order, a half-dozen men had died, or soon would.

The next morning they cautiously approached the small glen where the incident had occurred. During the struggle horses' hooves and men's boots had chewed up the soft ground, and he learned nothing from that. Before they began the journey back to Carthagen, Aurelius told Prefect Parthan, "If the centurion survives, demote him one rank. If he doesn't, make sure his wife gets his pension. Let's hope he doesn't."

# 21

# The Truth in a Lie

KET COULDN'T STOP shivering. The guardsmen had manacled his hands and ankles, and connected the two sets of manacles by a short length of chain. They'd finished by inserting a long spike through one of the chain links, then pounding it into
the ground in one of the horse stalls, leaving him there chained and naked. He tried to
burrow into the straw for warmth, but the cold ground sucked the heat out of his
bones. In the darkness of the stables he had no idea how much time passed, but he
felt as if he laid there for an eternity, shivering and pissing himself.

"Ket, me boy."

Ket recognized Obregon's voice. He tried to open his eyes, but the swelling
around one made that impossible. "What faffa . . ." The swelling around his mouth
also made it difficult to speak.

"Hold still, lad, let me check your legs."

Ket felt Obregon probing at his feet, ankles, and legs.

"Okay, nothing broken there. Come on, lad, let's get you to your feet."

Obregon gripped him beneath his armpits and grunted with effort. Ket got a knee
beneath him and helped a little. Then he got a foot on the ground next to the knee,
and with the big man's help he climbed to his feet and stood, but couldn't stand up
straight because of the length of chain connecting the hand and leg irons. Obregon
pressed him against the wall of the stall. "You gotta stand on your own, boy. I gotta
see if anything's broken."

Ket gripped the fence between stalls to stay on his feet while Obregon probed at
his ribs. He hit something sensitive and Ket cried out. The monk probed at that spot
for a few seconds. "Just a nasty bruise there."

He probed at Ket's face, paid close attention to his teeth and jaw, and the bones
around his eyes. When he finished, he declared, "Ok, no teeth missing, no broken
bones. Let's get you cleaned up."

Obregon rubbed him down with a damp rag, then tied a loincloth around his hips and groin.

"I brought a blanket," Obregon said. "I think that's all I can get away with. Don't burrow under the straw. That puts you in contact with the dirt, and the ground sucks all the heat out of you, even on a warm day. We'll wrap you in the blanket, then you lay on top of the straw."

Obregon helped him curl up in the blanket. "When you gotta piss get up and do it in the corner. Don't just lay there and piss in your cloth."

Ket didn't recall the monk leaving, but he drifted off into an uneasy sleep. He had a hazy memory of Obregon returning with water and small amounts of food, and he took care to obey the man and piss in the corner.

•  •  •  •

*The girl was no one, just the child of a merchant of modest means, except she bore that mark. To her it was nothing but some discolored skin on the inside of her right forearm, at least in the beginning. But to me it represented all the infinite possibilities of destiny. I had read about it, but never thought to see it in my time, never believed it might be anything but fantasy, legend, myth. Then I looked upon it for the first time, and it revealed itself to me, flashing images of power I could not fathom.*

*The mark is a capricious mistress, demanding, unyielding, unrepentant in its quest for power. It haunted her with the spirit of its maker. It tormented her with visions of evil. It cursed her with the need to release it. And in the end it betrayed her, as it betrays all those who fall under its spell.*

*Whatever her intended destiny she never met it. She died of the rotting scourge, but had she lived . . .*

*Author unknown*
*penned in the time of the Rotting Scourge*

Kainborne could not hide his impatience, wanted to whip the horse beneath him into a gallop and charge down into the Vale of Tramorth. "Why have we slowed down? Can we go no faster?"

Seated on a horse next to him, Zarkoffa rolled his eyes. "We've pushed the animals as hard as we can. They're exhausted, and if we don't slow the pace, they'll simply drop to the ground beneath us. That'll slow us more, and we'll get there even later. Do something to occupy your thoughts, and trust us to get you there when we can."

Zarkoffa had said as much the night before when Kainborne wanted to continue travelling through the night.

Two days ago a messenger had delivered a dispatch from Benedictus, and luckily Kainborne had been spending a few months at Dramoran, not Inversill. According to the abbot's frantic scrawl, the boy had gone berserk and tried to murder a monk, and it took six guardsmen to subdue him. If only Kainborne had made the journey each year as he had planned; if only he hadn't let almost three years lapse without personally checking on the boy, he would have controlled the situation much better than that stupid abbot. He tried to take Zarkoffa's advice, tried to think of other matters.

The chest of scrolls Macallan's great grandfather had accumulated proved to be a treasure trove. It required painstaking effort, and after almost six years, there still remained scrolls untouched and untranslated. But he had uncovered one that appeared to be well over a thousand years old. Its author had penned it at the time of the Rotting Scourge in a precursor to the language presently in use in the Duchies and the Lowlands. It was an old language still spoken in some remote villages, and it took months to translate.

The author believed the Dreadmark was the product of some sort of curse and mentioned its *maker*. If nothing more, it confirmed that the Dreadmark had been around for more than a millennium. But half the scroll had rotted away, and to Kainborne's overwhelming frustration, the narrative ended there.

"It won't be long now."

Zarkoffa's words brought Kainborne out of his reverie. The horses had just stepped off the road and onto the cart path that led to the monastery. Kainborne's patience with Benedictus had worn quite thin. "That fool abbot had better be waiting for me."

Zarkoffa shrugged. "We sent a rider ahead. He will be."

Zarkoffa had the right of it. As they approached the monastery, Benedictus stood framed in the main gate. A hundred paces before they reached him he trudged forward in an awkward shuffle. Out of sheer spite Kainborne pulled his horse to a stop, forcing the man to cross the entire distance. The abbot slipped once, fell into the mud, struggled to his feet, and trudged on. He stopped beside Kainborne's horse and gripped a saddle strap to support himself. Red faced, he wheezed and struggled to breathe.

"Master Kainborne, I'm so glad you've come. You can now tell us what to do with the boy."

Kainborne leaned down and growled, "If you had done this properly I shouldn't need to tell you what to do. We're going to discuss this in your study . . . now."

He straightened in the saddle. "Zarkoffa, with me."

He spurred his horse into a trot, heard the rest of the troop do likewise, and didn't stop until he could dismount inside the monastery wall. He'd been there before and no longer needed a guide to Benedictus's study. With Zarkoffa following him he went straight to it, walked in, and found a tray of chilled wine waiting for him.

He sat down in a chair and said, "Pour me some of that wine, and pour some for yourself."

Zarkoffa grinned, poured two goblets of wine, handed one to Kainborne, sat down in a cushioned chair, and rested his muddy boots on the seat of another chair. They sat there silently for some minutes sipping at the wine. Then Kainborne heard a commotion through the open study door. A second later Benedictus stepped through it, his fine robes streaked with mud, his red face shining with greasy sweat. Breathing heavily, he bent over, rested his hands on his knees and struggled to catch his breath.

Kainborne didn't allow him even a moment's respite. "Now, Reverend Brother Benedictus, you claim the boy tried to murder a monk. Why did he do that?"

"No . . . reason," the abbot said. "Just . . . went . . . mad. No . . . reason."

Kainborne shook his head. "No one tries to murder someone for no reason. Have the boy brought here. Let's see what he says."

"And," Zarkoffa said. "You said he *tried* to murder a monk. That means he didn't succeed. Why don't we have that monk brought here as well?"

There was a reason Kainborne employed Zarkoffa. "Yes, also summon the monk."

When the guards dragged the boy into the study in manacles and a loincloth, looking at the swelling on the lad's face and bruises about his body, it took every bit of control Kainborne had to not start screaming. Two guards stood on either side of the boy, restraining him by his elbows, one applying enough pressure to make the lad grimace.

Two monks followed them into the room, one a scrawny little fellow with a couple lines of scabrous welts across his face, the other a big man with a patch over his eye. Kainborne had seen the two before and it took a moment to recall their names: Markus and Obregon.

Kainborne growled at the two guards, "You two can leave."

One of them opened his mouth to say something, but Kainborne cut him off. "If you don't leave now—" He nodded to Zarkoffa. "—I'll have him remove you."

The two guards left the room. The boy remained standing in a crouch, swaying and unsteady on his feet. Kainborne focused on the two monks. "Who'd he try to kill?"

Markus stepped forward. "Me."

That didn't surprise Kainborne. "Why?"

Markus grimaced. "No reason, just went berserk."

The larger monk spoke. "Perhaps it was the switching you gave him. And he didn't try to kill anyone, just defended himself and the girl. Maybe lost control a bit."

Markus stiffened and turned on Obregon. "You weren't there."

"Yah," Obregon said, "but I know the boy. And I know you."

Zarkoffa lifted his boots off the chair and stood. He crossed the room, and as he passed the two monks, the larger one stepped to one side, as if he didn't want the man at his back. The assassin stopped at the boy and looked him over, then turned to Markus. "Boy's grown a lot, outweighs you by a couple of stone. Seems to me if he wanted to kill you, you wouldn't be standing here with us."

Markus snarled, "The guards stopped him before he could."

Zarkoffa grinned. "Yah, and you with not a mark on you, except maybe some welts on your ugly face."

The assassin turned back to the boy, put a finger beneath his chin, and forced him to look up. One eye remained swollen shut, and on the left side of his mouth both his upper and lower lip had puffed out considerably. Zarkoffa released the boy's chin, and stepped around behind him to examine his back. "Where'd he get these scars?"

Markus raised his chin proudly. "The boy can be quite recalcitrant, and occasionally needs a good switching to keep him in line."

"A switching?" Zarkoffa asked. "Looks more like you horse-whipped him. And some of these scars are old and healed over."

Kainborne had heard one thing they had yet to address. He aimed his question at Obregon. "You said defended himself and . . . the girl. What girl?"

Markus snarled, "The little trollop and the boy were rutting like cattle."

Obregon rolled his eyes. "I don't think either of them yet know how to rut."

That added another dimension to the story, but it didn't really matter. While carnal pleasures were not to Kainborne's taste, he couldn't fault the boy if he had the same unclean urges as other men. But if the lad got the girl with child, that would be a problem. And while Markus clearly had trouble restraining himself when punishing the boy, the lad had fought back. More importantly, he had reached an age when young men often showed the first signs of independence. Kainborne needed to quash that before it got out of hand.

During Kainborne's ruminations, the argument between Obregon and Markus grew quite heated, with Zarkoffa egging Markus on. "Enough," Kainborne shouted, and the room went silent.

"I need an animal," he said, "alive, healthy, and captive."

That produced a few curious looks.

Benedictus spoke haltingly. "We have some cattle and sheep, probably can get a goat or two from one of the steadings in the valley. And there's a dog or two about."

Kainborne shook his head. "No, too big, and not the right kind. Something I can keep in a small cage."

Markus said, "Maybe we have a rabbit in the kitchen they haven't slaughtered yet."

"No," Kainborne said. For what he wanted to do, the animal needed to be an aggressor, a predator, but he wasn't about to tell them that. "That won't work."

"Brother Pontifus," Obregon said. "He keeps hawks and falcons."

Benedictus added, "Or maybe a cat. There's a couple of strays about."

Either would work nicely, but he needed to keep the animal caged, which might prove impossible with a cat. A bird of prey would be ideal in so many ways, but Kainborne didn't like the connection to the boy's name. Though, when further discussion yielded no other possibilities, he put his concerns aside. A hawk it would be.

"Someone get me a hawk," he said, standing. "And tell this Brother What's-His-Name I need a feather plucked from the bird as well, freshly plucked, not something he picked up off the floor. Tomorrow I'll have a talk with the boy and you won't have any difficulty with him after that."

There were limits to what he intended to do, and Markus's continued torment of the boy could disrupt everything. He addressed his next words to the big monk. "Obregon, from now on you're in charge of the boy, no one else. Now, all of you, leave, except for the boy. And Obregon, you wait for him out in the hall."

One by one they filed out of the room, though Obregon glanced over his shoulder with a distrustful look. Once the door closed, Kainborne approached the boy. The lad stood leaning against a wall and appeared to be only partially conscious of his surroundings, which was ideal. Kainborne approached the boy and said, "Turn around. I want to see what he did to your back."

With the manacles impeding him, the boy shuffled as he turned. Kainborne didn't really care about the scars on the boy's back, but it was a good excuse to get him in a position where he couldn't see what Kainborne did. He retrieved a small sharp knife from his robes, and separated a lock of hair from the mop atop the lad's head. He only needed a few of the longer strands, so he traced the hairs to the boy's scalp, saying, "I need to brush your hair out of the way so I can see the back of your neck as well."

With a quick jerk of the knife, he cut a few strands of hair.

"Yes," he said. "Nothing I can do about those scars."

He folded the strands of hair into a small piece of paper and hid it in his robes.

Benedictus had assigned Kainborne the same room he'd occupied during his previous visits. It was one of the few rooms with a lock, which Kainborne required. On the room's bed, Zarkoffa had placed the small strongbox of tinctures along with the rest of Kainborne's luggage. While he sorted through it, Brother Pontifus arrived with a caged hawk and a plucked feather. Kainborne examined the feather carefully, and saw a hint of blood on the tip of its quill, which confirmed its freshness.

Brother Pontifus tried to give Kainborne instructions on caring for the bird, but Kainborne cut him off. "Find my man Zarkoffa and tell him what to do to keep the bird healthy during our ride back to Dramoran. After that, Duke Jarrod has a falconer who is more than capable of caring for the animal."

He dismissed the monk, who walked away muttering unhappily.

Kainborne locked the door to his room, a spartan cell not unlike those occupied by the monks. It contained a bed, plus a small writing table and chair. He placed the feather on the table. In his traveling gear he carried a sewing kit for making repairs. From it he selected a needle and placed it next to the feather. One of Duke Jarrod's distant ancestors had built the monastery about four hundred years earlier. He climbed up onto the bed, and from an exposed beam, using a knife he pried loose a small sliver of wood. He placed it on the table with the needle and feather.

He needed the boy seated in the chair facing north, his back to the south. To accomplish that he pulled the table out into the middle of the room, then repositioned the chair. He sat down at the table, retrieved the piece of paper from his robes, and unfolded it. From the three hairs it contained, he selected the longest, then carefully tied it into a loose witch's knot about twice the size of the tip of his thumb. He inserted the wood splinter into the witch's knot on the east side, then inserted the needle from the opposite direction on the west side; old wood and iron, to isolate or join. He inserted the quill of the feather into the north side of the knot, where the bird would be. The boy would sit on the south side, completing the sorcerer's compass. The splinter and the needle, east and west, would both isolate and join the hawk and the boy, north and south.

From his robes, he retrieved the key to the strongbox of tinctures, and opened it. He selected a special vial containing a silver-gray liquid, a powerful hallucinogen, then sat back and examined his work. He was ready for the boy.

# 22

# The Hawk

THE SWELLING HAD receded nicely. Ket could now open both eyes without difficulty and speak with no funny sounds coming out. And it was a relief to be rid of the manacles, and to wear his homespun shirt and pants along with simple boots. After a decent night's sleep on his pallet, Obregon told him to report to Kainborne's room.

Ket made his way there, knocked on the door, and heard a voice shout, "Enter."

He opened the door but stopped halfway through it. In the middle of the room Kainborne sat at a small table. A caged hawk on the table's surface looked Ket's way. The bird had a brownish head and back, rust sides, and an almost white breast. Kainborne pointed to a chair next to him. "Come in, close the door, and sit down."

Ket closed the door, crossed the room, then pulled the chair away from the table far enough to be well outside the man's reach. He sat down, and saw a feather on the table in front of him.

Kainborne waved him on impatiently. "Pull up close to the table and sit facing the hawk."

Ket gripped the chair and edged it forward, noticed that the feather appeared to be entangled with a splinter of wood and something shiny, perhaps a needle. A strand of what looked like hair tied the feather, wood and needle into a strange cross. Ket recalled a faint sting the previous day as Kainborne had brushed his hair aside to look at his neck. At the time he had assumed a few strands had snagged in a finger ring or something. But a quick glance at the man's hands revealed he wore no rings or jewelry, nothing on his wrists either. Ket thought it quite possible one of his hairs had been used to tie the splinter, needle, and feather.

Kainborne lifted a goblet off the table and extended it to Ket. "Drink this."

Ket shrugged and tried to sound respectful. "I'm not thirsty, good sir."

Kainborne's voice hardened. "Drink it, I said."

Ket hesitated, knowing he had no reason to trust this man.

Kainborne's eyes flashed with anger. "Drink it or I'll have Brother Markus come here and switch you until you do."

Ket reached out and accepted the goblet from the man's hands, lifted it to his lips and sipped. It tasted like good wine, the kind of wine they'd never serve a half-Scairn boy.

"Not just a sip, drink it all."

Thinking of Markus and his switch, Ket downed the wine, then placed the goblet on the table. Kainborne picked it up, looked into it, and nodded his approval.

"Now," Kainborne said, "look into the hawk's eyes."

Ket looked at the hawk, but the bird didn't seem much interested in him. He glanced at Kainborne, and the man said, "Look at the hawk's eyes and don't look away until I give you permission."

Again, Ket looked at the hawk and sat there for several minutes, waiting, not knowing what to expect. What did this strange man want of him?

The hawk reminded him of his dream, of soaring through the air with a freedom his kind would never know. While awake he felt sorry for the rabbit, but in the dream the kill had thrilled him. He recalled that dream with great pleasure, and at that moment, the eyes of the hawk in front of him seemed unusually large, and once again he soared through the heavens on powerful wings.

He caught a thermal, dipped his right wing to stay in the rising column of air, used it to climb even higher with no effort on his part. Joy filled his heart, for once again he was free.

• • • •

Kainborne watched the boy fidget as he stared at the hawk. The powerful hallucinogen he'd given the lad would take time to show any effects, and during that time he kept the boy focused on the bird. The boy sat there staring at the hawk, never looking away from it for fear of Kainborne's wrath, the animal ignoring him.

Kainborne almost drifted off to sleep, but when the boy suddenly stopped fidgeting, the time had come. The boy's jaw slowly dropped, and his mouth opened as if in awe of something. He sat deathly still, his eyes unblinking, clearly seeing something Kainborne could not. He knew the enchantment had taken effect when the hawk also froze and sat as unmoving as the boy, the two of them staring at one another.

Kainborne stood and walked around the table, moving slowly while looking at the boy and hawk from all angles. As he circled them, they took no notice of him, but stared at each other like statues frozen in time. When he completed the circuit, he again sat down to wait.

He had never used this enchantment before and did not know how long it might take. If it worked, it would bind the boy's spirit with that of the hawk. The bird would inherit any aggressiveness in the boy, leaving him quite malleable. It would also mute any carnal desire in the lad, so Kainborne need not worry that a young peasant girl might find herself with child, at least not one fathered by the boy.

Kainborne had other charms that were even more effective, but they'd leave the boy dangerously complacent. If he employed one of those the lad would not fear death, not avoid danger, not even defend himself if the need arose. And if left in place too long, such a charm would likely cause his death, even if only indirectly. Kainborne needed an enchantment he could leave in place for years, something that would produce subtle effects without endangering the lad.

Some instinct drew Kainborne's eyes to the charm on the table in front of the boy. A thin trail of smoke rose upward from the feather, but after a few seconds it split into two tracks. One rose toward the boy's face and entered his nostrils, while the other climbed toward the hawk's face and entered its nostrils. The grimoire Kainborne had consulted for the spell had mentioned nothing of that. But Kainborne had modified the spell to suit his own purposes, so the unexpected shouldn't surprise him. When the talisman he had constructed stopped emitting the trails of smoke, no sign of the feather remained. With a dreamy look on his face, the boy crossed his arms on the table in front of him, then leaned forward and rested his head on top of them. He appeared to slip into a state of quiet slumber.

Kainborne thought it best to let the boy sleep and awake on his own, but he didn't have long to wait. After some minutes, the lad lifted his head and slowly looked around the room in a confused daze. He froze when he saw Kainborne, his eyes blinking rapidly.

If the enchantment had failed, Kainborne would kill the bird to ensure no vestiges of it remained, then think of something else. He took care to not appear menacing. "What did you see?"

The tincture Kainborne had given the boy was extremely powerful, and would still affect his perceptions. It also induced a willingness to answer questions without dissembling.

"I flew," the boy said, "like a hawk. I killed a rabbit and ate it."

The melding of the boy's spirit with that of the bird had worked. All aggressiveness in the boy's nature would now transfer to the hawk, and he'd be docile and obedient.

Kainborne stood. "Good, you may go."

The boy stared at him dumbly, then stood and walked out of the room on unsteady legs.

The next morning, with Zarkoffa on his heels, Kainborne stepped into Benedictus's study. Brother's Markus and Obregon stood to one side, with Benedictus seated behind his ornate desk. As Kainborne entered the room, the abbot stood and gave him an ingratiating smile. "Master Kainborne, a pleasant morning to you, good sir. I hope your conversation with the young man went well."

Kainborne sat down in the chair he always occupied. "Quite well."

Zarkoffa again sat down and rested his boots on the seat of another chair.

Benedictus stepped out from behind his desk. "So we'll have no further difficulties with the boy?"

When Zarkoffa spoke, his words echoed Kainborne's thoughts. "Seems to me the only problem you had with the boy came about because you horse-whipped him."

Markus opened his mouth to speak, but Benedictus gave him a hard look and he held his tongue. Benedictus grimaced. "No one actually horse-whipped the boy. He was disobedient, and Brother Markus saw fit—"

Zarkoffa interrupted him. "Put scars on my back like that, and I just might kill someone."

Before the abbot replied, Kainborne intervened, looking at Markus as he spoke. "I don't care what you call it, the scars on the boy's back tell me you punished him with far too much vigor." Kainborne didn't care one whit for the boy, but he needed him safely squirreled away where no one of importance would ever pay the least bit of attention to him. It was now clear that abusing him would probably spur him to rebel, and that might take any number of unpredictable forms.

He addressed his next words to the abbot. "You'll have no trouble with the boy. I had a long talk with him and he'll be quite cooperative." There were limits to the enchantment, and they needed to be aware of them. "Though, I should add that while he will be docile under most circumstances, if pushed to an extreme, he will defend himself. So if Brother Markus's enthusiasm for the switch gets him killed, I don't want to hear about it."

Brother Markus's eyes flashed with indignation.

Kainborne stood. "We'll be leaving on the morrow."

Zarkoffa stood, crossed the room to Markus and loomed over the little monk. "And then there's the matter of the girl. When I come back, if I find you've mistreated her in any way, I'll be very unhappy."

The little monk's eyes widened and his indignation turned to stark fear.

Kainborne walked out of the room and Zarkoffa followed. Out in the hall, when Zarkoffa closed the door and they were alone, Kainborne asked, "What care you for the girl?"

The assassin shrugged. "Nothing. I just don't like that little shit of a monk Markus. If you ever want him dead, I'll do it for free."

"What if I want Obregon dead?"

Zarkoffa wrinkled his nose with distaste. "That'll cost you."

"Why Obregon and not Markus?"

Zarkoffa grinned. "Markus I can gut while looking him in the eyes. Obregon I gotta sneak up on from behind, real careful like. And I gotta finish him quick. He'll cost you a pretty penny."

• • • •

"What did that man do to you?"

That morning Obregon had focused the lesson on numbers, and his question perplexed Ket. "What man?"

The big monk frowned. "Kainborne, when you met with him alone, two months ago. What did he do?"

Ket tried to resurrect his memories of that meeting, and recalled only a confused kaleidoscope of images centered on the hawk. "He made me stare at a hawk."

"Ah!" Obregon said. "The hawk. Made you stare at it. What else did he do?"

Ket shook his head. "Nothing, just that. Made me stare at the hawk." Ket had some memories of soaring through the skies and killing a rabbit, but that couldn't be. And since Kainborne's visit, Ket's only dreams now were of the hawk, and he loved those dreams. The hawk loved it too, because it didn't get to fly except in Ket's dreams.

"He did something to you," Obregon said. "You ain't the same."

Ket spent the afternoon mucking out the stables, and while busy at that Peta came by carrying her bucket of water. "Would you like a drink of water?"

Ket accepted the cup of water, downed it in a few gulps, and handed it back to the girl. "Thank you, Peta."

He noticed that the topmost laces on the front of her shift remained untied, exposing soft skin. She saw him looking at her chest, gave him that shy smile, and he thought he should do something in return, but he couldn't think what.

Holding the bucket in her left hand, Peta planted her right fist on her hip. "Are you mad at me, Ket?"

"Mad?" Ket asked. "Why would I be mad at you?"

She wrinkled her nose. "You don't notice me anymore. It's like I ain't there unless I shout in yer ear."

That confused him, because something in him told him she had the right of it. "I'm acting different?"

She frowned. "I don't know. But you ain't the same. You ain't yerself."

Ket didn't know what to say to that. While he stood there trying to think of something, she turned on her heel and walked away, the water in her bucket sloshing from side to side. In the past, he had enjoyed watching her hips sway as she walked away from him, but he didn't care about that anymore.

Ket mucked out the stalls, then climbed up into the hayloft to retrieve a bale of hay. He came across his special little stash. He had to think carefully to recall that he had hoped it would help him stay alive when he left the monastery. The hawk wanted him to take it and go, and keep going until he left the entire valley. But that seemed like a lot of trouble, and they'd probably catch him and bring him back anyway, just as they had before. Ket retrieved the bale of hay and returned to his chores.

As the months passed, Peta grew distant, and the following summer married a farmer with a steading near the south end of the valley. Ket never saw her again.

Kainborne came the next year, and the year after that, though he spent less time with Ket each visit. But he seemed satisfied and less angry. Ket grew a few more inches and towered over Markus, though he still looked up a little to meet Obregon's eyes. As Ket's nineteenth birthday approached, he wondered if Kainborne would come again that year.

• • • •

*The Dreadmark is a demanding mistress. She is arduous, conniving, and deceitful, a duplicitous vixen of cunning deception. Strife is her lover, dissension her child, war her heritage. She need not deceive you, for she will entice you in subtle and beguiling ways, and you will deceive yourself. And when you believe you are most clever, when you think you have prevailed, it is then that you should look to your back for the veiled blade. Beware, man of mortal flesh, for she has no heart or soul. When you think to lead or cajole the Dreadmark, she leads you. When you think to benefit from the Dreadmark, you will follow the trail of your own foolishness, and it will lead you to oblivion.*

*Haptimus ahm Tarnasus*
*in the years of the Awakening*

*When I first read Haptimus ahm Tarnasus, I thought him a madman. But now I wonder if there isn't always some truth even in the ravings of a twisted mind. In the years immediately after Domaxus's passing, the seeming madness of my dear friend's ravings blinded me. I knew nothing of the Dreadmark then, but have learned much since, and I've come to understand that he saw what none of us could: a mark on his arm that I now know had been a portent heralding devastation and destruction. The curse of the Dreadmark made our world conform to its needs. I truly believe that now. It tempted, cajoled, and enticed those who thought to manipulate it. The witch who spawned the mark was a brilliant genius of corrupt intent, and even from the grave she tempts those who think to gain from the mark. She lures them to suckle at her breast, but all they gain is the vile, poisonous milk of their undoing.*

*Claudius ahm Carthagen* neh *Modain*
*penned some years after the Withering Wars*

Many in Carthagen knew an authentic scroll dating back to the time of the Withering Wars could always tempt Aurelius. Merchants were quick to seek him out if they uncovered something that might bring a profit, though they thought it nothing more than a rich man's keen interest in history, a mere hobby. Aurelius encouraged that fiction, because as long as they believed his accumulation of scrolls just an expensive diversion, no one—most importantly Divonia—took his collection seriously. He feared the day she might learn that some of those scrolls contained valuable and dangerous information.

A merchant had recently uncovered a small trove of scrolls in the ruins of an abandoned military outpost near the border with the Mountain Kingdom. It was close to Modain, the small village reputed to be Domaxus's birthplace, though no one had confirmed that. The nearness to Modain, and a few scrolls with handwriting that matched that of others penned by Claudius, testified to their authenticity. And one of those contained the first reputable reference to the Dreadmark that Aurelius had found.

In all his scrolls, Aurelius had come across only a few cryptic references to the Dreadmark, and discounted them as nothing more than superstitious drivel. But he had several scrolls penned by Claudius, who always wrote in a clear, concise, and thoughtful hand. And in that new scroll it sounded as if Claudius lent credence to the fearful Dreadmark. After reading that, Aurelius had gone through all his scrolls to find what few references to the Dreadmark did exist. And while some still appeared to be the ravings of madmen, when he considered the scroll penned by Claudius, they were all consistent. That bothered Aurelius.

Claudius firmly believed that the Dreadmark manipulated the world around it. Apparently, it influenced people and events in subtle ways. A powerful man might see something unusual in a child's birthmark, irrevocably changing the child's path through life. A guardsman might fall ill one evening, and through inattention allow an assassin to pass unchallenged. Claudius referenced several scrolls he had possessed three hundred years ago. But Aurelius had yet to find any of them, though he dearly wished he might. And then there was that reference to some sort of evil witch or sorceress. Aurelius recalled the scroll he'd translated, and its reference to the myth of the Scairn witch, and the Lowlands sorcerer. He now regretted burning the paper on which he'd scribbled the translation. He wanted to compare it with this new information, but to do that he'd have to translate it all over again, a task that would take hours he didn't have.

In Aurelius's time no one really believed in magic or sorcery, but apparently those of Claudius's time had; or perhaps they hadn't, but Claudius had come across some evidence to change his mind. Claudius was a man of thoughtful and sound reason, and it bothered Aurelius that he might give credence to such superstitious nonsense.

His thoughts turned to the recent skirmishes with Tarnasus. Since that first incident between the two centurions, four more had occurred. He had now confirmed several reports of clashes between Duchies soldiers and the Mythrians, both situations escalating almost daily. And Tarnasus and Andopolous clashed regularly, as did Carthagen and the Duchies. It was almost as if the Dreadmark did exist, as if it were a real thing now manifest somewhere in the domain of the Three Realms. An ancient portent manipulating them with malign and calculating intent would be a convenient excuse. Unfortunately, reality had more to do with stupid men doing stupid things. Thankfully, if such a thing as the Dreadmark had existed in the past, it didn't exist now, and he needn't lose sleep over it. He rolled up the scroll and hid it among others of less importance.

# 23

# Abduction

"JUST TWO HORSES today, boy."

Hefting the heavy saddle, Ket paused, surprised that only two guardsmen had come to the stables. "Just two?"

"Aye," one of them said. "The others ate something bad, and they got the trots."

His friend laughed. "Yah, they don't know which end to aim at the bucket. So it's just the two of us today."

"But it's rent day," Ket said. "Isn't that dangerous?"

The first one shook his head. "Nah. It's been rent day every six months for years, and ain't no one stupid enough to rob from the duke."

There seemed to be something wrong with that logic, but Ket couldn't fathom what.

Ket saddled the horses, and while doing so recalled his dreams of soaring high above the fields below. Sometimes he hunted and caught a rabbit, squirrel, or mouse. Sometimes he simply floated on a thermal, relishing the freedom of the heights with joy that filled his heart to bursting. The hawk loved it even more than Ket.

He finished saddling the two horses, carefully hitched two draft-horses to the wagon, and attached a lead-rope to the halter of one. Then he led them out of the stables, with the two soldiers following on their horses. When Brother Sylander joined them he grunted and sighed wearily as he climbed up into the open bed of the wagon. The guards nudged their horses into a walk, and Ket followed them through the gates of the monastery.

Ket thought *rent day* had been improperly named since it actually took three or four days. The farmers and stead-holders paid some coin, but they also paid in salt, pepper, firewood, eggs, ale, wine, grain, eels, fish, woven cloth—basically anything that might be of value to the monks and the duke. In late fall Ket and Sylander collected rents going down the south end of the valley. But with summer coming they headed up-valley, working their way north, stopping at three or four steadings each day. Sylander followed a well-established schedule, and the first night out they stayed at an inn in a large village on Lake Shielnagh. Sylander got a bed in the back of the inn and a hearty meal. Ket got a blanket on the floor near the common-room hearth, and scraps from the kitchen.

The next morning they worked their way further north, turned around about noon, and took a different route back. They spent the second night in the barn of one of the larger steadings.

On the third day out they rose with the sun, and slowly worked their way back toward the monastery. Near noon, they stopped at a small farm. While Sylander spoke with the farmer and recorded his payment in a ledger, the two guardsmen stood to one side talking quietly. As Ket hefted a sack of salt onto the bed of the wagon, he overheard one say, "You see 'em too?"

"Yah," his companion said. "Two of 'em. Rough looking assholes."

"Think they'll get brave?"

"Maybe. We best be careful, but we can handle 'em." To emphasize the point, he adjusted the position of the heavy sword buckled to his side.

Ket struggled with a small cask of ale, thinking their words should alarm him, but for a couple years now nothing had bothered him. The hawk didn't like that, and thought he should be more concerned.

The farmer also had a rack of split firewood for them. When Ket finished loading it onto the wagon, Sylander climbed onto the back of it, Ket took up the lead-rope, and led the horses and wagon out onto the valley road. The two guardsmen seemed a little tense as they headed down the road toward the monastery. They had about a two-league walk, with three more farms to visit, which would get them there just before dusk. At that point, the goods in the wagon towered over Ket, and to keep them from tumbling out he'd cinched them in place with ropes. Ket hoped Sylander would allow him to park the wagon in the stable, get dinner, and unload it in the morning. The hawk thought he should pay more attention to the road, but Ket didn't understand why.

They passed through a heavily wooded section of the valley near the river, and as they rounded a sharp bend in the road, two riders sat on horses blocking their way. Both guardsmen brought their horses to a halt and drew their swords. Ket brought the wagon to a stop behind them.

One of the guards said, "We're on the duke's business. Move aside."

One of the riders blocking the road nudged his horse forward a few paces. His bald head glistened in the sunlight, completely smooth without a hint of hair. Some sort of jewelry glinted in each of his ears, and a ring in his nose reflected the rays of the sun.

"Well now," he said in a thick accent. He stood up in his stirrups and craned his neck. "Is that a cask of ale I see in that wagon? It's been a hot, dry day, and I fancy a cup of that ale to quench me thirst."

The same guard who'd spoken before said, "The ale is the property of the Duke of Dramoran, and if you don't move aside, the only thing you'll taste is the point of me sword."

Ket sensed the hawk tense, and it wanted him to be ready for a fight, but he didn't know how to fight. The hawk didn't like his doubt and uncertainty.

The bald man grimaced. "Ahhh, it's gonna be the hard way, is it?"

The guardsman pointed his sword at the man. "Your choice."

The bald man shook his head sadly, raised his fingers to his lips, and emitted a sharp, piercing whistle.

Ket heard a hiss and a loud thud. One guardsman cried out, an arrow buried in his back. Another hiss, and an arrow punched through the neck of his companion. Both guardsmen tumbled from their saddles as one of the draft horses whinnied and reared. Ket turned and focused on the horse, using all his skills to calm it. He spotted Brother Sylander in the distance, running as if a blood-sucking demon were on his heels, his robes fluttering behind him. The monk disappeared into the surrounding forest, and only then did Ket hear the hawk shouting at him to run for his life.

He spun about, ready to abandon the horses and wagon, but a bowman stood not three paces from him, arrow nocked and drawn. The man shouted, "Do I kill him, Fallon?"

Ket dare not look away, but the bald man eased his horse forward into his narrowed range of vision. "No, just don't let him get away." He stood up in his stirrups and shouted at someone else. "Termik, find that monk and slit his throat."

The bowman relaxed his pull on the bow, but didn't un-nock the arrow or lower it. "Don't try to run, boy. I can drop you at a hundred paces."

Fallon dismounted, walked up to Ket, looked him up and down, and grinned. "Healthy young lad."

They tied Ket's hands behind his back, hobbled his ankles, blindfolded him, and threw him into the back of the wagon. It creaked, groaned, and clanked as they carried him and their loot away. He heard them talking, but only a word or two here and there, and none of it made sense.

When they came to a stop, they dragged him out of the wagon, removed his blindfold, and tied him to a tree. The four bandits spent about an hour ransacking the wagon, and they found several dozen eggs among the loot. They used firewood from the wagon to start a healthy fire, then cooked the eggs and ate their fill, washing them down with the ale. When they realized they had too many eggs, Fallon pointed his cup of ale at Ket. "We can't take eggs with us, so let the lad have some,"

Like the bandits, Ket ate his fill. They had never given him eggs at the monastery, and he thought it the best meal he'd ever eaten.

Apparently, the two bowmen didn't have mounts of their own, but with the acquisition of the two guardsmen's horses they now had saddled mounts. From their talk Ket learned Termik hadn't found Sylander in the forest, so the monk would live another day.

It was Termik who asked Fallon, "What you gonna do with the boy?"

Fallon rubbed his bald head and regarded Ket for a moment. "I hear Tarnasus has called in all their levies, but they ain't enough. They need more fighting men, and are paying good coin for volunteers. I think the lad here, he wants to be a big hero, don't you, boy? I think he wants to volunteer. And he needs us to get him to Tarnasus's bailiffs so he can. Let's be kind and do the boy a favor."

• • • •

The hawk didn't hunt at night; that was for owls. Ket perched on a branch waiting for dawn, his wings tucked tightly about him to conserve heat. Time had little meaning to him, though he recalled it had been important in another life.

The eyes that stared at him drew his attention and filled his view: amber eyes with vertically slit pupils, centered in an ancient face wrinkled beyond belief. Strange tattoos surrounded those eyes in an intricate pattern, then continued down the cheeks of an old woman's face.

"What are you?" she said. "When I look in your eyes I see Scairnessa. When I look in your soul I see Scairndraka. When I look in your heart I see a little boy damaged, wounded, and frightened. When I look in your spirit I see the raken, fierce, angry, and dangerous. What are you, strange boy? And why do you haunt my dreams?"

Ket didn't know how to answer the old woman's riddles. They confused him, frightened him, frustrated him, angered him. Or maybe the anger belonged to the hawk.

The woman's eyes dilated. "Ah, you are man-child, and yet you are not. You are Scairn-child, and yet you are not. You are fledgling hawk, and yet you are not. Are you the ket to our caerm, the raken to our lioness?"

The old woman disappeared and Ket saw a pretty Scairn girl with pale white skin, amber eyes, and vertically slit pupils. Dark hair surrounded her face, and he recalled seeing her somewhere before. He had a vague memory of her standing in a window high above him, watching him, while he played cat-and-mouse with a kitten.

"Yes!" the old woman said, her voice cracking with triumph, her wrinkled face reappearing. "She's seen you, has she? Was it in a dream like this? Or are you wandering the streets outside the palace right under my nose? Where can I find you, my little ket? Where are you hiding?"

A gruff voice interrupted them. "Wake up, boy."

Ket had trouble shrugging off the dream; couldn't recall most of it, just recalled that pretty girl's face, and that wrinkled, old face, and a string of unfathomable riddles. Somehow that old Scairn woman knew his name.

The bandits had been kind to him and bound his wrists in front of him before turning in for the night, allowing him to sleep in some comfort. He sat up and shook off the last remnants of the dream, though the hawk didn't want him to.

The bandits rekindled the fire. They cooked and ate more eggs, and again Ket truly enjoyed the meal. They bundled together a pack of supplies from the wagon and cinched it on the back of a draft horse. Then they put Ket bareback on the other draft horse, and tied his hands in front of him with a loop around the horse's neck. Ket now knew enough about horses to understand that if he fell, the loop meant the horse would drag him, trampling him beneath its hooves. Thankfully, Fallon and his men didn't seem in any great hurry and rode at a comfortable pace.

• • • •

Anyone who walked past the open door of Obregon's small cell would see him sitting at his desk apparently reading something. Hoping to calm his soul, he had adopted the habit of reading late each morning. That day he had selected an old book, a treasure from his past, hoping to lose himself in its familiar writings. But as the years had passed, he had found it more and more difficult to concentrate on the words in front of him. When he sat down to read, as so often happened, his crimes haunted him. His mind wandered to a past he would rather forget, a life filled with regret and shame, a life he had walked away from.

A high-pitched shout broke the stillness of the morning, startling him and pulling his thoughts back to the moment; probably just Markus upset with someone. The little shit always found something to be upset about. But then the shout came again, followed by several more shouts in a mixture of voices. It sounded like an argument far beyond any of Markus's petty squabbles.

Obregon sighed, closed the treasured book, and carefully returned it to the chest at the foot of his bed. He did not regret the interruption of those old memories.

He walked out of his cell and followed the shouts and noise to a small crowd gathered in the main courtyard just inside the monastery's gates. As he approached them he heard Benedictus shout, "What happened? Damn you, tell me."

Obregon recognized Sylander's voice as he whined, "Bandits. Yesterday. They killed the two guards, would have killed me if I hadn't escaped."

Obregon's size proved to be an advantage as he elbowed his way through the on-lookers to the center of the crowd. He found Benedictus standing over Sylander, the old rent-collector on his knees, weeping and sobbing like a child. "They were going to kill me, but I ran and hid. It was horrible. I suffered terribly while they hunted me. But I escaped. I escaped, even though I'm badly wounded."

Crawling through thick undergrowth had left scratches on his arms, legs, and face, with a trickle of blood here and there, but nothing serious.

Benedictus demanded, "What of the duke's rents?"

"They took it all," Sylander bawled. Another monk helped him climb to his feet. "They took everything, the horses, the wagon, everything."

Benedictus's eyes widened. He paled visibly, and threw his hands in the air as if pleading with some ancient god. "This will anger Kainborne. He'll be livid, might re-duce our endowments, could cut them off completely. We'll be destitute, we'll—"

Obregon interrupted him. "What of the boy?"

"Boy?" Benedictus demanded, spittle flying from his mouth. "What boy?"

Obregon aimed his question at Sylander. "Was Ket with you yesterday, leading the horses as usual?"

Sylander nodded his head frantically. "Yes. Yes. They took him away."

Benedictus shrieked and dropped to his knees. "We're ruined. Kainborne will be doubly angered."

Obregon stepped between him and Sylander, grabbed the older man by the front of his robes and pulled him close. "You say they took the boy away. You mean they took him alive?"

"I think so," Sylander said. "I think they tied him up and put him in the back of the wagon. But I'm not sure. I was hiding, had to hide in the forest all night long to make sure they didn't catch me. They hunted me through the entire night."

Obregon thought that unlikely. The bandits might make a cursory search, but they wouldn't stick around for long.

Now that Obregon had Sylander's attention, he forced the monk to describe the entire sequence of events. It sounded like the boy was still alive and a captive of the four bandits. Most of the rents Sylander had collected would be of little use to highwaymen, and the wagon would slow them down. Most likely they had traveled until sundown to put some distance between them and their crime, ransacked the wagon for what they could use, then moved on. But why take the boy? Why not just kill him?

Obregon left Benedictus and the other monks in the middle of the courtyard. As he walked away he heard them putting together a story for Kainborne, one that would absolve them of any negligence in the matter. It involved Ket betraying them to his secret friends the bandits. They returned the favor by helping him escape, with the boy and his bandit friends richer because of the duke's stolen rents. Benedictus intended to have the message sent immediately by messenger to Kainborne at Dramoran.

Obregon returned to his cell and opened the chest at the foot of his bed. To a cursory glance it contained a spare robe and other clothing, all threadbare and time worn. But the items on top hid old memories.

He lifted the tatty clothing in a single large bundle and tossed it on the bed. He retrieved two books to get them out of the way and carefully placed them on the small desk. That exposed several objects his fellow monks would not expect him to possess.

He removed his robes and tossed them aside, stripping down to the breeches and blouse he wore beneath them. From the chest he retrieved and donned a boiled leather cuirass with chest and back plates, and stiff leather shoulder harnesses. To his surprise, he had actually lost some weight during the intervening years, and he fit into it easily. Then he buckled matching boiled-leather bracers onto his arms, greaves on his lower legs, and a war skirt of leather plates around his waist. Last, and perhaps most important of all, he lifted an old sword harness out of the chest. He buckled the belt around his waist, felt the comforting weight of the gladius on his right hip, and a heavy trench knife on his left.

He slid the gladius out of the sheath and examined it. Scratched and pitted, its edges chipped from years of use; it could still take off a man's head if needed. He sighed. "You and me, old friend, it's been a long time."

He glanced down at the armor he'd donned. It bore no badges of rank, no symbols of status, was in fact cut and marked in many places. No one would mistake him for anything but a common hire-sword, and that was as it should be.

He sheathed the sword and marched out of his cell. He'd acquire gauntlets and any other items he needed as he traveled. A small cache of silver and copper coins should last him for several months. If he didn't find the boy in that time, it wouldn't matter.

In the kitchens he prepared a small bundle of food that would get him through the next few days, then made his way to the stables. He saddled the remaining guardsman's horse, stowed his meager provisions in its saddlebags, and added to that some oats for the horse. Then he mounted up and guided the animal out into the monastery's main courtyard. Benedictus and the other monks were too busy hatching their story to take notice of him, but had they looked his way, he doubted they would have recognized him. He rode out through the open gates, but said no farewells to the monastery in the Vale of Tramorth.

# 24

# A Season for War

"BLAST IT ALL!" Macallan swore as he stormed into Kainborne's workshop. "I begin to think she is barren."

Kainborne stood and bowed, struggling to shift his thoughts away from the scroll he'd been reading. "Barren, Your Grace? I . . . I don't understand."

"My wife," the archduke shouted. "Another month and she's still not with child. And I've gone to her bed every night since the beginning of spring. She must be barren."

Kainborne spoke carefully. "But she bore Clarahm."

Macallan shook his head. "That was nineteen years ago. I tried to conceive a spare back then too, almost succeeded twice, but she lost both children, one early on and the other at birth. She is barren. I am certain of it."

Kainborne stepped around his desk and approached the man, hoping to turn his thoughts in a different direction. "Perhaps a little more time is required. After all, it has only been three months. Summer will soon be upon us, the weather is warming, and it appears there'll be war in the Lowland Kingdoms."

Macallan rubbed his chin in thought. "Yes, there will be opportunities there, but also danger. It's all well and good if the Lowland Kingdoms want to butcher each other, especially if they kill enough men to reduce the size of those blasted armies they've assembled. If it ends after a battle or two, we needn't worry. But if it continues through winter and into next year, it'll likely spill over into the Duchies. That's why I've decided to take your recommendation and call in the levies."

Kainborne took care to show no outward satisfaction at Macallan's decision. There would be considerable opportunity for him if war spread through the Three Realms. "It is a prudent decision, Your Grace, if only to be prepared for next spring."

"I agree," Macallan said. "And send messengers to Dramoran, Lagasdale, and Gathgorme. They should do likewise."

Kainborne nodded. "I'll see to it immediately, Your Grace."

Macallan sighed. "But what of my son? Clarahm is a weak invalid and I need a strong heir I can count on."

The archduke paused for a moment, his eyes widening as some thought struck him. He lowered his voice. "It occurs to me I could father a child on some whore, then tell everyone my wife bore the brat. I can make my wife keep her mouth shut about it, and we can pay off the whore. Or better yet, dispose of her."

Macallan's last words almost sounded like a question. It occurred to Kainborne he could enhance his standing with the archduke by offering to handle such an unpleasant task. But that would establish a clear link between murder and his use of tinctures, which might be a serious problem when he next needed to eliminate someone who proved to be troublesome or inconvenient. As Kainborne hesitated, trying to think of a way to shift the discussion away from murdering some whore, Clarahm limped into the room. The iron tip of his wooden peg-leg thudded on the floorboards. Kainborne and Macallan never discussed his quest for a spare in front of the boy.

"Father," Clarahm said. "What has upset you so?"

In the last year the boy's complexion had paled considerably, and he now looked sickly as well as weak, an unavoidable side effect of the tinctures.

"Nothing," Macallan said, clearly uncomfortable in the boy's presence. "Nothing you should worry about." He turned away from his son and walked out of the room.

Clarahm grimaced and looked at Kainborne. "I'm not stupid. He's trying to conceive an heir so he can replace the invalid."

That the boy confided in Kainborne stunned him no end, and only a fool would ignore such an opportunity. "No, not at all. Your injury simply reminded him that mischance is always possible, and should something befall you, the family must be prepared. It's his duty to produce more than one male child. He has a moral imperative to the duchy. Trust me, it is no more than that."

That calmed Clarahm a little. "Ever since I lost the leg I've been weak with the aches in my bones. I'll never fulfill his wish for a strong heir."

Kainborne tried to adopt an air of sympathy. "But you have a keen mind."

Clarahm shook his head. "What good is that?"

At that moment Kainborne realized the young man did not have a confidant. His father had abandoned that role, and the lad had no one who might guide him and soothe his fears. Kainborne found it easy to draw the boy out, and they spoke at some length, the boy's trust growing with each word.

Kainborne had intended to return to Dramoran shortly, but now he thought it best to remain at Inversill for the entire summer. Given enough time, he would become the boy's most trusted confidant. And that could prove to be of considerable advantage, even if that trust did nothing more than make it easier to kill the lad when the time came.

••••

Obregon easily found the site of Ket's abduction; the rotting corpses of the two dead guards lay in a ditch by the road.

He dismounted and examined them carefully. The arrow wounds were obvious, though the bandits had retrieved their arrows. They had also rifled through the bodies and stripped them of any valuables, though they had left the guards' swords behind. That didn't surprise Obregon; if a man had no training with a sword, he'd be a fool to pick up an unfamiliar weapon. The two swords were medium length, longer than his gladius, but shorter than a heavy broadsword. Obregon selected the better of the two and kept it.

He would have no trouble tracking the wagon, but once the outlaws abandoned it, he'd be tracking hoofprints, a difficult task at best. It helped that the bandits had taken the two guards' horses, which Dramoran's master blacksmith had shod. Obregon examined the hoofprints on the road and determined he could distinguish the better quality of the steel shoes on Duke Jarrod's horses. And of the bandits' two horses, one was unshod, and the other had a broken steel shoe that left a distinct print in the road's dirt. That would help considerably.

He left the two bodies in the ditch where they lay, and followed the ruts left by the wagon's wheels. Late that afternoon he found the abandoned wagon and the site where they spent the night.

Deep inside he feared the bandits abducted Ket for no other reason than to enjoy some sort of cruel sport with him before killing him. To his great relief, he didn't find the boy's body, and saw no sign of bloodshed or mistreatment. That didn't mean they wouldn't kill him at a later time, but at least the boy had survived thus far. And the bandits had spent the night there, which meant they didn't fear serious pursuit.

Obregon had learned long ago that a man tracking hoofprints only moved at about half the pace of his quarry, as long as they felt no need to hurry. And if they did fear pursuit and traveled in haste, he'd fall even further behind.

He scavenged through the abandoned goods from the wagon, took what might be of use and put together a meal. Then he lit a fire and settled in for the night. He planned to arise in the twilight before dawn, and be on the trail as soon as he had enough light to track his prey. He'd have to be patient and hope for the best.

••••

With Ket in tow the bandits followed the river. They climbed northeast into the mountains, their intended destination some place called the Tri-Corner. Ket had never seen real mountains before, and as they traveled he marveled at the snow-covered peaks that emerged from the mists to the north. After three days of travel, massive spires of rock dominated the horizon, with snow dusting their heights.

They stopped at a place where two smaller rivers trickled down out of the mountains. The smaller rivers converged to form the larger river that meandered through the Vale of Tramorth. Stone bridges crossed each of the two rivers just upstream from their point of convergence.

Fallon paused, looked at Ket, and pointed east. "The Tri-Corner. We cross them two bridges, one after the other, and we'll be in the Lowland Kingdoms. No hangman waiting for us there."

The bowman Termik added, "That's because we ain't robbed nobody there."

Fallon grinned. "Least wise not yet."

They crossed the first of the bridges and traversed a strip of land toward the next. Ket asked, "They call this the Tri-Corner because the rivers meet here?"

Fallon shook his head and halted his horse. "No, this is the only place where all three realms meet." He craned his neck to look forward, then looked over his shoulder behind them. "This looks like halfway between them two bridges."

He gave Ket a superior look, the way Markus did when launching into a lecture. "The Three Realms, boy, they're like three wedges in a pie, and they all meet right here at the pie's center, the Tri-Corner."

He pointed north. "You got your Mountain Kingdom to the north. Them cat-eyed Scairn all think alike and stick together. And while their women are pretty and sweet, you cross 'em and they'll put a blade in yer gut just as quick as any man. And come winter, it's colder'n a witch's tit up there."

He pointed southeast. "And you got your Lowlands to the southeast: three city-states that rule all the smaller cities and villages. They'll cut each other's throats, but when it comes to an outsider, they band together like nothing you ain't never seen. And it's always warm there, only gets a little cold in winter, though if you got a pack of them constables after you, it can get real hot."

He pointed southwest. "And you got your Duchies to the southwest, which is easy pickins because each duchy is real independent and they ain't organized like them damn constables in the Lowlands. That's their weakness. But they never war among themselves; that's their strength."

"Hey Fallon," one of his bowmen said. "You forgot the Hinterlands."

"Oh yah," the bandit said. He pointed southwest again. "Beyond the Duchies you got the Hinterlands. Ventured there once, though didn't go far. Strange people!

Apparently they got cities and royals and all that stuff. And most of their royals got brown skin, some so dark they're almost black. But you don't never see them here because they stay away from us."

That piqued Ket's curiosity. "I saw a brown-skinned man once. He passed through the valley."

Fallon nodded. "Yah, his parents was probably poor folk from the Hinterlands. You know what *they* call the Three Realms?" He paused for dramatic effect. "They call us the Dreadlands. Don't ask me why, but that's what they call us."

Fallon's eyes brightened and he grinned. He dismounted, faced due north, spread his feet, and planted his fists on his hips. "Me left foot's in the Duchies, me right foot's in the Lowlands, and me dick's in the Mountain Kingdom. I'm in all three realms all at once. That means I'm a real Tri-Corner man."

"You know," Termik said. "With yer dick in the Mountain Kingdom, maybe that means you're gonna put your dick in one of them pretty mountain wenches."

Fallon's grin broadened and he nodded. "I never had me one of them Scairn women before, but I think me dick's a'callin." He hopped forward as if being pulled by his crotch. "Whoa! See what I mean? Soon as we drops off the lad, let's go a'lookin."

With all four bandits laughing, Fallon mounted up, and they continued on.

• • • •

With Councilor Janus and Senator Lucius waiting for him in the Blue Drawing Room, Aurelius loitered in the hallway, anxiously awaiting Brunasus. When the Captain of the Palace Guard finally rounded a corner at the far end of the corridor, to Aurelius's relief Tribune Denian accompanied him. The two men stopped a pace in front of Aurelius and saluted him.

Aurelius shook his head. "Put aside the formalities. Did you get confirmation?"

Denian nodded. "I saw it with my own eyes."

Six days ago, Aurelius and Brunasus had tasked Denian with clarifying the many rumors coming out of Tarnasus and Andopolous. They gave him command of a small group of scouts, and he and his men had traveled east, wearing civilian clothing that bore no insignia of rank or allegiance.

Aurelius aimed his question at Brunasus. "You've fully debriefed him?"

The man nodded. "Aye, Dominus Aurelius, and with few exceptions, it is as we feared when we sent him out."

Behind the two soldiers, Aurelius saw Porcia walking their way, marching like a general headed for war. Brunasus and Denian parted as she stepped between them. "You're not doing this without me, Brother."

"How did you know?"

She gave him a bored look and lied. "A woman's intuition." Her eyes flicked momentarily to Denian. The tribune tried to look away from her, but only looked exceedingly guilty.

Aurelius looked pointedly at Denian, then at Porcia. "The two of you? Really?"

Her bored look turned to petulance. "Do you disapprove?"

He shrugged. "Would you care if I did?"

The petulance turned to anger. "Of course, I care what you think."

He acknowledged her anger with a nod. "My apologies, Sister. And yes, I do approve, most wholeheartedly."

He pointedly looked Denian in the eyes. "I value him greatly." He let a hint if anger show in his face. "But he shouldn't have told you."

Porcia stepped between them and planted her fists on her hips. "He didn't. It was just obvious. Six days ago he returned from a meeting with you. He said about two words to me, changed into civilian clothing, told me he must leave on urgent business, and wouldn't tell me what it was about or where he was going. Then when he returned he went straight to Brunasus, and the two of them headed straight to you. It has something to do with the impending war between Tarnasus and Andopolous, doesn't it?"

Aurelius nodded, conceding the point. He said to Denian, "My apologies for doubting you."

Denian shrugged.

Porcia clearly intended to have the last word. "And in case you're wondering, I do approve of your somewhat questionable relationship with . . . that woman."

Aurelius had known from the start there were no secrets in the Deoclation Palace. "That woman's name is Hessian."

Denian and Brunasus found something of interest on the floor and focused on it.

Porcia gave Aurelius a triumphant grin. "Yes, and she's a Slum Boss. That must be rather exotic."

Aurelius ignored her, backed up a step and looked at the three of them. "Lucius and Janus are awaiting us. Naerin and Victicus will be here shortly, so we don't have much time."

He turned, opened the tall double doors to the drawing room, and stepped through them, the three of them following on his heels.

Janus and Lucius stood near a hearth at the far end of the room. Both men turned to face him as he walked toward them, and he stopped two paces short of them. "I apologize for making you wait, but today I wanted to discuss facts, not supposition."

He stepped aside and indicated Denian. "Tribune Denian has just returned from the east. He's been scouting incognito."

Janus didn't react in the slightest.

Lucius's eyebrows rose. "This should be interesting."

To Denian, Aurelius said, "I think you know what we need to hear, so just give it to us in your own words."

Denian nodded. "Tarnasus and Andopolous have called in all levies and both can now field armies about eight thousand strong, a little less than two legions each. They've both done a lot of hurried recruiting of late, but I'd say Tarnasus has a significant advantage. Ninety percent of their troops are properly trained, while Andopolous can only claim about sixty percent, and are rushing to train the rest. Andopolous has amassed one legion about ten leagues north of the city, and Tarnasus is marching one legion down there now to meet them. I don't think they'll be ready for battle in the next week, but they will be shortly after that."

Lucius nodded carefully and looked Aurelius in the eyes. "How do we stand?"

Aurelius spoke carefully. "Three legions, close to fifteen thousand men, all but four or five hundred fully trained."

Lucius's lips curled upward into a pained smile. "Then we hold the upper hand."

Aurelius shook his head. "Not if they combine forces."

Denian grimaced. "They're going to fight. There is no doubt of that. If they reconsider and ally against us, it'll only be after they've killed a few thousand men."

Janus spoke for the first time. "Might I recommend we keep our distance and let them fight? Their warring will only diminish their numbers, and if they do combine forces, we'll still have the upper hand."

"No," Aurelius said, making no attempt to conceal his anger. "If Tarnasus and Andopolous engage in open war, I see no way we can avoid being drawn into it."

Lucius dismissed his words with a smug scoff. "And what's wrong with that? In fact, if we're smart we'll let them fight it out. Then near the end of summer, when they're both weakened by a couple months of battles, we can march in and sweep up the pieces. It'll be the first time we've united all three cities under one rule since Domaxus. And the combined armies will give Macallan and Selene Barasha cause to temper any thoughts they might have regarding the Lowlands."

Aurelius heard Divonia's scheming in Lucius's words. He didn't think for a moment that she and the Chairman of the Primus Council were kindred souls, but they did agree on many things. With no real power beyond his lone seat in the Senatus, he could not compete with her pillow talk, not when she whispered in so many ears. And once again, she had outmaneuvered him.

The doors of the Blue Drawing Room opened and a servant stepped into the room. He approached Aurelius and bowed. "Dominus Aurelius, Ambassadors Naerin and Victicus have arrived. The Lady Divonia and Senatus Supreme Maximillian are on their way."

Aurelius would have liked another hour with Lucius before facing the two ambassadors. "Wait until my mother and brother are here, then show the ambassadors in."

Brunasus and Denian quickly departed, and Janus stepped to one side to observe. Aurelius noticed Porcia loosen a strap at the top of her gown, exposing a little more skin; too much, in fact. She saw him looking her way and rolled her eyes. A few moments later Divonia fluttered in, and gave Lucius a chaste kiss on the cheek. Max followed, petulant and surly, probably begrudging the time spent away from a goblet of wine. Then the servant escorted the two old men into the room. Naerin seemed immune to Porcia's charms, but as always Victicus immediately gravitated toward her.

The meeting proved to be quite contentious, which Aurelius had expected. But to his surprise, the two ambassadors directed their ire at Maximillian and Aurelius, not at each other. It left Aurelius wondering who was at war with whom.

# 25

# Volunteer

TRACKING HOOFPRINTS ALWAYS proved to be slow work, but when the quarry headed for a pinch-point, the situation improved considerably. After three days following the bandits it became obvious the Tri-Corner was their destination. Obregon abandoned the slow plodding work and rode ahead to the first of the two bridges. He crossed it, and just on the other side found clear evidence the bandits had gone that way. At that point they had only one way to go, so he rode straight to the second bridge and confirmed that they had crossed there as well. From there, he followed them up into a range of low mountains, and depending upon their ultimate destination, they'd have to cross at one of only three passes. Obregon increased his pace, and paused only occasionally to confirm he hadn't lost their trail. And when he knew for certain which pass they had chosen, he made much better time.

As he rode down out of the mountains on the other side, the number of possible destinations increased and his pace slowed. Tarnasus lay to the east, and Carthagen to the south, though it could be a mistake to assume they were headed for a large city. Highwaymen like those he tracked would find the pickings easier near small towns and villages. On the other hand, the Lowlands constabularies were well organized, with a fair amount of cooperation between cities. Highway robbery in the Lowland Kingdoms frequently proved to be a dangerous undertaking anywhere but the most remote parts of the countryside.

His quarry had to cross at least two rivers, which helped him confirm they traveled in an easterly direction toward another range of mountains. At that point their destination must be somewhere in the greater environs of Tarnasus.

Thankfully, he hadn't yet found the body of a young boy abandoned by the side of the trail.

• • • •

Ket didn't understand where his captors were taking him, or what purpose they had in mind. But so far they hadn't harmed him, and apparently they intended to release him unhurt. He decided that if an opportunity to escape came his way, he wouldn't pass it up. But barring that, he needed to be patient.

They entered a range of low-lying mountains and took a day crossing through it. When they came upon a small village on the other side, Fallon questioned the locals, asking after the bailiff recruiting volunteers for Tarnasus. Ket didn't know what a bailiff did, nor did he understand the word *recruiting*. They forded a river, then paid a ferryman to carry them across another, and Ket lost count of the days. Then one day they came upon a fairly large village and stopped at a public house on its outskirts. Fallon dismounted and went in while the rest waited outside. A few minutes later he emerged and said, "Got it."

They skirted the outskirts of the village and circled around it. As they approached the south side, dust swirled through the air, and a cloud of it hung above their destination. In the distance men marched about in squared off ranks, and horsemen rode here and there.

They dismounted and untied the loop of rope from the neck of Ket's horse. Then Termik untied his hands, and spun him about to face Fallon.

The bald man grinned. "Listen to me, boy. You do what I say and you'll come out of this alive. If you don't do what I say—"

Ket felt a sharp point press into his back. Termik leaned close and whispered, "You'll do what he says, won't you?"

The hawk wanted Ket to spin about and rip Termik's eyes out with his talons, but Ket didn't have any talons. "Yes, I'll do what he says."

Fallon's grin didn't change as he nodded. "I knew you was a smart boy. Now don't say nothing to no one unless I tells you to."

He spun about and led the way. Termik pushed Ket forward, tightly gripping his left elbow with one hand, and with the other pressing the sharp point of the knife against his back as a painful and constant reminder. They approached a man seated alone behind a wooden table, and no one standing in front of it. He seemed bored, but he perked up as they walked his way.

"Good sir," Fallon said. "The lad here, he wants to volunteer. Yer paying good coin for volunteers, right?"

The man frowned, looked Ket over, and lifted an eyebrow. "So you want to volunteer, do you?"

"Yah," Fallon said, "he wants to volunteer. Don't you, boy?"

Termik nudged Ket with the point of his knife. "Yes, I want to volunteer." He wanted to ask what he was volunteering for, but the sharp point of the knife told him that probably wasn't a good idea.

The man looked Ket over again, then looked up at Fallon. "You sure he wants to volunteer?"

Fallon placed both hands flat on the table and leaned on it. He made a point of looking left, then right. "I don't see as you got much choice in the matter. It's either the boy, or you're empty handed. And he asked us to get him here, said we could have his sign-up bonus in return for the trouble." Fallon's mouth curled up into a broad grin. "And of course, you're entitled to a share of it."

The bailiff leaned back in his chair and regarded Fallon for a long moment. Then he turned his attention to Ket. "You got any experience?"

Fallon answered for him. "What do you think? If he's got any experience, it's digging mud in a field somewhere."

The bailiff continued to regard Ket. "He's got shoulders. Let me see your hands, boy."

Ket extended his hands, palms up.

The bailiff nodded. "And he's got calluses. He'll do well on the shield wall, if he lives. What's your name, boy?"

Ket decided not to give him his full name. "Ket."

The man frowned. "That's a name?"

Ket shrugged. "It's all I got."

The man wrote Ket's name in some sort of ledger, and that was how Ket became a soldier in the regular army of Tarnasus.

• • • •

Tempers flared during the regular meeting of the Privy Council. With Macallan calling in his levies, the armies of Tarnasus and Andopolous facing off, and war imminent in the Three Realms, Selene had closed the borders of the Mountain Kingdom. Small towns and villages usually saw Scairnessa only in passing, but the large cities of Mythria, Carigleigh, and Darliff hosted significant populations of Lowlands and Duchies folk. Many of the foreigners were involved in some aspect of trade between the Three Realms. And at the almost complete shutdown of trade, quite a few of the foreign merchants joined forces with Scairn merchants to protest loudly. Selene relented to some degree, though she did so reluctantly.

Her concerns were somewhat lessened because the mounted patrols they had instituted six years earlier had matured into an organized border guard. She gave orders that they carefully monitor the comings and goings through the limited number of routes from the other two realms. She also stipulated that known tradesmen and merchants were to be allowed passage, but the patrols were to turn back anyone who might be a spy or thief. Caerie wondered how the captain of a patrol would make such a distinction, since a spy or thief would certainly take pains to not look like a spy or thief.

As the meeting broke up, Caerie encountered Nick in the hallway outside. He leaned close to her and whispered, "I heard you cut the Tregairn fellow loose. Life will be so much better now that you've sent him packing. He was worse than the Skelain boy."

Caerie grimaced, and didn't hide her anger as she hissed, "You disapprove of him too?"

Nick stepped back and held up his hands in surrender. "No, not at all. I don't care who you bed, but mother certainly does. And now maybe she'll stop making my life hell."

It had been unfair to turn her anger on Nick. "She's been a bit of a shrew lately, has she?"

Nick shook his head sadly. "Yes. But you know, you've got a temper just like hers." He turned and walked away.

"Caermorgan Mythchild."

At the sound of Melceinnia's voice, Caerie's heart rate ratcheted up. She turned toward the old woman. The tattoos on her face and chest made it difficult to read her the way one might glean another's mood or intent.

The priestess smiled. "A word with you, child, if it pleases you."

Caerie hated it when she used that particular phrase, and replied as she always did. "At your pleasure, mistress."

Melceinnia grinned and raised an eyebrow. "But not yours, eh?"

Caerie ignored the question. "In the temple?"

The old woman shook her head. "No, I'll walk with you. Where are we going?"

She reached out and entwined her arm with Caerie's. Apparently, they would stroll through the palace like two dear friends. Melceinnia didn't wait to hear Caerie's destination, but began walking, and Caerie had no choice but to accompany her.

"You know, child, it was wise of you to cut off your relationship with the Tregairn heir."

Caerie didn't want to have that conversation. "I only spoke with him yesterday. Does everyone already know about that?"

"Oh, girl, don't be naive. You are mythchild. If you so much as sneeze, for the next week your health is discussed in considerable detail in every shadowy corner of this city. And he's the heir to an important family. A lot of people read quite a bit into that."

Caerie sighed. "I suppose Mother will be pleased."

"Yes," Melceinnia said. "Everyone's life is easier when she's not upset. But the Tregairn boy is of no concern to me. I knew you would end it eventually. My interest is for another boy."

Caerie hated the way the old woman so easily aroused her curiosity. "What boy? Is it someone I know?"

Melceinnia looked her way and gave her an infuriating grin. "I think you know him quite well. I believe he's about your age, with unusually pale blue eyes."

Caerie tried to recall the few Scairnessa young men she knew or had met, but none had blue eyes. "A Scairnessa?"

Melceinnia's grin broadened and she turned to look straight ahead. "No."

That didn't make sense. If he didn't have amber eyes, he must be Scairnessa. Rather than argue with the old woman, Caerie simply said, "I don't know any boys with blue eyes."

"Hmm!" Melceinnia said. "Your words carry the ring of truth. Perhaps you don't know this young man, but he certainly knows you, could recall your image quite vividly, which makes me think he must be somewhere on the palace grounds."

Caerie stopped and looked at the old woman. For the first time she realized she stood taller than the priestess. "You're confusing me. You talk as if you know the fellow well, and also as if you've never met him. Where did you meet this boy?"

Melceinnia turned and faced her squarely, that infuriating smile still on her face. "In a dream, child, a young man who is neither Scairn nor Scairnessa. He soars through the skies with the hunger of a hawk and the heart of a ket, but walks this earth with the spirit of a raken."

The old woman's riddles angered Caerie even more than the infuriating smile. She opened her mouth to voice her displeasure, but before she spoke Melceinnia turned and walked away, leaving her standing there.

• • • •

The four bandits left Ket with the bailiff, talking of heading back the way they had come. They apparently planned to turn north at the Tri-Corner to sample the whores in the Mountain Kingdom. The bailiff handed Ket over to a man named Centurion, who led him to a group of about twenty men. Ket was clearly the youngest among them, and didn't know what to expect. Centurion gave Ket a sword belt with a sheathed sword buckled to it. The sword was a little longer than Ket's forearm, which seemed short compared to the swords the guardsmen had carried. It had a heavy double-edged blade, a sharp point, and no cross guard. Pits and blemishes marred the steel of the blade, with several chips taken out of its edges. He tested the edges—they were not sharp, though the point was. Centurion also handed him a couple of pieces of hard leather with straps on them, then turned to walk away.

"Uh," Ket said to the man's back. "Uh, Master Centurion, good sir."

The fellow stopped in his tracks, turned about, and gave Ket the oddest look. "Master Centurion? Where'd you come up with that?"

Ket wondered if he'd now get a switching. "That's . . . that's your name, isn't it?"

Some of the men standing nearby laughed. Master Centurion just gave him that odd look. "No. That ain't my name. That's my rank. The name's Garsian."

He threw his hands up in the air, swore an oath, and marched back to Ket. "They're giving me children now." He lifted one of the leather contraptions and waved it in front of Ket's nose. "Do you even know what this is?"

Ket shook his head. "No, good sir."

"I ain't 'good sir' neither. I'm just Centurion. Not Master Centurion, just Centurion. Or maybe Centurion Garsian. And this—" Again he waved the leather contraption in front of Ket. "This is a greave, boiled leather. It protects your lower leg, mainly your shin, especially when someone tries to shove a sharp blade beneath the shield wall and stick you with it."

He paused for a moment, calmed, and his voice softened. "Here, let me show you."

He showed Ket how to strap on the greaves. They had a leather flap that protected the top of his foot, though not his toes. Garsian showed him how to buckle on the sword belt, then pulled the sword from the sheath and held it up. "This is a gladius. This is your second-best friend, second only to your shield."

He handed the sword to Ket, then turned and marched away.

One of the other men called after him in a shrill voice, "Are we going to get any training?"

The centurion stopped, turned about and grinned. "You just got it." He didn't wait for any argument, but turned and walked away.

Ket sheathed the sword and didn't know what to do next. But as he stood there pondering that, the fellow who had asked about training turned, looked him over, and walked his way. Something about the man reminded Ket of Markus. Unlike the monk, the fellow stood a little taller than Ket, wasn't stick thin, and walked with a swagger. But watching him approach, Ket still thought of Markus. The man had wavy red hair cut shoulder length, with a thin moustache and short spotty beard. He stopped a pace in front of Ket, planted his fists on his hips, and loudly announced, "Well now, what have we got here?"

Someone said, "Just leave the boy alone, Bilsius."

Bilsius shook his head. "Look at him. The boy's daft. He's a dimwit, a fool."

Bilsius took half a step and leaned forward, his nose a finger's breadth from Ket's. "I can see it in your eyes. Yer a fool, ain't you?"

Ket felt the hawk's anger rising within him. "I uh—"

The man crossed his eyes, skewed his lips, and imitated Ket. "Duh, I uh. Duh."

Without warning he shoved Ket, and Ket stumbled back a step. Bilsius stepped forward. "He's weak and stupid, which means he'll get us killed." He leaned forward again and locked eyes with Ket. "You're weak and stupid. The shield wall is only as strong as the weakest shield, and that's you." The fellow regarded him with hate and anger. But looking out through Ket's eyes, the hawk saw only a weak and stupid man.

When Bilsius's hand shot out and slapped Ket's cheek, he started. The blow left behind a fiery burn. The hawk wanted to attack, wanted Ket to rip the man's face apart with his talons, but Ket backed up a step.

Bilsius stepped forward. "Stupid and weak."

His other hand shot out and slapped Ket's other cheek, leaving a fiery burn there as well. "We can't have stupid and weak. We have to be strong."

The hawk wanted Ket to gouge the man's eyes out with his beak, but Ket backed up a step.

Bilsius advanced. "You're going to be the weak link in the wall, and I won't put up with you."

When the man struck out again, Ket's hand moved as if it had a mind of its own. He caught the man's wrist, stopping the fellow's hand a fraction of an inch from his cheek. Their eyes met and Bilsius grinned, then he jerked his hand away, clearly confident he'd snap it out of Ket's grip. But Ket held on while Bilsius struggled for a moment. Then the man froze, and still looking Ket in the eyes, he frowned.

The hawk closed its talons with crushing force.

"Ahhh," Bilsius screamed. "You're hurting me. Ahhh! Stop it."

With his left hand he tried to pry Ket's fingers loose, but the hawk knew the kill was close at hand and squeezed harder.

"Stop," Bilsius cried, tears streaming down his cheeks. "You're crushing my wrist. Stop. Stop. Please stop. Please."

The hawk pressed their advantage while Ket forced Bilsius to his knees in the dirt. Time for the kill, and while Ket didn't have talons, he did have a sword. But Garsian had buckled the sword on his right side, and with his right-hand occupied crushing Bilsius's wrist, he reached across with his left to the sword. His hand gripped the hilt in a way that when he drew it, he'd hold the blade point down, perfect for jamming it down Bilsius's throat. But someone else's hand pressed down on Ket's hand, and wouldn't allow him to draw the blade. He froze and looked to his right.

Centurion Garsian stood next to him, an oddly neutral look on his face. He spoke calmly and softly, with a volume far lower than that of Bilsius's cries, but Ket heard every word. "You can kill him if you want, but if you do we have to hang you. It's your choice."

The Centurion lifted his hand off the hilt of Ket's gladius.

Ket stood there frozen, Bilsius screaming, Garsian looking into his eyes, the hawk demanding he free it and allow it to kill. He needed Obregon there to tell him what to do, though in his heart he knew exactly what the older man would advise. The hawk's need hammered at him, and it took all his strength of will, but he released his grip on the sword's hilt, released his grip on Bilsius's wrist, and lowered both hands to his sides.

Garsian nodded once.

Bilsius sat on the ground, clutching his wrist and crying like a child. "He tried to kill me. You need to punish him."

Garsian finally broke eye contact with Ket and looked down at Bilsius. "You punish him, if you can."

One of the other men standing nearby looked at Ket. "Guess he ain't so weak."

Another man looked at Bilsius. "Guess we know who is."

# 26

# A Soldier

THE ARMY OF Tarnasus issued Ket a boiled leather helmet, a pair of hobnail boots with heavy soles, and a pack containing a blanket, a tin plate, a tin cup, and an oiled water skin. The helmet had scratches and marks on it, the hobnails and soles of the boots were worn down a bit, the blanket had moth holes, and the plate and cup had dents in them that looked as if they'd recently been hammered out.

"Come on," one of the men said. "Let's get some dinner."

Ket lined up with the other men for dinner, which proved to be a cup of gritty ale and a plate of boiled potatoes and maze. Some of the surrounding men complained about the fare, but for Ket it was better than the kitchen scraps they fed him at the monastery.

That night he sensed that old woman with the tattoos surrounding her amber eyes. She haunted his dreams, searched for him, but never found him. At times the two ravens stalked his dreams, and they left him feeling unclean. The female raven constantly sought to find someone, demanding, "Where is he?" the hiss of her voice slithering through his thoughts. He also dreamed of the hawk flying high above. It was angry at him for not allowing it to kill Bilsius, but as it soared through the heights, its anger dissipated. Ket awoke in the morning feeling rested.

After feeding them breakfast, they lined Ket up with about fifty men all standing in squared-off ranks in front of Centurion Garsian. "Listen up, men."

The general grumbling of the crowd didn't lessen or cease, so Garsian shouted them into silence. He stood still for a few seconds, as if challenging anyone to grumble or speak, and then he addressed them. "You men are now soldiers in the Army of Tarnasus, and you're assigned to my centuria. You got two days to train. After that, a lot of you are going to decide you don't like being a soldier in the Army of Tarnasus. But if you try to change that, we got other soldiers who know how to hunt you down.

And we hang deserters where we find them, no hearing before a magistrate, no appeal. We just hang you then and there."

He held his silence for several seconds, letting that sink in. Then they brought forth a wagon loaded with heavy shields and issued one to each man. Ket had never seen their like before: slightly cylindrical in shape, when he fitted his left arm into its strap, the shield curved around him a little to right and left, but ran straight up and down.

Garsian divided them into eight-man groups, saying, "This is your tent group. You'll tent together, if you got a tent, and fight and eat together regardless."

He showed each group of eight how to line up side by side and butt the straight edges of their shields together to form an impenetrable wall, a shield wall. Ket recalled Obregon telling him he'd gotten the scars on his arm on the shield wall. He missed the big monk.

They taught them to hold the shield with their left arm, and the gladius in their right hand. They pushed forward against the back of the shield with all their strength to advance the line, and stabbed around the shield to encourage the enemy to back up and make room for them.

"Don't let the shield wall break or falter. If you do, you won't be the only one that dies."

They placed three more lines of eight men behind them, their shields butted together, but held over their heads to protect them all from rains of arrows. They spent that first day with opposing groups of eight pushing against each other to see who could make the other group give ground.

During the second day, they fought mock combat against more experienced soldiers. Behind the eight men of the enemy shield wall stood a second line of men armed with blunted javelin shafts, jabbing the shafts around the shields of their wall. They had dredged the tip of each shaft in charcoal dust, and if a trainee came away from a skirmish with charcoal marks, it meant he'd taken a javelin wound. During the morning Ket got a lot of charcoal marks on his arms, legs and torso, but as the day progressed he slowly learned how to stay alive, and came away from each skirmish with fewer marks.

At the end of the second day they assembled them into ranks and Garsian addressed them again. "Time for one last lesson. Time for me to teach you how to march. So here's your lesson: you put your right foot in front of your left foot, then your left foot in front of your right foot, and you do that in the direction we point, and you keep doing that until I tell you to stop. Okay, training done. Now, for the next two days, you get to practice what I just taught you about marching. Any questions?"

"Centurion Garsian." Ket recognized Bilsius's voice. "We get more equipment than this, don't we? This isn't enough."

Garsian rolled his eyes, shook his head, and groaned. "If you fight well and live, yes, you get more equipment, which gives you a better chance at living another day. If you fight poorly and live, no, you don't, which increases the odds you'll die in the next battle. And when you do, we scavenge your equipment from the battlefield and give it to someone else."

Ket now knew the source of the equipment and weapons he carried.

• • • •

Riding down the far side of the second range of mountains, when Obregon reached the foothills his pace slowed considerably. He kept his horse to a walk, with his eyes focused on the ground to either side. Occasionally, he stopped and dismounted to examine hoofprints. He now followed tracks several days old, and whenever the trail branched, he stopped and examined each direction carefully. Thankfully, the trail in front of him didn't see much traffic, and it hadn't rained recently, so he still had hoofprints to follow. But poor luck still forced him to backtrack a couple times and start over, and as the day progressed that occurred with increasing frequency. By late afternoon he was ready to give up and simply head for Tarnasus. That seemed to be their destination, and he'd just have to hope for the best.

Riding slowly and watching the ground, he heard a laugh somewhere in front of him, muffled by distance and a turn in the trail. He focused on the trail ahead as another laugh followed the first. Then one by one four riders emerged from the bend in the trail. Obregon immediately recognized their leader from Sylander's description. Completely bald without a hint of hair, his head the shape of a smooth egg, the man wore some sort of jewelry that glinted in each of his ears, and a ring in his nose that reflected the rays of the sun. The four men spotted Obregon and their laughter died.

Obregon wasn't about to convict them based on a bald head and some cheap jewelry, but as they approached he recognized the tack on the two horses taken from the guardsmen. And two of them carried unstrung bows strapped to their saddles. Two swordsmen and two bowmen; add that to the bald head and the duke's horses, and he had all the proof he needed.

When they approached to within about twenty paces, the bald man nodded to Obregon. "Good day, kind sir. The trail behind us is clear and dry. What do we face ahead?"

Obregon returned the fellow's gesture with a polite nod of his own. "Clear and dry, but there's a small caravan a few hundred paces back that might slow you." That was a lie, but the possibility of witnesses nearby might give them pause before considering an attack on a lone traveler.

As they passed each other, Obregon noticed the two bowmen fidgeting nervously. Up close, he confirmed their bows remained unstrung, so they couldn't simply nock an arrow and put it in his back. They'd have to stop, dismount, and string the bows, which should give him a little time. Once they had passed him he kept his head turned enough to see any quick motion out of the corner of his eye. And when he had ridden about fifty paces beyond them he stopped, dismounted, and pretended to check one of his horse's hooves while keeping an eye on the four highwaymen. Their leader paid him no heed, but the other three kept looking over their shoulders.

Once they passed out of sight, Obregon climbed into the saddle and spurred his horse into a trot. He rounded the bend in the trail, continued on for another fifty paces, then dismounted. Leading his horse by the reins, he took it well off the trail and out of sight of anyone passing by. He tied its reins to a tree limb, drew his sword, bent into a crouch, and headed back to the trail, using the cover of the forest canopy to remain concealed. As he approached the trail he heard two men speaking.

"Where'd he go?"

Through the brush Obregon saw the two bowmen talking. He crept forward, moving only when one of them spoke, using their words to cover any noise he made.

"He probably figured we was gonna rob him, and he's running like hell."

Obregon inched forward another step.

"Well he was right about that, but he's gone now and he ain't worth chasing."

The two bowmen had stopped, dismounted, and stood facing each other, each holding his horse's reins in one hand, and a strung bow in the other. One bowman mounted his horse and spurred it up the trail, heading back the way they had come. The other turned in the opposite direction, looking the way they thought Obregon had gone. The fellow shook his head and swore, "Blast and be damned!"

Obregon stepped out of the forest growth behind him. In one quick motion he swung his sword overhead in a two-handed grip, slamming the edge down on the top of the man's head. It cleaved his skull in two and he crumbled to the ground. Obregon grabbed the fellow's bow, pulled a couple arrows from the quiver attached to his saddle, then returned to the shadows of the forest. He waited in silence, and after a few minutes the other bowman returned looking for his companion.

Obregon had no great expertise with a bow, but he had trained extensively with every weapon possible. And while not a sharp-shooter, he nocked an arrow, raised the bow, and aimed. Even with only one good eye, at a distance of less than twenty paces, and an unmoving target, he fired the arrow with confidence. It punched into the second bowman's chest and knocked him out of the saddle.

Obregon moved quickly. He led the two men's horses off the trail and tied their reins to the tree next to his own mount. Then he returned to the trail, shouldered each of the bodies one at a time, and dumped them in the brush a dozen paces into the undergrowth.

He waited longer for the bald leader and the other swordsman to show up looking for their companions. But they eventually came, though they nudged their horses forward cautiously, swords drawn. Obregon waited, hidden in the forest undergrowth.

"I don't like it," the swordsman said. "Where are they?"

The bald leader glanced side to side before answering. "Probably chasing the big fellow on the horse." He didn't sound confident about that.

Obregon waited until they had gone about twenty paces past his position. He nocked an arrow and waited for a clear line-of-sight to the swordsman through the forest undergrowth, but the chance never came. He crept forward.

The bald leader dismounted to examine the trail, while his companion rode his horse a hundred paces farther down it. Obregon had a clear shot to the leader, but his one-eyed bow skills would not work well for the longer distance to the swordsman.

Obregon needed the leader alive, so he aimed at the fellow's gut and released the arrow. It punched into the man's stomach and he screamed. He dropped his sword and bent forward, clutching the arrow in his gut, groaning and wailing.

Obregon stepped out of the forest, nocked another arrow, and aimed at the swordsman in the distance. It was all bluff, but the man fell for it, spun his horse about, and spurred it into a gallop away from him.

The bald leader tried to run, but he moved in a bent over scrabble, and Obregon easily caught up to him. He kicked the man in the back, knocking him to the ground. Obregon heard the arrow shaft snap as the bandit leader rolled over and screamed. "What? Why?"

Obregon gave his heart a moment to slow, then sat down on a nearby rock to wait and watch the man struggle.

The fellow groaned and cried as he propped himself up on his elbows. "Who the bloody hell are you?"

Obregon answered by simply asking, "Where's the boy?"

Obregon watched realization flash in the man's eyes, but it quickly changed to calculation. "What boy?"

Obregon shook his head sadly. "That's a gut wound, which means you're gonna die slow and painful. Be honest with me and I'll make it easy for you."

The bandit shook his head. "The boy ran away."

"I don't believe you."

The man shrugged. "I guess I wouldn't believe me neither. The boy's a soldier now, and he's gonna be doing some fighting."

Obregon stood. "What legion, which legate?"

The bandit leader grimaced with pain. "I don't know that kind of stuff. Just turned him over to some little shit of a bailiff with high falutin airs."

Since all bailiffs were officious little shits, that didn't help any. Obregon questioned him further, but the man soon had trouble speaking and he passed out. Obregon stood, drew his sword, approached the man, and buried the point in his chest. Then for good measure, he pulled the trench knife and slit the bandit's throat.

He considered selling the three horses to augment the coins in his purse. But that would take time, and if anyone got suspicious he might find himself answering questions posed by unhappy constables. He unsaddled the bandits' three horses, removed their reins and tack, and set them free. At least he had acquired a good bow and a quiver full of arrows.

He mounted up and headed east.

• • • •

In the morning, Garsian assigned Ket and another recruit named Tobias to a tent group of experienced soldiers who'd lost two men in a recent battle. They lined up, got breakfast, shoveled it down quickly, then broke camp. Before marching, they stacked the heavy shields on horse-drawn wagons, and Ket was thankful he didn't have to carry his in addition to his other equipment. He noticed that more experienced veterans carried larger packs than his, and recalled Garsian's words. Apparently, those men had fought well and lived.

As they marched, the veterans gave the two newcomers bits and pieces of advice, and Ket realized that two days of training had barely scratched the surface of what they needed to know. At mid-morning, after fording a river, they broke to refill their water skins, chew on some salty jerky, and take a short breather.

In a group not far away, Ket heard Bilsius complaining loudly about something. One of the veterans hooked a thumb over his shoulder, pointing at the bully. "He ain't going to last long."

Tobias said, "He's been an asshole from the start, but Ket showed him a thing or two."

The veterans all perked up, and one of them said, "Tell us about it."

Tobias launched into a fairly colorful description of the incident where Ket faced down Bilsius. Ket wasn't ready for it when one veteran slapped him on the back so hard he almost tumbled off the rock where he'd parked his butt. "That's the way to handle an asshole like that."

Tobias lowered his voice and leaned close to Ket. "What did Garsian say to you when he stopped you from drawing your sword? His voice was too low. The rest of us couldn't hear."

Ket shrugged. "He said I could kill him if I wanted, but they'd have to hang me."

All the veterans nodded, and one of them said, "He was testing you."

An older veteran named Emparis said, "You'll probably have to kill that asshole anyway, but don't get into a fight. That's strictly prohibited. Anyone does any fighting and everyone involved gets punished. Twenty strokes to your back with a horse-whip for the first offense, fifty for the second, and the hangman's noose for the third. Just be careful, and when the time comes, do it quiet and right."

Ket wasn't sure what he meant by that, and his confusion must have been plain to see. The old fellow said, "There's lots of ways to get killed soldiering. One way is a gut wound." The man grimaced and shook his head. "Don't get a gut wound. Another way is to break the shield wall in battle. Do that, and we'll close it up without you, because if we don't, we get killed with you. If you pull your weight, do your job, but go down fighting anyway, we'll close it in front of you. Someone'll drag you back to the physikers in camp, and maybe you'll live."

He looked Ket in the eye. "Them what don't pull their weight put all of us in danger." He paused for a moment. "Pull your weight, because if you don't, and you go down, we'll close the wall behind you."

No one needed to tell Ket what would happen if they isolated him in front of the shield wall surrounded by enemy soldiers. But another thought occurred to him. If he didn't pull his weight, they might not wait for chance, or an enemy pike, to bring him down. It wouldn't be hard to trip one of your shield mates, then close the wall behind him. And it would be even easier if you orchestrated it with one of your comrades, and made sure that during the battle the fellow occupied the position between the two of you on the shield wall.

Ket looked Emparis in the eyes and nodded once. "I understand."

The veterans all smiled, nodded, then decided it was time to compare notes on whores. Ket didn't have anything to contribute to that conversation.

# 27

# The Shield Wall

KET MARCHED WITH the army through that first day, then through the next. As they pitched camp at the end of the second day, Garsian gathered the new recruits around him. "First, we establish camp, which means you're going to sweat. After that get dinner, and eat your fill. Then get as much sleep as you can, because at dawn tomorrow we fight, and you're going to need it."

The recruits dispersed and returned to their tent groups. Ket learned that a strong vanguard had preceded the main body of their army, clearing the roads and countryside of any opposing forces. With nothing to fear the previous night, they had simply bivouacked by the side of the road. But now, with the main enemy force close at hand, they erected tents and set up a proper camp surrounded by a palisade and deep ditch. Garsian tasked Ket with digging fire pits for a field kitchen, then helping the physikers set up a field hospital. They also laid out simple streets and pathways, which turned the field camp into a large village. It was hard work and it almost kept his mind off the coming battle.

When he returned to his tent group, they all lined up at one of the field kitchens, and Ket noticed the servings dished out were quite hearty. A veteran nudged Ket and nodded toward his plate of food. "Dead man gets a good last meal."

Tobias looked at his food and his eyes widened, but Emparis said, "Don't worry about it, lad. He's just having fun with you." Emparis's words did nothing to diminish the look on Tobias's face.

One of the other veterans nudged Ket with an elbow. "You didn't react, just sat there calm as could be. You've fought before, right?"

Ket shook his head. "No. Never." But the man's words made him wonder at his reaction. He should feel something about the coming battle, maybe butterflies in his stomach like when he feared a switching from Markus. But he felt nothing, perhaps because the hawk looked forward to the killing.

As they sat around the campfire and ate, the conversation remained muted, no talk of whores or gambling.

Everyone in their tent group looked up to Emparis, as did many others. "I'll soon be a twenty-year man," he told Ket. "Then I get to retire with a pension and a piece of land, maybe take me a wife."

Ket asked him, "Who are we going to fight?"

The veteran shrugged. "Don't know, but since we headed south and a bit east, I'm thinking Andopolous."

Ket didn't sleep well that night, which bothered him because Garsian had told them to get as much sleep as possible, and he took that to mean he'd have a better chance of living if he did. After lying awake for what seemed like hours, he climbed to his feet and made his way to the latrines to empty his bladder. The streets they had laid out in the camp were dimly lit by widely spaced braziers. As Ket walked back to his tent group, a shadowy figure stepped out into the street in front of him.

"You tried to kill me." Ket recognized Bilsius's shrill voice. "You need to be punished properly."

Ket knew he couldn't reason with the man, but recalling Emparis's words about the punishment for fighting, he had to try. "We have a battle tomorrow, and we both need to get some sleep."

Ket tried to step around the bully, but Bilsius shoved him and he stumbled backwards. Someone hit him from behind, tackling him, and he realized the man had brought a couple of friends. Two strangers lifted him to his feet, pinning his arms behind him, and Bilsius punched him in the gut, then hit him with a haymaker to his left cheek. Bilsius drew his fist back for another blow, but one of the two men pinning Ket's arms snarled, "That's enough. If you go too far, they'll want to know who did it, and you don't want twenty strokes any more than I do."

They left him lying in the dirt, laughing as they walked away, the hawk raging with murderous fury.

Ket lay there for a while, then checked his cheek and ribs. They hadn't broken anything, just left a few bruises. He struggled to his feet, staggered back to his blanket, and lay down. He tossed and turned for a while, but at some point must have slept, because a veteran woke him in the dark hours before dawn. "Get breakfast," the man said. "But eat light. You don't want a full stomach if you take a bad wound."

The kitchens gave the men a meal of hard bread smeared with white lard, and a mug of strong, hot tea. It was better than what Ket usually got in the monastery. As they ate, Emparis warned Ket and Tobias, "You should have gotten a couple months training, but the legion is under-manned, so you're going to have to stay alive and learn fast. We'll help you. Just do what we say, and above all don't get too brave and do something crazy. And don't turn and run. If you turn and run, you put us all in danger."

After breakfast they buckled on their greaves, bracers and sword belts. Emparis and the veterans carefully checked both Ket and Tobias, made a few adjustments, then they lined up at a wagon to receive their shields.

Tobias's hands shook so badly he needed help slipping his left forearm through the shield straps and tightening them properly. Again, a veteran noted Ket's unnatural calm. "You're a cold one, ain't you?"

Ket wanted to have fear, knew it could be dangerous to be completely fearless, but the hawk's anger overrode all emotion. It wanted to fight and kill, to free itself from all restrictions, to soar through the skies and hunt unimpeded. At that thought, Ket recalled the strange talisman on the table in Kainborne's room. It had been an assembly of wood-splinter, needle, and feather tied together by a strand of hair, possibly one of Ket's hairs. In his thoughts the hawk nodded knowingly, acknowledging his concern about Kainborne.

Emparis assembled their tent group in a line, with Ket and Tobias separated by two veterans on each side. "Remember," Emparis told them, "you don't respond to the battle horn. I do, and I tell you to advance or retreat a full step or half step. And no matter what, if the man on either side of you can't advance fully, you don't advance past him. We keep the shield wall together and tight at all times."

They joined a large assembly of tent groups and marched south over untilled fields, with only a hillock or tree here and there to break up a rolling landscape. Twilight had just lightened the sky when Ket first heard a faint roar in the distance, and as they moved closer, he thought he distinguished the occasional metallic ring, neigh of a horse, or shout from a man's throat.

Tobias asked, "What's that sound?"

One veteran said, "Light infantry and cavalry skirmishing and loosening up our friends from Andopolous. When we're ready, they'll withdraw to cover our flanks."

The sound of the preliminary fighting grew louder as they marched forward. They topped a small rise just as the shadows of twilight disappeared, and Ket saw mounted troops and infantry on both sides fighting in a chaotic brawl. He said, "It looks kind of brutal."

Emparis shook his head. "No, lad, that's more like nice talk at a fancy party. Brutal is when we butt shields with their heavy infantry, and you're ducking under sword points shoved through the gaps at you."

Emparis frowned, leaned close to Ket, and peered at his face. Ket realized that with the coming of daylight, the man now saw the swelling and bruise on his cheek. "What happened to you?"

Ket shrugged. "Fell down on my way back from the latrine last night."

Emparis's eyes narrowed. "You trip over Bilsius?"

Recalling the prohibition against fighting, Ket wanted to change the subject. He spotted two men wheeling a strange contraption forward. It looked like a giant cross-bow on wheels, constructed of wood and ropes. "What's that?"

A veteran answered. "A ballista. Fires a bolt with an arrowhead as long as your forearm and a shaft half as thick as your arm. Some of them throw rocks big enough to take your head off."

They lined up in a phalanx with their tent group in front, and three rows of men behind them all carrying shields. Then their phalanx joined many others in a long line spaced out in a checkerboard pattern. A horn blared and Emparis bellowed, "Shields up."

Ket drew his gladius with his right hand, and he and the others in the front line crouched down behind their shields. The three rows behind them lifted their shields overhead to protect them from arrows.

The horn blared again, but a note different from the first. "Advance," Emparis shouted.

Ket and his comrades took one full step forward.

The horn blared, Emparis shouted, and again they stepped forward. In that way they moved step by step toward the enemy force. Ket had been warned that lifting his head to look over his shield could earn him an arrow in the eye, so he kept his head down and imagined the enemy shield wall advancing toward them in the same meas-ured cadence. They moved forward that way for about fifty paces, and then some-thing thudded against Ket's shield. Someone shouted, "Arrows," as dozens of shafts thumped into shields all around him.

Emparis halted them and asked, "Anyone hurt?"

When no one answered they continued the advance. At one point the battle horn sounded a different note, Emparis shouted, "Javelins," and the men behind them grunted with effort as they threw their shafts.

They advanced another fifty paces, and finally met resistance as their shield wall butted against the enemy wall. "Half step," Emparis shouted.

Ket pressed his shoulder into his shield, and as he'd been taught, stabbed the blade of his gladius through the narrow gap between his shield and that of the man on his right. Advance, stab. Advance, stab. Advance, stab. Ket noticed the veteran on his right sometimes stabbing low, sometimes high, constantly varying the height of his thrust, and he tried to imitate him. An enemy blade sliced through the gap between shields, one of their opponents trying to do the same to them.

His mind drifted off into a strange, half-aware state. If it weren't for the stabbing, and the shouts and screams, advancing felt much like trying to push an old wagon out of thick, sticky mud. Ket simply put his shoulder to the shield and pressed forward; advance and stab, advance and stab.

Something massive slammed into his shield and an iron spike the length of his forearm punched through it just above his head. If he hadn't bent down to stab low an instant earlier, it would have split his head like a ripe melon. His shield felt overly heavy and he had trouble keeping it upright. With a ballista bolt stuck high in his shield, the weight of its shaft wanted to pull his shield down. It took all his strength to keep it upright and advance, to hold it from tilting forward and down, exposing them all. He struggled, gave up stabbing and concentrated on advancing, concentrated on holding his shield upright. The veteran on his left shouted, "Drop back. We'll close the line. Drop back."

Ket stopped advancing, stepped back a pace, and the wall closed in front of him as if by magic. The men behind him stepped around him with practiced ease. One of them stood over him, carrying a heavy axe. The fellow shouted, "Lower your shield."

Ket understood immediately what the man wanted. He pressed the bottom of his shield against the ground, then tilted it forward so the back-end of the bolt pressed into the dirt. The man swung the axe overhead in one quick motion, chopping through the bolt's shaft and leaving only the iron bolt-head still buried in Ket's shield.

"Return to your position," the fellow shouted.

It amazed Ket the way the men in his phalanx moved with precision amid the chaos, allowing him to step forward and return to his place on the shield wall. The morning continued in a blurry haze of advance and stab. Ket lost track of the time. His arms ached, his legs ached, and somewhere he got a nasty cut on his right forearm. It reminded him of the scars on Obregon's right arm.

At times they advanced easily, stepping forward with nothing opposing them. At other times they came to a complete halt, and the battle became a contest of stabbing and trying to push that damn wagon forward through all that mud. At some point they relieved Ket's phalanx with fresh troops, and he and his comrades withdrew to a makeshift camp well back from the fighting and out of range of any bowshot.

Ket got a drink of water and they offered him food, but exhaustion had killed any appetite he might have. He laid his shield on the ground, but didn't have the energy to clean the blade of his gladius, so he sat down on a rock to catch his breath, gladius in hand. He wasn't the only one to do that.

Centurion Garsian walked among the men under his command, checking them one after another. He sometimes shared a word with one or two, sometimes just nodded. He paused when he came to Ket, pointed to his shield and asked, "That yours?"

Ket looked at his shield, the heavy iron spike of the ballista's bolt still protruding from the split wood.

Seated nearby, Emparis stood. "It's his, all right. Didn't lower his shield so much as a hair, not even with the weight of that bolt's shaft hanging on it."

One of the other veterans added, "Couldn't blame him if he had lowered it, but might've lost a man or two. The boy even advanced five paces carrying the damn thing."

Garsian nodded.

Ket shrugged. "I don't think I really did anything to the enemy."

The centurion's eyes narrowed and he looked at the gladius in Ket's hand. "Raise your gladius. I want to see it clearly."

Ket lifted the blade for the man to inspect. Blood smeared the length of the steel, and also covered Ket's hand where it gripped the hilt. He recalled that during the battle he had feared the blood would make the hilt slippery, and had gripped it even tighter. And after hours of that, he thought he might have trouble letting go.

Garsian asked, "That your blood?"

The hawk hungered after the blood, but Ket shook his head. "No."

Garsian turned to Emparis. "Can I assume he didn't stab any of his comrades?"

Emparis answered with a grin.

Garsian slapped Ket on the back. "You fought well, lad. You fought well."

He turned and walked away.

After getting some rest, Ket returned to the shield wall and fought for the rest of the afternoon. Then the armies of Tarnasus and Andopolous disengaged. When Andopolous withdrew a few leagues to the south, Ket and his comrades marched after them in pursuit. They established a new camp, and reengaged two days later. The second battle lasted four days, and for Ket it proved to be a grueling grind of advance and stab, alternating with periods of retreat and stab. At that point, the higher-ups decided they would neither march nor fight, but stay in place for a time.

Ket thought he might get to relax and rest up, but Centurion Garsian had other ideas. The new recruits spent a week learning to fight with just a gladius and a small round shield. They also practiced with the gladius and a knife in their off-hand, sometimes a long dagger, sometimes a heavy trench knife. Sometimes they put aside the gladius and practiced with a medium-length sword.

Ket's only training and experience were in techniques for the shield wall. He stumbled around at first like a clumsy oaf, especially with the hawk distracting him. But then he realized the hawk's lightning-fast reflexes drew his eyes to his opponent's weaknesses. It might spot a slight misstep, or an overextended sword-thrust. The hawk didn't understand them as mistakes, but Ket did, and the hawk drew on that knowledge to pull Ket's attention in the right direction. At one point, when his instructor overextended his sword in a slashing blow, instead of resisting the stroke, Ket stepped in and batted the back of his blade, forcing him to overextend even further. Ket quickly tapped him in the side of the head with the hilt of his sword to score the point, then disengaged.

The man paused and hesitated, frowning. Then he grinned and nodded. "Well done, lad. You've fought before, eh?"

Ket shook his head. "No, sir, never."

The man's grin broadened. "Well that's even better. Keep at it and you'll be a real fighter. But you shouldn't have disengaged. Knock me half-conscious with yer hilt, then gut me with the knife in your off-hand, or crush my voice box with the edge of yer small shield. At a moment like that, don't back off."

The man attacked.

After that, as Ket learned to fight with the hawk, instead of resisting it, his fighting skills improved rapidly. Training was not as grueling as an actual battle, but it did keep the recruits busy. Practice and drill. Ket learned that after doing that for a while, they did more practice and drill. Later they trained with javelins and pikes, and Ket learned to think of himself as a soldier.

# 28

# A Time of War

BEFORE HE PASSED out, the bandit leader had not been completely forthcoming with Obregon. He hadn't given him specifics as to exactly what they had done with the boy. Obregon had only learned that they'd turned him over to an officious bailiff. Carthagen and Andopolous were too far south. Tarnasus was the nearest of the three city-states to the mountain passes they had traversed, so it had to be Tarnasus. And since Tarnasus and Andopolous had pulled in all their levies, and now offered recruitment bonuses to fill out the legions they needed, it didn't take a genius to figure out the bandits' motive in taking the boy alive.

Obregon no longer tried to track hoofprints and headed due east at a steady pace his horse could maintain. In a large village west of Tarnasus, he made a few inquiries and learned they had established a recruiting post somewhere to the south. He headed straight in that direction, and as he passed through the center of the village, he spotted the cloud of dust on the horizon. It didn't take long to find the bailiff seated at a table with a journal and a quill pen in front of him, a bored look on his face. He probably had a small purse of coin to pay the signup bonuses, but the ground in front of the table remained empty; no men standing there to take advantage of the city's generosity. A single guard stood to one side conversing with the bailiff.

Obregon walked up to the table and stopped in front of it.

The bailiff perked up. The guard perked up and stepped forward, standing about an arm's length to Obregon's right.

The bailiff looked him up and down, his eyes finishing with a quick glance at the scars on Obregon's forearms. Obregon was probably the first to approach the table wearing leather armor and a sword.

The bailiff's eyebrows rose. "I'm authorized to pay extra for a man with experience. What rank?"

Obregon shook his head. "That's the past. I'm not here to sign up. I just want a little information."

The bailiff sighed and placed his hand flat on the table in front of him, his fingers spread. "I'm not in the business of giving out information. If you ain't here to sign up, then you're wasting my time. So go away, old man. Or I'll have my friend here—" He nodded toward the guard. "—make you go away."

Obregon hadn't tested his reflexes in a long time, but the guard on his right was clearly an amateur. The fellow stood there relaxed and unconcerned, expecting no trouble from the *old man*. With his right hand, Obregon grabbed the hilt of his gladius, and pulled the blade from the sheath. He slammed the butt of the hilt into the guard's nose, sending a spray of blood flying. As the man crumbled, Obregon used his left hand to pull the trench knife from the sheath on his left hip. Then he brought the blade down and punched its tip into the table between the bailiff's fingers. The bailiff and Obregon both froze, the bailiff's eyes wide with fear. The guard crumbled to the ground, groaning.

Obregon leaned forward and looked the bailiff in the eyes. "I'm not here to hurt you. In fact, I don't care about you one way or another. I just want a small amount of information, and if you give it to me, we'll part friends. If not, I'm going to cut off your fingers one at a time until you do. Do you understand me?"

With his eyes blinking rapidly, the bailiff nodded.

"Good," Obregon said. "A bald man with a ring in his nose and shiny earrings. He had three companions plus a young boy. Do you remember him?"

The bailiff nodded.

Obregon learned that Ket had involuntarily volunteered for the Army of Tarnasus. The bandits and the bailiff had probably split his signup bonus, but Obregon didn't care about that. The bailiff didn't know to which legion they had assigned Ket, nor to which centuria. But he did confirm that Ket had probably marched south to fight against Andopolous. The guard would simply have to live with a crooked nose, and Obregon didn't cut off any of the bailiff's fingers.

• • • •

Without exhausting their levies, the four dukes had assembled an army of five thousand soldiers. Kainborne had nothing to contribute as Macallan planned his campaign against Mythria. But while the archduke met with his two most senior knights, huddled over maps in his study, Kainborne stood in the background and found small opportunities to influence matters to his advantage.

"I'm splitting the force," Macallan told them. "We'll send half to Lagasdale. He can attack Carigleigh from the west. We'll take the other half, go north, and assault Darliff from the south."

"Excellent," one knight said. "A two-pronged attack. They'll be forced—"

The lady of Inversill marched into the room, her back rigid, her anger palpable. "I would have a word with my husband, now." She pointed at the two knights. "You two, leave."

Lady Claireen had never displayed anger in Kainborne's presence, and that she did now surprised him.

Macallan stepped toward her and lowered his voice. "My dear lady wife, this is not a good moment. Perhaps later we can discuss what has upset you."

She didn't budge, didn't move, her back so rigid it seemed to vibrate like steel struck by a hammer. She remained silent, said not a word, and after several seconds Macallan turned to the two knights. "Perhaps it's best if you do leave. We can continue this later today."

The two knights hurriedly left the room. Kainborne turned to follow, but the lady stopped him. "Not you, Kainborne. Perhaps you can inject some sanity into my husband."

Until that moment, Kainborne's relationship with Claireen had been limited to a polite nod, word, or greeting here and there. And she had relied on him to relieve Clarahm of the pains that troubled him. But her words sounded as if she looked upon him as a potential ally, and the possibilities in that were endless.

Kainborne hesitated and glanced at Macallan for permission. The archduke gave him a surreptitious nod and said, "Perhaps you should close the door."

Kainborne closed it and turned, choosing to remain near the door to observe.

Claireen didn't wait for an invitation to speak. "You stopped coming to my bed and have been working your way through every whore in Inversill."

Macallan shrugged. "You've never before objected to a little whoring."

She spit her words at him. "You've never before tried to beget a bastard on one."

His eyes widened. The archduke had not been at all circumspect in his desire to conceive a bastard heir, and it appeared word of his efforts had reached his wife. Or perhaps she had bribed one of the prostitutes.

Claireen continued. "I know what you're doing. You think I'll be silent if you claim I bore the child, but I won't. I will make sure every one of your liege lords knows the parentage of the child. I'll shout it far and wide. I'll tell their wives, and their children, and they'll all know their new lord will be the son of a whore."

She spun about, marched to the door, opened it, and stormed out of the room.

Macallan shook his head. "Damn and blast it all. If she spills the truth, it'll not sit well with my liege lords."

Kainborne frowned, taking care to hide his great relief. At least now he wouldn't have to kill the little bastard. He thought it wise to give Macallan more reason to abandon his foolish plans. "And with war imminent, you'll need their support now more than ever."

"Aye," Macallan said. "You have the right of it there . . ."

He hesitated, and the sour look on his face brightened. "But what if I take a mistress? Perhaps the daughter of one of my liege lords, a young pretty one. I could father a bastard on her, then recognize the boy as legitimate. Any of my liege men would relish the thought of a descendant rising to the position of Archduke of the Four Duchies. Why, they'll present their daughters to me like cattle at an auction."

The archduke stood straighter and puffed his chest out. "Yes, that'll work nicely."

With a lively and invigorated step, he marched out of the room.

Kainborne considered his options. If Macallan were successful, Kainborne might have to ensure that the bastard heir died by *eating bad meat*. Or barring that, Kainborne could simply kill Clarahm and addict the new heir to his tincture.

Kainborne's months at Inversill proved to be quite productive. He slowly developed a relationship with Lady Claireen, and she came to consider him a trusted advisor. Clarahm confided in him regularly, and grew emotionally dependent upon him as a confidant. It certainly helped that when the lad's joints ached to the point of leaving him bedridden, he needed Kainborne's tincture to suppress the pain and give him a measure of relief. And of course, neither he nor his father understood he had become addicted to the tincture, and it was that addiction that actually caused his malady.

As summer melted the snows in the mountains of Mythria, Kainborne rode north with Macallan and his army. Jarrod and his levies joined them in the foothills.

· · · ·

A month into summer, Centurion Garsian gave Ket a cuirass with boiled leather chest and back plates, and hard leather overlapping flaps on his shoulders. When he tried it on it felt too large, but Ket learned that was by intent, allowing room for layers of cloth padding to improve comfort and soften any blows. While Emparis and the veterans helped him adjust the padding and fit, Ket noticed Bilsius watching them closely, an angry sneer on his face. The man still wore only the basic equipment issued to all recruits at their enlistment.

Ket passed the months of summer and much of autumn that way: march, fight, train. Autumn and winter in the Lowlands were mild compared to the other two realms, and he lost count of the number of battles in which he fought. As winter approached, Centurion Garsian gave him a heavy trench knife. Its sheath fit nicely on the left side of his sword belt opposite the gladius. Bilsius's pack had grown a little, but Ket's had grown considerably, and Bilsius clearly didn't like that.

Garsian frequently gave them free time to do as they pleased. The veterans and Tobias spent those hours among the camp followers, and they spent their pay on ale, wine, and women. That didn't appeal to Ket, though he did join them once because they goaded him into it. He drank a little ale and spent an hour with a prostitute. Everything worked, and he felt pleasure in the act, but he clearly didn't experience the same desire as the other men. He recalled that at one time he had thought of Peta that way; not as a whore, but a girl that attracted him in a pleasant and exciting way. But the minute those thoughts surfaced, the hawk's anger flared, so he spent his free time oiling his leather armor, or sharpening his knife and gladius.

Near the end of summer, one evening after dinner, Ket sat near a fire slowly running an oilstone up and down the edge of his gladius. His thoughts drifted to Obregon, Peta, Markus, the dark man, his mum. He missed Obregon, Peta, and his mum, and had concluded the dark man knew something about her death, something that no one should know. Those thoughts brought the hawk's anger forth, and Ket found comfort in the fury that welled in his chest.

"Keep running that stone up and down that blade, and you'll grind the whole thing away."

Ket put the fury aside, focused on the moment, and looked up. Emparis and the men from the tent group had returned from an evening of drinking and camp followers. They grunted and groaned as they took seats around the fire.

Tobias sat next to Ket, and sounded a little uncomfortable. "You know, some of the men think you're kind of strange. You don't like drinking or women. You don't never have any fun."

One veteran said, "He ain't a lover of men, 'cause we'd know if he was."

Another said, "I don't care if he's a lover of sheep. When he's next to me on the shield wall, I don't have to worry about that side."

Emparis said, "Some here think you like the killing. Every now and then a man comes along, and for him the killing takes the place of drink and women. It's his pleasure, but I don't think that's it with you, is it?"

Ket tried to understand his own feelings on the matter and shook his head. "No. It's just that I'm supposed to kill, so I kill. I don't care about that any more than I don't care about the other things." He thought it wise not to mention the hawk's ever-present fury.

A veteran looked pointedly at Emparis. "Word around camp has it we ain't going to fight Andopolous no more."

Emparis nodded. "Garsian thinks our higher-ups are talking with their higher-ups, maybe join forces with them."

At a nearby campfire Bilsius's voice rose in a high-pitched whine. "Carthagen? We're marching to Carthagen? We can't win against Carthagen. They'll slaughter us."

Tobias said, "Why are we still putting up with him?"

His words reflected Ket's own thoughts.

One veteran said, "We're under-manned in both legions. We need every man we can get, even one like him."

Another said, "Especially if we're going to face Carthagen. Otherwise . . ." He didn't finish the thought.

Two days later they broke camp and marched due west.

"Yah," Emparis said as he shouldered his pack. "It's gonna be Carthagen."

That was when the desertions began, not a lot, not by the hundreds. But each morning, when they climbed out of their blankets, the count of soldiers in the legion had declined by a small number. Apparently, Bilsius felt that his own fortunes were no longer best served by military service. A week later, as they prepared for their first battle with Carthagen, he vanished in the middle of the night.

· · · ·

As the Duchies armsmen retreated, taking their wounded and dead with them, Damuel sat astride his horse and worried that the situation would only deteriorate further. With the Lowlands city-states warring among themselves, and Macallan's armies assaulting Mythria on two fronts, it appeared the Three Realms were in for years of instability. The merchants and tradesmen had complained rather loudly.

One of Damuel's lieutenants rode toward him at a trot and halted his horse beside him. "Two dead, my lord, and six wounded."

Damuel cocked his chin toward the retreating Duchies forces, now barely visible in the twisting, turning passes of the mountainous countryside. "And them?"

The young man glanced down the trail. "We estimate four or five dead, and quite a few more than that wounded."

Damuel nodded. "They're getting better. They're learning, aren't they?"

The young lieutenant sighed. "I fear so, my lord."

The duchies armsmen were learning how to fight in the rugged terrain of the Mountain Kingdom. The traps Damuel's men set for them proved less effective every day, and the foreigners had learned to navigate the trails and passes without exposing themselves.

Damuel returned to the camp he used as a base of operations. Colonel Amian awaited him in his pavilion, a career officer for whom Damuel had the greatest respect. They conferred for about an hour, and as the meeting broke up, Amian said, "My lord, we've been fighting these skirmishes and forays for a month now. We've tested their strength and know it well. They can't truly press us."

Damuel agreed. "And Kailill reports similar results on the western front. I fear more what we will face next spring, after they've had a winter to reevaluate their tactics and incorporate what they've learned. And if they come at us in greater numbers . . ."

Amian nodded. "Aye, my lord. We'll have no real trouble with them before winter drives them out of these mountains. Why don't you return to Darliff and your son? We have this in hand, and if something unforeseen does arise, I'll have a courier on your doorstep the next morning."

When Damuel retired he lay awake for a time thinking about that. Amian was eminently competent and able. And barring something dramatically unforeseen, the Duchies would make no headway in Mythria, at least this year. Amian could do without Damuel for a few weeks, perhaps even longer. He fell asleep thinking of Anthon's smile, and Zalestria's body.

Damuel arose early the next morning and rode to Darliff. He, Zalestria, and Anthon had temporarily taken up residence there to be near the fighting on the southern front. While not as large as Mythria, Darliff still boasted all the amenities of a great city.

Damuel arrived late in the afternoon, and as he stepped through the door of their hired apartment, Anthon rushed him and leapt into his arms. "Papa, papa." The six-year-old boy was growing rapidly into his father's stature. "Can I be a soldier when I grow up like you?"

Only a few steps behind the boy, Zalestria answered him. "Your father is a great man, so you can be anything you want. Why, who knows, we live in a time of portentous change. You might stand closer and closer to the throne every day."

Damuel narrowed his eyes and gave her an unhappy look. He didn't want her putting such ideas in the boy's head. It was a disagreement they'd had many times. "I'm not going to discuss that right now. In fact, I'm going to wash the smell of horse off me."

Zalestria leaned close to him and delicately traced a finger across his lower lip. It constantly amazed him the way her mere touch sent that thrill through his body. He wanted to grab her and fuck her up against the wall right then and there, but she gave him a chaste kiss on the cheek. "As soon as I heard you'd arrived, darling, I ordered the servants to draw you a hot bath. I'll be waiting for you."

A half-hour later washed, shaved, and hair combed but still a bit wet, he donned an evening robe. And with Anthon napping under the care of his nursemaid, Zalestria quickly had him out of that robe. After weeks apart, his passion and desire consumed him.

Damuel lay in bed as Zalestria stood and crossed the room completely naked. She poured two glasses of chilled wine, returned to the bed, and handed him one.

As he sipped his wine, she gave him one of those calculating looks. "You know, darling, your officers hold you in extremely high regard."

She frequently broached the same subject after they rutted, the same disagreement, and he wondered how that statement would provide the opening she sought. He also wondered how she knew what his officers thought of him. "Have you spoken to any of them recently?"

She dismissed the question with a wave of her hand. "Just occasionally. You know, when a young officer delivers a dispatch to our door, or something like that. Just ordinary little daily encounters. But they do regard you highly, and I think you should remember that the next time . . . you and Selene don't see eye to eye. Many of your officers will support you no matter what. And with their backing, you can face her from a stronger position."

*No matter what*, Damuel thought. He needed to roll those words around in his thoughts to glean her meaning. No doubt she had thanked the young officer who delivered the dispatch by carnally worshiping with him. Damuel didn't waste time trying to learn who among his officers she spread her legs for, but he did wonder how many on any given day. That would be one way to gain their support, or, for that matter, to have him murdered.

# 29

# First Battle

WITH WINTER APPROACHING, the air in the foothills of the Mountain Kingdom took on a decided chill. Kainborne tightened the straps on his cloak, shivered, and huddled closer to the fire. He hated sleeping in a blanket on the ground, hated the food, hated everything about a soldier's camp. But when Macallan expounded on the pleasure of ". . . eating game you've killed with your own bow that very day," Kainborne had perfected his lies. "Oh, Your Grace, I am but the poorest of bowmen, so I cannot enjoy the enormous pleasure of the kill. But I do relish and look forward to fresh game prepared over an open fire. It's so much more delectable."

Staring at the fire, Kainborne mumbled, "More like burnt meat badly charred by an incompetent cook."

One of Macallan's servants perked up. "Pardon, Master Kainborne?"

"Nothing," Kainborne growled, making no attempt to disguise his surly mood. The man's bloody servants probably loved burnt food as much as the archduke.

A shout from one of the perimeter guards drew everyone's attention.

Kainborne stood, and when someone else shouted, "It's the archduke," he hurried toward the commotion. But as the first riders appeared at the trailhead, their heads bent with exhaustion, he knew the news would not be good.

Macallan had enacted his plan to put half his men under the command of Lagasdale, with orders to attack Carigleigh from the west, while he assaulted Darliff from the south with the other half. Unfortunately, the narrow trails and steep passes of the mountainous terrain did not lend itself to open warfare. And the Scairn had refused to cooperate and come down from their high-country refuges and meet the Duchies armies in a fair fight. They had forced Macallan to resort to smaller battles and skirmishes, and reports from Lagasdale told of the same difficulties there. At least with the strength of their present force, they had established a defensible base camp from which to operate. And they hadn't repeated the debacle in which Clarahm had lost his leg.

Jarrod and the archduke rode into camp, Macallan's mood bordering on rage. "Blast those bloody Scairn. We haven't gotten within five leagues of Darliff. They wait in ambush, and our numbers do us little good when they fight like cowards from hidden redoubts."

Kainborne sent a servant to bring cups of strong brandy for Jarrod and Macallan. And once the archduke calmed down, they adjourned to the comfort of his pavilion to reevaluate the campaign.

Warming his hands near a hot brazier, Jarrod gulped at his brandy, then shook his head sadly. "It may be mid-autumn, but it'll soon start snowing up here."

Macallan's mood had shifted from open rage to seething anger. "Aye, we have no choice. The bloody Scairn probably relish fighting in the snow. And if we give them that advantage, we'll pay a dear price for that. We'll have to withdraw, and try again next spring."

It was time for Kainborne to help them see a more productive path. "Your Graces, if I may be so bold as to make a suggestion, there are better and more profitable alternatives."

Both dukes perked up, and Macallan waved his cup of brandy at Kainborne. "Speak up, man, speak up."

Kainborne paused for dramatic effect. "As we stand here speaking, the armies of Tarnasus and Andopolous are fighting one pitched battle after another. They are weakening each other, but will probably finish by combining forces against Carthagen."

Originally from Carthagen himself, Kainborne knew how they thought. "With that kind of turmoil, there is probably far more to be gained in the Lowland Kingdoms than in these mountains. And we need not wait for next summer to gain it. Winter in the Lowlands will not be warm and cozy, but at least there's no snow, biting chill, or bitter frost. Call in the rest of the levies, and the spoils of Carthagen could be ours for the taking."

Macallan pointed at Kainborne with his cup of brandy, splashing it on the carpets of the pavilion. "But I want Scairn blood. They took my son's leg."

Jarrod frowned and Kainborne said, "Take the spoils of Carthagen this winter, and you can come back for Mythria with even greater strength next spring."

Macallan froze and his eyes narrowed in thought. Kainborne had gotten through to the man.

They broke camp, and Macallan marched his army down out of the mountains. In the foothills Kainborne, Jarrod, and his armsmen turned southwest toward Dramoran, while Macallan headed south to Inversill. They allowed their horses to proceed at a slow walk, all looking forward to a warm hearth after three months in the higher elevations. Autumn had arrived some weeks earlier, and even in Dramoran the air had taken on a chill. Winters in Dramoran could be harsh, but nothing compared to Mythria.

In the Lowland Kingdoms, Tarnasus and Andopolous had fought several battles. And while Tarnasus had won more than they'd lost, their success had been far from overwhelming. Neither city had emerged from the bloodletting as a clear and undisputed victor. And if they didn't soon turn their attention to Carthagen, their war would devolve into a contest of grinding attrition. Each day, the chaos of war created more opportunities for Kainborne.

They reached the gates of Dramoran in early afternoon. Tired and sore, Jarrod retired to his apartments, so Kainborne headed for his workshop. He found the oaf sitting in a chair and snoring. Kainborne kicked the chair. The oaf started awake and jumped to his feet.

"Master Kainborne, I'm at your service."

"Yah, I know," Kainborne said. "Go to the kitchen and tell the cook I'm hungry. Tell her to send a maid with something to eat, and don't you even consider touching it."

As the oaf scurried out of the room, Kainborne eyed the pile of unopened missives on his desk. Given that he'd been gone for four months, he would have expected more. To his relief, there were only about a dozen, and he thought he could get through them in short order. He sat down, grabbed one at random, and opened it, an update from one of his contacts in Carthagen telling him that Tarnasus and Andopolous might soon be at war. His contact had written it at the beginning of summer and it contained nothing he didn't already know. The next letter was similarly out of date, but the third sparked his interest since it had come from Benedictus.

> My dear Master Kainborne.
>
> I hope this missive finds you well. I am concerned that you
> have not responded to my earlier message about the missing
> boy. I know he is of some importance to you, and regret that
> we've been unable to locate him, though we have spared no expense in trying. I await your instructions.
>
> Yours always in service,
> Most Reverend Brother Benedictus

Missing boy? Kainborne's heart raced as he scrabbled through the remaining letters on his desk, searching for the man's *earlier message*. He found it, ripped it open, and read it carefully. It related a story that the boy had secretly befriended a band of highwaymen, and plotted with them to murder Jarrod's guards and steal his rents, then escape with them into the countryside. The abbot also suspected that Brother Obregon had conspired with them, since he vanished the day after the boy's disappearance.

Kainborne stood, and clutching the letter in his hand, he marched out of his workshop. He found Zarkoffa in the stables with a couple of guards overseeing the care of their mounts. Kainborne's anger must have been obvious, because the assassin raised an eyebrow as he approached.

"With me," Kainborne hissed. "Now."

Zarkoffa addressed one of the guards. "Please make sure the stable boy sees to my horse properly."

The fellow nodded.

Kainborne spun about, and with Zarkoffa following, marched out into the middle of Dramoran's castle yard. He stopped, turned to face the man, and extended the letter toward him. "Read this."

Zarkoffa eyed the paper suspiciously, reached out, and took it from Kainborne's hand. He stared at the writing for several seconds, standing in unnatural stillness like a statue. When he finally moved, he shook his head. "The boy may be missing, but I don't believe any of the rest of this garbage."

"Why not?"

Zarkoffa shrugged. "The boy isn't a conniver or a sneak, but Benedictus and his bloody monks are."

Kainborne agreed with him on that. Zarkoffa wasn't aware of the compulsion Kainborne had induced in the boy with his spell, but that made it even less likely any of Benedictus's claims about the boy were true. "Go there and find out exactly what did happen. And if the boy's not dead, then go wherever you must to find him. And if you can't bring him back, then make sure he is dead."

Zarkoffa grinned. "What about Benedictus?"

Kainborne wanted to tell the man to strangle the damn abbot, but he'd hold that option in reserve until he knew the truth. "Use whatever means you deem necessary to get the truth out of him and his damn monks. But leave him alive, at least for now."

• • • •

Advance and stab, retreat and stab, advance and stab, retreat and stab. As enemy swords hammered against Ket's shield, and arrows punched into it, he put his shoulder to it, dug his heels in, and pressed forward. Sweat blinded him, but he didn't need to see well to advance his shield and stab around it.

Ket had learned that even in the tiny world behind his shield, he could actually gauge to some degree the success of a battle, or at least the success of their portion of the shield wall. If they advanced more than they retreated, that was good. But against Carthagen they seemed to advance and retreat in equal measure, and he thought the battle might have deteriorated into a grinding stalemate.

They had moved Ket to the right edge of their eight-man-wide phalanx. Emparis told him that was Garsian's recognition that they could depend on him to hold steadfast at one of the more difficult slots on the shield wall, and he intended to prove them right.

The curved blade on the end of an enemy pike hooked the top of his shield and tried to pull it down. He found himself in one of those rare moments when he pulled on the top of his shield with his left arm instead of pushing, while pressing the lower half of it forward with his hip. His shield twisted, and for an instant he caught a glimpse of an enemy soldier's eyes. He jammed the point of his gladius into the fellow's face, and closed the gap in the wall. In that exchange he'd somehow dislodged the pike pulling on his shield.

Advance and stab, retreat and stab. Like so many other battles, the hawk's fury kept Ket going beyond exhaustion and fatigue. He wondered if he would have survived through the summer without its rage to give him strength.

At mid-day they relieved his phalanx with fresh troops, and Ket and his shield mates withdrew to a rearward camp to rest. He actually slept for a brief period, but Emparis shook him awake. Their phalanx returned to the fighting.

He finished the day sitting on a rock by their campfire, his battered shield laying on the ground nearby. He focused on cleaning blood off his right arm, gladius, face, shoulders, legs. The rest of his tent group sat nearby. They hadn't lost anyone that day.

When Tobias spoke, he sounded weary and fearful. "Did we win or lose?"

Emparis answered him. "Neither, stalemate. But against Carthagen, that's pretty good."

• • • •

Zarkoffa rode his horse through the gates of the monastery. He stopped in front of the stables, remained in the saddle, and shouted, "Atticus, get out here. Now."

Apparently, the monks had all learned to recognize his voice because he didn't have to shout a second time. In a few seconds the old fellow rushed out through the stable doors, his robes flapping behind him. "Master Zarkoffa, what are you doing here?"

Zarkoffa dismounted. "What I'm doing here is none of your bloody business." He handed the old monk the reins. "Take care of my damn horse."

He shielded his eyes and glanced at the sun. He'd arrived about mid-morning, but it would be just like that lazy abbot to still be in bed. "Send someone to find Benedictus, and if he's not in his study, tell him to get his ass there without delay. I'll be waiting for him. And if I have to wait long I'm going to be real unhappy."

It occurred to him that old Atticus was quite pliable and might come in handy. "And I want you and Markus there as well."

Zarkoffa marched straight to the abbot's study and found no sign of Benedictus. Out of pure spite he sat down in the chair behind the abbot's desk, leaned back, and crossed his ankles on top of the desk. He pulled the knife from his belt and picked at his fingernails.

The abbot's study had two entrances. Zarkoffa waited about five minutes, then one door slammed open and Benedictus huffed into the room, breathing heavily. "Master Zarkoffa . . . welcome to . . . Tramorth."

The other door swung open, and Markus marched into the room, though he did so with too much confidence to suit Zarkoffa. Old Atticus followed on Markus's heels, bent over and scurrying like a rodent.

Zarkoffa pointed at Markus and Atticus. "Both of you, leave and close the door, but wait just outside until you hear from me."

Markus frowned, but he and Atticus obeyed.

Zarkoffa stabbed the point of the dagger into the desk, stood, walked around the desk, and closed the door through which Benedictus had come. The abbot trembled visibly as Zarkoffa returned to the chair, sat down, and again crossed his ankles on top of the desk. "Now tell me exactly what happened to the boy."

Benedictus gulped, then started talking. Zarkoffa remained silent and purposefully did not interrupt the man as he told a story much in keeping with that in his letter to Kainborne: The boy had conspired with bandits, and Obregon had probably helped him.

When the abbot finished, Zarkoffa said, "Leave, close the door, and wait outside."

As soon as Benedictus closed the door, Zarkoffa bellowed, "Markus, get in here."

The door opened and the monk stepped into the room. Atticus followed, but Zarkoffa shouted, "Not you, Atticus. Just Markus. Get out, but don't go far."

The old man scurried out of the room, closing the door as he did so.

Zarkoffa said, "Tell me exactly what happened to the boy."

While Markus told his story, as he'd done with Benedictus, Zarkoffa did not interrupt or question him, but remained silent through the telling. Markus's story matched Benedictus's exactly. In fact, it matched it much too closely, as he had suspected it would.

Zarkoffa shouted. "Benedictus, Atticus, get in here."

Both doors opened, and the two monks rushed into the room. At that point Markus's confidence had completely disappeared and he looked just as frightened as the other two.

"This Brother Sylander," Zarkoffa said, "the one who collects rents, I want to talk to him."

Benedictus and Markus both shared a frightened look, then Markus stepped forward eagerly. "I'll go get him."

He turned to leave, but Zarkoffa said, "No. Stay where you are."

Markus turned back to face him. Zarkoffa thought it obvious Markus wanted to retrieve Sylander so he could coach him on the way, probably brow-beat him as well to make sure he held to their story.

Zarkoffa shook his head. "No, I think it best if Brother Atticus retrieved him."

Atticus glanced about uncertainly, and didn't move until Zarkoffa shouted, "Go."

The man spun and disappeared through the door with a speed Zarkoffa would not have believed. Some minutes later he returned with another old monk. At that point they all looked much the same.

"Now," Zarkoffa said, "Brother Sylander stay, and the rest of you get out. But close the doors and wait outside."

Sylander didn't wait to be asked, but immediately told the same story Benedictus and Markus had related. As he spoke, Zarkoffa calmly lifted his boots off the desk, stood, and walked around the desk to face the man squarely. The old fellow continued to recite his story without interruption, his eyes darting back and forth between Zarkoffa and the door.

Zarkoffa spoke in a soft voice. "Shut up, you damn fool."

The man's eyes widened and he went silent.

"Now," Zarkoffa said, "you're going to tell me the truth, not that drivel you're spewing."

Zarkoffa thought he might have to threaten the old fellow, but Sylander babbled like a fishwife gossiping with her cronies. Halfway through the telling Zarkoffa smelled urine, and realized the man had pissed himself. It took some questioning, but in short order he assembled the real story of the boy's disappearance, including a reasonable description of the bandits.

Zarkoffa called the rest of them back into the room, gave Atticus orders to return to the stables, provision his horse for a journey of several days, and told him to prepare a horse-drawn cart that Sylander could handle. He'd prefer to make the old man walk, but they needed to cover a couple of leagues and that would take forever. Atticus scurried out of the room to comply.

Zarkoffa made the remaining three stand there while he sat down at Benedictus's desk, rifled through the drawers, and found a piece of stationary that seemed rather luxurious for a monastery. Then he carefully penned a detailed description of the actual events of that day, concluding that no one really knew why Obregon had disappeared.

He folded the letter, then stood. "Benedictus, Markus, don't let me see you again. Sylander, come with me."

He marched out of the room with the old monk following on his heels. He stopped at the barracks and gave the letter to a guard. "Get on a horse right now and ride to Dramoran as fast as you can. Deliver this to Master Kainborne." He gave the fellow a look to put a little fear in him, and to ensure that he wouldn't dally or delay.

By that time, Atticus had his horse and the cart ready. Zarkoffa mounted up, and with Sylander driving the cart, they headed north up the road that meandered through the valley. He made the monk show him the site of the theft and abduction, but after more than four months, nothing of interest remained. Questioning Sylander further, Zarkoffa learned that while hiding in the forest, the monk had seen the bandits leave the area travelling north up the road. He left Sylander there and rode north.

He spent a couple of days riding up and down the road, inquiring at steadings and holdings. He questioned anyone he encountered, but came up with nothing. A hot meal and a decent night's sleep would help him think better, so near the north end of the valley he stabled his horse at an inn. He'd reevaluate the situation in the morning.

While eating dinner in the common room, he overheard two patrons mention something about bandits. Zarkoffa knew something about him made strangers cautious. But a few coins loosened their tongues, and he learned that travelers on the road had been having trouble of late with a lone highwayman.

# 30

# Deserter and Turncoat

ADDRESSING THE PRIMUS Council, Lucius sounded quite defensive. "They bloodied our nose, but that's all."

Carthagen's legions had fought the Army of the East, as the combined forces of Tarnasus and Andopolous were now called. The battle had lasted four days, and it had not gone well. Invictus General Hadrius sat silently fuming as Lucius spoke, though the look he gave the Chairman of the Primus Council made it clear he had much to say.

Aurelius intended to give him a chance to speak his mind, but not just yet. He stood and didn't wait to be recognized. "Senator Lucius, as I recall, you told us to expect a clear and easy victory." Aurelius sat down.

Lucius dismissed Aurelius's words with an angry wave of his hand. "It was far from a victory for them. They lost as many men as us."

One of the other senators mumbled loud enough for everyone to hear. "But not a victory for us."

Someone swore an epithet, another shouted, and the Primus Council erupted into a chorus of yelling and cursing. Most of the senators stood, and more than one senator shook a fist at another. Lucius contributed to the general chaos by bellowing that everyone should shut up and sit down. Aurelius thought it telling that General Hadrius sat quietly and did not join in the commotion, though the disgust visible on his face made his feelings clear.

Some years ago, Aurelius had watched his father deal with a similar situation. And while he didn't have the esteem of the Senatus Supreme to project authority, he nevertheless imitated him now. He slowly and calmly stood, and remained standing in place without saying a word, without making any gestures, or meeting anyone's eyes. He tried to adopt a look of sadness and disapproval.

Nothing changed at first. Then one senator took note of his silent stance, glanced around, and sat down. Then another did the same, and another, and in a matter of seconds, the only members of the council standing were Aurelius, Lucius, and two senators still shouting at the top of their lungs. One of them glanced Aurelius's way and froze, looked about, then sheepishly sat down. It took his opponent a few seconds to catch on, then he did the same. Still standing, Lucius stared daggers at Aurelius for a long moment, then silently lowered himself into his seat.

It was time for Hadrius to speak his mind. Aurelius had not prompted the general earlier because his fuming anger meant he'd likely just start shouting. But at that moment the man sat silently watching Aurelius, the scowl he'd displayed a few minutes ago replaced by a curious frown.

Aurelius gave him a nod. "Invictus General Hadrius, we had an advantage in numbers, plus our supply lines are short and simple, while theirs are long and stretched thin. Please stand and tell us why the expected easy victory did not come to pass." Aurelius sat down, marveling at the silence that enveloped them all.

Hadrius stood, took a deep breath, then spoke. "We engaged our main force with theirs much too early. We should have harried them for several days and met them in smaller skirmishes. That would have forced them to use up their supplies, while making it impossible for them to replenish them. And don't forget, their troops have been fighting in real battles for months now. They're all experienced veterans, while this battle was the first time most of our troops have engaged in any kind of massed combat. We paid the price for that inexperience."

At that point, just about everyone had a question or two for the general. But instead of shouting them out, they followed protocol by standing and waiting to be recognized by Lucius. That allowed him to control the dialog somewhat, so they never addressed the real issue: Lucius and Divonia wanted to boast of a quick and easy victory, so they and their faction had forced Hadrius to engage prematurely. But that was now a well-known secret, and the debacle had created a critical mass of senators who would not allow that to happen again. At least no one tried to blame Hadrius.

As the meeting of the council broke up, Hadrius approached Aurelius. He lowered his voice. "You reminded me of your father in there."

Aurelius smiled. "I'll take that as a compliment."

Hadrius smiled back, but appeared uncomfortable. "It was. And we all miss your father."

He broke eye-contact with Aurelius and turned his head to his left. Aurelius followed his gaze and saw Maximillian leaving the chamber. His brother appeared unsteady on his feet, and only then did Aurelius realize the meeting had proceeded as if Max hadn't been there.

• • • •

Zarkoffa returned to the monastery, stabled his horse, then commandeered the cart and horse Sylander had driven, plus a monk's robe with a serviceable hood. If his plan worked, he'd only need his knife, so he left his sword strapped to his saddle in the stables. He collected an old chest, a cracked ale cask someone had discarded, plus other odds and ends, and piled them into the back of the cart. None of it had any real value, but it only needed to *look* like he had something worth stealing. He donned the monk's robe—it nicely hid the knife at his belt—and pulled the hood over his head. Then he climbed into the cart, and headed up the road to the north end of the valley.

He spent three days slowly meandering up and down the road between the inn where he stayed at night, and the far north reaches of the valley. Nothing happened during the first two days, but late on the third, while headed back to the inn, he drove the cart around a sharp bend in the road, and found a stranger on a horse blocking his way. The man had a sheathed sword strapped to his saddle.

Zarkoffa brought the cart to a halt, raised his voice, and spoke with a fearful tremble. "Uh . . . good sir . . . you're blocking my way."

The man glanced casually to his left, then to his right. "Yah, I guess I am."

Zarkoffa was rather pleased with the whiny tremble he produced. "If it pleases you, good sir, please move aside a bit so I may pass."

The man shook his head. "But it doesn't please me."

He sighed, lifted his right foot out of the stirrup, over the horse's rump, and slowly dismounted. He reached up to the sword strapped to the saddle and pulled it from the sheath. Then he took two steps forward, raised the sword, and placed the tip of the blade beneath Zarkoffa's chin. "Kindly step out of the cart and let me see what you've got there."

Zarkoffa continued his act. "Please don't hurt me, good sir." He climbed out of the cart, begging and pleading, moving like an old man with aged joints. If he stood up straight he'd stand taller than the highwayman, but he remained hunched over so he didn't appear large or imposing. "I doubt any of my meager possessions will interest a man of your means."

The fellow elbowed him aside. "Let me be the judge of that."

The man had so much confidence he turned his back on Zarkoffa, placed his sword in the cart's bed, and reached for the cracked ale cask. Zarkoffa slipped his hand beneath his robes and pulled the knife from its sheath. He stepped forward, gripped the man's hair from behind with his left hand, and touched the edge of the blade to his throat. The man froze.

Zarkoffa spoke in the same tone he used with the damn monks. "If you want to live, don't say or do anything. There's a length of rope next to that cask. Hand it to me."

The fellow retrieved the rope and offered it behind his back.

Zarkoffa didn't take the rope, but kicked the man's feet out from under him, and drove him face-down onto the ground. Zarkoffa had pre-tied loops in the rope, and sitting on the fellow, with his blade pressed to the side of his neck, it took only a moment to secure his hands behind his back. With a knee in the middle of the man's back, Zarkoffa once again touched the blade to the man's throat. "I don't care about you one way or another. But I believe you have some information I want, and if you help me, I'll let you live. If you don't, I'll cut your throat."

The man nodded his head rapidly. "Whatever you want."

"Exactly," Zarkoffa said. "About four months ago, you and three companions murdered two of Duke Jarrod's soldiers, stole his rents, and abducted a young boy. What did you do with the boy?"

The fellow shook his head. "I don't know anything about that. Not murder. I wouldn't do that."

Zarkoffa flicked his wrist, snapping the tip of the blade sideways and opening a gouge in the man's cheek. The man cried out, then gritted his teeth and remained silent.

Zarkoffa sighed. "If you really know nothing, then you're of no use to me. Give me some reason to let you live."

At that point the highwayman grew quite talkative. He told of how they had turned the boy over to a bailiff enlisting recruits for the Army of Tarnasus. Zarkoffa found it interesting that on their return, someone attacked them and killed the fellow's three accomplices.

"Okay," Zarkoffa said. "You get to live, for now, but you're going to show me where your friends died."

The bandit grimaced. "I'm not sure I can find it again."

Zarkoffa knew the kind of incentive the man needed. "Find it for me, and you get to live. Otherwise . . ."

Zarkoffa tossed the fellow's sword aside, emptied the cart, made the highwayman climb into it, and hog-tied him there. He gagged him with a dirty rag and a length of rope, then tied the reins of the fellow's horse to the back of the cart and returned to the monastery.

He retrieved a guardsman from the barracks, hustled him to the stables, and pointed at the highwayman hog-tied in the cart. "Watch him until I come back. He talks to no one, and no one talks to him. I'll be back shortly." Zarkoffa leaned close to him and growled, "Understand?"

The guard nodded, his eyes wide with fear.

Zarkoffa didn't have time to go looking for the stable master, so he simply bellowed, "Atticus."

The monk appeared out of the shadows, scurrying like a rat. "Yes, Master Zarkoffa."

Fear encouraged idiots like the old man to obey without question. "Saddle my horse and provision it for several days' journey." He pointed at the highwayman's horse. "And provision that horse as well."

Zarkoffa returned to Benedictus's study, kicked the abbot out of the room, and penned an update for Kainborne. That done, he returned to the stables and gave the guard watching the highwayman instructions to take the message to Kainborne immediately.

By that time Atticus had provisioned the horses as instructed. With the bandit's hands still tied behind his back, Zarkoffa helped him climb onto his horse. Then, holding the reins of the bandit's horse, he climbed into the saddle of his own horse, and they rode out through the gates of the monastery headed for Tarnasus.

• • • •

Aurelius changed into simple street clothing and joined Denian with an armed escort. They rode across the city to the edge of Campo Adrina. Aurelius had spent nine years carefully nurturing the trust of the three slum bosses, and had succeeded to some degree, though the level of trust was different with each boss. Interestingly enough, his not-so-secret relationship with Hessian had helped only a little in that regard, even with her. He and she shared a strange kind of mutual attraction without much trust. And interestingly enough, by starting a relationship with no trust, they had nowhere to go but up.

When he and the three bosses needed to meet, they gathered face-to-face in a large inn at the edge of the slum, rather than in a dank basement in the middle of it. That considerably reduced the danger of assassination. Before Aurelius's arrival, the bosses always stationed guards around the inn and cleared its common room. Denian's men joined the guards, as much to keep an eye on them as to prevent any undue interruption of their meeting. And when a meeting ended, Aurelius always compensated the innkeeper with a couple of silver coins.

Hessian had sent Aurelius a note telling him she had some important intelligence regarding the Army of the East, sparking his interest. When he stepped into the common room he spotted her seated with two men at a table at the far end. That day she wore her slum-boss outfit: a man's blouse open down the front almost to her naval, skin-tight men's pants, and knee-high boots. She had decorated her face with

     J. L. Doty

black lip paint and dark makeup that surrounded her eyes, her black hair arranged in a disarray of spikes and ringlets. In one hand she held the bowl of a pipe with the end of its long stem tucked in the corner of her mouth.

When Aurelius stepped into the room, she looked his way, winked, sucked on the pipe, then blew a sequence of smoke rings at him. And with each puff of smoke, she carefully shaped her mouth in a provocative way. Behind her stood Ganda, one of her senior lieutenants. No one would mistake him for anything but a thug.

Tenato sat on her left, boss of the Regalia Slum. His curly white hair, pale white skin, and skeletally thin features set him apart from most Carthagenians. On her right sat Bapo-Anto, boss of the North End Slum. Bapo-Anto would never win a prize for beauty. He stood only chest-high to Aurelius, but probably outweighed him because he carried heavy muscle in the arms, shoulders, chest, and legs. Regardless of his short stature, Aurelius would not want to face him in a fair fight. A scar bisected his mouth from his upper right cheek to his lower left jaw. And someone had once struck him in the face so hard they had shattered the orbit of his left eye. A field of stitch-scars surrounded the eye, so someone had attempted to repair it. But the bones on that side of his face had healed to produce a badly distorted eye socket. His left eye now occupied a position a little lower and to one side of where it should be. He probably had some vision through it, because it did track when he changed the direction of his gaze. But it didn't track in concert with the right eye, which could be quite unnerving.

Aurelius crossed the room, stopped at the table, and nodded. "Hessian, Bapo-Anto, Tenato."

The two men nodded, but Hessian gave him a pouting frown. "I'm upset with you."

He thought he knew what was coming. "I'm sorry. What did I do?"

She lifted an eyebrow. "You haven't seduced me yet."

Technically speaking that was true, at least regarding who had done the seducing. He still took care to never find himself alone with her unless the circumstances were right. She could be unpredictable.

He pulled an empty chair away from the table, stepped around it, and sat down. "Your note said you have some important intelligence for me."

She shook her head. "Not me. This is Bapo-Anto's play."

She glanced over her shoulder. "Ganda."

The thug turned, walked to a door in the back of the room, and opened it. He leaned through the open doorway and said, "We're ready."

A tall, thin fellow stepped through the open door and crossed the room with Ganda behind him. Ganda took his place behind Hessian. The tall fellow stepped up and stood beside Bapo-Anto, but did not sit down.

Up close, Aurelius got a better look at the newcomer. He had a full head of thick red hair, with a scraggly moustache and beard that looked like a poor attempt at a goatee.

Bapo-Anto looked Aurelius in the eyes and cocked his head toward the man standing next to him. "Until recently me friend here fought for Tarnasus, but he decided that was a dangerous way to make a living."

Aurelius kept the look on his face neutral. "A deserter?"

Bapo-Anto grinned, his left eye appearing to look at the fellow standing beside him while his right eye stared directly at Aurelius. "Aye, but more'n that. He's Carthagenian."

Aurelius nodded. "A deserter and a turncoat."

Tenato spoke, his voice a distorted crackle. "I don't like turncoats."

Bapo-Anto frowned. "I wouldn't call him a turncoat exactly. He just took money to do some fighting for 'em. And what's wrong with taking money? We all do it, don't we?"

"Yah," Aurelius said. "I suppose we do. Who is he?"

Bapo-Anto turned his head to look at the man standing next to him. He carefully looked him up, then down, and if one could interpret his distorted features correctly, he didn't appear to like what he saw. "He's an old friend, used to work for me a few years back. Name's Bilsius, but we calls him Flick, because you can't trust him."

"So," Aurelius said. "You can't trust him, and he's going to give me information, and I have no way of knowing if it's true or not. What good is that?"

Bapo-Anto lifted a finger and shook it from side to side while shaking his head along with it. "No, you misunderstood me. It's *you* who can't trust him. I can trust him, because if he don't tell me the truth, I'll cut his throat. So you ask the questions, he tells me the answers, and you get to listen."

Hessian leaned forward. "Flick'll tell the truth, because if he doesn't, I'll do unpleasant things to him for a couple of days before Bapo-Anto cuts his throat."

The red-haired fellow swallowed hard, and Aurelius thought the three slum bosses had nicely made their point. And with that distorted logic, Aurelius questioned the fellow. Or rather, he asked Bapo-Anto questions, Bapo-Anto relayed the questions to Flick, the man answered, and Aurelius got to listen to his words. It didn't take him long to determine that the fellow had probably been an infantryman of low rank, if any rank at all. Aurelius did learn that the rank-and-file soldiers in the Army of the East had little or no confidence they could defeat Carthagen. But when the fellow mentioned he fought on the shield wall, Aurelius said, "Show me your forearms."

Flick's eyes narrowed with distrust. "Why?"

Bapo-Anto snarled. "Just do what he fucking says."

Flick extended both arms and slid the sleeves of his tunic up to his elbows. Aurelius saw no scars there, and even the best of soldiers picked up a cut or two on their right arm when stabbing their gladius around the edge of their shield. That meant this fellow hid behind his shield, which made him a weak point in the shield wall. In the legions, a man's shield mates would not tolerate that, and had their own ways of removing a coward like him from the equation. But he had survived almost two seasons of battles against Andopolous, and that didn't add up.

It wouldn't work to ask a direct question like, "Why did your shield mates let a coward like you survive an entire season of battles?" Instead, he skirted the issue, asked a series of indirect questions, and learned what he wanted. He and his generals had suspected that the Army of the East was under-manned, but he now knew it for a certainty. And if they allowed cowards like this fellow to survive, the shortage must be close to critical. But beyond that, the fellow had little to offer. On the other hand, that he stood there at all was an interesting piece of information. The legions were adept at catching and hanging deserters. That they had failed to catch this fellow, and their lack of confidence that they could defeat Carthagen, probably meant he wasn't the only one to turn tail and run.

Aurelius didn't want any of the slum bosses to think he owed them anything, and they wouldn't have picked up on the manpower issue or the desertions. He looked Bapo-Anto in his good eye. "So far he hasn't told me anything I don't already know. Next time, bring me an officer, preferably one of some reasonable rank, otherwise it's not worth the trip."

Flick bristled, opened his mouth to say something, but Bapo-Anto fired an elbow out to the side and caught the deserter in the gut. Flick grunted and doubled over.

Aurelius stood, sliding his chair back with his legs. "Is there anything else?"

Hessian carefully placed her pipe on the table and stood. "I'll see you to the door."

She stepped around the table, took his arm, and made him walk casually with her across the room like a couple at a grand ball. The inn had a small vestibule at its main entrance that served as a cloakroom. As they stepped into it, Hessian turned to face him, and he realized she had him alone in that small room. Knowing her, she had intentionally maneuvered him into that situation.

She pointed a finger at him as if scolding a naughty child. "You learned something in there that pleased you. I don't know what, but I can tell you did. After all, at this point I know you rather well, don't I?"

She arched an eyebrow and smiled. "And in Campo Adrina, everything has its price. That means you owe me."

He spoke cautiously. "As long as the price is reasonable, what do I owe you?"

She leaned forward and stopped with her lips a finger's breadth from his. "A kiss."

Before he could react, she wrapped her arms around his neck and pressed her lips against his. He realized he was an amateur caught up in a game with a consummate professional, though he did enjoy the taste of her. And a piece of him wanted to relax his guard and just spend the afternoon with her.

She ended the kiss, grinned, and said, "I think you owe me a lot more than a kiss."

He turned away from her and crossed the short distance to the outer door, paused there and looked over his shoulder. "Okay, I owe you more." He gave her a lurid grin. "Perhaps sometime you'll get to collect it."

He moved quickly, opened the door, and stepped out into the street. Denian and his men gathered up their horses, and as Aurelius climbed into the saddle, he saw her standing in the inn's doorway. She smiled, winked, and blew him a kiss. "Trust me. You will enjoy it."

Denian leaned close to him and lowered his voice. "Uh, Your Grace . . . you have something black smeared on your lips."

Aurelius wiped his lips with his sleeve and spurred his horse into a trot.

# 31

# Defeat

THE MAN ON Ket's left went down, opening a gap in the shield wall. In that situation he had learned to change the cadence from advance and stab, to hold, shuffle, stab, hold, shuffle, slash, and keep doing that until he closed the gap in the wall. He and his mates quickly closed the opening, but at the last moment a gladius chopped into his left thigh. The wound would have been far more serious had not his skirt of boiled leather segments taken the bite out of the blow. But the cut opened a bad slash, and he stumbled as pain shot up his leg, though he didn't fall.

The cadence of the shield wall shifted to a steady repeat of retreat and stab, retreat and stab. A sharp crack and the sound of splintering wood startled Ket, and the man on his right cried out. A ballista bolt twice as long as his arm and half as thick had split the man's shield, and skewered his chest. He fell toward Ket, went down, and took Ket with him.

• • • •

Seated on his horse on a rise overlooking the battlefield, Aurelius watched the carnage below. The battle had raged for three days: one day of stalemate, a second day of begrudging progress, and a third day with a slow but steady crawl toward victory.

He glanced at the sun, noted that only about two hours remained before sunset.

On a horse next to him, Hadrius spoke as if reading his thoughts. "It will be done before sunset. They may put together a few skirmishes or raids tomorrow, but not a concerted battle, nothing we can't handle."

The man sounded melancholy, a general who didn't rejoice in victory, or perhaps a man who fought to achieve victory, but didn't rejoice in the price they paid. Aurelius thought that a good thing, and he decided he liked Hadrius.

"What of next week?" Aurelius asked. "And the week after that, and the month after that?"

Hadrius shook his head. "Your information was correct. They were badly under-manned. And I must thank you for ensuring Lucius didn't try to play general again. We executed a proper battle plan and weakened them before engaging their main force. Do have your spies monitor the situation, but I doubt they can put together even three legions between them."

Aurelius needed to make sure the general understood him. "We'll need them when we face the Duchies. And after that we may have to fight the Mythrians. Keep the killing to a minimum. If a man resists, or is sorely wounded to the point where death is a kindness, then so be it. But accept surrender and take as many captives as possible, and I'll want to talk to the officers. Treat them well, because I fear we're going to need them."

Hadrius nodded. "You and I think alike on that issue, though your mother is more . . ."

Aurelius finished the thought for him. "Bloodthirsty."

Hadrius winced. "That was not the word I sought."

Aurelius couldn't hide a smile. "But it does work, doesn't it?"

Hadrius ignored his question. "Let us hope many down there live, though some will have no choice but the pit."

Aurelius grimaced. "I hate that tradition."

• • • •

Something awakened Kainborne from a sound sleep. He'd been having a wonderful dream in which he marched victorious into Carthagen and exacted revenge upon his old enemies.

"Fire! Fire!"

That shout, even muffled and distant, sobered him as no other word could. With stone walls, wooden beams, plank floors, and tapestries hung everywhere, fire might easily turn a castle into a raging inferno.

He sat up, threw the covers off, rolled out of bed, and while he pulled on a robe, he considered what might be of value in his bedroom. He had a small strongbox of tinctures, but he could replace them. The chest of old scrolls Macallan had gifted him had been too large to store in his workshop, so he'd had servants place it in a corner of his bedroom. And purely as a matter of convenience, he'd stored all the scrolls he'd removed from it in a closet near his bed, where he kept his most valuable scrolls. Those he could not replace. He'd have to get a crew of servants up to the room to carry it all to safety before the fire spread.

He rushed to the door of his room and opened it, thinking to call for help. But he saw no flames roaring through the halls, and only smelled traces of smoke. He heard more shouts, but muffled and distant, so he concluded he faced no immediate danger. His heart calmed.

He turned and walked back into his room, pulled on a pair of shoes, then headed for the lower floors. As he made his way down a stairway to the second floor, he saw the flickering orange glow of flames flashing through a small window. He stopped there, glanced down at the castle yard, and his heart went cold. The fire had completely engulfed the west tower. Flames licked out through the windows of his workshop on the first floor. A line of servants and soldiers had formed a bucket brigade that snaked across the ground, an ill-fated attempt to quash the flames. He ran down the stairs as he had never run before.

The bucket brigade didn't really put the fire out; it simply ran its course. Kainborne wasn't able to enter his workshop until just after dawn. Everything in it now lay in ruins, but with one exception, none of it really mattered. He found the blackened and twisted wire remnants of the hawk's cage, and all that remained of the bird were a few badly charred bones, talons, and feathers.

Kainborne didn't know what to expect. The scroll in which he'd found the formula for the spell had also documented a different formula for breaking the enchantment. But Kainborne had modified the original formulary, and the scroll mentioned nothing about the effect on the boy if the predator died before properly dissolving the sorcerous connection between the two. With no corporal body tying the hawk's spirit to the mortal world, Kainborne feared it would be trapped in the boy's soul. Better if the boy died with the bird, but he didn't think that likely. He just didn't know what to expect, and that infuriated him. He could only hope Zarkoffa found the boy and brought him back—or killed him.

· · · ·

The hawk screamed and dove for Caerie's muzzle, going for her eyes. She batted it aside with a forepaw, careful to keep her claws retracted. She crouched, lowered herself almost to her belly, knowing her fur would blend into the tall grasses of the savanna, and hopefully confuse the bird for a few seconds as it wheeled around for another attack. The hawk had gone murderously insane, screeching its anger and hatred, but something in Caerie warned her to only defend herself, and not kill it.

As it came for another pass, she leapt, using the power of her haunches to launch her high into the air, retracting her claws to avoid harming the bird. But in that instant she transformed from lioness to Scairn and caught the hawk in her hands. She fell to the ground in a tumble, focusing on the clutch of her fingers as she rolled, careful not to loosen her grip. As she struggled to her feet, holding its wings tightly against its body, it ripped at her arms with its talons, shredding the skin there. She looked into its eyes, noted their unusual shade of pale blue, and the bird calmed.

Caerie thrilled at the freedom of flight, had experienced nothing like it before, wanted to soar through the heavens and never stop. She dipped a wing and swung about on a thermal, sharing her joy with the young peasant boy—

That woman's voice came to her again, slithering through her thoughts like the hiss of a snake. "No, child, it is too soon."

The man agreed, his voice cold like a steel blade on the harshest of winter nights. "The time will come, but not now."

Caerie gasped and sat up in bed. Soaked in sweat and breathing heavily, she struggled for air, felt dirty and unclean, as if she had fallen into a cesspool of hatred. She remembered almost nothing of the dream, though the terror of it still haunted her. And she recalled the unusually pale blue eyes of a hawk. Hawks didn't have blue eyes. And Melceinnia had spoken of a boy with unusually pale blue eyes. Were the two connected? And what games did that damn priestess hope to play?

• • • •

The hawk's rage consumed Ket, devoured him the way a big cat might swallow a tiny mouse; too small to be a meal, just an afterthought. The hawk flapped its wings, the muscles of its shoulders straining to climb higher and higher, the ground below shrinking into the distance. It wanted to kill, to rend flesh, to hurt anyone it found, but above all it wanted to taste the blood of its captor, the being who had imprisoned it in another spirit.

Ket struggled to be free of its fury, to control it, and he realized that something had changed. The hawk's rage was not his, was not an intimate part of his own soul the way it had been for so long now, didn't blossom within him, but remained separate and distinct. He saw it, understood it, a primal need to dominate the skies, anger that it lived locked in a cage of steel wire. Imprisoned in the dungeon of another spirit, it feared that it would never hunt again. And that it could do so only through Ket's dreams, drove it to despair.

Ket understood the hawk, understood its anger and fears, and when the girl entered his soul, he thought he might find peace. In the hawk's body the two of them together soared through the heavens, and her presence gave him joy. He released the hawk and gave it the freedom to rule the heights. But in his heart he knew only his death could free it completely. Then something intervened and ripped him and the girl apart.

• • • •

Ket slammed awake and cried out, saw only darkness surrounding him. He tried to sit up but butted his forehead against something hard. He lay back and took several breaths, struggling to recall his last seconds in the battle. But his mind kept returning to the soaring heights, and some sort of battle with a lioness, and the strange, unclean presence of that woman and man. He tried to focus, and by carefully ordering his thoughts, he found he could ignore the hawk and recall his last memories of the battle. The man next to him had gone down, a ballista bolt pinning his shield to his chest, and he'd taken Ket down with him. After that, he recalled nothing.

The hawk had left him, and yet it still commanded all his thoughts, both waking and dreaming. The bird's perceptions distracted Ket. Its focus zoomed in on an object, then shifted abruptly to something else, frequently startling him. But that was also how it helped him fight, and he knew his life depended on learning to make use of the bird's instincts, though now was not the time for that. Its interference angered him, so he shook his head, trying to clear his mind.

In the dark he reached down and touched the gash in his thigh. It hurt, but he'd lived with worse. The hawk regarded the pain with disdain, as if it thought he should stop whining and shake it off. Blood around the wound had dried, so some hours had passed. Exploring with his hands, he learned he lay on the churned dirt of the battlefield. Above him, the cylindrical curve of his shield partially protected his head, torso, and thighs. His lower legs protruded from the bottom of his shield, and something pinned his ankles to the ground. That angered him, so he kicked until he freed his ankles, realizing the impediment had been a dead body.

He pushed on the shield and it moved a little. His frustration overcame him, and he pushed harder, lifting it up and shoving it to one side. Above him the false light just before dawn colored the skies. A cold, stiff hand plopped onto his face, a hand connected to an arm that ended in splintered bone and torn meat.

"We got a live one here."

At the sound of the shout Ket tried to freeze, but the hawk's anger pushed him to action and he sat up. Cold steel touched the side of his throat, and glancing to his right he saw several inches of a blade that rested on his shoulder, a blade held by someone behind him.

"Don't move, boy, or I'll take your head off."

A man wearing no armor or uniform stepped in front of him. He wore common street clothing that reminded Ket of the homespun he'd grown up wearing, and the fellow aimed a crossbow at Ket's chest. "Stand up, boy."

The blade lifted off his shoulder. Ket rolled over onto his hands and knees. He paused for a moment, hoping to spot his gladius. Someone said, "Don't even think about it, boy."

It didn't really matter. Ket saw no sign of his blade, and wasn't sure what he'd do with it against a crossbow. His thigh complained as he struggled to his feet, facing the man who'd been behind him with the sword. Like the other fellow, he wore simple clothing.

Once on his feet, Ket glanced around and realized any resistance would have been futile. Four men surrounded him, one with a crossbow, one with a sword, and two with cudgels. The swordsman held the point of his blade to Ket's chest, and the crossbowman aimed his bolt at Ket's face. The two men carrying clubs pinned his arms behind his back, stripped him of his cuirass, greaves, bracers, and other armor, and tied his hands with a length of rope. Then they led him to a small group of captives seated on the ground, all with their hands tied. Ket didn't recognize anyone from his phalanx.

When Ket sat down one captive said, "It's the pit for us."

Ket didn't know what that meant. "What's the pit?"

The man shook his head and closed his eyes. "The fighting pit." He would say no more.

Ket sat there for several hours as they added more captives to the group. At midday, a stocky fellow with a short club tied to his belt stopped nearby and looked them over. "My name's Crenselus," he bellowed. "I'm the pit boss. I'm in charge of you, and you do what I say. Now stand up, all of you."

Hampered by the wound in his thigh and his hands tied behind his back, it took Ket a little longer to get to his feet than most of the others. One of his comrades struggled with a badly wounded leg and couldn't make it. Crenselus walked up to the fellow and planted his fists on his hips. "Someone cut his throat."

One of Crenselus's men pulled a knife, but someone shouted, "Hold there," and they froze. A tribune on a mounted horse guided the animal at a walk among them, and stopped near Crenselus. "No killing," he said. "You get two per cohort. That's the custom, but no killing."

Crenselus shrugged. "They're going to the pit. They're gonna die anyway."

The tribune shook his head. "Maybe in the pit, but not here. Leave him for the physikers."

The pit boss lined up his captives, then secured them to a long length of rope, the prisoners spaced about three paces apart. With a guard of ten men, most carrying clubs, Crenselus marched them off the battlefield. Ket had spent much of the summer and autumn marching, and easily slipped into the cadence of putting one foot in front of the other, though the uneven gait of marching with a limp tired him faster than normal. When a guard walked past Ket, the hawk focused on him, focused on his cudgel, focused on the knife at his belt. Ket might have missed the knife had not the hawk made him aware of it.

On that battlefield, Ket's relationship with the hawk had transformed. He and it had been at odds for years, ever since that day in Kainborne's room in the monastery when the man had made Ket look into the hawk's eyes. Ket didn't know how or why, but a few hours ago he had come to terms with the animal. Now he no longer resisted the hawk, and the bird no longer fought him. And he thought that might help considerably the next time he fought for his life.

They marched west for about four leagues, then crossed a bridge over a wide river. In late afternoon they approached a small cluster of one-story mud and wattle huts. Ket thought they were approaching a large village or steading. But as they passed through it, the buildings didn't end, and changed from mud and wattle to heavy beam and wood plank. They walked further, and he realized the village extended to the horizon. As they marched deeper into the massive village, the road they walked grew crowded with pedestrians, men on horses, and horse-drawn carriages. On either side, buildings constructed of stone alternated with wooden structures, some with a second floor.

Such an enormous village amazed Ket. "What is this place?" he asked.

A guard butted him between the shoulder blades with his cudgel, and Ket stumbled. "It's Carthagen, you damn fool."

Ket had never seen a city before. His life up to then had consisted of the castle at Glenmoore, the monastery, and the Army of Tarnasus stretched out and marching down a long road, or lined up for battle. He tried to take in every sight and sound, but it overwhelmed him. To stop his head from spinning, he tuned it out and focused on the ground in front of him. If Ket escaped, he'd have no way of navigating the streets of the city.

Crenselus and the guards led the captives to a wrought-iron gate between two buildings. Thuggish looking guards stood on either side of it. The pit boss nodded to the guards and they opened the gate. Beyond it they marched through a narrow space between buildings, then through a door, down a flight of stairs, and into a large room with a dirt floor. Dim tapers lit the subterranean chamber poorly, and a haze of greasy, strange-smelling smoke hung in the air. The guards used their cudgels to line the captives up with their backs to a stone wall.

Crenselus walked up the stairs and shouted, "We're ready!"

A few minutes later he reappeared followed by a woman and two men, all three of them rather odd looking. The woman had painted her lips with some sort of black coloring and wore men's breeches and boots. One of the men looked like a tall, ghostly skeleton. The other was a short fellow, heavily muscled, with a scar across his mouth, and a misshapen eye socket that badly distorted his features. The hawk spotted a dagger on the woman's hip, a knife on the ghost's belt, a stubby club dangling from the short-man's waist.

With Crenselus leading them, they stopped at the first prisoner on the rope, conversed for a few seconds, then moved on to the next. In that way, they slowly worked their way down the line. When they reached Ket, Crenselus said, "He's wounded, may be useless." He used his cudgel to tap Ket's wounded thigh, and Ket grimaced at the shock of pain.

The short fellow with the damaged face leaned forward and peered at Ket's thigh. "Doesn't look too deep. Give it a week to heal. If it festers, just cut his throat. If it heals, he's a strapping lad. Be fun watching him in the pit."

# 32

# The Fighting Pit

THE DAY AFTER Carthagen's victory, Obregon rode into one of the surviving camps of the Army of the East. Perhaps a thousand men remained in that camp, and no sentry challenged him, which attested to the magnitude of their defeat. He knew how soldiers thought, and he walked among them speaking as one soldier to another. He claimed he wanted to find his son, a young man named Ket with unusually pale blue eyes. Without that single striking feature, it would have been useless to ask after one otherwise ordinary-looking boy. He spent hours at it, and late in the afternoon, while describing Ket to an older veteran, the man said, "Healthy lad, right? A little taller than most, well-muscled, broad shoulders, but not a big man like you."

Obregon tried not to get his hopes up. "Yah, that sounds like him."

The veteran nodded. "He was in my centuria, different phalanx. Didn't say much. Funny thing, wasn't interested in women and drink, but he fought well."

"He would," Obregon said. "Do you know if he survived?"

The man shook his head. "They was in the thick of it. No one came out of that. He's either dead or captured. Sorry, old man."

Obregon continued working his way through the survivors, but came up with nothing more. He mounted his horse, rode down to the battlefield, and noted the way Carthagen's army treated the prisoners: no death stroke unless absolutely necessary, physikers attending to the wounded, regardless of allegiance. It's what Obregon would have done, because Carthagen would soon need those men to defend against the Duchies, and maybe the Mythrians as well.

Obregon wasn't about to search through all the bodies, because if Ket had died, it didn't really matter. On the other hand, if captured, he'd end up in Carthagen one way or another.

• • • •

The highwayman told Zarkoffa that while returning from Tarnasus, someone had ambushed him and his companions. The attack had come in the foothills on the far side of the mountains just west of the city. Travelling at the fastest pace the horses could handle, it took them a week to get there. But the fellow didn't recall the exact location, so once in the vicinity they slowed. At one point the bandit stopped them, glanced around, shook his head, and said, "No, this isn't it." They moved on.

They did that several times until they finally rounded a sharp bend in the trail and came upon a badly decomposed body. The fellow lay by the edge of the trail. His shiny bald head had dried in the sun and turned black, but remained shiny and bald. He still retained the nose ring, but someone had relieved him of the earrings and other baubles.

Zarkoffa dismounted to examine the body. There appeared to be an abdominal wound of some sort, but the fellow had died by a sword thrust to his chest. Then his assailant had cut his throat for good measure.

To make sure the captive bandit didn't escape, Zarkoffa hog-tied him again. Then he searched the surrounding forest. It took more than an hour, but he eventually found two bodies. Their assailant had dumped them in the brush a dozen paces into the undergrowth. Both had decomposed as badly as the bald fellow. Their attacker had split one fellow's head with a sword or axe, nearly cleaving it in two. The broken stub of an arrow's shaft still protruded from the other's chest. Given the body's present state of decay, without that evidence Zarkoffa would not have been able to determine the cause of death.

Zarkoffa returned to the hog-tied highwayman and drew his knife. Laying helpless on the ground, the man said, "You said if I found it for you, I get to live."

Zarkoffa grudgingly nodded. "You're right, I did, and I owe you that."

Zarkoffa extended the knife toward the man's tied hands. The man breathed a sigh of relief.

Zarkoffa said, "But I lied."

The highwayman's eyes widened and he screamed, "No, please no."

Zarkoffa gripped his hair and pulled up, arching the man's back. He slashed the knife across his throat, cutting it deeply. The fellow gurgled and spit blood, choked and coughed for a few minutes, then he went silent. Zarkoffa left him there in the trail next to his companion. He'd sell the fellow's horse and tack to add a few coins to his purse.

As Zarkoffa headed down the trail to Tarnasus, he thought he now knew where Obregon had disappeared to.

• • • •

Ket's captors forced him and the other prisoners to sit down on the dirt floor, their backs to a wall, five guards watching over them. With his hands still tied behind his back, Ket found it impossible to get comfortable. But curling up his right leg allowed him to extend his left leg out straight, taking pressure off the wound in his thigh.

Exhaustion weighed heavily on him, and he closed his eyes, hoping he might actually sleep. But then he heard that whiney voice. "I thought that was you."

Ket opened his eyes. Bilsius stood over him, a smug grin on his face. One guard asked, "You know this one, Flick?"

"Yah," Bilsius said. "He's an old friend of mine. Stand him up."

Two guards grabbed Ket by his elbows and armpits and lifted him to his feet. Bilsius leaned close to him. "You tried to murder me."

The guard asked, "Why'd he try to murder you?"

Bilsius snarled, "He's a coward."

The hawk wanted Ket to attack, but Ket hesitated. Then he realized Bilsius would enact his revenge regardless, so Ket said, "Sorry I failed." He snapped his head forward, butted the asshole in the right eye, connected nicely with the edge of the eye socket.

Bilsius screamed and staggered back, a trail of blood dripping down his cheek. Reaching up, he ran his hand across his face, smearing the blood. He looked at his fingers, then pointed at Ket. "See what I mean. He's a maniac."

He stepped forward, drew his fist back, and punched Ket in the gut. Ket's abdominal muscles spasmed, he doubled over, and the two guards holding him released him, dropping him to the floor. A cudgel slammed into his shoulder, another into his back. The other prisoners broke into an uproar, screaming and shouting, but Bilsius and his friends ignored them. With no one to stop them, they'd likely beat Ket to death, intended or not. The hawk raged, its perceptions distracting Ket, focusing on an object, then shifting abruptly to something else. Ket spotted a knee, kicked out, connected with it solidly, and heard ligaments snap. The fellow screamed and tumbled to the floor. Ket rolled aside as a club thudded into the dirt floor where his head had been an instant earlier, but another club grazed the side of his temple and his senses reeled.

"What the bloody hell do you think you're doing?"

The roar of that voice brought everyone to a stop. Ket scrabbled about on the dirt floor, couldn't get to his feet with his hands tied and his senses spinning. Unable to defend himself, he knew they'd now kill him.

That voice roared again. "You flaming idiots, you bloody fucking fools!"

Ket's senses steadied and he focused again. Crenselus stood over him, screaming at the top of his lungs. "Who's responsible for this?"

One guard sheepishly lowered his eyes and mumbled, "Flick."

The pit boss spun toward Bilsius. "This was your idea?"

Bilsius flinched. "What does it matter? They're condemned anyway."

In a blinding instant Crenselus cocked his arm back and swung out, hitting Bilsius with a haymaker punch to the nose. Blood sprayed, and Bilsius tumbled backward like a tree toppled in the forest. He landed on the floor and bounced once. He groaned, struggled back up onto his elbows, but his eyes rolled around and his head wobbled about.

Crenselus stood over him and spoke softly. "Yah, they're condemned, but they die in the fighting pit, not here. I'm going to call in a physiker to see to the lad, and you're paying for it. And you get no wages until the lad's ready to fight."

Ket had some bruises, but with a couple day's rest, the physiker thought the blow to his head would be fine. He applied a greasy salve to the wound in Ket's thigh, and told Ket to hope it didn't fester.

• • • •

When the carriage came to a stop in front of the inn, Damuel snugged his cloak about him and opened the door in its side. An icy wind blasted him in the face as he stepped out onto the cobblestones of the street, and snow crunched beneath his boots. Wheeled transport would soon be useless in Mythria, and they'd resort to sleds as they did every winter in the mountains.

Flakes of white slanted sideways through the air as he shouted up to the driver. "I'll be at least a couple of hours. Stable the horses with the inn, get in out of the cold, and get yourself a warm mug of mulled wine."

Inside the inn, Damuel brushed snow off his shoulders and stomped his boots. The innkeeper took his cloak and led him to a private room. General Kailill awaited him, along with two of his senior lieutenants and two of Damuel's, one of them Colonel Amian. When they had deployed to Darliff and Carigleigh, they'd abandoned their ritual of sharing dinner and drinks once a month, but had resurrected it upon their return to the city of Mythria.

The five men greeted him warmly. They downed several drinks, then dined on roasted bighorn. They spiced the food and drink with stories of past exploits, many of which were actually true. After dinner the innkeeper served them a bottle of strong brandy. If they remained true to form, one bottle would not be enough, nor two.

The atmosphere grew somber, and the four lieutenants looked to Kailill, who swirled the brandy in his glass thoughtfully. He clearly had something to say and would obviously speak for all five of them.

Kailill looked Damuel in the eyes. "Your Grace, it occurs to me we could do a better job of fighting this war if we actually treated it like a war."

Damuel kept the look on his face neutral. "You know I value any advice you offer." He took a moment to meet eyes with each of the other men. "That goes for all of you."

Kailill relaxed a little, and a hint of tension Damuel had not been aware of left the room. He got the impression he had just passed a test.

Kailill continued. "We could be a lot more effective if we took the fight to the Duchies, rather than waiting here in our mountain passes. Hit and run tactics. Venture forth with moderately sized forces, strike, then withdraw. All the better if they chase us into *our* winter strongholds."

Damuel raised his drink and sipped. "I'm listening. Tell me more."

Kailill did all the talking, with only the occasional comment from one of their subordinates. Damuel asked several questions and threw out some ideas of his own. But when they finished, he asked the most important question of all. He looked pointedly at the four lieutenants. "Does he speak for all of you in this?"

Not one of them hesitated, and all four nodded.

In the carriage on the way back to the palace, Damuel considered that discussion carefully. No one had said anything overtly, but in their words he had heard underlying discontent with the way Selene had dictated their actions, forcing them to fight a war piecemeal. Discontent with the Crown could be a dangerous thing. No wonder they had been overly circumspect, then relieved that Damuel listened without judgement. And their discontent had sounded far too much like the pillow talk Zalestria whispered in his ear after they rutted.

Once back in their apartments he related a highly edited version of that discussion to Zalestria, curious to see her reaction. He finished with, "Are they thinking with their brains, or is someone encouraging them to think with their cocks."

She grinned, leaned close and kissed him on the cheek. "Darling, I learned long ago that sometimes you have to get a man to think first with his cock, then point the way so he can start thinking with his brains."

That was about as close as he might ever get to an open admission that she was fucking some, if not all, of his officers.

• • • •

Ket spent an unpleasant night sitting on the floor of that dank basement. The guards woke them all in the morning, and from the groggy looks on the other prisoner's faces, they had slept no better.

Their captors fed them a surprisingly good meal of hot venison stew with a crust of hard bread and a cup of ale. Bilsius had said they were condemned, and Crenselus had agreed with him, saying, ". . . but they die in the fighting pit, not here."

Ket glanced at the man next to him on the rope, an older veteran. "This the last meal for us condemned men?"

The fellow shrugged. "More like they want us healthy so we fight better. More entertaining if we fight better."

Ket asked, "The fighting pit?"

The fellow nodded, silently chewing his food.

From him, and a couple of other veterans nearby, Ket learned that Domaxus the Conqueror had slaughtered his opposing armies by executing every survivor. But that left the Lowlands with a terrible shortage of men, no one to till fields and bring in crops, so they instituted the custom of the fighting pit. The victor of a war selected two healthy men from each losing cohort, about twenty men per legion, and they died in the pit fighting the winner's champions. That allowed the winner to punish the loser in an appropriate manner, but not devastate its male population.

Ket didn't want to die a condemned man. "What if you beat their champion?"

One veteran said, "Don't know. Never heard of that."

Another said, "It ain't never happened. And if you try, they make it worse for you."

They finished eating and sat in silence for a couple of hours. With a full stomach Ket dozed off, but boots thudding on the stairway woke him. Crenselus had arrived with more guards.

"On your feet," he bellowed.

Those who were slow to rise received encouragement from the guards' cudgels. Then they hustled them up the stairs and out onto a busy street. Crenselus marched them south, and occasionally a citizen of Carthagen raised a fist at them or shouted an epithet. But to Ket's surprise, most of the people in the streets eyed them with curiosity, not malice or hate.

The wound in Ket's thigh had closed and no longer seeped fluids . The surrounding skin remained a healthy pink, not the angry red of festering. Marching across the city didn't bother him, and his limp had lessened considerably, so maybe they wouldn't cut his throat.

On the south side of the city they crested a small rise, the road ended, and Ket got his first look at the fighting pit. Beneath him stretched a vast open-air amphitheater that began with a grassy slope directly in front of him. Slanting downward, the grass ended about two hundred paces from him. Beneath that, native rock had been carved into tiered, circular shelves, seats that surrounded a round, flat expanse of dirt a hundred paces across: the fighting pit. A hundred or more heavy wooden posts stood in a ring around the edge of the pit, like silent sentries protecting the onlookers from the combatants. Each rose out of the ground to about the height of a tall man, and Ket wondered at their purpose.

A cluster of carpenters appeared to be putting the finishing touches on a small wooden structure in the center of the tiered seating. It offered shaded seating, probably for someone special.

The veteran behind him said, "Common folk get to sit on the grass slope. They'll bring wine, ale, and food, and have a good time."

Ket concluded the rich people and nobles sat on the tiered, stone shelves. But the grassy slope and stone shelves didn't circle the entire fighting pit. On the far side a single-story stone structure enclosed about a quarter of it. Ket didn't know how to interpret what he saw there. Some sort of mechanical structure covered its flat stone roof, and the front of it appeared to be segmented into a series of cells faced with iron bars.

Ket pointed. "What's that?"

The veteran grimaced. "The cages."

Ket couldn't hide his confusion. "What are they for?"

The man shook his head. "You'll see."

Crenselus marched them down onto the floor of the fighting pit. And now much closer to the stone structure, Ket confirmed his conclusion that it consisted of a row of narrow cells fronted by iron bars; *cages*, the veteran had called them. The pit boss paced back and forth while the guards lined the prisoners up about fifty paces from the cages.

One guard said, "We're ready, boss."

Crenselus stopped pacing, faced the prisoners squarely and planted his feet, his fists on his hips. He slowly looked up and down the rope line, nodded, then raised his hands to the heavens. "Look at this place, will you? Ain't it magnificent?"

He lowered his hands. "Though it ain't been put to use since I was a boy. But I do have fond memories of it."

He looked at the prisoners and his eyes narrowed. "First, I got a little demonstration for you."

He spun about and bellowed, "One up."

Ket heard a clanking, clattering mechanical sound. The bars of one cage rose straight up into the mechanical contraption on the roof, opening the cage to the ground of the fighting pit.

Crenselus put a hand to his mouth and shouted, "Down."

A loud clack startled Ket. The bars of that cage dropped, and thudded against the dirt floor of the pit, once again sealing the cage.

The pit boss bellowed, "Two up."

The process repeated, but with the bars of two cages rising into the roof.

"Down," he shouted, and the bars thudded down.

Crenselus turned back to the prisoners. "Clever, ain't it?"

The man nodded as if agreeing with himself. "When you're put in a cage, you'll get basic armor to match your opponents: greaves and bracers. One man to a cage, and you're going to live there for the rest of your life. When the time comes, they'll open a cage . . . or two, or maybe ten, and no one knows which cages they're gonna open. If your cage opens and you don't want to fight, just sit there. They'll come and drag you out, and you'll die a lot worse than if you'd come out on yer own. Come out and fight well, and we'll give you a quick end."

He pointed to the ground at his feet. "There'll be a table right here, always covered with lots of arms: swords, shields, battle axes, the works. Your opponents will also be out here waiting for you. When your cage opens, come out and arm up. I mean it. Take whatever you want, but don't take too long about it, because there ain't no rule says they gotta wait for you to arm up. If they want, they can rush you and take your head off before you're ready."

He paused to let that sink in. "They might let one of you out against ten of them, or they might let five of you out against one of them, but that really don't never happen. Just remember one thing: when your cage opens, there ain't no rules except one: the only way you're getting out of the fighting pit is dead. So fight hard, and you'll earn a quick and easy death."

The two veterans on the rope-line on either side of Ket appeared to have adopted him. The one on his right hissed, "Remember that lad, come out and fight well so you can die quick."

The one on his left said, "Exactly. You don't want to die slow."

They put Ket in a holding cell with five other prisoners. He hadn't spotted it before because it wasn't part of the complex of fighting cages, but situated off to one side. It confined those with minor injuries so they could heal first, then fight better and provide more entertainment. Like the cages, it opened directly onto the floor of the fighting pit. But it was large enough to hold several men, and its bars swung outward on hinges instead of ratcheting up into the roof.

That first day, Ket stood at the open bars of the holding cell and looked out at the fighting pit. The curve of the structure containing the one-man cages arced around the pit, allowing him to see all but the few cages closest to his cell. He heard that mechanical clanking sound and watched the bars of one cage rise into the roof. Crenselus and his guards removed one man from the rope line, untied his hands, and unceremoniously shoved him into the cage. The bars dropped to the floor of the pit like a headsman's axe.

They repeated that, one man at a time, until every cage contained a prisoner. About ten men still remained on the rope line. They stuffed them into another holding cell opposite the one in which Ket stood.

After two days tied to that rope, Ket took some time to stretch and work the kinks out of his muscles. The men in the cell with him didn't bother. They fed them well, gave each man a blanket, and Ket had no trouble falling asleep.

# 33

# A Quick End

STRANGELY ENOUGH, KET slept well for a condemned man, and perhaps because of that he awoke easily when someone snarled, "Blast, this is wrong."

Ket opened his eyes to the false light just before dawn. He quietly rolled out of his blanket and stood to see what had awakened him. The cell faced northeast, and the sun would soon rise over the lip of the amphitheater. He gripped the bars and looked out at the grounds of the fighting pit.

The pit remained empty except for two men standing at the bars of one cage. One man wore ankle length robes, and Ket wasn't sure what that meant in Carthagen, but the fellow didn't look at all like a monk. When the two men stepped to the entrance of the next cage and peered through its bars, Ket glimpsed expensive looking shoes, which eliminated the monk idea.

The other fellow stood taller than the not-monk, wore breeches, shiny knee-high boots, steel spurs, a blouse with a ruffled collar, and a cuirass of polished boiled leather that appeared more decorative than functional. Metal emblems and badges decorated his chest. Over that he had donned a black cloak held in place by a large metal clasp. He had dark hair cut long enough to hide the upper half of his ears, and sported no whiskers.

Ket knew his type: a rich man.

In the complete silence of an early, still morning, the rich man's words carried far. "This disgusts me. It's an atrocious waste of innocent men's lives."

The two men stepped up to the next cell and peered in.

The not-monk fellow nodded with such deference, it was clear the rich man outranked him by a considerable margin. He spoke more quietly than the rich man, and Ket didn't hear his words.

The rich man shook his head. "No, my proposal failed. The Senatus will not outlaw this travesty. I had some support, but not enough."

Again, the not-monk spoke too softly for Ket to catch all his words, but he did hear him address the rich man as, "Dominus Aurelius . . ." That meant the fellow held some sort of rank in the nobility of Carthagen.

They stepped to the next cage, peered in, and Ket waited there unmoving, his hands gripping the bars of the cell. He wondered if they'd stop at his cell, or move on before then. If they did stop, and they shared words with him, he'd have to decide if he should address the fellow like a peasant, or speak properly as Obregon had taught him.

. . . .

It took everything Aurelius had to control his anger as he looked into a cage and saw a lone man wrapped in a blanket on a wooden cot. They had won a war that cost the combined cities of the Lowlands a couple thousand fighting men. Now they would waste more lives in a senseless festival of death.

He shook his head and said to Janus, "We might as well just murder them, line them up and hang them one after another."

Janus shrugged. "That might be more cruel than a quick death in the pits, my lord."

Aurelius glanced over Janus's shoulder and saw a man standing at the bars of the holding cell for the injured. The fellow stood with his head bowed, his hands gripping the bars of his cell. Aurelius stepped around Janus and walked to the cell, and as he approached, the fellow looked up, looked him in the eyes. The man's youth struck a chord of anger in Aurelius's heart, and the unnatural paleness of his blue eyes startled him.

The young man smiled pleasantly. "Your Grace, kind of you to look in on the condemned."

Aurelius started and noticed that Janus did as well. The young fellow had spoken with a refined tongue and a Carthagenian accent. "You're from Carthagen?"

The lad shook his head. "No, my lord, my first time here. In fact, my first time in any city. It's . . . a bit overwhelming."

Aurelius didn't understand. "But you speak as if—"

"Dominus Aurelius!"

At the sound of someone calling his name, Aurelius turned, saw Crenselus walking his way. "Dominus Aurelius, the crowds from the city are arriving, and we need to clear the fighting pit."

Aurelius glanced back at the young man, confused by the lad's words.

Again, the young man smiled pleasantly. "Will you stay and enjoy the festivities?"

Aurelius shook his head. "No, I don't have to. That's my brother's responsibility. I intend to have nothing to do with this."

Aurelius allowed Crenselus to lead him and Janus away, but his encounter with the young man disturbed him greatly.

• • • •

Carthagen rounded up all prisoners not destined for the pit, relieved them of their weapons, and confined them in a camp on the north end of the city. After the politicians and generals negotiated terms, they'd return their weapons and integrate them into the Army of Carthagen to fight the Duchies. Obregon again used the excuse of an old man searching for his son, but while a few recalled the young man with pale blue eyes, none knew his fate.

He spent one night sleeping under the stars, then rose with the sun and headed across the city. At a cheap inn on the south side, he stabled his horse, then joined the crowds in the streets walking to the fighting pit. He didn't share their festive mood.

He traded words with a few guards in the amphitheater. Recognizing him as an old soldier and one of their own, they allowed him to take a seat in the back row of the tiered shelves. That put him about fifty paces from the floor of the pit. He should have remembered to bring a pillow to cushion his butt on the hard stone.

• • • •

Ket stood at the bars of the cell and watched a group of six guards carry a heavy wooden table onto the grounds of the fighting pit. They struggled with its weight, moving in short, choppy steps, frequently putting it down to rest for a few seconds. The guards placed the table about twenty paces in front of the cages, and a few seconds later another guard drove a horse-drawn wagon out to them, the bed of the wagon laden with arms. They piled the table with weapons just as Crenselus had promised.

When Ket's time in the fighting pit came, he didn't want stiff muscles to slow him, so he spent an hour stretching. Again, the men in the cell with him didn't bother. With no possibility of real exercise, he resolved to stretch his muscles as frequently as possible, and it appeared to help with the thigh wound.

As the morning progressed, crowds of commoners slowly filled the grassy slope at the top of the amphitheater. They came bearing food and drink, sat down on the slope, and enjoyed themselves. In late morning the carved stone shelves closer to the pit filled with people who looked elegant and refined. Most brought a pillow to cushion their butt when they sat on the stone. Vendors walked among rich and poor alike, selling something, though Ket could not guess what, probably some sort of refreshment. The combined mass of thousands of people produced a background roar that had built so slowly, Ket hadn't noticed it.

About midday, the guards brought food to the holding cells and the cages. Ket accepted his, but returned to the bars to watch the events of the day transpire, eating while standing there. To Ket's surprise, the men in the cages accepted the food. With the possibility of battle so close, Ket would have declined.

The sun had moved past its zenith when horns blared and the background roar of the crowd went silent. A procession of men and woman in brightly colored clothing walked slowly down the grassy slope, then down a central aisle of stairs carved into the tiered stone seats. They stepped into the shade of the wooden structure the carpenters had assembled and sat down. The crowd roared, a deafening thunder that pounded at Ket's ears. He glanced over his shoulder, surprised that none of the men sharing his cell took any interest in the events transpiring in the pit.

The cheers of the crowd died, and in the silence Ket heard faint voices in the distance. Men in officious looking robes stood at the base of the tiered seating, shouting into speaking horns. But all had aimed their horns away from Ket, directing their words at the crowd, and he couldn't decipher anything they said. Armed guards took up positions at the perimeter of the fighting pit, and Ket noted that the lowest row of tiered seats sat on the ground of the pit. Nothing but those guards separated the spectators from the ground where men would fight for their lives.

One of Ket's cellmates bumped against him. He glanced around, and saw that the other men in the cell had gathered at the bars to watch the action. He returned his attention to the fighting pit.

An iron gate opened at the far side of the pit. A large man stepped out onto the fighting ground, one of the city's champions. He wore greaves and bracers and carried a sword and shield. The gate closed, and the crowd went wild.

The man walked calmly to the shaded wooden structure, stopped in front of it, and bowed deeply. Again, the crowd roared and cheered. The champion turned around to face the cages, the arms table the only thing between him and his opponents.

Ket's heart raced as he waited several seconds for something to happen. Then he heard that clanking, clattering mechanical sound, and the bars of one cage rose upward. It had only lifted a few feet when the cage's occupant rolled out beneath it, and rushed to the table of arms. He wore basic armor like the champion, hurriedly strapped on a sword belt, and lifted a shield. But the champion didn't rush him, just stood there calmly while the fellow armed up. Of course, it would be a better fight that way, more entertaining for the crowd if the condemned man were properly armed and could fight well before the champion cut him down.

The champion walked calmly forward, and he and the condemned man met in the middle of the pit. They squared off, crouched, and circled. Then the champion raised his sword high and brought it down on the man's shield, striking the first blow. They struck back and forth, blow after blow after blow, the crowd screaming and roaring. Ket had spent months training with sword and shield, and thought the two men evenly matched in skill, though the champion had an advantage in size.

The champion over-committed on a stroke and the hawk helped Ket spot the mistake. But the condemned man didn't take advantage of it. Ket had now seen enough of his fighting to know he had the skills to do so, and could have inflicted a minor wound to the champion's shoulder. It wouldn't have necessarily meant victory, but he had passed up a small success that might have evened the odds a little. A fight like that often consisted of small victories that eventually produced a win. Ket didn't understand why the condemned man had ignored such an opportunity.

The two men in the pit fought on, and when the condemned man made a mistake, the champion also passed up the opportunity. Ket didn't understand.

The champion eventually inflicted a nasty gash on his opponent's upper left arm, and as pain and blood-loss weakened the prisoner, his strength faded. Then the champion got inside his guard and stabbed the tip of his sword into the fellow's gut. The man fell to his knees, dropped his sword, bent over and clutched his abdomen.

The champion approached the condemned man and stopped a pace behind him. He looked up at the mass of onlookers and raised both arms high, his sword held in his right hand, his shield strapped to his left forearm. The crowd roared its approval, a sound like thunder on a stormy day, and the champion nodded. He shouted something at the condemned man, but the crowd's cheers drowned out his words. On his knees and bent over, the prisoner responded by straightening out of his crouch. He did not stand but remained kneeling, and stretched his chin toward the heavens, exposing his neck.

The champion tossed his shield aside, gripped the hilt of his sword in both hands, and swung it in a broad, flat arc. It chopped through the man's neck and sent his head flying to one side. The crowd cheered and screamed. For a few seconds the prisoner's headless body remained on its knees, motionless and upright, then it toppled forward. His chest slammed into the ground and bounced once, blasting a small cloud of dust outward. The condemned man had fought well, and been granted a quick end.

To raucous cheers and applause, the champion picked up his shield and walked off the grounds of the pit. Two guards then led a horse and cart to the dead man. They stripped him of his weapons and armor, tossed his head and body onto the cart, and carried him away. Then a group of jugglers, acrobats, and entertainers entered the pit. While they performed, workers tidied up the grounds. Guards collected the dead man's weapons and armor, cleaned his blood off them, and returned the arms to the weapons table. The performers provided a nice intermission that allowed one to make a quick trip to the privy or get some refreshment. Throughout the afternoon they alternated such entertainment with contests of death. Ket watched two more men die in individual combat.

As dusk approached and the shadows lengthened, several guards rushed out carrying bundles of torches. They placed one torch atop each of the poles surrounding the pit and lit it, and while a hundred or more torches illuminated the fighting grounds, the flickering light also deepened its shadows.

They finished the day with a melee of four champions and four condemned men. During that free-for-all, one champion stumbled, opening a cut on his knee. But the four champions defeated their opponents handily. At that point, the shadows were much too deep to continue the fighting.

The only injury a champion had taken that day was the self-inflicted knee-wound on the man who had stumbled. Ket didn't understand.

• • • •

On the second day, the fighting opened with a four-on-four melee, and not one of the four champions took even a minor wound. The acrobats and entertainers provided a short intermission, and following that a lone champion walked out onto the ground of the fighting pit, a large brute carrying only a battle axe. Ket had watched him fight the day before, and the fellow had finished by splitting his opponent's head, putting him out of his misery. Dying under the blows of that axe was not a quick way to go, regardless of how well one fought.

As Ket watched, the brute bowed to the nobles in the shade of the wooden structure, then turned to face the cages. The mechanical apparatus atop them made that ratcheting sound, and the bars of a single cage rose upward, but nothing happened. No prisoner appeared from the darkness of the cage, and after a hundred heartbeats, the crowd grumbled unpleasantly.

Half a dozen guards rushed across the pit, stormed into the open cage, and dragged the prisoner out into the sunlight. The crowd shouted and jeered, hooting catcalls and screaming epithets. The guards bludgeoned and beat the prisoner, then dragged him to one of the tall poles that surrounded the pit. They stood the condemned man up with his back to the pole, and tied his hands behind him. Apparently, they had another use for the tall poles, something other than supporting a torch for the last contest of the day. They tied ropes around the prisoner's chest and ankles to keep him upright, then exposed his abdomen, and slit his stomach muscles. Entrails spilled out of his abdomen and dropped to the ground, hanging from his gut by lengths of intestine. They left him there, alive and staring at his own guts.

The champion again bowed to the nobles, turned to face the cages, and as the bars ratcheted up from one, a prisoner rushed out, armed up, and fought to his death. More acrobats and entertainers followed, and more contests of death. They finished the second day with a one-on-one contest, again lighting the torches to make the most of the last hour of daylight.

At least a dozen times that day a combatant made a minor mistake, and his opponent didn't take advantage of it. Were they not as skilled at fighting as Ket assumed? But he had practiced with some of those prisoners, knew how hard they trained, knew they had the skills, but must not be using them. Or maybe the condemned men just didn't care, while the champions didn't think they needed to worry about it.

At the end of each day, a physiker came to examine the injured men in the holding cell. Ket thought it ironic that regardless of the man's diagnosis, it was really no more than a death sentence given another name. If the wound had festered, they dragged the patient out and cut his throat. If it had healed, he went into the cages to die in the pit. If it hadn't healed, but appeared to be improving, it bought the patient another day, but the cages and the pit awaited him regardless.

As darkness settled over the fighting pit, the flames in the torches dwindled, and the shadows deepened. Ket sat next to the cell bars with his back to a wall, pondering what he had seen. He didn't feel like sleeping, and as time passed, he heard a couple of his cellmates snoring. At random intervals, the poor fellow they'd tied to the post and gutted emitted a piteous groan, audible only because of the stillness of the night.

The crunch of gravel outside the holding cell drew Ket's attention, the footsteps of someone moving furtively. He looked up and saw a dark figure standing on the other side of the bars. "Is that you, young man, you with the pale blue eyes?"

Ket recognized the rich man's voice. He should probably stand up and bow or something, but bowing properly had never been part of Obregon's lessons. "Yah," Ket said. "It's me."

"I have a question."

Ket shrugged. "Ask away."

"You're Carthagenian. Why did you join Tarnasus?"

Ket almost shrugged again, but it was a useless gesture in the dark. "They held a knife to my back."

"The bailiff and his guards?"

Ket shook his head. "No, a highwayman and his companions. They shared the signup bonus with the bailiff. And I'm not Carthagenian."

"Then what are you?"

Ket spoke softly, almost a whisper, "Scairndraka."

The rich man emitted a sharp intake of breath, and lowered his voice. "You don't look Scairn, but if that's true, a wise man once told me to never use that word because it's a mean, nasty word with a very unkind intent."

Ket nodded. "A wise man once told me the same. Now please go away. I have to get some sleep."

The dark figure stood at the cell bars for several seconds, then turned and quietly walked away.

Ket laid down and tried to sleep, but the snores of his cellmates and moans from the gutted man kept him awake for a time. He eventually slept, and got up the next morning to watch the fighting in the pit for a third day.

At the beginning of the second match that day, as the bars on one cage rose slowly upward, for several seconds nothing happened. Ket thought he might see a repeat of the gutted man. But then a tall fellow ducked beneath the cage's bars, stepped out onto the ground of the pit, and casually walked to the arms table. He didn't take his time, but neither did he rush. At the table he carefully strapped a shield on his left arm, and selected a medium length sword.

One of Ket's cellmates leaned against the bars next to him and shook his head. "This ain't gonna be good."

Another man joined the two of them and nodded. "Yah, there's always one."

The champion out-massed the condemned man, but the tall fellow's arms gave him an advantage in reach. They squared off, traded a few blows, and Ket knew immediately this match would be different. The tall fellow fought with determination, was possibly fighting to win. Ket noticed the crowd cheered with less fervor, their cries muted compared to the thunderous roar of previous matches.

At the next round of blows, the condemned man slipped inside the champion's guard, his blade slicing across the champion's hip and scoring first blood. The champion disengaged and backed up three paces, limping slightly, the smear of blood on his breeches visible to all. The crowd went silent as the two men stared at each other for several long seconds. Then the champion nodded, and the look on his face hardened. The two opponents bent and approached each other in a crouch, the champion moving with more caution.

The man standing at the bars next to Ket said, "Once it's started, once a blow has been struck, law says no one can end it until it's done."

The champion's attitude of casual indifference disappeared. He now moved carefully and fought with determination. The two men traded a series of blows and he cut the tall prisoner on his left thigh just above the knee. The condemned man back stepped, limping badly. They engaged again, and the champion cut the prisoner on his right shoulder, then on his right forearm. At that point the prisoner had trouble swinging his sword properly, and in the next series of blows the champion batted his blade aside. Ket thought he would stab the fellow in the chest and finish it. But the champion chopped downward, cutting deeply into the prisoner's left calf. The condemned man collapsed to his hands and knees on the ground. The champion stood over him, placed the edge of his sword against the man's neck, and waited unmoving.

Several of Ket's cellmates now stood at the bars near him. One of them said, "It's done."

Four guards rushed out into the fighting pit, hefted the prisoner between them, and like the gutted man tied him to a post, but they didn't gut him. Several other champions marched out onto the grounds, one carrying a war hammer. He stopped in front of the condemned man, and the roar of the crowd returned as he swung the hammer downward. He shattered the man's right ankle, and the fellow screamed. Then the champion swung the hammer again and shattered the prisoner's left ankle. To the thunderous roar of the crowd, the champions all walked off the field.

Ket watched three more contests that day. At the end of each, the champion of that combat, after defeating his opponent, walked over to the tall fellow and broke something: a leg, an arm, a finger. But they never cut him with a blade, and Ket realized they didn't want him to bleed out. Near the end of the day, one of Ket's cellmates grabbed his arm and spun him away from the cell's bars. Facing him squarely, the fellow said, "Yer thinking about it, ain't you?" He shook his head. "Don't, because that's what happens if you hurt a champion."

He nodded toward the pit. "A week from now, maybe even two weeks, he'll still be alive because they'll keep him alive, his fucked-up arms and legs festering and pussing. They won't let him die until they've squeezed the last bit of life out of him. They won't let him die."

He shook his head again. "Don't even think about it. Just fight well, and die quick and clean."

The lesson of the pit was clear and simple: fight well and earn a quick death, but don't dare fight to win. Ket wondered if he could accept that, but the hawk responded with absolute fury. The thoughts it pushed into his head were fight, kill, die, no compromise, no half way. Nothing else would be acceptable.

                J. L. Doty

At the end of that day, the physikers declared Ket fit for combat, and they transferred him to an empty cage. In the cage he found greaves and bracers lying on a
wooden cot. He used the cot's blanket to wipe the blood off them, then tried them
on. They fit reasonably well.

# 34

# Execution

KET SAT ON the wooden cot in the dark of his cage. For three days he'd watched the fighting in the pit, and sleep now eluded him.

There appeared to be eight champions. He had now seen each of them fight repeatedly and recognized them, though mostly by their stature and fighting skills. Four of them fought only in melees of two or more, while the other four fought only in single combat. There might be more champions of which Ket remained unaware, but in three days of fighting only the eight had appeared in the pit.

Ket considered the melees he'd watched. Four condemned men who had probably never trained together faced four champions who had undoubtedly trained as a team. The prisoners fought four individual combats that happened to be occurring simultaneously, while the champions fought a single battle involving eight men. They fought as a team, just the way Ket had fought with the veterans on the shield wall. Sometimes the champions so outclassed the prisoners it had been almost comic the way they had struggled to avoid killing one of their opponents too early. Ket concluded that if the champions stepped onto the grounds of the pit with the sole intent of killing their opponents as quickly as possible, the melees might end in mere seconds. No entertainment value in that.

The one-on-one contests were a different story. The team element didn't come into play, but all four of the individual champions had repeatedly ignored opportunities so obvious even Ket would have spotted them after only a few weeks of training.

At first he had struggled with the champions' indifference to the fight, and the prisoners' willingness to be butchered. But they had clearly demonstrated the lesson of the fighting pit: fight well and earn a quick death. Fight poorly, and suffer the fate of the gutted man. Fight to win and suffer an even worse fate.

That was the lesson: fight well, but don't fight to win. Ket struggled to accept that while the hawk berated him for his foolishness.

The gutted man continued to moan, though his pain must have increased because now he occasionally cried out. The poor fellow with broken arms and legs constantly sobbed and whimpered. Ket tried to tune them out, but the sound of footsteps outside his cage drew his attention. In the dark a shadowy figure approached and stopped one pace from the bars. Perhaps the rich man had come back, but then Bilsius spoke in his usual whine. "Won't be long now."

Ket didn't respond, simply remained seated on his cot and didn't move.

"Me and Crenselus have a little surprise for you tomorrow, and you ain't gonna like it."

Ket kept his silence.

"Say something, asshole."

Ket remained still.

"Blast you. You're going to die tomorrow, so say something."

Ket didn't move, and after several seconds Bilsius walked away, emitting a stream of curses.

Ket hadn't counted the cages exactly, though he estimated there were about twenty, but they only killed eight prisoners a day. That meant some prisoners sat in their cage for two or three days, never knowing when the bars would rise. Ket imagined sitting there, heart pounding and gut muscles clenched at the beginning of each contest, waiting to see if his bars rose off the floor of the pit. Do that for a couple of days and any man might be ready to die.

Bilsius had taunted Ket in the hope of striking fear into his heart, but instead he had helped Ket decide how he would die. He wasn't foolish enough to think four months of training made him a highly skilled combatant, but it did make him competent, and he had a few advantages they weren't counting on. He and the hawk would fight as a team, he'd fight to kill, and Bilsius had unintentionally warned him his time would come tomorrow, had warned him to be prepared. Ket intended to heed that warning.

• • • •

Divonia's shouts echoed through the halls, and at times like that, servants and retainers throughout the Deoclation Palace sought an excuse to be elsewhere. Aurelius glanced around his small study. Divonia didn't like the place, thought it was beneath him and avoided it. And for that reason, he had used it many times to avoid her.

"Hide," he said to no one. "At least admit it to yourself. You're hiding from your mother."

Unfortunately, while the closed door and thick walls dimmed the sound of her anger, when she fully lost control, no door in the palace was thick enough to completely mute her shouts. Sometimes she continued until her voice cracked and sounded coarse, and stopped only then.

Aurelius sighed. He couldn't avoid his responsibilities forever, should at least attempt to calm her. He had just about steeled himself to stand and do so, when the door to his study swung open and Porcia swept into the room. She spoke in a breathless rush. "You must come. Mother is livid, and she's throwing things at Max."

Aurelius grimaced. "It's him again, is it?"

"Yes, it's always him, and now he can't even stand on his own feet. If he tries, in a step or two he literally falls down."

Aurelius stood. She turned to lead the way, but he caught her hand, pulled her toward him, and wrapped her in his arms. She stiffened for a moment, then broke into tears.

After some seconds she stifled the tears, took a breath, and pushed away from him. "He's been doing that a lot lately, and it's getting worse. Please come with me now. I can't control Mother the way you can."

She turned and walked through the door. He didn't need her to lead the way—he could simply head for the shouting—but he followed her nevertheless.

In Max's apartments they found Divonia standing over him, she screaming at the top of her lungs; he sitting on the floor with his back to a wall, his legs sprawled out in front of him. His head lolled from side to side, and his eyes wouldn't focus. Splashes of vomit discolored the front of his blouse and his trousers, and a puddle of it stained the floor next to him. Broken shards of glass and pottery littered the floor, remnants of the items Divonia had thrown at Max.

Lucius stood nearby, his carefully nurtured look of refined statesman marred by the anger and disgust that clouded his features.

Divonia immediately turned her ire on Aurelius. "Where have you been?"

Aurelius spoke without raising his voice. "I'm here now, and you should bring the volume down several notches."

Her eyes flashed. She pointed at Max and spoke through gritted teeth. "Do something about him."

Aurelius looked at his brother. "Let's just find some servants to help us, and put him in bed with a bucket to puke in."

Divonia shook her head. "But he's due at the fighting pit."

Aurelius shrugged. "Well they'll just have to proceed without him."

Divonia's volume returned to full blast. "They can't."

Lucius stepped forward. "They can, but right now we're in negotiations with Andopolous and Tarnasus. In the pit we're executing prisoners from their army, and if the family supremus doesn't show its respect by sending a representative, it could be disastrous."

Divonia's eyes widened, and Aurelius didn't like the look she gave him. "You'll have to go in his stead. You can take his place."

A knot of anger crawled up Aurelius's throat. "Me? I refuse to have anything to do with that disgusting carnival of depravity."

Lucius nodded and spoke calmly. "That would work. Everyone in this city respects you, and you've represented the family many times in the past."

Porcia took their side against him. "And we can spread the word that Max ate something that gave him a jippy tummy."

Aurelius shook his head. "No one will believe that."

His mother had calmed considerably. "No, they won't, but it'll still work."

Aurelius could have avoided this by finding some excuse to absent himself from the city during the executions in the fighting pit. He sighed. "All right. Since I have no choice, I'll do it."

Divonia gave him a smug smile. She had attended the fighting every day, and returned to the palace each evening energized and excited. The blood-letting clearly thrilled her. While Porcia, like him, had completely avoided the pit.

If Aurelius had to attend, then he wanted a little revenge on both of them. "But I have two conditions."

Divonia lifted an eyebrow and spoke cautiously. "Whatever you wish."

Porcia eagerly agreed with her. "Yes."

Aurelius pointed at Divonia. "You will not attend with me."

She scowled.

Aurelius pointed at Porcia. "And you will."

She scowled.

• • • •

In the morning they served Ket a hearty breakfast, standard fare for the fighting pit. He ate lightly and put most of the food aside. He would have done that even if Bilsius hadn't warned him with his gloating. The food would keep. And if Bilsius had lied, or something forced them to change their plans and he didn't fight that day, he could eat his fill after the last contest of the day. And if he lived to see the next day, he'd do the same.

He recalled the way he'd gone into his first battle with no real fear, and the way the veterans in the Army of Tarnasus had wondered at that. But that had changed with his last battle, changed with his shifting relationship with the hawk, and fear now clutched at his gut. He stood, took a few deep breaths, and went through his stretching routine, trying to calm his heart and his fears. That helped a little.

He crossed the length of his cage, gripped the bars of his cell, and looked at the grounds of the fighting pit. The arms table lay about twenty paces in front of him, and he could easily pick out the individual arms at that distance. He spotted a mid-length sword like that he'd trained with, a dagger that appeared to have a blade about twelve inches long, a large trench knife, a round shield. No javelins or other throwing weapons; they wanted close-in, hard combat. He didn't pay any attention to heavier weapons like a battle-axe or a war-hammer, because he hadn't trained with those.

The arms table itself appeared to be constructed of heavy oak planks, its top surface thicker than the breadth of his hand and supported by four heavy posts. He recalled that six guards had struggled with its weight, and suspected it would require all his strength to topple it onto its side. He could pound a battle axe into that table, or bludgeon it with a war hammer, and not split the thing or break it apart. And then it occurred to him no one had made use of the table itself as a weapon.

The sun rose higher in the sky as the commoners filled the grassy slope at the top of the amphitheater. Then the people in fine clothing sat on their pillows on the carved stone shelves. To Ket's relief, the background noise from the crowd finally drowned out the moans and cries the gutted man and broken man constantly emitted.

When the guards brought the prisoners their mid-day meal, Ket did not turn it down as he had originally planned. That might make him stand out as different from the other prisoners. Above all, he needed them to consider him just another condemned man who would die in the pit like all the others. He accepted the meal, drank the sweet tea, nibbled on a few bites of bread, but left most of it with his uneaten breakfast. To quell the butterflies in his stomach, he went through his stretching routine again. The hawk considered him weak.

The horns blared, the nobles walked down the slope of the amphitheater to the wooden structure, and sat in the shade. The men in officious robes shouted into their speaking horns, and the armed guards took up their positions at the perimeter of the fighting pit. The first champion stepped into the pit, bowed to the nobles, and turned to face the cages. Ket took several deep breaths and tensed, his stomach muscles tight and rigid. His heart threatened to pound out of his chest as he heard that mechanical clanking, clattering sound, and he could not look away from the bars of his cage. He waited . . . waited . . . and they did not rise.

•   •   •   •

As the guards carried the first body out of the pit, Aurelius forced himself to watch and not look away.

"Smile and wave," Porcia said, "and get that scowl off your face. At least pretend you're enjoying yourself."

He looked her way. "Are you?"

She wrinkled her nose. "No, not in the least. I don't like this any more than you do, but I can pretend."

To demonstrate, she smiled, waved at the people on her left, turned her head slowly, and waved at the people on her right. For a moment she glanced at Aurelius and her eyes hardened. "And don't misjudge my smiling demeanor, because I'm not going to forgive you for making me attend this butchery."

Aurelius tried to imitate her, and like her, he smiled and waved to his left and right.

Porcia shook her head sadly. "At least you've progressed from a scowl to a grimace, and one can almost pretend it's a smile."

Aurelius needed to broach a subject with her, but he had to tread carefully. "This thing with Denian, is it serious?"

Her eyes flashed with anger. "It could be, but not yet. Why? You said you approve of him."

Aurelius killed the scowl on his face and gave her a genuine smile. "I do, unequivocally. But if it does get serious, let me know. I'll talk to Max, and make sure you're given a substantial dowry."

Her look softened.

A thought occurred to him. "I suppose I should promote him as well."

Her eyes widened. "Don't you dare. If he got a promotion because of me, he'd be very angry. That would ruin everything."

Aurelius held up his hands in surrender. "Okay, no promotion he doesn't properly earn. But definitely the dowry."

She smiled, leaned toward him, and kissed him on the cheek.

The entertainers rushed out onto the grounds of the pit, and Aurelius thought of that young half-Scairn boy. The poor kid would die in the pit, and Aurelius could do nothing about it, though for all he knew the young man had already fought his battle and died.

"Why so glum, Brother?"

Porcia's question fueled his anger. "I met someone a couple nights ago, a young boy condemned to the pit, can't be more than eighteen, nineteen, maybe twenty. We're murdering innocents now."

Porcia sighed. "That is sad. Is there nothing you can do?"

He shook his head. "No, nothing. Once he's in the pit, his fate is sealed. But I'll not give up. We can't call ourselves civilized when we do this. Maybe I can convince Max, and he can use his influence as the Senatus Supreme."

Porcia spoke in a weary tone. "Max has wasted any influence he might have had. He can no longer help you."

"Yah," Aurelius said. "There is that."

The intermission ended, was followed by a four-on-four melee, another intermission, then another single combat. At that point, Aurelius glanced at the sun, guessed enough daylight remained for one more contest. *One more execution*, he thought.

· · · ·

As the entertainers rushed off the grounds of the fighting pit, Ket took several deep breaths, and carefully stretched his muscles. He tried to quell the butterflies in his gut, but failed. Guardsmen hurriedly planted blazing torches atop the posts that surrounded the pit. It would be the last contest of the day, and if Bilsius hadn't lied, Ket would now have to fight for his life. He intended to fight to win, but somehow he had to make sure they killed him before they tied him to a post next to the broken man.

Ket's cage faced north, and from it he couldn't see the exact position of the sun, but guessed dusk was not far off. He stayed a pace back from the bars, and hidden in the darkness of his cage, he carefully examined the weapons on the arms table. Each time the guards returned a dead man's weapons to the table, Ket made sure they hadn't moved those he wanted, or if they had, he located them one more time. Throughout the day he had repeated that exercise after each contest.

Ket stepped up to the bars and focused on the gate through which the champions always entered. So far, they had never done two melees in one day, and they had already performed a four-on-four earlier, so the fellow who stepped through that gate would be one of the four single-combat champions.

Ket watched the gate closely, and when it opened, a swordsman stepped out carrying a sword and a round shield. Ket had seen him fight several times now, and they were equally matched in height and weight. The fellow certainly had more experience than Ket, at least in the fighting pit. But since Carthagen hadn't fought battle after battle throughout the summer and autumn, Ket thought it possible he had more experience on a battlefield. He didn't think the skills he'd learned on the shield wall would do him any good that day.

Several seconds passed. Oddly enough, they didn't close the champion's gate, and the swordsman dallied there. Then the brute with the battle axe stepped through the gate. Ket had also seen the big axe man fight, and the fellow depended on his strength to make up for his lack of speed.

The big brute slapped the swordsman on the back, saluted him, and they both shared a laugh. Then the gate closed and they marched toward the wooden structure where the nobles sat.

• • • •

Caerie stood at the window, looking at the gardens below. It was not the anniversary of her first vision, so she didn't expect to see anything beyond the flowers and their blossoms, no visions of the young man.

She no longer lived in the nursery, but had returned there every year on that anniversary. And without fail, she had seen that peasant boy standing beneath the aged oak tree. She had watched him grow into a strong young man, watched the lion cub grow into a powerful lioness, and the fledgling raptor into a fearful raken. But with each passing year the ravens had come as well, and more and more they dominated the vision. More and more the female raven slithered through Caerie's thoughts like a snake leaving a polluted trail of desecrated ground in its wake. The woman's desires always left Caerie feeling degraded and unclean.

Caerie didn't understand why she had returned to the window that day. Something had troubled her now for days, a nameless dread that had started as a nagging ache in her soul, and grown steadily until she could no longer stand it. She didn't feel pain, but rather fear and anxiety that now bordered on terror. She felt in her heart that something was about to happen, and she didn't know what.

She heard the rustle of garments behind her and recognized Melceinnia's voice. "What is it, child? What troubles you so? I can feel it, and it's not natural."

# 35

# Fight to Win

WHEN THE GATE closed with two champions in the fighting pit, the crowd went insane. Ket tried to tune out the roar of shouts and screams so he could think. Two of them! Did that mean a small melee and Ket would fight beside another prisoner? Would it be two-on-two, two-on-one, or two-on-something?

The clanking, clattering mechanical sound interrupted Ket's thoughts, and the bottom of his cage's bars lifted slowly off the floor of the pit.

The change in expectations did not change his plans. For four days, the champions had never rushed the prisoners while they selected arms, which meant Ket could simply walk out calmly and take his time selecting weapons at the arms table, just like the broken man. But that might alert them he and the hawk had different plans. If he had any hope of succeeding, he needed to give them the impression that he, like all the other prisoners, would fight well to be granted a quick end, but would not fight to win. Give them what they expect, and don't surprise them until time for the kill, if he lived that long.

He stepped to the back of the narrow cage, spread his feet and braced. And when the bottom of the bars had risen to about waist height, he charged, hit the ground and shoulder rolled out into the fighting pit. As he raced to the arms table, the two champions took notice and walked calmly toward him. He glanced quickly over his shoulder and saw that no other cage's bars had risen; it would be two-on-one.

At the table he skidded to a stop and grabbed a medium length sword much like the one he'd trained with. He wouldn't have bothered to buckle on the sword's belt and sheath, but he needed it to carry another weapon, so he strapped it on. He selected a sheathed heavy trench knife, and jammed it into the belt over his right hip. He scanned the table for other weapons, saw a dagger he didn't think would be of use, a mace he wasn't trained to use, a gladius and other weapons, but at that point he had run out of time.

The two champions had crossed the distance to the table, separated, and came around it from both sides. Ket grabbed a small round shield, jammed his left forearm into its straps, and pulled the sword from the sheath. He wasn't ready to commit yet, wasn't ready to fully engage, but they wanted to box him between them, and it would be suicide to let that happen.

Of the two, Ket decided he'd rather have the slower brute at his back, though he feared the massive battle axe far more than the sword. He charged the swordsman. The man clearly hadn't expected that, and he hesitated. At the last instant Ket swerved slightly to one side, let the fellow swing his blade at him, deflected it with his shield, and rushed past him. He dug his heels in, and turned to face his two opponents. He now had the swordsman and table between him and the brute, which momentarily put the axe man out of play. Ket charged in and swung his sword. The swordsman deflected it with his shield and swung back. Ket deflected that with his shield and they disengaged.

The swordsman paused, smiled, and shouted above the roar of the crowd, "Well played, lad."

Ket grimaced, struggling to catch his breath. "I'm going to fight well." He didn't add that he would also fight to win.

The swordsman nodded. "Then we'll be kind."

Ket had already seen the type of kindness the brute's battle axe delivered, and didn't think it would be any better beneath the swordsman's blade. And Ket didn't want a quick and kind death. He wanted to live, and the hawk agreed with him on that. But he knew only one fate awaited him in the fighting pit that day. He would fight with everything he had, and if he did win, he didn't see any way to stop them from tying him up next to the broken man. But better that, than to merely give up. The hawk agreed with him on that too.

Ket noticed the shadows in the pit lengthening. Dusk was not far off, and he hoped he might use that to his advantage. He sidestepped, putting more of the table between him and the axe man. The swordsman didn't like that. He charged, trying to drive Ket away from the table with heavy, overhanded blows. Ket deflected one sword strike with his shield, and the next with his sword, their blades ringing like a hammer striking an anvil. It took all of Ket's skill to deflect the next blow, and the next. Then the hawk cried out a warning, and he realized in a panicky instant he'd lost track of the brute.

Ket let his knees buckle, twisted, blindly threw his shield up behind him, felt its edge smack into something, and dove sideways. He hit the ground in the shadow beneath the table and rolled, scrambled to the other side, and jumped to his feet. The table now separated him from both the swordsman and the axe man.

Only then did Ket feel the sharp pain in his left shoulder. Blood dripped down onto his shield straps. He lifted the shield and the shoulder complained like blazes, but the hawk's anger and spirit helped him ignore the pain. He flexed his arm, could still use it, though for how long he couldn't guess.

Across the table the swordsman grinned. The brute gave Ket a determined look, a stream of blood running down his face from a gash just above his eye, probably put there by the edge of Ket's shield. And though it didn't appear to hinder the man, he kept wiping at the blood to keep it out of his eyes. A red smear on the tip of his axe blade told Ket it was the brute who had sliced his shoulder. An inch or two one way or another, and it would have taken off Ket's arm.

The two men turned away from each other and sprinted around the table, circling it to come at Ket from opposite sides. Ket didn't want to face that axe, so he shuffled sideways toward the swordsman and met him just as he came around the end of the table. The fellow swung his blade in a high arc, slicing down toward Ket's face. Ket deflected it with his shield and struck back, trading blow after blow with the man, back stepping and drawing him away from the table. He'd chosen a direction that also drew him and the swordsman away from the big axe man, keeping the brute behind the swordsman and out of play.

As Ket tensed to strike the next blow, to his amazement, the hawk suddenly thrust his arms out to the sides and down, a suicidal move. But air pressure beneath his flight feathers lifted his feet off the ground. The hawk raised its talons in front of Ket and ripped out at the swordsman. Then his feet hit the ground and he almost stumbled.

The swordsman cried out, staggered backwards, and froze. Three deep gashes traced lines of blood across his face, and an eyeball hung on his cheek, suspended from the socket by sinews of bloody tissue.

Ket didn't understand; he hadn't swung his sword. And even if he had, it couldn't inflict three wounds in a single strike. But the three front talons on a hawk's claw could.

The swordsman looked at Ket with his one good eye, then raised his face to the heavens and screamed his fury at the sky.

• • • •

Caerie screamed as something cut into her left shoulder, sending a wave of pain crashing through her soul. She collapsed, but someone caught her and lowered her gently to the floor. Tears streamed down her cheeks as she looked up into Melcein-nia's face. Caerie desperately sucked air into her lungs and wondered where the pain had come from.

Caerie's field of view dimmed and narrowed just as her father's face appeared next to the priestess's. "By the ancient spirits, what in hell is going on here?"

The old woman raised her hand, blood dripping from her fingers. "A cut in her left shoulder, a wound delivered by no blade, no person . . . a spirit wound, I think."

Carrie's father demanded, "What are you babbling about, old woman?"

Melceinnia ignored him and looked into Caerie's eyes. "Are you with him now, child, the boy with blue eyes? Is he there inside you?"

Nausea gripped Caerie's gut and she swallowed hard. She had never felt such pain and it overwhelmed her. "I . . . don't know . . . blue eyes."

The priestess's brows furrowed with anger. "But there is a boy, isn't there?"

Caerie felt something in her soul, something aligned with her spirit, and she struggled to speak. "I . . . a boy . . . maybe."

"Blast you, woman," her father shouted. "Talk to me, damn it."

Melceinnia's head turned and looked at him. "Bring her, now, and follow me."

• • • •

Boredom had set in, another contest, another execution. Aurelius felt guilty that he'd grown bored at the blood-sport of killing innocent men. But the boredom came as a welcome relief to the anger that washed through him with each man's death.

For the last contest of the day, the guards in the pit placed lit torches atop the posts. Then an axe man and a swordsman stepped through the champion's gate, marched forward, stopped in front of Aurelius and Porcia, and bowed. The crowd roared; the two champions turned to face the pit, and the bars of one cage lifted.

As the bars clattered upward, nothing happened for several seconds. Then the condemned man erupted from his cage in a shoulder roll and sprinted to the arms table. Aurelius thought he looked rather young, but from a distance of almost a hundred paces, and in the fading light, he couldn't be sure of that.

Porcia sighed. "I think he's younger than all the rest. I can't look." She turned her head toward Aurelius and looked away from the fighting. Her eyes glistened, though she held back her tears.

The roar of the crowd surged, drawing Aurelius's attention back to the fighting pit. He leaned forward, squinting, hoping to glimpse the color of the young man's eyes, but the distance was far too great for that. He mumbled, "It could be."

The young fellow engaged with the swordsman, trading a frantic series of blows back and forth, blades clanging together and thudding against shields. When they finished, the young man had put the table between him and the axe man, a shrewd move.

Aurelius stood.

Porcia looked up at him. "What's wrong?"

"Nothing," he said, shaking his head. "Or maybe everything. I can't see well enough from here."

He edged past Porcia to the main aisle that ran down the middle of the seats, then walked down the few steps to the floor of the fighting pit. The guards that lined the perimeter of the pit faced inward toward the combatants, and remained unaware of Aurelius, who stood only a few paces behind them.

He heard the clash of blades, the shouts of the crowd now a deafening roar, and realized he'd missed some of the action. The young man now faced both champions with the table between him and them. A smear of bright red darkened the left shoulder of his tunic. He lifted his shield, testing the arm, and Aurelius thought he glimpsed blue eyes, or perhaps that had just been his imagination.

He squinted harder and stepped forward, bumping into one of the perimeter guards. The man looked his way, started, and stepped back a pace. He shouted to be heard above the crowd. "Uh, Your Grace, you shouldn't be here. It's dangerous. Please stand behind us."

At that moment, the shadows deepened as the sun finished its descent, and twilight enveloped them all. Aurelius's temper flared. "Nonsense." He brushed the man aside and took another step forward.

The guards, now aware of his presence, stepped forward to maintain a line of defense between him and the combatants.

The sound of sword blades clashing pulled Aurelius's attention back to the fight. The young man had drawn the swordsman away from the table, again keeping the axe man out of the action. In the fading light, the flickering shadows of the torches made it almost impossible to see anything. The lad seemed to rear up, as if suspended on the wings of a giant raptor. Aurelius damned the bloody shadows as he squinted harder, heard a bone-chilling scream, and all three combatants froze.

The swordsman stood a few paces from the boy, his face and chest covered in blood. Behind him the axe man had halted, clearly as stunned as the swordsman and the boy. Then the boy charged.

• • • •

When Ket had faced the two champions earlier, and traded a few simple words with the swordsman, he now realized that had been a mistake. It had given them a moment to evaluate the situation, to think and plan how to attack him as a team. He needed to keep the chaos going unchecked, so he charged the wounded swordsman, aiming to pass him on the side of his ruined eye.

Neither of his opponents expected the move, and he closed the few paces to the man before either could react. Instead of engaging the swordsman fully, he slapped him aside with his shield, and buried the point of his sword in his solar plexus. He didn't look back as he passed the fellow, moving with too much speed to yank his blade free, forcing him to leave it behind. He gained two full paces toward the axe man before the brute reacted. The fellow raised his axe, but Ket slammed into him with his shield.

He'd gotten inside the man's guard, put all his strength behind his shield, and like his months on the shield wall, he plowed forward; advance, advance, advance. Ket pushed onward, forcing the man to retreat one step, two steps, three steps, hoping to keep him constantly off balance. Then they both plowed into something, Ket tumbled to the dirt, and slammed his ribs against a heavy wooden table leg. As blades and armor clattered to the ground around him, Ket realized he'd driven the axe man back to the arms table.

Ket scrambled to his feet and spun to face the brute just as the man swung his axe in a broad, flat arc. Ket ducked, desperately throwing his shield up. The axe connected with it, splintering the wood and ripping it loose from his arm. The force of the blow threw Ket to one side.

He rolled over onto his knees just in front of the table, looked up, and saw the brute standing over him. With a grin of triumph on his blood-smeared face, the big man raised the axe high over his head in a two-handed grip, and swung it down.

Ket fell back and rolled under the table. An ear-splitting crack shook the table as he scrambled beneath it. He tumbled out from under the table on the other side and jumped to his feet.

He and the axe man faced each other across the table, the axe's blade buried in its surface. The brute grinned, gripped the axe handle, and pulled. But it didn't budge. He pulled again, and still it didn't move.

Ket reached for the trench knife he'd jammed into his belt, but he'd lost it somewhere in the struggle and had nothing to fight with. As the big man pulled on the axe's handle, grunting like an ox, Ket scanned the weapons on the table, looking for something he could use. He spotted a mace, grabbed it, pulled it back, leaned forward over the table, and swung out, smacking the mace into the side of the brute's head.

Ket expected the fellow to fall unconscious to the ground, but the axe man only staggered back a half-dozen steps. He stopped and shook his head, blinking his eyes, staggering about, but refused to go down.

Ket scrabbled through the weapons on the table, shoving useless items aside. He found a dagger, gripped its hilt, and unsheathed it. He swept out with his arm, clearing an area atop the table, blades and other weapons clattering to the ground. Then he back-stepped several paces, dug his heels into the dirt, and charged forward. He closed the distance to the table, hopped onto its surface, then leapt into the air. But in an instant he knew it wasn't enough, knew he'd fall a few paces short of the brute, would be at the man's mercy. Then the hawk again forced Ket's arms out to his sides, and his wings carried him the extra distance.

The axe man seemed to clear his head and his eyes focused just as Ket crashed into him. He jammed the dagger into the big man's shoulder as his momentum slammed the fellow backward onto the ground. Ket landed on top of him and the brute's head bounced hard off the dirt. The fellow hesitated and had trouble focusing his eyes.

Ket pushed off the man, struggled to his knees, sat on the man's chest, and yanked the blade out of his shoulder. Then he raised the dagger in both hands, and drove it into the asshole's eye. The axe man stiffened and arched his back. Ket ground the blade around, scrambling the brute's brains. The big man spasmed, jerked and kicked, but Ket held on, grinding the knife through his skull. Then the brute heaved once, and lay still.

Ket looked over his shoulder at the swordsman, fearing the man might have recovered enough to attack. But the fellow lay on his side, silent and unmoving. Ket's sword bisected his midsection, with several inches of it protruding from his back.

Ket couldn't get up, couldn't stand, struggled to suck enough air into his lungs. He looked down at his arms and torso and legs. Blood seeped from a dozen wounds, most of which he didn't recall taking. The axe man lay beneath him, his remaining eye staring blankly at Ket.

Ket tumbled off the axe man, rolled onto his back on the ground, and simply tried to breathe, to suck air into his lungs and calm his racing heart. He raised his right hand to wipe the sweat and blood out of his eyes, realized he still gripped the hilt of the dagger, its blade dripping red blood and gray specs of the brute's brains. He had gripped it so tightly he'd taken it with him, though he hadn't intended to.

It was the silence that got his attention. The roar of the crowd had disappeared, and not even the background rumble remained, just complete, absolute silence so still it seemed born of the dead.

# 36

# Obregon

CAERIE HAD SWORN that she would not scream again, but then something pierced her chest beneath her right arm, and she cried out. She might have been able to handle the pain, but there were no enemies to cringe away from, no opponents to fight. It was like stumbling blindfolded through a room of vipers, never knowing when one might next strike, or how deep or painful the wound would be.

Caerie shook her head, trying to clear her thoughts of the boy and the hawk. She focused on her surroundings, realized her father had carried her to her bed, its sheets now soaked in blood.

Standing over Caerie, her mother gripped her hand with crushing force and shouted, "What is going on? She's bleeding in a dozen places and it's not like there are assassins here to do that to her."

Melceinnia probed at the new wound. "I know not, Crown Mother."

"Damn it!" Selene pleaded. "You're the one who's supposed to know about all this weird and strange stuff."

Melceinnia grimaced. "I may have a guess."

Selene didn't lower her voice one notch. "Then bloody well spit it out."

The old priestess spoke hesitantly. "I have read of it, and until now thought it just superstitious drivel. If it is real, it hasn't happened for generations."

Selene gritted her teeth. "Don't give me a damn lecture."

Caerie's father said, "When I carried her out of the nursery, you said something about spirit wounds. What did you mean by that?"

Melceinnia swallowed and shook her head. "I think her spirit is entwined with that of another, and he is under attack. Every wound he receives, she receives. I think she eases some of his pain, protecting him by taking it upon herself. But I'm not certain of any of this."

Selene demanded, "And who is this . . . *him*?"

The old woman looked Caerie in the eyes. "Only she can answer that question. But look at her. I think it's over now."

Caerie didn't argue with the old woman, but something deep within her told her the battle was far from over.

· · · ·

"What in bloody hell do you think you're doing?"

At Crenselus's shout, Ket raised his head, though he could barely focus. The pit boss marched across the pit toward him, Bilsius trailing in his wake, his nose a swollen ruin from the punch Crenselus had given him. Far behind them, Ket saw the rich man standing on the grounds of the pit, a line of guards arranged protectively in front of him. The fellow tried to push them aside, but they restrained him and wouldn't allow him to pass.

Crenselus stopped on one side of Ket, Bilsius on the other. The pit boss leaned over Ket, spittle flying from his mouth as he screamed. "You're not supposed to kill them. They're supposed to kill you. You're the one who's supposed to bloody well die. What in blazes were you thinking, you bloody idiot?"

Ket didn't know what to say. "I . . . I'm sorry."

Crenselus's eyes bulged as if about to pop out of his skull. "You're sorry? You're bloody fucking sorry?" He straightened, looked up toward the darkening sky and announced, "He's sorry. He's bloody fucking sorry. Well that makes it all better, doesn't it?"

The man raised an arm and used his sleeve to wipe the sweat and spittle off his face. He looked down at Ket. "You're sorry, and I'm oh so pleased that you're sorry. But that doesn't make it all better, though I do know how to fix it."

He looked pointedly at Bilsius, both of them standing over Ket. "Somebody cut this idiot's bloody fucking throat."

The rich man shouted, "Nooo!"

Bilsius calmly said, "Gladly."

Ket looked at Bilsius as the fellow reached for a knife at his belt and pulled it, a heavy blade with a single edge.

Bilsius grinned, and when he spoke, his ruined nose made the whine even more irritating. "You ain't gonna like this, but I am."

The hawk reminded Ket of the dagger in his right hand. As Bilsius leaned forward, Ket rolled his way and jammed the dagger through the top of his foot, pinning it to the ground as if pegged there by a giant steel nail.

Bilsius screamed, dropped the knife, bent and reached for the dagger pinning his foot.

Ket got to his hands and knees and scrambled to Bilsius's blade. He grabbed it, rolled again and jumped to his feet behind Bilsius just as the man pulled the dagger out of his foot. The hawk guided Ket's actions. He gripped the asshole's hair, pulled back, reached around, and dragged the edge of the blade across his throat, cutting deeply into the flesh. Bilsius gurgled and choked blood as Ket kicked him aside and charged at Crenselus.

The pit boss's eyes widened. Ket plowed into him, jamming the blade upward just beneath his solar plexus, burying it to the hilt and aiming for the heart. Ket held on to Crenselus as the man grunted and coughed, and for a moment they stood face to face, looking each other in the eyes. The pit boss's mouth opened and he struggled to speak. "You . . . bloody . . . fucking . . . idiot."

Ket released him, and as he dropped away and fell to the ground, Ket held onto the hilt of the blade and it slid out of the man's chest. The eerie silence remained. He looked around, and didn't know what to do next.

A guard shouted, "He's dangerous. Kill him."

The rich man struggled with some of the guards and again shouted, "Nooo!"

The guards that ringed the fighting pit all charged toward Ket, and the crowd went berserk, letting out a roar that exploded like thunder. Ket let the hawk guide him. He turned toward the rich man, dug his heels in, and ran straight at him, straight at the guards that separated them. The guards all carried sword and shield, and Ket carried only a single knife. Apparently, the hawk thought it was time for him to die, but he damn well wasn't about to accept a quick and clean end. The hawk thought him a fool, a stupid fledgling.

The distance between Ket and the guards closed rapidly, several of the guards raising their swords high. Ket's death might or might not be quick, but it certainly would not be clean. And then Ket dreamed of soaring through the heavens on glorious wings.

•  •  •  •

Caerie and the boy rode together on the wings of the hawk's spirit, the lioness in her soul content to go where they chose. The pain disappeared as peace and contentment washed through her, and she would gladly let that single instant last a lifetime. But then she realized that the end of pain for her meant the boy would now feel it all, and sorrow soured her contentment.

They plowed into someone, a tall Scairnessa man.

• • • •

When the guard shouted, "He's dangerous. Kill him," fear crawled up Aurelius's throat and he shouted, "Nooo!" But they ignored him, and the roar of the crowd returned. The guards closed in on the lad, a hundred of them charging at the young man from all directions, all carrying swords.

The boy turned toward Aurelius and charged, running headlong at the guards and straight to his own death. Aurelius again shouted, but his words drowned in the crowd's cheers. He had to stop this, tried to rush forward, but the guards had closed ranks in front of him, blocking him, protecting him. He stepped back several paces while they advanced on the lad, desperately seeking a way to get past the guards as the light of day faded.

He lost sight of the young man in the flickering shadows of a hundred torches. For a brief instant he thought he saw the wings of a massive raptor skim just over the heads of the guards, but that must be a trick of the dancing shadows. And then something slammed into him and knocked him to the ground in a tumble.

• • • •

Everything hurt, and the pain of Ket's wounds felt as if it had blossomed tenfold in just seconds. He struggled to his feet, moving like an old man, still gripping the heavy knife. Only a pace away, the rich man also climbed to his feet, his back to Ket. The guards in front of the fellow were all focused on the center of the pit, and apparently none were aware of Ket. He didn't understand how he'd gotten past them.

Ket staggered forward, intending to slit the man's throat the way he'd slit Bilsius's. But in the few words they had shared the man had been kind, and seemed sad and melancholy. The hawk agreed when Ket decided not to kill him.

Like the guards, the man looked toward the shadows at the center of the pit. Ket staggered forward behind him, reached over the man's left shoulder, and with his left hand gripped his chin. In the same instant, he reached over the fellow's right shoulder and put the edge of the blade to his throat. The man froze.

Once again the crowd had gone silent, no cheers, shouts or screams. A guard glanced over his shoulder and saw Ket holding the knife at the rich man's throat. "He's behind us."

The guards spun about to face Ket and the rich man. Ket leaned on the fellow, needing his strength to remain standing. Ket swallowed and could barely speak. "Stay back," he said, and the guards hesitated.

For a few seconds no one moved, then the rich man spoke softly. "What next, young man?"

Ket tried to think, but couldn't come up with anything. "I . . . don't know. I'm . . . just trying . . . to stay alive."

"I may be able to help you there," the rich man said, still speaking softly. "I give you my word that if you release me, you will not be harmed."

Ket didn't know if he should believe him. "Maybe you should tell your guards that."

"Okay," the man said. "But I'd really appreciate it if you didn't cut my throat while I do so."

Ket nodded, a useless gesture standing behind the man. "Okay."

The rich man raised his voice. "This young man defeated his opponents in fair combat in the fighting pit. By that, he has earned the right to live. I've given him my word that if he releases me unharmed, he gets to live free and unpunished. And I order you men to honor my word."

Ket tried not to sway on his feet, knew he was close to collapse. "How do I know I can trust you?"

The rich man hesitated. "I . . . uh . . . gave you my word."

The hawk's anger boiled up in Ket's chest, and he spoke louder than intended. "How do I know your word is good? I'm just a peasant and you're some rich guy."

The guards tensed, but the rich man held his hands out as if pushing them away and they didn't advance.

Ket heard the crunch of gravel as someone approached behind him. He glanced over his shoulder and saw a big man wearing leather armor. The fellow stood about five paces away, though the shadows hid his features.

"Stay away from me," Ket shouted. "Come near me and I'll cut his throat."

The man nodded, edged sideways, and walked in a wide circle around Ket and the rich man. Ket saw a patch covering one eye, recognized the broad shoulders and heavy build of the man, and couldn't believe it when Obregon stopped in front of him.

The rich man tensed in Ket's arms and said, "Invictus Gener—"

"No!" Obregon shouted, his face shifting to a mask of rage as he took one step forward. "That man is dead. He died long ago, and his soul rots in the deepest of hells."

Obregon took several breaths, visibly struggled to calm down, and looked Ket in the eyes. "If this man gives you his word, you can trust him. He'll die before allowing his word to be broken. I give you *my* word on that."

Only then did Ket realize he'd learned to trust the old man, though he'd never before learned to trust anyone but his mum. Ket's knees shook. His hands trembled, and he didn't want to cut the rich man's throat by accident, so he dropped the knife.

His vision faded, his knees weakened further, his eyes saw only a deep well of darkness before him, and he fell into it.

· · · ·

As the young man slumped to the ground, the guards rushed forward and the crowd screamed its collective anger. Aurelius thought the pit guards might murder the lad right in front of him. He knelt down, placed one hand on the boy's chest, and raised the other to halt the guards. He shouted to be heard above the crowd. "Bring a physiker, and get a pallet or stretcher. I'm taking him to the palace, and I want him treated well. That's an order." A few of the guards scowled at that.

Many of the guards had turned and now faced outward, holding the crowd back.

Aurelius glanced around, saw no sign of the old man with the patch over one eye, but spotted Porcia marching his way. When she reached him, she stood over him and the boy, and put her fists on her hips. She had to shout to be heard. "What are you going to do with him?"

Aurelius shook his head. "I don't know. But I gave him my word no one'll kill him, and the only way I can guarantee that is to take him to the palace under guard."

He glanced around, realized if they didn't move quickly, the crowd would turn into an angry mob. "Stay by him. If we're separated or I'm needed elsewhere, make sure the guards protect him."

She bent and leaned forward. "I think half of them want to kill him. You sure they'll obey me?"

He had the same concern. "If it comes to that, turn all imperial and bark orders at them like you're the queen of something. I've seen you do it before."

She flashed a look of exasperation at him, turned to a guard tribune, and did the imperial queen thing. "You and forty of your men, with me and Dominus Aurelius, now. And stay close to us at all times."

Two guards showed up with a stretcher, and they bundled the boy onto it. They dare not try to take the lad through a crowd of twenty thousand angry onlookers. But the amphitheater had a little-used private exit behind the cages, and the guard tribune led Aurelius to it. They followed a narrow path by the river, and emerged at the edge of the city. The lad did not look well.

Three times Aurelius had glimpsed the wings of a large raptor in the pit, each time for only a fraction of a second. It had to have been a trick of the light and shadows, because no one else appeared to have shared his hallucination. And there had been no hawk or eagle in the pit. He glanced up at the sky, but darkness had enveloped the city. He thought it would be best not to dwell on such lunacy.

# 37

# Aurelius's Lie

CAERIE AWOKE AND gasped, fear clutching at her heart as she wondered from where the next attack would come. She tried to lift a hand to her face to wipe the tears from her eyes, but her arms wouldn't move; someone had tied them down. A little experimentation confirmed that they had also restrained her legs, and a strap of some kind across her brow prevented her from lifting her head.

Her father's face and shoulders appeared in her field of view as he leaned over her. He smiled. "You're awake. How do you feel?"

A question to which Caerie wasn't sure she had the answer. "I . . . uh . . ."

His smile didn't falter. "That's the most coherent thing you've said for a couple of hours. Now stop, put away the fear, take a breath, think it through, and tell me how you feel."

Caerie looked in his eyes and found comfort there. Sander deVries, the consort of no consequence, a man with no power and only one responsibility: father potential heirs in the Crown Mother's womb. But still, the best father a girl could want. Those who thought him nothing more than a useless breeding stud didn't know him as Caerie and her brothers did.

She took that breath as instructed, and only then understood the pain had disappeared, though weariness flooded every muscle in her body. "I . . . don't hurt anywhere, but I think if I'm allowed to rise . . . I'll be weak as a kitten."

He nodded. "I thought as much. Let's get you out of these restraints. But while I remove them, don't try to sit up. The physikers say you'll just swoon if you move too quickly."

He first removed the strap across her forehead, then the ties on her wrists and arms, then those on her legs. Recalling glimpses of blood-soaked sheets, she raised her head to look at her torso and legs, and saw nothing but clean and unsoiled bedding. As he put a strong arm behind her back and helped her sit up, she asked,

"Was it all just a dream?" But then she spotted the bloody sheets piled in the corner.

Her father nodded and said, "I guess I don't need to answer that question."

He got her into a comfortable sitting position. And seeing that window only a few paces from her, she realized they had put her in her old bed in the nursery.

She looked her father in the eyes. "The nursery?"

He smiled and shrugged. "You were bleeding rather badly, and it was the closest bed at hand." He grinned. "You still fit in the smaller bed, but just barely."

A hundred questions fluttered through her thoughts, and she didn't know which to ask first.

He didn't wait for her to ask even one. "Melceinnia called them spirit wounds, said your spirit was entwined with that of a blue-eyed boy, that he was under attack, and you shared his wounds, helping him in some way." He wrinkled his nose. "She was pretty vague about a lot of it, probably because she doesn't really understand what's happening to you, and she doesn't want to admit it."

Caerie felt stronger with each passing second. "That is so like her."

He continued. "In any case, the attacks suddenly stopped. Then she and your mother cleaned you up, and told me there is now no sign of any wounds, as if they never existed."

He glanced over his shoulder, a guilty look on his face. "I'm under strict instructions to alert them instantly should you awake. They're going to be very upset that I didn't." He leaned close to her and whispered. "But what do those women know?"

He straightened, reached out, and gripped a bell-pull. "Are you ready?"

Caerie took a deep breath, let it out slowly, and nodded.

He gave the bell-pull a yank. An instant later, a handmaid stepped into the room. He gave her instructions to tell Selene and the priestess that Caerie had regained consciousness. The servant disappeared.

Caerie's father reached out, took her hand in his, and gave it a gentle pat.

Selene blew into the room like a mountain whirlwind, the old priestess behind her. Caerie's mother stopped on the left side of her bed, and Melceinnia on the right. "Now," the Crown Mother said, projecting her royal persona. "You're going to tell us about this blue-eyed boy."

"Uh," Caerie said. "I don't know any blue-eyed boy."

• • • •

When they reached the palace, with no better plan at hand, Aurelius sent Porcia to get his personal physiker, then led the guards carrying the lad's stretcher to his own apartments. He directed them to place the young man's stretcher on a table, then chased everyone out of the room. The physiker arrived a short time later and immediately went to work examining the boy, Aurelius kept his mouth shut and tried not to appear impatient. At least the man spoke as he worked, which kept Aurelius somewhat informed.

"Bad wound to his shoulder, deep cut, I'm surprised he could fight with that. Nasty stab wound in his right side, though it looks like his ribs deflected the blade, so hopefully it's not too deep. I'm going to leave the shoulder and stab-wound open. We'll close them in a day or two, but we'll have to keep them moist, maybe dab them with a little strong brandy."

The physiker sighed and turned to face Aurelius. "A bunch of small wounds, and he's lost a lot of blood."

Aurelius asked, "The shoulder wound?"

The physiker shrugged. "That, and accumulated loss from all his injuries. If nothing festers, he'll live. On the other hand, if it goes bad, he might survive, but the odds are against him."

Aurelius had seen many a soldier die when the simplest of wounds putrefied. "I understand. Just do what you can."

As the physiker turned back to the young man, on the far side of the room Porcia hurried through the doorway, clearly in a rush. She flashed Aurelius a warning look and rolled her eyes.

Divonia stepped into the room behind her. "There you are, Aurelius. I was about to retire, but I heard you'd returned from the fighting pit with a guest. I also heard today's contests ended in absolute chaos. They say someone actually defeated a champion."

She crossed the room in a flourish, stopped on the other side of the young man, and wrinkled her nose. "He stinks, and he's filthy."

Aurelius hoped she didn't get too inquisitive. "Yes, he's injured."

"Who is he?"

Aurelius was not stupid enough to admit he knew nothing about the young man. Time for a small lie. "A good friend. One of our men."

Her nose remained wrinkled as she scowled. "He looks like a common—"

He had to grow the lie a little. "Oh . . . he's an officer."

She shook her head. "He doesn't look like an officer."

Aurelius had no choice but to lie even more. "He was working undercover for me. The stink is part of his disguise, helps him blend in."

"Oh," she said, wrinkling her nose and covering it with a small handkerchief. "Well, I hope your friend is okay." She frowned, and looked more closely at the young man. "He is rather handsome. When he's well again . . . and properly dressed, introduce me."

She spun about and walked out of the room, her gown fluttering behind her.

Porcia walked around the table, took Aurelius by the arm, and guided him across the room to the point farthest from the physiker. She rolled her eyes and lowered her voice. "I suppose Mother can look past anything if it means a good fuck. Is he really an officer?"

Aurelius lowered his voice to match hers. "I don't know."

"Then who is he?"

He shook his head. "I don't know that either, though I think he and I have a mutual acquaintance, an old man who used to mean a lot to me. But other than that, I don't know anything about him."

She let out a quiet chuckle. "Oh Brother, what a tangled web we weave. Let's hope this nobody you've adopted doesn't wake up one morning with Mother next to him in bed. You know what they're saying on the streets?"

He shook his head, didn't want to hear it.

She grinned. "They say he single-handedly defeated five champions."

"That's ridiculous."

She turned serious. "Yes, but no one's ever defeated *any* champion before. And he did defeat two all by himself. I saw that with my own eyes."

The physiker cleared his throat, clearly wanting their attention.

Aurelius and Porcia returned to the young man's side.

"I've stitched up the small wounds," the physiker said. "I'll close the last two tomorrow."

He left Aurelius and Porcia alone with the patient.

Porcia looked at the lad and sighed. "Mother's right: he stinks."

Aurelius's frustration surfaced. "He's been locked in a tiny little cell for days. I don't imagine they wheeled a big metal tub in there for him, and gave him sweet-smelling perfumes like those you put in your bath water."

She ignored him. "And his clothing is . . . well . . . he looks like a peasant."

Aurelius had to agree with her on that. "But he speaks well, and has a Cartha-genian accent."

Porcia shook her head. "He stands out like . . . well . . . like a peasant in a palace."

Aurelius knew he could count on her, but to do so he must ask for it. "I need your help. If I'm not available I need you to watch over him for me, please."

She lifted an eyebrow. "You need me to help you maintain your lie."

"That too."

Her eyes narrowed as she considered him. "He means a lot to you?"

He owed her the full truth. "I don't know what he means to me, but I think he means a lot to an old friend."

She turned toward the young man on the stretcher, and looked him over carefully. "We'll have to get him some decent clothing. And speaking of decent clothing, what happened to you?"

She pointed at Aurelius's chest.

He looked down, saw that something had shredded the front of his cloak, and the ceremonial leather cuirass he wore bore deep scratches. He recalled his hallucination, and didn't want to believe the talons of a raptor had cut into his cloak and scarred his cuirass. It would be best not to mention anything about large raptors in the fighting pit. Porcia wouldn't believe him any more than he trusted his own eyes.

To answer her question he said, "I don't know. Must have torn it somehow in all the excitement."

Porcia looked again at the lad on the stretcher. "As to accommodations, let's find him a bedroom in the far reaches of the palace. And we'll make sure Mother doesn't know where it is."

• • • •

Kainborne reread Zarkoffa's first message. Four highwaymen had stolen the duke's rents and abducted the boy, and Zarkoffa intended to investigate.

When Kainborne had first read that, the message had infuriated him; no boy, no knowledge of his whereabouts, nothing. Kainborne had even considered travelling to Tramorth himself, but then the assassin's second message arrived. Zarkoffa had captured one of the highwaymen—apparently the only one still alive—and learned that he and his companions had enlisted the boy in the Army of Tarnasus. With the guidance of the captured bandit, the assassin intended to follow their trail.

Tarnasus and Andopolous had spent the summer pitting their armies against one another, then combined forces against Carthagen. If the boy had died on some battlefield, then that would be the end of it, though it would vex Kainborne to never know his fate. But if the lad still lived, then who better to find him than Zarkoffa? Time and again the man had proven quite resourceful.

Kainborne briefly considered going to the Lowlands himself. He had excellent contacts in Carthagen, and they might put him in touch with people in Tarnasus, those he could count on to be motivated by the proper amount of coin. But with his services in demand by both Jarrod and Macallan, Kainborne dare not take the chance of an extended absence. On the other hand, with Macallan marshalling his forces against the Lowlands, he could point out the advantage of personally rallying his contacts, and how his presence in Carthagen would prove highly beneficial to the archduke. He'd have to think on that, make sure he had all the right pieces in place before proposing such an option.

• • • •

The light of a half-moon barely penetrated the darkness of the amphitheater. Aurelius halted his horse at the top of the grassy slope where commoners enjoyed the festivities in the pit. Far below him a few torches sputtered in the wee hours of the morning, bright spots in a dim well of gloom. Denian brought his horse to a stop beside him. For what he must do, Aurelius did not want a full escort.

Both men dismounted and Denian grimaced. "Are you sure you don't want me to take care of this, Your Grace? You can watch the horses while I do so."

Aurelius shook his head. "No. This is my responsibility, my duty."

Denian extended his hand. "Then I'll watch the horses, Your Grace."

Aurelius handed him the reins of his horse, and started down the slope, moving cautiously in the darkness. He made his way to a torch mounted on a pole at the top of the tiers of carved stone seats. Before he got there he heard a man snoring, and beneath the light of the torch he found a guard curled up on the top tier of the seats. He thought he might sneak past the fellow, but the man stirred and looked up. Seeing Aurelius standing over him, he scrambled to his feet.

"Here now," he said. "The fighting pit is closed for the night. You can't—"

He frowned and leaned forward, squinting at Aurelius in the flickering light of the torch. "Ah, Your Grace, I'm sorry. I didn't—"

Aurelius shook his head. "Think nothing of it, man. And there's no need for me to mention anything about . . ." He nodded toward the seat where the man had been sleeping.

The fellow grimaced. His centurion would probably dock him a week's pay for dereliction of duty. Good! The guard now owed Aurelius a favor, and he'd repay it by keeping his mouth shut.

Aurelius tried to give the fellow the politician's smile Porcia delivered so easily. "I'm just here to look over the pit. Don't get much chance to do that when all the crowds are here."

Aurelius didn't wait for a reply, but turned and left the guard standing there. No torches lit his way as he walked down the central aisle of stairs carved into the tiered stone. When he stepped onto the floor of the pit he turned and stayed behind the ring of posts. As he followed the circumference of the pit, the groans coming from the man they had gutted grew louder. He approached the poor fellow, and the smell of feces and rotting bowels assailed his senses. No one wanted to listen to the groans, or smell the stench, and Aurelius hoped that even hardened guards would drift to other parts of the pit. He stopped in front of the man, careful not to step on his entrails.

The fellow wheezed and groaned, struggling to breathe. A sheen of greasy sweat covered his face, and snot drizzled from his nose.

Aurelius retrieved the dagger from the sheath on his belt. He looked at the blade, a thin spike about the length of his hand. Then he looked the prisoner in the face. "I'm sorry."

He stepped around behind the poor soul, and buried the blade in his chest, aiming for the heart. The fellow jerked once, then went still.

Aurelius withdrew the blade and watched the man's chest carefully for several seconds. The man no longer drew breath.

Aurelius had done what he could. Now for the poor fellow with the broken arms and legs.

# 38

# Tribune Justicus

AS WORD TRICKLED up from the battlefields to the south, there had been no need to spend any time in Tarnasus. If the boy still lived, he'd be with the army.

A few days south of the city, Zarkoffa encountered wagons transporting wounded north, and from them he learned that Tarnasus had combined forces with Andopolous to defeat their common enemy. He turned west, crossed a low mountain range, and encountered more refugees east of Carthagen. The city had handily defeated the combined army.

One day later, Zarkoffa rode through the remnants of the battlefield. Even he found the stench of so many rotting bodies overpowering, and was glad to leave behind the squawks of the carrion-eaters.

He spent the night deep in the forest and well away from the road. As a matter of caution, he didn't light a fire, which made for an uncomfortable night shivering in his blanket.

He rose with first-light and rode into the outskirts of Carthagen. With Kainborne's contacts at his disposal, he should be able to get a message to the man. And they might also be of use in finding the boy.

• • • •

At first-light Obregon climbed out of bed, opened the shutters in his room, and looked out at the city. The previous night he'd followed Aurelius and the guards carrying Ket. He'd shadowed them through the private exit at the back of the amphitheater, and kept at a discreet distance all the way back to the palace. Then he sought out this inn and hired a room on the second floor. In the distance, the spires of the Deoclation Palace dominated the horizon. He thought he could trust Aurelius to do well by the boy, but it wouldn't hurt to stick around and make sure.

• • • •

Its bloodlust sated, the hawk found contentment coasting on a thermal, rising higher with the warm air into a diamond-clear sky. The bird and Ket were alone for once. The absence of the girl saddened him, but the absence of the malevolent thoughts of the man, and the snake-like hiss of that woman's voice, did not. Nor did Ket miss the strange old woman with tattoos around her eyes, and her weird and unsettling riddles.

The dream of coasting on a thermal ended, and Ket realized he lay on his back on something soft, clearly not the ground of the fighting pit. He had a vague memory of a physiker working on him, recalled the bite of the man's stitching needle as he said something about closing wounds. He had a hazy recollection of Obregon and the rich man, but he found those memories impossible to resurrect with any clarity. He opened his eyes, blinked rapidly at the harsh glare of sunlight slanting through a window, and said the first thing that came to mind. "Uhhh!"

He heard soft footsteps, then a beautiful woman from the gentlefolk leaned over him and looked him in the eyes. She had brownish blond hair arranged in a complicated thing atop her head. "Ah, you're awake. Welcome back to the world, young man. How do you feel?"

They'd wrapped his left arm in some sort of sling and bandages, and immobilized it completely against his chest. He could move his right arm, but doing so hurt. In fact, he hurt all over. But he thought he should *speak properly* to one such as her, so he lied. "I'm fine, really, but where am I? And I mean no offense, but . . . who are you?"

Her eyes brightened. "Aurelius was right. You do speak well, and definitely with a Carthagenian accent." She frowned. "That's one thing we don't have to worry about. But as to your questions, you're in the Deoclation Palace, and I'm Domina Porcia, of the family supremus. Let me help you sit up."

She leaned forward to adjust his pillow, which put her chest right in front of his face, limiting his view to breasts, skin, and nipples. He closed his eyes, squeezed them tightly shut, and felt rather flushed as she put an arm behind his back. He tried to help her as she got him into a sitting position, smelled strange scents like a flower garden, but unlike that as well. Ket waited until the operation had been fully completed before opening his eyes.

He glanced around and saw stone walls surrounding him. He looked down, saw a bed, white sheets, a blanket. He marveled at the feel of the sheets, so smooth and soft.

"What's your name?"

The woman standing beside his bed wore a gown that fully clothed her, but clung so intimately to her body she might as well have been naked. It drew his eyes to all sorts of places he shouldn't look, though he did want to look. He recalled his experience with the prostitute among the camp followers of the legion, and couldn't believe he hadn't enjoyed himself back then. Again he felt flushed, but he focused on her face and took great care not to look at the other parts. "Uhhh . . . Ket."

She shook her head. "It doesn't come across well when you keep saying 'Uhhh.' You should work on that. And you say your name is Ket?"

"Yes."

She shook her head. "That's not a name. Who has a name like that?"

"Me."

"Well what kind of name is that?"

"My name."

Her frown deepened and she scowled. "And who are you?"

"I'm nobody. I'm just a peasant."

She wrinkled her nose and grimaced as if she'd just tasted sour milk. "A peasant! You're serious?"

He nodded.

She sucked in a deep breath and sighed. "Oh dear. We have a lot more work to do than I thought. Let me think."

She turned around and walked across the room, then turned and walked back, her head tilting in thought one way, and then the other, as if having a conversation with herself. She stopped at Ket's bed. "I think I have it. Ket is not a name that'll work around here, so you're now Justicus. Or better yet, Lord Justicus."

She frowned and shook her head. "No, on second thought, Lord Justicus will raise too many questions about your family. So we'll leave it at Justicus."

Her face brightened and she smiled. "Yes, that works nicely. And Aurelius told Mother you're an officer. I don't know much about military matters, but I do have a friend who's a tribune, so you'll be Tribune Justicus. How does that sound?"

Ket didn't know what to say, though he almost said, "Uhhh," but caught himself before doing so. "That sounds fine."

# 39

# The Mark of the Dread

*The mark of the dread deceives and manipulates, bends and shapes all to its purpose. It is a cunning mistress of artifice and betrayal. She offers the fulfillment of all desires and hopes, a siren of carnal need and material delight, and yet she gives naught but destruction and damnation. Those who think to manipulate are manipulated. Those who think to deceive are deceived. And those who think to wield the flame to fire the crucible, learn to their horror that their machinations suit only the Dreadmark.*

*Author unknown*
*penned in an unknown time long ago*

· · · ·

Here ends
*Dread Child*

Book 1
*The Dreadmark Covenants*

# Dramatis Personae
## *Dread Child*

The Three Realms
- The Four Duchies
    - Inversill, preeminent among The Four Duchies
    - Dramoran, second only to Inversill
    - Lagasdale
    - Gathgorme
- The Lowland Kingdoms (Lowland City-States)
    - Carthagen
    - Tarnasus
    - Andopolous
- The Mountain Kingdom (Mythria)

Personae Dramoran
- Jarrod—newly invested Duke of Dramoran
- Kadmarkh—Lord of Glenmoore
- Kainborne—principal advisor and councilor to Jarrod
- The oaf—Kainborne's much-abused assistant
- Zarkoffa—the assassin Kainborne frequently employs

Personae Inversill
- Claireen—Macallan's wife and lady
- Clarahm—son of Macallan and Claireen
- Macallan—archduke of Inversill, and ruler of The Four Duchies

Personae Mythria
- Amian—a Colonel, one of Damuel's trusted lieutenants

- Caerie—daughter of Selene and Sander, also known as Caermorgan Mythchild
- Damuel—Selene's brother, an Unchosen, previously Damueltarn Mythchild
- Kailill—Command General of Mythria's armies
- Melceinnia—High Priestess of Myth and Legend
- Nick—son of Selene and Sander and Caerie's older brother, also known as Nicklairan Mythchild
- Palmath—Chancellor of the Exchequer
- Sander—Selene's Crown Consort
- Selene—Crown Mother of the Throne of Myth and Legend
- Zalestria—a young priestess recently elevated from her novitiate's robes, and Damuel's lover

Personae Tramorth

- Antiphinees—a monk with an unwholesome liking for young boys
- Christolus—a monk who grows vegetables in the monastery garden
- Fallon—the leader of the highwaymen who kidnap Ket
- Markus—an unpleasant monk who must educate Ket
- Obregon—a kind monk who must educate Ket
- Pontifus—a monk who raises hawks and falcons
- Sylander—a monks who collects rents from the farmers and stead holders in the valley
- Termik—one of Fallon's henchmen
- Thadamous—a young boy frequently the brunt of Markus's ire
- Willowby—a monk with an unwholesome liking for young boys

Personae Carthagen

- Aurelius—Maximillian's younger brother
- Bapo-Anto—Boss of the North End Slum
- Brunasus—Captain of the Deoclation Palace Guard
- Crenselus—Pit Boss of the Fighting Pit
- Denian—a young tribune and trusted lieutenant of Aurelius
- Divonia—wife of Marius and his widow
- Dominatia—an old madam of a bordello
- Garrien—a nobleman hanged for betraying the city to Macallan
- Hadrius—Invictus General and Aurelius's ally
- Hessian—Boss of the Campo Adrina Slum, and Boss of Bosses
- Lascivien—a young madam of a bordello

- Marius—Senatus Supreme who dies early in book 1
- Martonian—one of Kainborne's unsavory contacts in the city
- Maximillian—oldest son of Marius and Divonia, and heir to the Senatus Supreme
- Parthan—a prefect commanding patrols on the border with Tarnasus
- Pleasuria—a young madam of a bordello
- Porcia—Aurelius's younger sister
- Tenato—Boss of the Regalia Slum

Personae Tarnasus
- Bilsius—an unpleasant and whiney soldier, known as Flick in the slums of Carthagen
- Emparis—a wise veteran in the army
- Garsian—a centurion in the army
- Victicus—Ambassador to Carthagen

Personae Ancient
- Cerciea—the flame
- Damodian—the crucible
- Decritos—author of an old scroll
- Domaxus—the Conqueror, who exterminated three duchies
- Haptimus—author of an old scroll
- Octovian—Invictus General and commander of Domaxus's armies
- Plantonin—author of an old scroll

Personae Andopolous
- Naerin—Ambassador to Carthagen

# Acknowledgements

I'D LIKE TO thank Clyde, Dan, Dave, Jaime, Steve, and Tory for fixing all my dotted t's and crossed i's, and for their invaluable insight, criticism and advice, Karen for both supporting my dream and being my most valuable critic, and all the wonderful readers and fans out there, many of whom are now good friends.

# Books by J. L. Doty

**Series: The Dreadmark Covenants**
Dread Child (available 3/1/2024)
Dread Spirit (6/1/2024)
Dread Soul (9/1/2024)
Dread Lord (12/1/2024)
**Series: The Treasons Cycle**
Of Treasons Born
A Choice of Treasons
**Stand Alone Novel**
The Thirteenth Man
**Series: The Gods Within**
Child of the Sword
The SteelMaster of Indwallin
The Heart of the Sands
The Name of the Sword
**Series: The Dead Among Us**
When Dead Ain't Dead Enough
Still Not Dead Enough
Never Dead Enough
**Series: The Blacksword Regiment**
A Hymn for the Dying
A Dirge for the Damned
A Prayer for the Fallen
A Requiem for the Forsaken
**Series: Commonwealth Re-contact Novellas**
Tranquility Lost

# About the Author

JIM IS A full-time SF&F writer, scientist and laser geek (Ph.D. Electrical Engineering, specialty laser physics), and former running-dog-lackey for the bourgeois capitalist establishment. He's been writing for over 30 years, with 19 published books. His first success came through self-publishing when his books went word-of-mouth viral, and sold enough that he was able to quit his day-job, start working for himself and write full time—his new boss is a real jerk. That led to contracts with traditional publishers like Open Road Media and Harper Collins, and his books are now a mix of traditional and self-published.

The four novels in his new coming-of-age epic fantasy series, *The Dreadmark Covenants*, are scheduled for release beginning in early 2024.

Jim was born in Seattle, but he's lived most of his life in California, though he did live on the east coast and in Europe for a while. He now resides in Arizona with his wife Karen and Julia, a little being who claims to be a cat. But Jim is certain she's really an extra-terrestrial alien in disguise.

Visit the author's website at https://www.jldoty.com/
Contact the author at jld@jldoty.com

www.ingramcontent.com/pod-product-compliance
Lightning Source LLC
Chambersburg PA
CBHW030802200726
48285CB00014B/506